SEPTIMUS HEAP

✠ BOOK ONE ✠

Magyk

SEPTIMUS HEAP

⊹⊢ BOOK ONE ⊣⊹

Magyk

ANGIE SAGE

ILLUSTRATIONS BY MARK ZUG

BLOOMSBURY

First published in Great Britain in 2005 by Bloomsbury Publishing Plc
38 Soho Square, London, W1D 3HB

Published in America by HarperCollins Children's Books,
a division of HarperCollins Publishers, 1350 Avenue of the Americas,
New York NY 10019

A CIP catalogue record of this book is available from the British Library

Hbk ISBN 0 7475 7587 8
Export pbk ISBN 0 7475 7820 6

All papers used by Bloomsbury Publishing are natural, recyclable products made
from wood grown in well-managed forests. The manufacturing processes conform to
the environmental regulations of the country of origin.

Printed in Great Britain by Clays Ltd, St Ives plc

1 3 5 7 9 10 8 6 4 2

www.septimusheap.co.uk
www.bloomsbury.com

For Lois,
with love and thanks for
all your help and encouragement—
this book is for you.

⊹⊱ CONTENTS ⊰⊹

Magyk

BLEAK CREEK

THE CASTLE

THE FOREST

THE RIVER

THE RAMBLINGS

ONE WAY BRIDGE

NORTH GATE

JANNIT MARTEN'S BOAT YARD

THE MOAT

HOLE-IN-THE-WALL TAVERN

WIZARD TOWER

TRACK OF RUBBISH CHUTE

SOUTH GATE

RAVEN'S ROCK

GREAT ARCH

MUNICIPAL RUBBISH DUMP

THE PALACE

SALLY MULLIN'S TEA AND ALE HOUSE

THE CASTLE

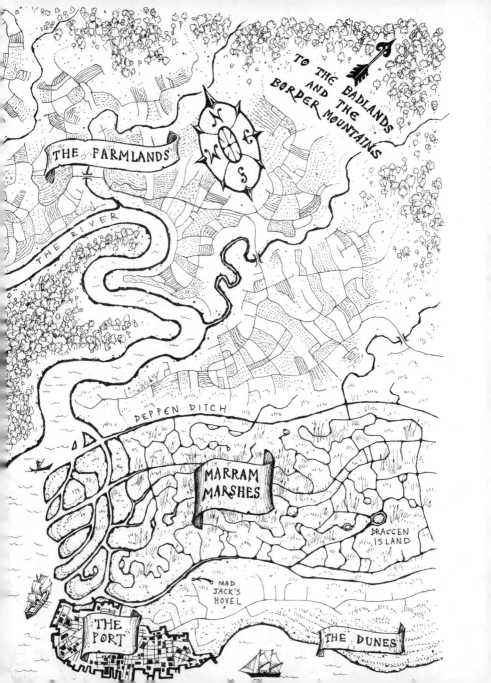

SOMETHING IN THE SNOW

S*ilas Heap pulled his cloak* tightly around him against the snow. It had been a long walk through the Forest, and he was chilled to the bone. But in his pockets he had the herbs that Galen, the Physik Woman, had given him for his new baby boy, Septimus, who had been born earlier that day.

Silas drew closer to the Castle, and he could see the lights flickering through the trees as candles were placed in the windows of the tall narrow houses clustered along the outside walls. It was the longest night of the year, and the candles would be kept burning until dawn, to help keep the dark at bay. Silas always loved this walk to the Castle. He had no fear of the Forest by day and enjoyed the peaceful walk along the narrow track that threaded its way through the dense trees for mile after mile. He was near the edge of the Forest now, the tall trees had begun to thin out, and as the track began to dip down to the valley floor, Silas could see the whole Castle spread before him. The old walls hugged the wide, winding river and zigzagged around the higgledy-piggledy clumps of houses. All the houses were painted bright colors, and those that faced west looked as if they were on fire as their windows caught the last of the winter sun's rays.

The Castle had started life as a small village. Being so near to the Forest the villagers had put up some tall stone walls for protection against the wolverines, witches and warlocks who thought nothing of stealing their sheep, chickens and occasionally their children. As more houses were built, the walls were extended and a deep moat was dug so that all could feel safe.

Soon the Castle was attracting skilled craftsmen from other villages. It grew and prospered, so much so that the inhabitants began to run out of space until someone decided to build The

Ramblings. The Ramblings, which was where Silas, Sarah and the boys lived, was a huge stone building that rose up along the riverside. It sprawled for three miles along the river and back again into the Castle and was a noisy, busy place filled with a warren of passages and rooms, with small factories, schools and shops mixed in with family rooms, tiny roof gardens and even a theater. There was not much space in The Ramblings, but people did not mind. There was always good company and someone for the children to play with.

As the winter sun sank below the Castle walls, Silas quickened his pace. He needed to get to the North Gate before they locked it and pulled up the drawbridge at nightfall.

It was then that Silas sensed *something* nearby. Something alive, but only just. He was aware of a small human heartbeat somewhere close to him. Silas stopped. As an Ordinary Wizard he was able to sense things, but, as he was not a particularly good Ordinary Wizard, he needed to concentrate hard. He stood still with the snow falling fast around him, already covering his footprints. And then he heard something—a snuffle, a whimper, a small breath? He wasn't sure, but it was enough.

Underneath a bush beside the path was a bundle. Silas picked up the bundle and, to his amazement, found himself gazing into the solemn eyes of a tiny baby. Silas cradled the baby in his arms and wondered how she had come to be lying in the snow on the coldest day of the year. Someone had wrapped her tightly in a heavy woolen blanket, but she was already very cold: her lips were a dusky blue and the snow dusted her eyelashes. As the baby's dark violet eyes gazed intently at him, Silas had the uncomfortable feeling that she had already seen things in her short life that no baby should see.

Thinking of his Sarah at home, warm and safe with Septimus and the boys, Silas decided that they would just have to make room for one more little one. He carefully tucked the baby into his blue Wizard cloak and held her close to him as he ran toward the Castle gate. He reached the drawbridge just as Gringe, the Gatekeeper, was about to go and yell for the Bridge Boy to start winding it up.

"You're cutting it a bit fine," growled Gringe. "But you Wizards are weird. Waddyou all want to be out for on a day like this I dunno."

"Oh?" Silas wanted to get past Gringe as soon as he could, but first he had to cross Gringe's palm with silver. Silas quickly found a silver penny in one of his pockets and handed it over.

"Thank you, Gringe. Good night."

Gringe looked at the penny as though it were a rather nasty beetle.

"Marcia Overstrand, she gave me an 'alf crown just now. But then she's got class, what with 'er being the ExtraOrdinary Wizard now."

"*What?*" Silas nearly choked.

"Yeah. Class, that's what she's got."

Gringe stood back to let him pass, and Silas slipped by. As much as Silas wanted to find out why Marcia Overstrand was suddenly the ExtraOrdinary Wizard, he could feel the bundle beginning to stir in the warmth of his cloak, and something told him that it would be better if Gringe did not know about the baby.

As Silas disappeared into the shadows of the tunnel that led to The Ramblings, a tall figure in purple stepped out and barred his way.

"Marcia!" gasped Silas. "What on earth—"

"Tell *no one* you *found* her. She was *born* to you. *Understand?*"

Shocked, Silas nodded. Before he had time to say anything, Marcia was gone in a shimmer of purple mist. Silas spent the rest of the long, winding journey through The Ramblings with his mind in turmoil. Who was this baby? What did Marcia have to do with her? And why was Marcia the ExtraOrdinary Wizard now? And as Silas neared the big red door that led to the Heap family's already overcrowded room, another, more pressing question came into his mind: What was Sarah going to say to yet another baby to care for?

Silas did not have long to think about the last question. As he reached the door it flew open, and a large red-faced woman wearing the dark blue robes of a Matron Midwife ran out, almost knocking Silas over as she fled. She too was carrying a bundle, but the bundle was wrapped from head to toe in bandages, and she was carrying him under her arm as if he were a parcel and she was late for the post.

"Dead!" cried the Matron Midwife. She pushed Silas aside with a powerful shove and ran down the corridor. Inside the room, Sarah Heap screamed.

Silas went in with a heavy heart. He saw Sarah surrounded by six white-faced little boys, all too scared to cry.

"She's taken him," said Sarah hopelessly. "Septimus is dead, and she's taken him away."

At that moment a warm wetness spread out from the bundle that Silas still had hidden under his cloak. Silas had no words for what he wanted to say, so he just took the bundle out from under his cloak and placed her in Sarah's arms.

Sarah Heap burst into tears.

✢ 2 ✢

SARAH AND SILAS

The bundle settled down into the Heap household and was called Jenna after Silas's mother.

The youngest of the boys, Nicko, was only two when Jenna arrived, and he soon forgot about his brother Septimus. The older boys slowly forgot too. They loved their little baby sister and brought home all kinds of treasures for her from their Magyk classes at school.

Sarah and Silas of course could not forget Septimus. Silas blamed himself for leaving Sarah alone while he went out to fetch the baby's herbs from the Physik Woman. Sarah just blamed herself for everything. Although she could hardly remember what had happened that terrible day, Sarah knew she had tried to breathe life back into her baby and had failed. And she remembered watching the Matron Midwife wrapping her little Septimus from head to toe in bandages and then running for the door, shouting over her shoulder, "Dead!"

Sarah remembered that all right.

But Sarah soon loved her little baby girl as much as she had loved her Septimus. For a while she was afraid that someone would come and take Jenna away too, but as the months passed and Jenna grew into a chubby, gurgling baby, Sarah relaxed and almost stopped worrying.

Until one day when her best friend, Sally Mullin, arrived breathless on the doorstep. Sally Mullin was one of those people who knew everything that was going on in the Castle. She was a small, busy woman with wispy ginger hair that was forever escaping from her somewhat grubby cook's hat. She had a pleasant round face, a little chubby from finishing off too many cakes, and her clothes were generally covered in sprinkles of flour.

Sally ran a small cafe down on the pontoon beside the river.

The sign over the door announced:

THE SALLY MULLIN TEA AND ALE HOUSE
CLEAN ACCOMMODATION AVAILABLE
NO RIFFRAFF

There were no secrets in Sally Mullin's cafe. Anything and anyone arriving at the Castle by water was noticed and commented on, and most people coming to the Castle did prefer to arrive by boat. No one apart from Silas liked the dark tracks through the Forest that surrounded the castle. The Forest still had a bad wolverine problem at night and was infested with carnivorous trees. Then there were the Wendron Witches, who were always short of cash and had been known to set traps for the unwary traveler and leave them with little more than their shirt and socks.

Sally Mullin's cafe was a busy, steaming hut perched precariously over the water. All shapes and sizes of boats would moor up at the cafe pontoon, and all sorts of people and animals would tumble out of them. Most decided to recover from their trip by having at least one of Sally's fierce beers and a slab of barley cake, and by telling the latest gossip. And anyone in the Castle with half an hour to spare and a rumbling tummy would soon find themselves on the well-trodden path down to the Port Gate, past the Riverside Amenity Rubbish Dump, and along the pontoon to Sally Mullin's Tea and Ale House.

Sally made it her business to see Sarah every week and keep her up to date with everything. In Sally's opinion Sarah was much put-upon with seven children to care for, not to mention Silas Heap, who did very little as far as she could see. Sally's stories usually involved people Sarah had never heard of and would never meet, but Sarah looked forward to Sally's visits all the same and enjoyed hearing about what was going on around her. However, this time what Sally had to tell her was different. This was more serious than everyday gossip, and this time it did involve Sarah. And, for the first time ever, Sarah knew something about it that Sally did not.

Sally swept in and closed the door conspiratorially behind her.

"I've got some terrible news," she whispered.

Sarah, who was trying to wipe breakfast from Jenna's face, and everywhere else that the baby had sprayed it, *and* clean up after the new wolfhound puppy all at the same time, was not really listening.

"Hello, Sally," she said. "There's a clean space here. Come

and sit down. Cup of tea?"

"Yes, please. Sarah, can you believe this?"

"What's that, then, Sally?" asked Sarah, expecting to hear about the latest bad behavior in the cafe.

"The Queen. The Queen is dead!"

"What?" gasped Sarah. She lifted Jenna out of her chair and took her over to the corner of the room where her baby basket was. Sarah lay Jenna down for a nap. She believed that babies should be kept well away from bad news.

"*Dead*," repeated Sally unhappily.

"No!" gasped Sarah. "I don't believe it. She's just not well after her baby's birth. That's why she has not been seen since then."

"That's what the Custodian Guards have been saying, isn't it?" asked Sally.

"Well, yes," admitted Sarah, pouring out the tea. "But they *are* her bodyguards, so they must know. Though why the Queen has suddenly chosen to be guarded by such a bunch of thugs, I *don't* understand."

Sally took the cup of tea that Sarah had placed in front of her.

"Ta. Mmm, lovely. Well, *exactly* . . ." Sally lowered her voice and looked around as though expecting to find a

Custodian Guard propped up in the corner, not that she necessarily would have noticed one amid all the mess in the Heaps' room. "They *are* a bunch of thugs. In fact, they are the ones who *killed* her."

"Killed? She was *killed*?" exclaimed Sarah.

"*Shhh*. Well, see here . . ." Sally pulled her chair closer to Sarah. "There's a story going around—and I have it from the horse's mouth . . ."

"Which horse would that be, then?" asked Sarah with a wry smile.

"Only Madam Marcia"—looking triumphant, Sally sat back and folded her arms—"that's who."

"*What?* How come you've been mixing with the Extra-Ordinary Wizard? Did she drop by for a cup of tea?"

"Almost. Terry Tarsal did. He had been up at the Wizard Tower delivering some really weird shoes that he had made for Madam Marcia. So when he had stopped moaning about her taste in shoes and how much he hated snakes, he said that he had overheard Marcia talking to one of the other Wizards. Endor, that little fat one, I think. Well, they said the Queen had been shot! By the Custodian Guards. One of their Assassins."

Sarah could not believe what she was hearing.

"*When?*" she breathed.

"Well, this is the really *awful* thing," whispered Sally excitedly. "They said she was shot on the day her baby was born. Six whole months ago, and we knew nothing about it. It's terrible . . . terrible. And they shot Mr. Alther too. Dead. That's how come Marcia took over . . ."

"Alther's *dead*?" gasped Sarah. "I can't believe it. I really can't . . . We all thought he'd retired. Silas was his Apprentice years ago. He was lovely . . ."

"Was he?" asked Sally vaguely, eager to get on with the story. "Well, that's not all, see. Because Terry reckoned that Marcia had rescued the Princess and had taken her away somewhere. Endor and Marcia were just chatting, really, wondering how she was getting along. But of course when they realized Terry was there with the shoes, they stopped. Marcia was very rude to him, he said. He felt a bit strange afterward, and he reckoned she'd done a Forget Spell on him, but he'd nipped behind a pillar when he saw her muttering and it didn't take properly. He's really upset about that as he can't remember whether she paid him for the shoes or not."

Sally Mullin paused to draw breath and have a large gulp of tea.

"That poor little Princess. God help the little one. I wonder where she is now. Probably wasting away in some dungeon somewhere. Not like your little angel over there . . . How is she doing?"

"Oh, she's just fine," said Sarah, who usually would have talked at length about Jenna's snuffles and new tooth and how she could sit up and hold her own cup now. But just at that moment Sarah wanted to turn the attention away from Jenna—because Sarah had spent the last six months wondering who her baby really was, and now she knew.

Jenna was, thought Sarah, surely she must be . . . *the baby Princess.*

For once Sarah was glad to wave good-bye to Sally Mullin. She watched her bustle off down the corridor, and, as Sarah closed the door behind her, she breathed a sigh of relief. Then she rushed over to Jenna's basket.

Sarah lifted Jenna up and held her in her arms. Jenna smiled at Sarah and reached out to grab her charm necklace.

"Well, little Princess," murmured Sarah, "I always knew you were special, but I never dreamed you were our own Princess." The baby's dark violet eyes met Sarah's gaze and she looked solemnly at Sarah as if to say, *Well, now you know.*

Sarah gently laid Jenna back in her baby basket. Her head was spinning and her hands shook as she poured herself another cup of tea. She found it hard to believe all that she had heard. The Queen was dead. And Alther too. Their Jenna was the heir to the Castle. The Princess. What was happening?

Sarah spent the rest of the afternoon torn between gazing at Jenna, *Princess* Jenna, and worrying about what would happen if anyone found out where she was. Where was Silas when she needed him?

Silas was enjoying a day's fishing with the boys.

There was a small sandy beach in the bend of the river just along from The Ramblings. Silas was showing Nicko and Jo-Jo, the two youngest boys, how to tie their jam jars onto the end of a pole and dip them in the water. Jo-Jo had already caught three tiddlers, but Nicko kept dropping his and was getting upset.

Silas picked Nicko up and took him over to see Erik and Edd, the five-year-old twins. Erik was daydreaming happily and dangling his foot in the warm, clear water. Edd was poking at something under a stone with a stick. It was a huge water beetle. Nicko wailed and clung on tightly around Silas's neck.

Sam, who was nearly seven, was a serious fisherman. He had been given a proper fishing rod for his last birthday, and there were two small silver fish laid out on a rock beside him. He was about to reel in another. Nicko squealed with excitement.

"Take him away, Dad. He'll frighten the fish," Sam said
crossly.

Silas tiptoed off with Nicko and went to sit beside his oldest
son, Simon. Simon had a fishing rod in one hand and a book in
the other. It was Simon's ambition to be the ExtraOrdinary
Wizard, and he was busy reading all of Silas's old magic books.
This one, Silas noticed, was called *The Compleat Fish-Charmer*.

Silas expected all his boys to be some kind of Wizard; it
was in the family. Silas's aunt was a renowned White Witch
and both Silas's father and uncle had been Shape-Shifters,
which was a very specialized branch, and one that Silas hoped
his boys would avoid, for successful Shape-Shifters became
increasingly unstable as they grew older, sometimes unable to
hold their own shape for more than a few minutes at a time.
Silas's father had eventually disappeared into the Forest as a
tree, but no one knew which one. It was one of the reasons
why Silas enjoyed his walks through the Forest. He would
often address a remark to an untidy-looking tree in the hope
that it might be his father.

Sarah Heap came from a Warlock and Wizard family. As
a girl, Sarah had studied herbs and healing with Galen, the
Physik Woman in the Forest, which was where she had met

Silas one day. Silas had been out looking for his father. He was lost and unhappy, and Sarah took him back with her to see Galen. Galen had helped Silas to understand that his father, as a Shape-Shifter, would have chosen his final destination as a tree many years ago and would now be truly happy. And Silas too, for the first time in his life, realized he felt truly happy sitting next to Sarah by the Physik Woman's fire.

When Sarah understood all she could about herbs and healing, she had said a fond good-bye to Galen and joined Silas in his room in The Ramblings. And there they had stayed ever since, squeezing in more and more children while Silas happily gave up his Apprenticeship and worked as a jobbing Ordinary Wizard to pay the bills. Sarah made herb tinctures at the kitchen table when she had a spare moment—which did not often happen.

That evening, as Silas and the boys made their way up the beach steps to go back to The Ramblings, a large and menacing Custodian Guard, dressed in black from head to toe, barred their way.

"Halt!" he barked. Nicko started to cry.

Silas stopped and told the boys to behave.

"Papers!" shouted the Guard. "Where are your papers?"

Silas stared at him. "What papers?" he asked quietly, not wanting to cause trouble with six tired boys around him needing to go home for supper.

"Your papers, Wizard scum. The beach area is forbidden to all without the required papers," sneered the Guard.

Silas was shocked. If he had not been with the boys, he would have argued, but he had noticed the pistol that the guard was carrying.

"I'm sorry," he said. "I didn't know."

The Guard looked them all up and down as if deciding what to do, but luckily for Silas he had other people to go and terrorize.

"Take your rabble out of here and don't come back," snapped the Guard. "Stay where you belong."

Silas hurried the shocked boys away up the steps and into the safety of The Ramblings. Sam dropped his fish and started to sob.

"There there," said Silas, "it's all right." But Silas felt that things were most certainly not all right. What was going on?

"Why did he call us Wizard scum, Dad?" asked Simon. "Wizards are the best, aren't they?"

"Yes," said Silas distractedly, "the best."

But the trouble was, thought Silas, there was no hiding it

if you were a Wizard. All Wizards, and only Wizards, had them. Silas had them, Sarah had them and all the boys except Nicko and Jo-Jo had them. And as soon as Nicko and Jo-Jo went to the Magyk class in school they would have them too. Slowly but surely, until there was no mistaking it, a Wizard child's eyes would turn green when he or she was exposed to Magyk learning. It had always been something to be proud of. Until now, when suddenly it felt dangerous.

That evening, when at long last all the children were asleep, Silas and Sarah talked late into the night. They talked about their Princess and their Wizard boys and the changes that had overtaken the Castle. They discussed escaping to the Marram Marshes, or going into the Forest and living with Galen. By the time dawn broke and at last they fell asleep, Silas and Sarah had decided to do what the Heaps usually did. Muddle through and hope for the best.

And so, for the next nine and a half years, Silas and Sarah kept quiet. They locked and barred their door, they spoke to only their neighbors and those they could trust and, when the Magyk classes were stopped at school, they taught the children Magyk at home in the evenings.

And that is why, nine and a half years later, all the Heaps except one had piercing green eyes.

⊹⊱ 3 ⊰⊹
THE SUPREME CUSTODIAN

It *was six in the* morning and still dark, ten years to the day since Silas had found the bundle.

At the end of Corridor 223, behind the big black door with the number 16 stamped on it by the Numerical Patrol, the Heap household slept peacefully. Jenna lay curled up snugly in her small box bed that Silas had made for her from driftwood washed up along the riverbank. The bed was built neatly into a big cupboard leading off a large room, which was in fact the only room that the Heaps possessed.

Jenna loved her cupboard bed. Sarah had made some bright

patchwork curtains that Jenna could draw around the bed to
keep out both the cold and her noisy brothers. Best of all, she had
a small window in the wall above her pillow that looked out onto
the river. If Jenna couldn't sleep, she would gaze out of her window for hours on end, watching the endless variety of boats that
made their way to and from the Castle, and sometimes on clear
dark nights she loved to count the stars until she fell fast asleep.

The large room was the place where all the Heaps lived,
cooked, ate, argued and (occasionally) did their homework, and
it was a *mess*. It was stuffed full of twenty years' worth of clutter
that had accumulated since Sarah and Silas had set up home
together. There were fishing rods and reels, shoes and socks,
rope and rat traps, bags and bedding, nets and knitting, clothes
and cooking pots, and books, books, books and yet more books.

If you were foolish enough to cast your eye around the
Heaps' room hoping to find a space in which to sit, the chances
were a book would have found it first. Everywhere you looked
there were books. On sagging shelves, in boxes, hanging in bags
from the ceiling, propping up the table and stacked up in such
precariously high piles that they threatened to collapse at any
moment. There were storybooks, herb books, cookery books,
boat books, fishing books, but mainly there were the hundreds
of Magyk books, which Silas had illegally rescued from the

school when Magyk had been banned a few years back.

In the middle of the room was a large hearth from which a tall chimney snaked up into the roof; it held the remains of a fire, now grown cold, around which all six Heap boys and a large dog were asleep in a chaotic pile of quilts and blankets.

Sarah and Silas were also fast asleep. They had escaped to the small attic space that Silas had acquired a few years back by the simple means of knocking a hole up through the ceiling, after Sarah had declared that she could no longer stand living with six growing boys in just one room.

But, amid all the chaos in the big room, a small island of tidiness stood out; a long and rather wobbly table was covered with a clean white cloth. On it were placed nine plates and mugs, and at the head of the table was a small chair decorated with winter berries and leaves. On the table in front of the chair a small present, carefully wrapped in colorful paper and tied with a red ribbon, had been placed ready for Jenna to open on her tenth birthday.

All was quiet and still as the Heap household slept peacefully on through the last hours of darkness before the winter sun was due to rise.

However, on the other side of the Castle, in the Palace of the Custodians, sleep, peaceful or not, had been abandoned.

The Supreme Custodian had been called from his bed and had, with the help of the Night Servant, hurriedly put on his black, fur-trimmed tunic and heavy black and gold cloak, and he had instructed the Night Servant how to lace up his embroidered silk shoes. Then he himself had carefully placed a beautiful Crown upon his head. The Supreme Custodian was never seen without the Crown, which still had a dent in it from the day it had fallen from the Queen's head and crashed to the stone floor. The Crown sat crookedly on his slightly pointed bald head, but the Night Servant, being new and terrified, did not dare to tell him.

The Supreme Custodian strode briskly down the corridor to the Throne Room. He was a small, ratlike man with pale, almost colorless eyes and a complicated goatee beard that he was in the habit of spending many happy hours tending. He was almost swamped by his voluminous cloak, which was heavily encrusted with military badges, and his appearance was made faintly ridiculous by his crooked, and slightly feminine, Crown. But had you seen him that morning you would not have laughed. You would have shrunk back into the shadows and hoped he would not notice you, for the Supreme Custodian carried with him a powerful air of menace.

The Night Servant helped the Supreme Custodian arrange himself on the ornate throne in the Throne Room.

He was then waved impatiently away and scuttled off gratefully, his shift nearly over.

The chill morning air lay heavily in the Throne Room. The
Supreme Custodian sat impassively on the throne, but his
breath, which misted the cold air in small quick bursts, betrayed
his excitement.

He did not have long to wait before a tall young woman
wearing the severe black cloak and deep red tunic of an
Assassin walked briskly in and bowed low, her long slashed
sleeves sweeping across the stone floor.

"The Queenling, my lord. She has been found," the Assassin
said in a low voice.

The Supreme Custodian sat up and stared at the Assassin
with his pale eyes.

"Are you sure? I want *no mistakes* this time," he said menacingly.

"Our spy, my lord, has suspected a child for a while. She
considers her to be a stranger in her family. Yesterday our spy
found out that the child is of the age."

"What age exactly?"

"Ten years old today, my lord."

"*Really?*" The Supreme Custodian sat back in the throne
and considered what the Assassin had said.

"I have a likeness of the child here, my lord. I understand

she is much like her mother, the ex-Queen." From inside her tunic the Assassin took a small piece of paper. On it was a skillful drawing of a young girl with dark violet eyes and long dark hair. The Supreme Custodian took the drawing. It was true. The girl did look remarkably like the dead Queen. He came to a swift decision and clicked his bony fingers loudly.

The Assassin inclined her head. "My lord?"

"Tonight. Midnight. You are to pay a visit to—where is it?"

"Room 16, Corridor 223, my lord."

"Family name?"

"Heap, my lord."

"Ah. Take the silver pistol. How many in the family?"

"Nine, my lord, including the child."

"And nine bullets in case of trouble. Silver for the child. And bring her to me. I want *proof*."

The young woman looked pale. It was her first, and only, test. There were no second chances for an Assassin.

"Yes, my lord." She bowed briefly and withdrew, her hands shaking.

In a quiet corner of the Throne Room the ghost of Alther Mella eased himself up from the cold stone bench he had been sitting on. He sighed and stretched his old ghostly legs. Then he gathered his faded purple robes around him, took a deep breath and walked out through the thick stone wall of the Throne Room.

Outside he found himself hovering sixty feet above the ground in the cold dark morning air. Instead of walking off in a dignified manner as a ghost of his age and status really should, Alther stuck his arms out like the wings of a bird and swooped gracefully through the falling snow.

Flying was about the only thing that Alther liked about being a ghost. Flying, or the Lost Art of Flyte, was something that modern ExtraOrdinary Wizards could no longer do. Even Marcia, who was determined to fly, could do no more than a quick hover before crashing to the ground. Somewhere, somehow, the secret had been lost. But all ghosts could, of course, fly. And since he had become a ghost, Alther had lost his crippling fear of heights and had spent many exciting hours perfecting his acrobatic moves. But there wasn't much else about being a ghost that he enjoyed, and sitting in the Throne Room where he had actually *become* one—and consequently where he had had to spend the first year and a day of his ghosthood—was one of his least favorite occupations. But it had to be done. Alther made it his business to know what the Custodians were planning and to try and keep Marcia up to date. With his help she had managed to stay one step ahead of the Custodians and keep Jenna safe. Until now.

Over the years, since the death of the Queen, the Supreme Custodian had become more and more desperate to track down the Princess. Every year he would make a long—and much dreaded—trip to the Badlands, where he woud have to report his progress to a certain ex-ExtraOrdinary Wizard turned Necromancer, DomDaniel. It was DomDaniel who had sent the first Assassin to kill the Queen, and it was DomDaniel who had installed the Supreme Custodian and his henchmen to scour the Castle and search for the Princess. For while the Princess remained in the Castle, DomDaniel dared not come near. And so, every year, the Supreme Custodian would promise DomDaniel that *this* year he would be successful. *This* year he would get rid of the Queenling and at last deliver the Castle up to its rightful Master, DomDaniel.

And this was why, as Alther left the Throne Room, the Supreme Custodian wore what his mother would have called a silly grin on his face. At last, he had done the job he was sent to do. Of course, he thought, his silly grin changing to a smug smile, it was only due to his superior intelligence and talent that he had discovered the girl. But it wasn't—it was due to a bizarre stroke of luck.

When the Supreme Custodian took over the Castle, one of

the first things he did was to ban women from the Courthouse. The Ladies' Washroom, which was no longer needed, had eventually become a small committee room. During the past bitterly cold month, the Committee of the Custodians had taken to meeting in the former Ladies' Washroom, which had the great advantage of a wood-burning stove, rather than the cavernous Custodian Committee Room, where the chill wind whistled through and froze their feet to blocks of ice.

And so, unknowingly, for once the Custodians were one step ahead of Alther Mella. As a ghost, Alther could only go to the places he had been to in his lifetime—and, as a well-brought-up young Wizard, Alther had never set foot in a Ladies' Washroom in his life. The most he was able to do was hover outside waiting, just as he had done when he was alive and courting Judge Alice Nettles.

It had been late one particularly cold afternoon a few weeks ago when Alther had watched the Custodian Committee take themselves into the Ladies' Washroom. The heavy door, with LADIES still visible in faded gold letters, was slammed behind them, and Alther hovered outside with his ear to the door, trying to hear what was going on. But try as he might, he was not able to hear the Committee decide to send their very best spy, Linda Lane, with her interest in herbs and healing, to live in Room 17, Corridor 223. Right next door to the Heaps.

And so neither Alther nor the Heaps had any idea that their new neighbor was a spy. And a very good one too.

As Alther Mella flew through the snowy air pondering how to save the Princess, he absentmindedly turned two almost perfect double loops before he dived swiftly through the drifting snowflakes to reach the golden Pyramid that crowned the Wizard Tower.

Alther landed gracefully on his feet. For a moment he stood perfectly balanced on the tips of his toes. Then he raised his arms above his head and spun around, faster and faster until he started to sink slowly through the roof and down into the room below, where he misjudged his landing and fell through the canopy of Marcia Overstrand's four-poster bed.

Marcia sat up in a fright. Alther was sprawled on her pillow looking embarrassed.

"Sorry, Marcia. Very ungallant. Well, at least you haven't got your curlers in."

"My hair is naturally curly, thank you, Alther," said Marcia crossly. "You might have waited until I had woken up."

Alther looked serious and became slightly more transparent than usual.

"I'm afraid, Marcia," he said heavily, "this won't wait."

✢ 4 ✢
MARCIA OVERSTRAND

Marcia Overstrand *strode out of* her lofty tower bedroom with adjoining robing room, threw open the heavy purple door that led onto the landing and checked her appearance in the adjustable mirror.

"Minus eight-point-three percent!" she instructed the mirror, which had a nervous disposition and dreaded the moment when Marcia's door was flung open every morning. Over the years the mirror had come to read the footsteps as they crossed the wooden boards, and today they had made the mirror edgy. Very edgy. It stood to attention and, in its eagerness to please, made Marcia's reflection 83% thinner so that she resembled something like an angry purple stick insect.

"Idiot!" snapped Marcia.

The mirror recalculated. It hated doing math first thing in the morning, and it was sure that Marcia gave it nasty percentages on purpose. Why couldn't she be a nice round number thinner, like 5%? Or, even better, 10%. The mirror liked 10%s; it could do *them*.

Marcia smiled at her reflection. She looked good.

Marcia had on her winter ExtraOrdinary Wizard uniform. And it suited her. Her purple double silk cloak was lined with the softest indigo-blue angora fur. It fell gracefully from her broad shoulders and gathered itself obediently around her pointy feet. Marcia's feet were pointy because she liked pointy shoes, and she had them specially made. They were made of snakeskin, shed from the purple python that the shoe shop kept in the backyard just for Marcia's shoes. Terry Tarsal, the shoemaker, hated snakes and was convinced that Marcia ordered snakeskin on purpose. He may well have been right. Marcia's purple python shoes shimmered in the light reflected from the mirror, and the gold and platinum on her Extra-Ordinary Wizard belt flashed impressively. Around her neck she wore the Akhu Amulet, symbol and source of the power of the ExtraOrdinary Wizard.

Marcia was satisfied. Today she needed to look impressive. Impressive and just a little scary. Well, quite a bit scary if necessary. She just hoped it wouldn't be necessary.

Marcia wasn't sure if she could do scary. She tried a few expressions in the mirror, which shivered quietly to itself, but she wasn't sure about any of them. Marcia was unaware that most people thought she did scary very well indeed, and was in fact a complete natural at scary.

Marcia clicked her fingers. "Back!" she snapped.

The mirror showed her her back view.

"Sides!"

The mirror showed her both side views.

And then she was gone. Down the stairs two at a time, down to the kitchen to terrorize the stove, which had heard her coming and was desperately trying to light itself before she came through the door.

It did not succeed, and Marcia was in a bad temper all through breakfast.

Marcia left the breakfast things to wash themselves up and strode briskly out of the heavy purple door that led to her rooms. The door closed with a soft, respectful clunk behind her as Marcia jumped onto the silver spiral staircase.

"Down," she told the staircase. It began to turn like a giant corkscrew, taking her slowly down through the tall Tower, past seemingly endless floors and various doors that all led into rooms occupied by an amazing assortment of Wizards. From the rooms came the sounds of spells being practiced, chanted incantations, and general Wizard chitchat over breakfast. The smells of toast and bacon and porridge mixed strangely with the wafts of incense that floated up from the Hall below, and as the spiral stairs came gently to a halt, Marcia stepped off feeling slightly queasy and looking forward to getting out into the fresh air. She walked briskly through the Hall to the massive, solid silver doors that guarded the entrance to the Wizard Tower. Marcia spoke the password, the doors silently swung open for her, and in a moment she was through the silver archway and outside into the bitter cold of a snowy midwinter morning.

As Marcia descended the steep steps, treading carefully on the crisp snow in her thin pointy shoes, she surprised the sentry who had been idly throwing snowballs at a stray cat. A snowball landed with a soft thud on the purple silk of her cloak.

"Don't do that!" snapped Marcia, brushing the snow off her cloak.

The sentry jumped and stood to attention. He looked terrified. Marcia stared at the waiflike boy. He was wearing the ceremonial sentry uniform, a rather silly design made from thin cotton, a red and white striped tunic with purple frills around the sleeves. He also wore a large floppy yellow hat, white tights and bright yellow boots, and in his left hand, which was bare and blue with cold, he held a heavy pikestaff.

Marcia had objected when the first sentries arrived at the Wizard Tower. She had told the Supreme Custodian that the Wizards did not need guarding. They could look after themselves perfectly well, thank you very much. But he had smiled his smug smile and blandly assured her that the sentries were for the Wizards' own safety. Marcia suspected he had put them there not only to spy on the Wizards' comings and goings but also to make the Wizards look ridiculous.

Marcia looked at the snowball-throwing sentry. His hat was too big for him; it had slipped down and come to rest on his ears, which conveniently stuck out at just the right places to stop the hat from falling over his eyes. The hat gave the boy's thin, pinched face an unhealthy yellow tinge. His two deep gray eyes stared out from under it in terror as the boy realized that his snowball had hit the ExtraOrdinary Wizard.

He looked, thought Marcia, very small to be a soldier.

"How old are you?" she said accusingly.

The sentry blushed. No one like Marcia had ever looked at him before, let alone spoken to him.

"T-ten, Madam."

"Then why aren't you in school?" demanded Marcia.

The sentry looked proud. "I have no need of school, Madam. I am in the Young Army. We are the Pride of Today, the Warriors of Tomorrow."

"Aren't you cold?" Marcia asked unexpectedly.

"N-no Madam. We are trained not to feel the cold." But the sentry's lips had a bluish tinge to them, and he shivered as he spoke.

"Humph." Marcia stomped off through the snow, leaving the boy to another four hours on guard.

Marcia walked briskly across the courtyard, which led away from the Wizard Tower, and slipped out of a side gate that took her onto a quiet, snow-covered footpath.

Marcia had been ExtraOrdinary Wizard for ten years to the day, and as she set off on her journey her thoughts turned to the past. She remembered the time she had spent as a poor Hopeful, reading anything she could about Magyk, hoping for that rare thing, an Apprenticeship with the ExtraOrdinary

Wizard, Alther Mella. They were happy years spent living in a small room in The Ramblings among so many other Hopefuls, most of whom soon settled for Apprenticeships with Ordinary Wizards. But not Marcia. She knew what she wanted, and she wanted the best. But Marcia still could hardly believe her luck when she got her chance to be Alther Mella's Apprentice. Although being his Apprentice did not necessarily mean she would get to be the ExtraOrdinary Wizard, it was another step closer to her dream. And so Marcia had spent the next seven years and a day living at the Wizard Tower as Alther's Apprentice.

Marcia smiled to herself as she remembered what a wonderful Wizard Alther Mella had been. His tutorials were fun, he was patient when spells went wrong and he always had a new joke to tell her. He was also an extremely powerful Wizard. Until Marcia had become the ExtraOrdinary Wizard herself she hadn't realized just how good Alther had been. But most of all, Alther was just a lovely person. Her smile faded as she remembered how she came to take his place, and she thought about the last day of Alther Mella's life, the day the Custodians now called Day One.

Lost in her thoughts, Marcia climbed the narrow steps leading up to the broad, sheltered ledge that ran just below the

Castle wall. It was a fast way of getting across to the East Side, which was what The Ramblings were now called, and which was where she was headed today. The ledge was reserved for the use of the Custodian Armed Patrol, but Marcia knew that, even now, no one stopped the ExtraOrdinary Wizard from going anywhere. So, instead of creeping through endless tiny and sometimes crowded passageways as she used to many years ago, she moved speedily along the ledge until, about half an hour later, she saw a door that she recognized.

Marcia took a deep breath. This is it, she said to herself.

Marcia followed a flight of steps down from the ledge and came face-to-face with the door. She was about to lean against it and give it a shove when the door took fright at the sight of her and flew open. Marcia shot through it and bounced off a rather slimy wall opposite. The door slammed shut, and Marcia caught her breath. The passageway was dark; it was damp and smelled of boiled cabbage, cats' pee and dry rot. This was not how Marcia remembered things. When she had lived in The Ramblings the passageways had been warm and clean, lit by reed torches burning at intervals along the wall and swept clean every day by the proud inhabitants.

Marcia hoped she could remember the way to Silas and Sarah Heap's room. In her Apprentice days she had often rushed past their door, hoping that Silas Heap would not see her and ask her in. It was the noise that she remembered most, the noise of so many little boys yelling, jumping, fighting and doing whatever little boys do, although Marcia wasn't quite sure what little boys did—as she preferred to avoid children if at all possible.

Marcia was feeling rather nervous as she walked along the dark and gloomy passageways. She was beginning to wonder just how things were going to go for her first visit to Silas in more than ten years. She dreaded what she was going to have to tell the Heaps, and she even wondered if Silas would believe her. He was a stubborn Wizard, and she knew he didn't like her much. And so, with these thoughts going around in her head, Marcia walked purposefully along the passageways and paid no attention to anything else.

If she had bothered to pay attention, she would have been amazed at people's reactions to her. It was eight o'clock in the morning, what Silas Heap called rush hour. Hundreds of pale-faced people were making their way to work, their sleepy eyes blinking in the gloom and their thin, cheap clothes pulled around them against the deep chill of the damp stone walls. Rush hour in the East Side passageways was a time to avoid. The crush would carry you along, often way past your turning

until you managed to somehow wriggle through the crowd
and join the stream in the opposite direction. The rush hour
air was always full of plaintive cries:

"Let me off here, *please!*"

"Stop *pushing* me!"

"My turning, my *turning!*"

But Marcia had made the rush hour disappear. No Magyk
was necessary for this—just the sight of Marcia was enough to
stop everyone in their tracks. Most people on the East Side had
never seen the ExtraOrdinary Wizard before. If they had seen
her at all, it would have been on a day trip to the Wizard Tower
Visitor Center, where they might have hung around the courtyard all day, hoping to catch a glimpse if they were lucky. For
the ExtraOrdinary Wizard to be walking among them in the
dank corridors of the East Side was unbelievable.

People gasped and shrank away. They melted into the shadows of the doorways and slipped away down side alleys. They
muttered their own small spells to themselves. Some froze and
stood stock-still like rabbits caught in the glare of a brilliant
light. They gazed at Marcia as though she were a being from
another planet, which she may well have been for all the sim-
ilarities between her life and theirs.

But Marcia did not really notice this. Ten years as the

ExtraOrdinary Wizard had insulated her from real life, and however much of a shock it had been when it first happened, she was now used to all giving way before her, to the bowing and the respectful murmuring that surrounded her.

Marcia swept off the main thoroughfare and headed down the narrow passage that led to the Heap household. On her travels Marcia had noticed that all the passages now had numbers that replaced the rather whimsical names they had had before, such as Windy Corner and Upside-Down Lane.

The Heaps' address had previously been: Big Red Door, There and Back Again Row, The Ramblings.

Now it appeared to be: Room 16, Corridor 223, East Side. Marcia knew which one she preferred.

Marcia arrived at the Heaps' door, which had been painted regulation-black by the Paint Patrol a few days ago. She could hear the noisy hubbub of a Heap breakfast going on behind the door. Marcia took some deep breaths.

She could put off the moment no longer.

AT THE HEAPS

pen," *Marcia told the black Heap
door.* But, being a door belong-
ing to Silas Heap, it did nothing of the
sort; in fact, Marcia thought she saw it
tighten up its hinges and stiffen its lock.
So she, Madam Marcia Overstrand,
ExtraOrdinary Wizard, was reduced
to banging on the door as hard as
she could. No one answered. She tried
again, harder and with both fists, but there was still no reply.
Just as she was considering giving the door a good kick (and
serve it right too) the door was pulled open, and Marcia came
face-to-face with Silas Heap.

"Yes?" he said abruptly as if she were no more than an irritating salesperson.

For a brief moment Marcia was lost for words. She looked past Silas to see a room that appeared to have been recently hit by an explosion and was now, for some reason, packed full of boys. The boys were swarming around a small, dark-haired girl who was sitting at a table covered in a surprisingly clean white cloth. The girl was holding on to a small present wrapped in brightly colored paper and tied with red ribbon, laughing and pushing away some of the boys who were pretending to grab it. But one by one the girl and all the boys looked up, and a strange silence fell upon the Heap household.

"Good morning, Silas Heap," said Marcia a little too graciously. "And good morning, Sarah Heap. And, er, all the little Heaps of course."

The little Heaps, most of whom were no longer anything like little, said nothing. But six pairs of bright green eyes and one pair of deep violet eyes took in every detail of Marcia Overstrand. Marcia began to feel self-conscious. Did she have a smudge on her nose? Was some of her hair sticking up in a ridiculous fashion? Perhaps she had some spinach stuck in her teeth?

Marcia reminded herself that she had not had spinach for breakfast. Get on with it, Marcia, she told herself. You're in charge here. So she turned to Silas, who was looking at her as if he hoped she would soon go away.

"I said *good morning*, Silas Heap," said Marcia irritably.

"Indeed you did, Marcia, indeed you did," said Silas. "And what brings you here after all these years?"

Marcia got straight to the point.

"I've come for the Princess," she said.

"*Who?*" asked Silas.

"You know perfectly well *who*," snapped Marcia, who didn't like being questioned by anyone, least of all by Silas Heap.

"We don't have any princesses here, Marcia," said Silas. "I should have thought that was pretty obvious."

Marcia looked around her. It was true, it was not somewhere you would ever expect to find a princess. In fact, Marcia had never seen such a mess before in her entire life.

In the middle of the chaos, by the newly lit fire, stood Sarah Heap. Sarah had been cooking porridge for the birthday breakfast when Marcia had pushed her way into her home, and into her life. Now she stood transfixed, holding the porridge pan in midair and staring at Marcia. Something in her gaze told Marcia that Sarah knew what was coming. This, thought Marcia, is not going to be easy. She decided to dump the tough act and start over again.

"May I sit down, please, Silas . . . Sarah?" she asked.

Sarah nodded. Silas scowled. Neither spoke.

Silas glanced at Sarah. She was sitting down, white-faced and trembling, and gathering the birthday girl up onto her lap, holding her closely. Silas wished more than anything that Marcia would go away and leave them all alone, but he knew they had to hear what she had come to say. He sighed heavily and said, "Nicko, give Marcia a chair."

"Thank you, Nicko," said Marcia as she sat down gingerly on one of Silas's homemade chairs. The tousle-haired Nicko gave Marcia a crooked grin and retreated into the bunch of his brothers, who were hovering protectively around Sarah.

Marcia gazed at the Heaps and was amazed how alike they all were. All of them, even Sarah and Silas, shared the same curly straw-colored hair, and of course they all had the piercing green Wizard eyes. And in the middle of the Heaps sat the Princess, with her straight black hair and deep violet eyes. Marcia groaned to herself. All babies looked the same to Marcia, and it had never occurred to her how very different the Princess would look from the Heaps when she grew older. No wonder the spy had discovered her.

Silas Heap sat himself down on an upturned crate. "Well, Marcia, what's going on?" he said.

Marcia's mouth felt very dry. "Have you got a glass of water?" she asked.

Jenna scrambled down from Sarah's lap and came over to Marcia, holding a battered wooden cup with teeth marks all around the top.

"Here, have my water. I don't mind." She gazed at Marcia admiringly. Jenna had never seen anyone like Marcia before, no one as purple, as shiny, as clean and expensive-looking, and certainly no one with such pointy shoes.

Marcia looked at the cup dubiously, but then, remembering who had given it to her, she said, "Thank you, Princess. Er, may I call you Jenna?"

Jenna did not reply. She was too busy staring at Marcia's purple shoes.

"Answer Madam Marcia, poppet," said Sarah Heap.

"Oh, yes, you may, Madam Marcia," Jenna said, puzzled but polite.

"Thank you, Jenna. It's nice to meet you after all this time. And please, just call me Marcia," said Marcia, who could not help thinking how much Jenna looked like her mother.

Jenna slipped back to Sarah's side, and Marcia forced herself to take a sip of water from the chewed cup.

"Out with it, then, Marcia," said Silas from his upturned

box. "What's going on? As usual we seem to be the last to know over here."

"Silas, do you and Sarah know who, er . . . Jenna . . . is?" asked Marcia.

"Yes. We do. Jenna is our daughter, that's who she is," said Silas stubbornly.

"But you guessed, didn't you?" said Marcia, directing her gaze at Sarah.

"Yes," said Sarah quietly.

"So you will understand when I say that she is not safe here anymore. I need to take her. Now," Marcia said urgently.

"No!" yelled Jenna. "No!" She scrambled back onto Sarah's lap. Sarah held her tightly.

Silas was angry. "Just because you're the ExtraOrdinary Wizard, Marcia, you think you can just walk in here and mess up our lives like it doesn't matter. You most certainly are *not* taking Jenna away. She is ours. Our only daughter. She is perfectly safe here, and she stays with us."

"Silas," sighed Marcia, "she is *not* safe with you. Not anymore. She has been *discovered*. You have a spy living right next door to you. Linda Lane."

"Linda!" gasped Sarah. "A *spy*? I don't believe it."

"You mean that awful old gasbag who is always around

here prattling on about pills and potions and drawing endless pictures of the kids?" asked Silas.

"Silas!" remonstrated Sarah. "Don't be so rude."

"I'll be more than rude to her if she *is* a spy," declared Silas.

"There's no 'if' about it, Silas," said Marcia. "Linda Lane most definitely *is* a spy. And I'm sure the pictures she has been drawing are proving very useful to the Supreme Custodian."

Silas groaned. Marcia pressed home her advantage.

"Look, Silas, I only want the best for Jenna. You have to trust me. "

Silas snorted. "Why on earth should we trust you, Marcia?"

"Because I have trusted *you* with the Princess, Silas," said Marcia. "Now you must trust me. What happened ten years ago must not happen again."

"You forget, Marcia," said Silas scathingly, "that we don't *know* what happened ten years ago. No one ever bothered to tell us."

Marcia sighed. "How *could* I tell you, Silas? It was best for the Princess's, I mean Jenna's, sake that you did not know."

At the mention of Princess yet again, Jenna looked up at Sarah.

"Madam Marcia called me that before," she whispered. "Is that *really* me?"

"Yes, poppet," Sarah whispered back, then she looked Marcia in the eye and said, "I think we *all* need to know what happened ten years ago, Madam Marcia."

Marcia looked at her timepiece. This had to be quick. She took a deep breath and started.

"Ten years ago," she said, "I had just passed my final exams and I'd gone over to see Alther to thank him. Well, soon after I arrived a messenger rushed in to tell him that the Queen had given birth to a baby girl. We were so pleased—it meant that the heir to the Castle had at last arrived.

"The messenger summoned Alther to the Palace to conduct the Welcome Ceremony for the baby Princess. I went with him to help him carry all the heavy books, potions and charms that he needed. And to remind him in what order to do things as dear old Alther was becoming a little forgetful at times.

"When we arrived at the Palace we were taken to the Throne Room to see the Queen, who looked so happy—so wonderfully happy. She was sitting on the throne holding her newborn daughter, and she greeted us with the words, 'Isn't she beautiful?' And those were the last words that our Queen spoke."

"No," muttered Sarah quietly.

"At that very moment a man in a strange black and red

uniform burst into the room. Of course I know now that he was wearing the uniform of an Assassin, but at the time I knew nothing of the kind. I thought he was some kind of messenger, but I could see from the Queen's face that she was not expecting him. Then I saw that he was carrying a long silver pistol, and I felt very afraid. I glanced at Alther, but he was fussing with his books and hadn't noticed. Then . . . it was all so unreal somehow . . . I just watched the soldier very slowly and deliberately raise the pistol, take aim and fire it straight at the Queen. Everything was so horribly silent as the silver bullet passed straight through the Queen's heart and embedded itself in the wall behind her. The baby Princess screamed and tumbled from her dead mother's arms. I leaped forward and caught her."

Jenna was pale, trying to understand what she was hearing. "Was that *me*?" she asked Sarah in a low voice. "Was *I* the baby Princess?"

Sarah nodded slowly.

Marcia's voice trembled slightly as she carried on. "It was terrible! Alther was starting on the SafeShield Spell when there was another shot, and a bullet spun him around and threw him to the floor. I finished Alther's spell for him, and for a few moments all three of us were safe. The Assassin fired his next bullet—it was one for the Princess and me this time—but it skittered off the invisible shield and shot straight back at him, catching him in the leg. He fell to the floor, but he still kept hold of his pistol. He just lay there and stared at us, waiting for the spell to end, as all spells must.

"Alther was dying. He took off the Amulet and gave it to me. I refused. I was sure that I could save him, but Alther knew better. He just very calmly told me that it was time for him to go now. He smiled and then—and then he died."

The room was silent. No one moved. Even Silas stared deliberately at the floor. Marcia continued in a low voice.

"I—I couldn't believe it. I tied the Amulet around my neck and gathered up the baby Princess. She was crying now, well, we both were. Then I *ran*. I ran so fast that the Assassin had no time to fire his pistol.

"I fled to the Wizard Tower. I couldn't think where else to go. I told the other Wizards the terrible news and asked for their protection, which they gave us. All afternoon we talked about what we should do with the Princess. We knew she could not stay in the Tower for long. We could not protect the Princess forever, and anyway, she was a newborn baby who needed a mother. It was then that I thought of you, Sarah."

Sarah looked surprised.

"Alther often talked to me about you and Silas. I knew you had just had a baby boy. It was the talk of the Tower, the seventh son of the seventh son. I had no idea then that he had died. I was so sorry to hear that. But I knew you would love the Princess and make her happy. So we decided that you should have her.

"But I couldn't just walk over to The Ramblings and give her to you. Someone would have seen me. So, late in the afternoon, I smuggled the Princess out of the Castle and left her in the snow, making sure that you, Silas, would find her. And that was it. There was nothing more I could do.

"Except, after Gringe had flustered me into giving him a half crown, I hid in the shadows and watched for you as you came back. When I saw the way you held your cloak and the way you walked as if you were protecting something precious, I knew that you had the Princess and, do you remember, I told you, 'Tell *no one* you *found* her. She was *born* to you. *Understand?*'"

A charged silence hung in the air. Silas stared at the floor, Sarah sat motionless with Jenna, and the boys all looked thunderstruck. Marcia stood up quietly, and from a pocket in her tunic she took a small red velvet bag. Then she picked her way across the room, being careful not to step on anything, particularly a large, and none too clean, wolf that she had just noticed asleep in the middle of a pile of blankets.

The Heaps watched, mesmerized, as Marcia walked solemn-ly over to Jenna. The Heap boys parted respectfully as Marcia stopped in front of Sarah and Jenna and knelt down.

Jenna stared with wide-open eyes as Marcia opened the velvet bag and took from it a small gold circlet.

"Princess," said Marcia, "this was your mother's and now it is yours by right." Marcia reached up and placed the gold circlet on Jenna's head. It fitted perfectly.

Silas broke the spell. "Well, you've done it now, Marcia," he said crossly. "The cat's really out of the bag."

Marcia stood up and brushed the dirt off her cloak. As she did so, to her surprise, the ghost of Alther Mella floated through the wall and settled himself down beside Sarah Heap.

"Ah, here's Alther," said Silas. "He won't be pleased about this, I can tell you."

"Hello, Silas, Sarah. Hello, all my young Wizards." The Heap boys grinned. People called them many things, but only Alther called them Wizards.

"And hello, my little Princess," said Alther, who had always called Jenna that. And now Jenna knew why.

"Hello, Uncle Alther," said Jenna, feeling much happier with the old ghost floating next to her.

"I didn't know that Alther came to see you too," Marcia said, somewhat put out, even though she was rather relieved to see him.

"Well, I was his Apprentice first," snapped Silas. "Before you elbowed in."

"I did *not* elbow in. You gave up. You *begged* Alther to annul your Apprenticeship. You said you wanted to read bedtime stories to the boys instead of being stuck in a turret with your nose in a dusty old spell book. You really do take the biscuit sometimes, Silas," glowered Marcia.

"Children, children, don't argue now." Alther smiled. "I love you both the same. All my Apprentices are special."

The ghost of Alther Mella shimmered slightly in the heat of the fire. He wore his ghostly ExtraOrdinary Wizard cloak. It still had bloodstains on it, which always upset Marcia when she saw them. Alther's long white hair was carefully tied back into a ponytail, and his beard was neatly trimmed to a point. When he had been alive, Alther's hair and beard had always been a mess—he could never quite keep up with how fast it all seemed to grow. But now that he was a ghost, it was easy. He'd sorted it all out ten years ago and that was the way it had stayed. Alther's green eyes may have sparkled a little less than they had when he was alive, but they looked around him as keenly as ever. And as they gazed at the Heap household he felt sad. Things were about to change.

"Tell her, Alther," demanded Silas. "Tell her she's not having our Jenna. Princess or not, she's not having her."

"I wish I could, Silas, but I can't," said Alther, looking serious. "You have been discovered. An Assassin is coming. She will be here at midnight with a silver bullet. You know what that means . . ."

Sarah Heap put her head in her hands. "No," she whispered.

"Yes," said Alther. He shivered and his hand strayed to the small round bullet hole just below his heart.

"What can we do?" asked Sarah, very quiet and still.

"Marcia will take Jenna to the Wizard Tower," said Alther. "Jenna will be safe there for the moment. Then we will have to think about what to do next." He looked at Sarah. "You and Silas must go away with the boys. Somewhere safe where you won't be found."

Sarah was pale, but her voice was steady. "We'll go into the Forest," she said. "We will stay with Galen."

Marcia looked at her timepiece again. It was getting late.

"I need to take the Princess now," she said. "I must get back before they change the sentry."

"I don't want to go," whispered Jenna. "I don't have to, do I, Uncle Alther? I want to go and stay with Galen too. I want to go with everyone else. I don't want to be on my own." Jenna's lower lip trembled, and her eyes filled with tears. She held on tightly to Sarah.

"You won't be on your own. You'll be with Marcia," said Alther gently. Jenna did not look as though that made her feel any better.

"My little Princess," said Alther, "Marcia is right. You need to go away with her. Only she can give you the protection you will need."

Jenna still looked unconvinced.

"Jenna," said Alther seriously, "you are the Heir to the Castle, and the Castle needs you to keep safe so that you can be Queen one day. You must go with Marcia. *Please.*"

Jenna's hands strayed to the golden circlet that Marcia had placed on her head. Somewhere inside herself she began to feel a little bit different.

"All right," she whispered. "I'll go."

++ 6 ++
TO THE TOWER

J enna could not believe what was happening to her. She hardly had time to kiss everyone good-bye before Marcia had thrown her purple cloak over her and told her to stay close and keep up. Then the big black Heap door had unwillingly creaked itself open, and Jenna was whisked away from the only home she had ever known.

It was probably a good thing that, covered as she was by Marcia's cloak, Jenna could not see the bewildered faces of the six Heap boys or the desolate expressions on the faces of Sarah and Silas Heap as they watched the four-legged purple cloak swish around the corner at the end of Corridor 223 and disappear from view.

Marcia and Jenna took the long way back to the Wizard Tower. Marcia did not want to risk being seen outside with Jenna, and the dark winding corridors of the East Side seemed safer than the quick route she had taken earlier that morning. Marcia strode briskly along, and Jenna had to run beside her to have any hope of keeping up. Luckily all she carried with her was a small rucksack on her back with a few treasures to remind her of home; although, in the rush she had forgotten her birthday present.

It was midmorning by now and the rush hour was over. Much to Marcia's relief the damp corridors were almost deserted as she and Jenna traveled quietly along them, fluently taking each turn as Marcia's memory of her old trips to the Wizard Tower came back to her.

Hidden under Marcia's heavy cloak, Jenna could see very little, so she concentrated her gaze on the two pairs of feet below her: her own small, chunky feet in their scruffy brown boots and Marcia's long, pointy feet in their purple python skins striding over the dank gray slabs beneath them. Soon

Jenna had stopped noticing her own boots and had become mesmerized by the purple pointed pythons dancing before her—left, right, left, right, left, right—as they crossed the miles of endless passageways.

In this way the strange pair moved unnoticed through the Castle. Past the heavy murmuring doors that hid the many workshops where the people from the East Side spent their long working hours making boots, beer, clothes, boats, beds, saddles, candles, sails, bread, and more recently guns, uniforms and chains. Past the cold schoolrooms where bored children chanted their thirteen times-tables and past the empty, echoing storerooms where the Custodian Army had recently taken away most of the winter stores for its own use.

At long last Marcia and Jenna emerged through the narrow archway that led into the Wizard Tower courtyard. Jenna caught her breath in the cold air and stole a look out from under the cloak.

She gasped.

Rearing up in front of her was the Wizard Tower, so high that the golden Pyramid crowning it was almost lost in a wisp of low-lying cloud. The Tower shone a brilliant silver in the winter sunlight, so bright that it hurt Jenna's eyes, and the purple glass in its hundreds of tiny windows glittered and sparkled

with a mysterious darkness that reflected the light and kept
the secrets hidden behind them. A thin blue haze shimmered
around the Tower, blurring its boundaries, and Jenna found it
hard to tell where the Tower ended and the sky began. The air
too was different; it smelled strange and sweet, of magical spells
and old incense. And as Jenna stood, unable to stir another
step, she knew that she was surrounded by the sounds, too soft
to be heard, of ancient charms and incantations.

For the first time since Jenna had left her home she was
afraid.

Marcia put a protective arm around Jenna's shoulders,
for even Marcia remembered what it was like to first see the
Tower. Terrifying.

"Come on, nearly there," murmured Marcia encouragingly,
and together they slipped and slid across the snow-covered
courtyard toward the huge marble steps that led up to the
shimmering, silver entrance. Marcia was intent upon keeping
her balance, and it was not until she reached the bottom of the
steps that she noticed there was no longer a sentry on guard.
She looked at her timepiece, puzzled. The sentry change was
not due for fifteen minutes, so where was the snowball-throwing boy she had told off that morning?

Marcia looked around, tutting to herself. Something was

wrong. The sentry was not here. And yet he *was* still here. He was, she suddenly realized, between the Here and the Not Here.

He was nearly dead.

Marcia made a sudden dive toward a small mound by the archway, and Jenna fell out of the cloak.

"Dig!" hissed Marcia, scrabbling away at the mound. "He's here. Frozen."

Underneath the mound lay the thin white body of the sentry. He was curled up into a ball, and his flimsy cotton uniform was soaked with the snow and clung coldly to him, the acid-bright colors of the bizarre uniform looking tawdry in the cold winter sunlight. Jenna shivered at the sight of the boy, not from the cold but from an unknown, wordless memory that had flitted across her mind.

Marcia carefully brushed the snow from the boy's dark blue mouth while Jenna lay her hand on his white sticklike arm. She had never felt anyone so cold before. Surely he was already dead?

Jenna watched Marcia lean over the boy's face and mutter something under her breath. Marcia stopped, listened and looked concerned. Then she muttered again, more urgently this time, "Quicken, Youngling. Quicken." She paused for a

moment and then breathed a long slow breath over the boy's
face. The breath tumbled endlessly from Marcia's mouth,
on and on, a warm pale pink cloud that enveloped the boy's
mouth and nose and slowly, slowly seemed to take away the
awful blue and replace it with a living glow. The boy did not
stir, but Jenna thought that now she could see a faint rise and
fall of his chest. He was breathing again.

"Quick!" whispered Marcia to Jenna. "He won't survive
if we leave him here. We'll have to get him inside." Marcia
gathered the boy into her arms and carried him up the wide
marble steps. As she reached the top, the solid silver doors to
the Wizard Tower swung silently open before them. Jenna
took a deep breath and followed Marcia and the boy inside.

⊹ 7 ⊹
WIZARD TOWER

It was only when the doors of the Wizard Tower had swung closed behind her and Jenna found herself standing in the huge golden entrance Hall that she realized just how much her life had changed. Jenna had never, ever seen or even dreamed of a place like this. She knew that most other people in the Castle would never see anything like it either. She was already becoming different from those she had left behind.

Jenna gazed at the unfamiliar riches that surrounded her as

she stood, entranced, in the massive circular Hall. The golden walls flickered with fleeting pictures of mythical creatures, symbols and strange lands. The air was warm and smelled of incense. It was filled with a quiet, soft hum, the sound of the everyday Magyk that kept the Tower operating. Beneath Jenna's feet the floor moved as if it were sand. It was made up of hundreds of different colors that danced around her boots and spelled out the words WELCOME PRINCESS, WELCOME. Then, as she gazed in surprise, the letters changed to read, HURRY UP!

Jenna glanced up to see Marcia, who was staggering a little as she carried the sentry, step onto a silver spiral staircase.

"Come on," said Marcia impatiently. Jenna ran over, reached the bottom step and started to climb the stairs.

"No, just wait where you are," explained Marcia. "The stairs will do the rest."

"Go," said Marcia loudly and, to Jenna's amazement, the spiral staircase started turning. It was slow at first, but it soon picked up speed, whirling around faster and faster, up through the Tower until they reached the very top. Marcia stepped off and Jenna followed, jumping dizzily, just before the steps whirled back down again, called by another Wizard some-where far below.

Marcia's big purple front door had already sprung open for

them, and the fire in the grate hastily burst into flames. A sofa arranged itself in front of the fire, and two pillows and a blanket hurled themselves through the air and landed neatly on the sofa without Marcia having to say a word.

Jenna helped Marcia lay the sentry boy down on the sofa. He looked bad. His face was pinched and white with cold, his eyes were closed and he had begun to shiver uncontrollably.

"Shivering's a good sign," said Marcia briskly, then clicked her fingers. "Wet clothes off."

The ridiculous sentry uniform flew off the boy and fluttered to the floor in a garish damp heap.

"You're rubbish," Marcia told it, and the uniform dismally gathered itself together and dripped over to the rubbish chute, where it threw itself in and disappeared.

Marcia smiled. "Good riddance," she said. "Now, dry clothes on."

A pair of warm pajamas appeared on the boy, and his shivering became a little less violent.

"Good," said Marcia. "We'll just sit with him for a while and let him warm up. He'll be fine."

Jenna settled herself down on a rug by the fire, and soon two steaming mugs of hot milk appeared. Marcia sat down beside her. Suddenly Jenna felt shy. The ExtraOrdinary Wizard was sitting next to her on the floor, just like Nicko did. What should she say? Jenna couldn't think of anything at all, except that her feet were cold, but she was too embarrassed to take her boots off.

"Best get those boots off," said Marcia. "They're soaking."

Jenna unlaced her boots and pulled them off.

"Look at your socks. What a state," Marcia tutted.

Jenna went red. Her socks had previously belonged to Nicko, and before that they had been Edd's. Or were they Erik's? They were mostly darns and far too big for her.

Jenna waggled her toes by the fire and dried her feet.

"Would you like some new socks?" asked Marcia.

Jenna nodded shyly. A pair of thick, warm purple socks appeared on her feet.

"We'll keep the old ones though," said Marcia. "Clean," she told them. "Fold." The socks did what they were told; they shook off the dirt, which landed in a sticky pile on the hearth, then they neatly folded themselves up and lay down by the fire next to Jenna. Jenna smiled. She was glad Marcia hadn't called Sarah's best darning rubbish.

The midwinter afternoon drew on, and the light began to fade. The sentry boy had at last stopped shivering and was sleeping peacefully. Jenna was curled up by the fire, looking at one of Marcia's Magyk picture books when there was a frantic banging on the door.

"Come *on*, Marcia. Open the door. It's me!" came an impatient voice from outside.

"It's Dad!" yelled Jenna.

"Shh . . ." said Marcia. "It might not be."

"For goodness' sake, open the door, will you?" said the impatient voice.

Marcia did a quick Translucent Spell. Sure enough, to her irritation, outside the door stood Silas and Nicko. But that wasn't all. Sitting next to them, with its tongue lolling out and drool dribbling down its fur, was the wolf, wearing a spotted neckerchief.

Marcia had no choice but to let them in.

"Open!" Marcia abruptly told the door.

"Hello, Jen." Nicko grinned. He stepped carefully onto Marcia's fine silk carpet, closely followed by Silas and the wolf, whose madly wagging tail swept Marcia's treasured collection of Fragile-Fairy pots crashing to the floor.

"Nicko! Dad!" yelled Jenna and hurled herself into Silas's arms. It felt like months since she had seen him. "Where's Mum. Is she all right?"

"She's fine," said Silas. "She's gone to Galen's with the boys. Nicko and I just came by to give you this." Silas fished around in his deep pockets. "Hang on," he said. "It's here somewhere."

"Are you mad?" Marcia demanded. "What do you think you are *doing*, coming here? And get that wretched wolf away from me."

The wolf was busy dribbling over Marcia's python shoes.

"He's not a wolf," Silas told her. "He's an Abyssinian wolfhound descended from the Maghul Maghi wolfhounds. And his name is Maximillian. Although, he might allow you to call him Maxie for short. If you're nice to him."

"Nice!" spluttered Marcia, almost speechless.

"Thought we might stay over," Silas carried on, tipping out the contents of a small grubby sack over Marcia's ebony and jade Ouija table and sifting through them. "It's too dark now to go into the Forest."

"Stay? *Here?*"

"Dad! Look at my socks, Dad," said Jenna, waggling her toes in the air.

"Mmm, very nice, poppet," said Silas, still fishing around in his pockets. "Now where did I put it? I *know* I brought it with me . . ."

"Do you like my socks, Nicko?"

"Very purple," said Nicko. "I'm frozen."

Jenna led Nicko to the fire. She pointed at the sentry boy. "We're waiting for him to wake up. He got frozen in the snow, and Marcia rescued him. She made him breathe again."

Nicko whistled, impressed. "Hey," he said, "I reckon he's waking up now." The sentry boy had opened his eyes and was staring at Jenna and Nicko. He looked terrified. Jenna stroked his shaven head. It was bristly and still a little cold.

"You're safe now," she told him. "You're with us. I'm Jenna, and this is Nicko. What's your name?"

"Boy 412," mumbled the sentry.

"Boy Four One Two . . . ?" Jenna repeated, puzzled. "But that's a number. No one has a number for a name."

The boy just stared at Jenna. Then he closed his eyes again and went back to sleep.

"That's *weird*," said Nicko. "Dad told me they only had numbers in the Young Army. There were two of them outside just now but he made them think we were Guards. And he remembered the password from years ago."

"Good old Dad. Except," she said thoughtfully, "I suppose he's not my dad. And you're not my brother . . ."

"Don't be daft. 'Course we are," said Nicko gruffly. "Nothing can change that. Silly Princess."

"Yes, I suppose," said Jenna.

"Yes, of *course*," said Nicko.

Silas had overheard the conversation. "I'll always be your dad, and Mum will always be your mum. It's just you have a first mum as well."

"Was she really a Queen?" asked Jenna.

"Yes. *The* Queen. Our Queen. Before we had these Custodians here." Silas looked thoughtful and then his expression cleared as he remembered something and took off his thick woolen hat. *There* it was, in his hat pocket. Of course.

"Found it!" Silas said triumphantly. "Your birthday present. Happy birthday, poppet." He gave Jenna the present she had left behind.

It was small and surprisingly heavy for its size. Jenna tore off the colored paper and held a little blue drawstring bag in her hand. She carefully pulled open the strings, holding her breath with excitement.

"Oh," she said, not able to keep the disappointment out of her voice. "It's a pebble. But it's a really nice pebble, Dad. Thanks." She picked out the smooth gray stone and put it in the palm of her hand.

Silas lifted Jenna onto his lap. "It's not a pebble. It's a pet rock," he explained. "Try tickling it under its chin."

Jenna wasn't quite sure which end its chin was, but she tickled the rock anyway. Slowly the pebble opened its little black eyes and looked at her, then it stretched out four stumpy legs, stood up and walked around her hand.

"Oh, Dad, it's *brilliant*," gasped Jenna.

"We thought you'd like it. I got the spell from the Roving Rocks Shop. Don't feed it too much though, otherwise it will get very heavy and lazy. And it needs a walk every day too."

"I'll call it Petroc," said Jenna. "Petroc Trelawney."

Petroc Trelawney looked as pleased as a pebble can look, which was pretty much the same as he had looked before. He drew in his legs, closed his eyes and settled back down to sleep. Jenna put him in her pocket to keep him warm.

Meanwhile Maxie was busy chewing the wrapping paper and dribbling down Nicko's neck.

"Hey, get *off*, you dribble-bucket! Go on, lie *down*," said Nicko, trying to push Maxie onto the floor. But the wolf-hound wouldn't lie down. He was staring at a large picture on the wall of Marcia in her Apprenticeship Graduation gown.

Maxie began to whine softly.

Nicko patted Maxie. "Scary picture, hey?" he whispered to the dog who wagged his tail halfheartedly and then yelped as Alther Mella appeared through the picture. Maxie had never got used to Alther's appearances.

Maxie whimpered and burrowed his head under the blanket that covered Boy 412. His cold wet nose woke the boy up with a start. Boy 412 sat bolt upright and stared around him like a frightened rabbit. He didn't like what he saw. In fact, it was his worst nightmare.

Any minute now the Young Army Commander would come for him and then he would be in real trouble. Consorting with the enemy—that was what they called it when someone talked to Wizards. And here he was with two of them. *And* an old Wizard ghost by the look of it. Not to mention the two weirdo kids, one with some kind of crown on her head and the other with those telltale green Wizard eyes. And the filthy dog. They'd taken his uniform too and put him in civilian clothes. He could be shot as a spy. Boy 412 groaned and put his head in his hands.

Jenna reached over and put her arm around him. "It's all right," she whispered. "We'll look after you."

Alther was looking agitated. "That *Linda* woman. She's told them where you've gone. They're coming here. They're sending the *Assassin*."

"Oh, no," said Marcia. "I'll CharmLock the main doors."

"Too late," gasped Alther. "She's already in."

"But how?"

"Someone left the door open," said Alther.

"Silas, you idiot!" snapped Marcia.

"Right," said Silas making for the door. "We'll be off, then. And I'll take Jenna with me. She's obviously not safe with you, Marcia."

"What?" squeaked Marcia indignantly. "She's not safe anywhere, you fool!"

"Don't you call me a fool," spluttered Silas. "I am just as intelligent as you, Marcia. Just because I am only an Ordinary—"

"*Stop it!*" shouted Alther. "This is not the time to argue. For goodness' sake, *she's coming up the stairs.*"

Shocked, everyone stopped and listened. All was quiet. Far too quiet. Except for the whisper of the silver stairs steadily turning as they brought a passenger slowly up through the Wizard Tower right to the very top, to Marcia's purple door.

Jenna looked scared. Nicko put his arm around her. "I'll keep you safe, Jen," he said. "You'll be all right with me."

Suddenly Maxie put his ears back and gave a bloodcurdling howl. Everyone's hair stood up on the backs of their necks.

Crash! The door burst open.

Silhouetted against the light stood the Assassin. Her face was pale as she surveyed the scene before her. Her eyes glanced coldly about her, searching for her prey. The Princess. In her right hand she carried a silver pistol, the one that Marcia had last seen ten years ago in the Throne Room.

The Assassin stepped forward.

"You are under arrest," she said menacingly. "You are not required to say anything at all. You will be taken from here to a place and—"

Boy 412 stood up, trembling. It was just as he had expected— they had come for him. Slowly he walked over toward the Assassin. She stared at him coldly.

"Out of my way, boy," snapped the Assassin. She struck out at Boy 412 and sent him crashing to the floor.

"Don't do that!" yelled Jenna. She rushed over to Boy 412, who was sprawled on the floor. As she knelt down to see if he was hurt, the Assassin grabbed her.

Jenna twisted around. "Let go of me!" she yelled.

"Keep still, *Queenling*," sneered the Assassin. "There's some-one who wants to see you. But he wants to see you—*dead*."

The Assassin raised the silver pistol to Jenna's head.

Crack!

A Thunderflash flew from Marcia's outstretched hand. It knocked the Assassin off her feet and threw Jenna clear of her grasp.

"Begird and Preserve!" shouted Marcia. A brilliant white sheet of light sprung up like a bright blade from the floor and encircled them, cutting them off from the unconscious Assassin.

Then Marcia threw open the hatch that covered the rubbish chute.

"It's the only way out," she said. "Silas, you go first. Try and do a Cleaning Spell as you go down."

"*What?*"

"You heard what I said. Get *in*, will you!" snapped Marcia, giving Silas a hefty shove through the open hatch. Silas tumbled into the rubbish chute and then, with a yell, he was gone.

Jenna pulled Boy 412 to his feet. "Go on," she said and pushed him headfirst into the chute. Then she jumped in, closely followed by Nicko, Marcia and an overexcited wolfhound.

✠ 8 ✠

THE RUBBISH CHUTE

When Jenna threw herself into the rubbish chute she was so terrified of the Assassin that she did not have time to be afraid of the chute. But as she tumbled uncontrollably downward into the pitch blackness she felt an overwhelming panic well up inside her.

The inside of the rubbish chute was as cold and slippery as ice. It was made from a highly polished black slate, seamlessly cut and joined by the Master Masons who had built the Wizard Tower many hundreds of years ago. The drop was steep, too steep for Jenna to have any control over how she fell, so she tumbled and twisted this way and that, rolling from side to side.

But the worst thing was the dark.

It was thick, deep, impenetrable black. It pressed in on Jenna from all sides and although she strained her eyes desperately to see anything, anything at all, there was no response. Jenna thought she had gone blind.

But she could still hear. And behind her, coming up fast, Jenna could hear the swish of damp wolfhound fur.

Maxie the wolfhound was having a good time. He liked this game. Maxie had been a little surprised when he had jumped into the chute and not found Silas ready with his ball. He was even more surprised when his paws didn't seem to work any-more, and he had briefly scrabbled around trying to find out why. Then he had bumped his nose on the back of the scary woman's neck and tried to lick a tasty morsel of something off her hair, but at that point she had given him a violent shove that had flipped him over onto his back.

And now Maxie was happy. Nose first, paws held in close, he became a streamlined streak of fur, and he overtook them all. Past Nicko, who grabbed at his tail but then let go. Past Jenna, who screamed in his ear. Past Boy 412, who was curled into a tight ball. And then past his master, Silas. Maxie felt uncomfortable going past Silas, because Silas was Top Dog and Maxie was Not Allowed in Front. But the wolfhound had no choice—he sailed by Silas in a shower of cold stew and car-rot peelings and carried on down.

The rubbish chute snaked around the Wizard Tower like a giant helter-skelter buried deep inside the thick walls. It dropped steeply between each floor, taking with it not only Maxie, Silas, Boy 412, Jenna, Nicko and Marcia but also the remains of all the Wizards' lunches, which had been tipped into the chute that afternoon. The Wizard Tower was twenty-one stories high. The top two floors belonged to the ExtraOrdinary Wizard, and on each floor below that there were two Wizard apartments. That's a lot of lunches. It was wolfhound heaven, and Maxie ate enough scraps on his way down the Wizard Tower to keep him going for the rest of the day.

Eventually, after what felt like hours but was in fact only two minutes and fifteen seconds, Jenna felt the almost vertical drop level out, and her pace slowed to something that was bearable. She did not know it, but she now had left the Wizard Tower and was traveling below the ground, out from the foot of the Tower and toward the basements of the Courts of the Custodians. It was still pitch-black and freezing cold in the chute, and Jenna felt very alone. She strained her ears to hear any sounds that the others might be making, but every-one knew how important it was to keep quiet and no one

dared to call out. Jenna thought that she could detect the swish
of Marcia's cloak behind her, but since Maxie had hurtled past
her she had had no sign that there was anyone else with her
at all. The thought of being alone in the dark forever began to
take hold of her, and another tide of panic started to rise. But
just as Jenna thought she might scream, a chink of light shone
down from a distant kitchen far above, and she caught a
glimpse of Boy 412 huddled into a ball not far in front of her.
Jenna's spirits lifted at the sight of him, and she found herself
feeling sorry for the thin, cold sentry boy in his pajamas.

Boy 412 was in no state to feel sorry for anyone, least of all
himself. When the mad girl with the gold circle on her head
had pushed him into the abyss he had instinctively curled
himself up into a ball and had spent the entire descent down
the Wizard Tower rattling from side to side of the chute like
a marble in a drainpipe. Boy 412 felt bruised and battered but
no more terrified than he had been since he awoke to find
himself in the company of two Wizards, a Wizard boy and a
Wizard ghost. As he too slowed down when the chute leveled
out, Boy 412's brain began to work again. The few thoughts
that he managed to put together came to the conclusion
that this must be a Test. The Young Army was full of Tests.
Terrifying Surprise Tests always sprung on you in the middle

of the night, just as you had fallen asleep and made your cold narrow bed as warm and comfortable as was possible. But this was a Big Test. This must be one of those Do-or-Die Tests. Boy 412 gritted his teeth; he wasn't sure, but right now it felt horribly like this was the Die part of the test. Whatever it was, there wasn't much he could Do. So Boy 412 closed his eyes tightly and kept rolling along.

The chute took them ever downward. It turned left and traveled underneath the Custodian Council Chambers, bore right to take in the Army Offices and then straight on where it burrowed through the thick walls of the underground kitchens that served the Palace. This was where things became particularly messy. The Kitchen Maids were still busy clearing up after the Supreme Custodian's midday banquet, and the hatches in the kitchen, which were not far above the travelers in the rubbish chute, opened with alarming frequency and showered them with the mixed-up remains of the feast. Even Maxie, who had by now eaten as much as he possibly could, found it unpleasant, especially after a solidified rice pudding hit him square on the nose. The youngest Kitchen Maid who threw the rice pudding caught a glimpse of Maxie and had nightmares about wolves in the rubbish chute for weeks.

For Marcia it was a nightmare too. She wrapped her

gravy-splattered purple silk cloak with the custard-coated fur lining tightly around her, ducked a shower of brussels sprouts and tried to rehearse the One-Second Dry Clean Spell to use the moment she got out of the chute.

At last the chute took them away from the kitchens, and things became slightly cleaner. Jenna briefly allowed herself to relax, but suddenly her breath was taken away as the chute dipped sharply down under the Castle walls toward its final destination at the riverside rubbish dump.

Silas recovered first from the sharp dip and guessed they were coming to the end of their journey. He peered into the darkness to try to see the light at the end of the tunnel, but he could make nothing out at all. Although he knew that by now the sun had set, he had hoped that with the full moon rising some light would be filtering through. And then, to his surprise, he slid to a halt against something solid. Something soft and slimy that smelled disgusting. It was Maxie.

Silas was wondering why Maxie was blocking up the rubbish chute when Boy 412, Jenna, Nicko and Marcia cannoned into him in quick succession. Silas realized that it was not just Maxie who was soft, slimy and smelled disgusting—they all did.

"Dad?" Jenna's scared voice came out of the darkness. "Is that you, Dad?"

"Yes, poppet," whispered Silas.

"Where are we, Dad?" asked Nicko hoarsely. He hated the rubbish chute. Up until his leap into it Nicko had had no idea that he was terrified of confined spaces; what a way to find out, he thought. Nicko had managed to fight his fear by telling himself that at least they were moving and they would soon be out. But now they had stopped. And they weren't out.

They were *stuck*.

Trapped.

Nicko tried to sit up, but his head hit the cold slate above him. He stretched out his arms, but they both met the ice-smooth sides of the chute before he could straighten them. Nicko felt his breath coming faster and faster. He thought he might go mad if they didn't get out of there *fast*.

"Why have we stopped?" hissed Marcia.

"There's a blockage," whispered Silas, who had felt past Maxie and come to the conclusion that they had fetched up against a huge pile of rubbish that was blocking the chute.

"Bother," muttered Marcia.

"*Dad*. I want to get out, Dad," gasped Nicko.

"Nicko?" whispered Silas. "You okay?"

"No . . ."

"It's the rat door!" said Marcia triumphantly. "There's a

grille to keep the rats out of the chute. It was put up after
Endor found a rat in her hot pot. Open it, Silas."

"I can't get to it. There's all this rubbish in the way."

"If you'd done a Cleaning Spell like I'd asked you, there
wouldn't be, would there?"

"Marcia," hissed Silas, "when you think you are about to
die, a spot of housekeeping is not a number-one priority."

"*Dad*," said Nicko desperately.

"I'll do it, then," snapped Marcia. She clicked her fingers and
recited something under her breath. There was a muffled *clang*
as the rat door swung open and a *swish* as the rubbish oblig-
ingly hurled itself out of the chute and tumbled down onto the
dump.

They were free.

The full moon, which was rising above the river, shone its
clear white light into the blackness of the chute and guided
the six tired and bruised travelers out to the place they had all
been longing to reach.

The Riverside Amenity Rubbish Dump.

✢ 9 ✢
SALLY MULLIN'S CAFE

It was the usual quiet winter's evening in Sally Mullin's cafe. A steady buzz of conversation filled the air as a mixture of regular customers and travelers shared the large wooden tables that were gathered around a small wood-burning stove. Sally had just been around the tables sharing jokes, offering some newly baked slabs of barley cake and refilling the oil lamps that had been burning all through the dull winter afternoon. She was now back behind the bar, carefully pouring out five measures of Springo Special Ale for some newly arrived Northern Traders.

When Sally glanced over at the Traders she noticed to her surprise that the usual look of sad resignation Northern Traders were known for had been replaced by broad grins. Sally smiled. She prided herself on running a happy cafe, and if she could get five dour Traders laughing before they even had their first tankard of Springo Special, then she was doing something right.

Sally brought the ale over to the Traders' table by the window and set it skillfully down in front of them without spilling a drop. But the Traders paid no attention to the ale, for they were too busy rubbing the steamed-up window with their grubby sleeves and peering out into the gloom. One of them pointed at something outside, and they all broke out into raucous guffaws.

The laughter was spreading around the cafe. Other customers began coming to the windows and peering out until soon the entire clientele of the cafe was pushing for a place by the long line of windows that ran along the back.

Sally Mullin peered out to see what was causing the merriment.

Her jaw dropped.

In the bright light of the full moon, the ExtraOrdinary Wizard, Madam Marcia Overstrand, was covered in rubbish and dancing like a madwoman on top of the municipal rubbish dump.

No, thought Sally, that's not possible.

She peered through the smeary window again. Sally could not believe what she saw. There indeed was Madam Marcia with three children—*three children*? Everyone knew that Madam Marcia could not abide children. There was also a wolf and someone who looked vaguely familiar to Sally. Now, who was it?

Sarah's no-good husband, Silas I'll-Do-It-Tomorrow Heap. That's who it was.

What on earth was Silas Heap doing with Marcia Overstrand? With three of the children? On the *rubbish dump*? Did Sarah know about this?

Well, she soon would.

As a good friend to Sarah Heap, Sally felt it was her duty to go and check this out. So she put the Washing-up Boy in charge of the cafe and ran out into the moonlight.

Sally clattered down the wooden gangway of the cafe pontoon and ran through the snow up the hill toward the dump. As she ran, her mind came to an inescapable conclusion.

Silas Heap was eloping with Marcia Overstrand.

It all made sense. Sarah had often complained about how

Silas was obsessed with Marcia. Ever since he had given up his Apprenticeship to Alther Mella and Marcia had taken it over, Silas had watched her amazing progress with a mixture of horror and fascination, always imagining that it could have been *him*. And since she had become ExtraOrdinary Wizard ten years ago, Silas had, if anything, been worse.

Completely obsessed with what Marcia was doing, that's what Sarah had said.

But of course, mused Sally, who had now reached the foot of the huge pile of rubbish and was painfully scrabbling her way up, Sarah was not entirely innocent either. Anyone could see that their little girl was not Silas's child. She looked so different from all the others. And once when Sally had very delicately tried to bring up the subject of Jenna's father, Sarah had very quickly changed it. Oh, yes, something had been going on between the Heaps for years. But that was no excuse for what Silas was doing now. No excuse at all, thought Sally crossly as she stumbled her way up toward the top of the dump.

The bedraggled figures had started making their way down and were heading in Sally's direction. Sally waved her arms at them, but they appeared not to have noticed her. They seemed preoccupied and were staggering a little as if they were dizzy. Now that they were nearer, Sally could see that she was right about their identities.

"*Silas Heap!*" Sally yelled angrily.

The five figures jumped out of their skins and stared at Sally.

"*Shush!*" four voices whispered as loud as they dared.

"I will not *shush!*" declared Sally. "What do you think you are doing, Silas Heap? Leaving your wife for this . . . *floozie*." Sally waggled her forefinger disapprovingly at Marcia.

"*Floozie?*" gasped Marcia.

"*And* taking these poor children with you," she told Silas. "How *could* you?"

Silas waded through the rubbish to Sally.

"*What* are you talking about?" he demanded. "And will you please *be quiet!*"

"*Shush!*" said three voices behind him.

At last Sally quieted down.

"Don't do it, Silas," she whispered hoarsely. "Don't leave your lovely wife and family. Please."

Silas looked bemused. "I'm not," he said. "Who told you that?"

"You're not?"

"*No!*"

"*Shushhh!*"

* * *

It took most of the long stumble down the dump to explain to Sally what had happened. Her eyes widened and her mouth fell open as Silas told her what he had to in order to get her on their side—which was pretty much everything. Silas realized that they not only needed Sally's silence; they could do with her help too. But Marcia wasn't so sure. Sally Mullin was not exactly the first person she would have chosen to help. Marcia decided to step in and take charge.

"Right," she said authoritatively as they reached the solid ground at the foot of the dump. "I think we can expect the Hunter and his Pack to be sent after us any minute now."

A flicker of fear passed over Silas's face. He had heard about the Hunter.

Marcia was practical and calm. "I've filled the chute back up with rubbish and done a Lockfast and Weld Spell on the rat door," she said. "So with any luck he'll think we're still trapped in there."

Nicko shuddered at the thought.

"But it won't delay him long," continued Marcia. "And then he'll come looking—and asking." Marcia looked at Sally as if to say, *And it will be you he'll be asking.*

Everyone fell quiet.

Sally returned Marcia's gaze steadily. She knew what she

was taking on. She knew it would be big trouble for her, but Sally was a loyal friend.

She would do it.

"Right, then," said Sally briskly. "We'll have to get you all far away with the pixies by then, won't we?"

Sally took them down to the bunkhouse at the back of the cafe where many an exhausted traveler had found themselves a warm bed for the night, and clean clothes too if they needed them. The bunkhouse was empty at this time of day. Sally showed them where the clothes were kept and told them to take as much as they needed. It was going to be a long, cold night. She quickly filled a bucket with hot water so that they could wash off the worst of the mess from the chute and then rushed out, saying, "I'll see you down at the quay in ten minutes. You can have my boat."

Jenna and Nicko were only too pleased to get rid of their filthy clothes, but Boy 412 refused to do anything. He had had enough changes that day, and he was determined to hang on to what he had, even if it was a pair of wet and filthy Wizard pajamas.

Eventually Marcia was forced to use a Clean-Up Spell on him, followed by a Change of Dress Spell to get him into the thick fisherman's sweater, trousers and sheepskin jacket plus a bright red beanie hat that Silas had found for him.

Marcia was cross at having to use a spell for Boy 412's outfit. She wanted to save her energy for later, as she had an unpleasant feeling that she might need it all to get them to safety. She had of course used a little energy on her One-Second Dry Clean Spell, which, due to the disgusting state of her cloak, had turned into a One-Minute Dry Clean Spell and still hadn't got rid of all the gravy stains. In Marcia's opinion, the cloak of an ExtraOrdinary Wizard was more than just a cloak; it was a finely tuned instrument of Magyk and must be treated with respect.

Ten minutes later they were all down at the quay.

Sally and her sailing boat were waiting for them. Nicko looked at the little green boat approvingly. He loved boats. In fact, there was nothing Nicko loved better than being out in a boat on the open water, and this looked like a good one. She was broad and steady, sat well in the water and had a pair of new red sails. She had a nice name too: *Muriel*. Nicko liked that.

Marcia looked at the boat dubiously. "How does it work, then?" she asked Sally.

Nicko butted in. "Sails," he said. "She sails."

"Who sails?" asked Marcia, confused.

Nicko was patient. "The *boat* does."

Sally was getting agitated.

"You'd better be off," she said, glancing back at the rubbish dump. "I've put some paddles in, just in case you need them. And some food. Here, I'll untie the rope and hang on to it while you all get aboard."

Jenna scrambled in first, grabbing Boy 412 by the arm and taking him with her. He resisted for a moment but then gave in. Boy 412 was getting very tired.

Nicko jumped in next, then Silas propelled a somewhat reluctant Marcia off the quay and into the boat. She sat down uncertainly by the tiller and sniffed.

"What's that awful smell?" she muttered.

"Fish," said Nicko, wondering if Marcia knew how to sail.

Silas jumped in with Maxie, and *Muriel* settled a little lower down in the water.

"I'll push you off now," said Sally anxiously.

She threw the rope to Nicko, who skillfully caught it and stowed it neatly in the prow of the boat.

Marcia grabbed at the tiller, the sails flapping wildly, and *Muriel* took an unpleasantly sharp turn to the left.

"Shall I take the tiller?" Nicko offered.

"Take the what? Oh, this handle thing here? Very well, Nicko. I don't want to tire myself." Marcia wrapped her cloak around her and, with as much dignity as she could muster, shuffled awkwardly around to the side of the boat.

Marcia was not happy. She had never been in a boat before, and she had no intention of ever getting in one again if she could possibly help it. There were no seats for a start. No carpet, no cushions even and no *roof*. Not only was there far too much water outside the boat for her liking, but there was a little too much inside too. Did this mean it was sinking? And the smell was unbelievable.

Maxie was very excited. He managed to tread on Marcia's precious shoes and wag his tail in her face at the same time.

"Shove over, you daft dog," said Silas, pushing Maxie up to the prow where he could put his long wolfhound nose into the wind and sniff all the water smells. Then Silas squashed himself in beside Marcia, much to her discomfort, while Jenna and Boy 412 curled up on the other side of the boat.

Nicko stood happily in the stern, holding on to the tiller, and confidently set sail for the open reaches of the river.

"Where are we going?" he asked.

Marcia was still too preoccupied with her sudden proximity to such a large amount of water to answer.

"Aunt Zelda," said Silas, who had discussed things with Sarah after Jenna had left that morning, "we'll go and stay with Aunt Zelda."

The wind caught *Muriel*'s sails and she picked up speed, heading toward the fast current in the middle of the river. Marcia closed her eyes and felt dizzy. She wondered if the boat was meant to lean over *quite* so much.

"The Keeper in Marram Marshes?" Marcia asked rather feebly.

"Yes," said Silas. "We'll be safe there. She's got her cottage permanently Enchanted now, after she was raided by the Quake Ooze Brownies last winter. No one will ever find it."

"Very well," said Marcia. "We'll go to Aunt Zelda."

Silas looked surprised. Marcia had actually agreed with him without an argument. But then, he smiled to himself, they were all in the same boat now.

And so the little green boat disappeared into the night, leaving Sally a distant figure on the shore, waving bravely. As she lost sight of *Muriel*, Sally stood on the quay and listened to the sound of the water lapping against the cold stones. Suddenly she felt quite alone. She turned and started to make her way back along the snowy riverbank, her path lit by the yellow light shining from her cafe windows a short distance away. A few customers' faces gazed out into the night as Sally hurried back to the warmth and chatter of the cafe, but they appeared not to notice her small figure as she tramped through the snow and made her way up the gangway to the pontoon.

As Sally pushed open the cafe door and slipped into the warm hubbub, her more regular customers noticed that she was not her usual self. And they were right; unusually for Sally, she had only one thought on her mind.

How long would it be before the Hunter arrived?

✛ IO ✛
THE HUNTER

It took precisely eight minutes and twenty seconds for the Hunter and his Pack to arrive at the Riverside Amenity Rubbish Dump after Sally had waved *Muriel* off at the quay. Sally had lived through each one of those five hundred seconds with a mounting dread in the pit of her stomach.

What had she *done*?

Sally had said nothing when she returned to the cafe, but something about her demeanor had caused most of her customers to quickly drink up their Springo, gulp down the last crumbs of barley cake and melt speedily into the night. The only customers Sally had left were the five Northern Traders, who were on their second measures of Springo Special and were talking softly among themselves in their mournful singsong accents. Even the Washing-up Boy had disappeared.

Sally's mouth was dry, her hands were shaking and she fought against her overwhelming desire to run away. Calm down, girl, she told herself. Tough it out. Deny everything. The Hunter has no reason to suspect you. If you run now, he'll *know* you're involved. And the Hunter will find you. He always does. Just sit tight and keep cool.

The second hand of the big cafe clock ticked on.

Click . . . Click . . . Click . . .

Four hundred and ninety-eight seconds . . . Four hundred and ninety-nine seconds . . . Five hundred.

A powerful searchlight beam swept across the top of the rubbish dump.

Sally ran to a nearby window and stared out, her heart pounding. She could see a swarm of black figures milling around, silhouetted in the beam of the searchlight. The Hunter had brought his Pack, just as Marcia had warned.

Sally stared intently, trying to make out what they were doing. The Pack was gathered around the rat door, which Marcia had jammed shut with the Lockfast and Weld Spell. To Sally's relief the Pack seemed to be in no hurry; in fact, it looked as though they were laughing among themselves. Some faint shouts drifted down to the cafe. Sally strained her ears. What she heard made her shiver.

". . . Wizard scum . . ."

". . . Rats trapped by a rat door . . ."

". . . Don't go away, ha ha. We're coming to get you . . ."

As Sally watched she could see the figures around the rat door becoming increasingly frantic as the door held fast against all their efforts to pull it free. Standing apart from the Pack was a lone figure watching impatiently whom Sally rightly took to be the Hunter.

Suddenly the Hunter lost patience with the efforts to free the rat door. He strode over, grabbed an axe from one of the Pack and angrily attacked the door. Loud metallic clangs echoed down to the cafe until eventually the mangled rat door was tossed to the side, and one of the Pack was sent into the chute to dig out the rubbish. A searchlight was now trained directly into the chute, and the Pack gathered around the exit. Sally could see the glinting of their pistols in the glare of the lights. With her heart in her mouth, Sally waited for them to discover that their prey had fled.

It didn't take long.

A disheveled figure emerged from the chute and was roughly

grabbed by the Hunter who, Sally could tell, was furious. He
shook the man violently and threw him aside, sending him
sprawling down the slope of the dump. The Hunter crouched
down and peered disbelievingly into the empty rubbish chute.
Abruptly, he motioned for the smallest of the Pack to go into
the chute. The man chosen hung back reluctantly, but he was
forced in, and two Pack Guards with pistols were left at the
entrance.

The Hunter walked slowly to the edge of the rubbish dump to
regain his composure after finding that his prey had eluded
him. He was followed at a safe distance by the small figure of
a boy.

The boy was dressed in the everyday green robes of a
Wizard Apprentice, but unlike any other Apprentice, he wore
around his waist a red sash with three black stars emblazoned
on it. The stars of DomDaniel.

But at that moment the Hunter was unaware of Dom-
Daniel's Apprentice. He stood quietly, a short, solidly built
man with the usual cropped Guard haircut. His face was brown
and lined from all his years outdoors spent hunting and tracking down prey of the human kind. He wore the usual Hunter
attire: dark green tunic and short cloak with thick brown

leather boots. Around his waist was a broad leather belt from which hung a sheathed knife and a pouch.

The Hunter smiled a grim smile, his mouth a thin, determined line turned down at the edges, his pale blue eyes narrowed to a watchful slit. So it was to be a Hunt, was it? Very well, there was nothing he liked better than a Hunt. For years he had been slowly making his way up through the ranks of the Hunting Pack, and at last he had reached his goal. He was a Hunter, the very best of the Pack, and this was the moment he had been waiting for. Here he was, hunting not only the ExtraOrdinary Wizard but also the Princess, the *Queenling* no less. The Hunter felt excited as he anticipated a night to remember: the Sighting, the Trail, the Chase, the Close and the Kill. No problem, thought the Hunter, his smile broadening to show his small pointed teeth in the cold moonlight.

The Hunter turned his thoughts to the Hunt. Something told him that the birds had flown from the rubbish chute, but as an efficient Hunter he had to make sure that all possibilities were covered, and the Pack Guard he had sent inside had been given instructions to follow the chute and check all exits back up to the Wizard Tower. The fact that that was probably impossible did not trouble the Hunter; a Pack Guard was the lowest of the low, an Expendable, and would do his duty or die in the attempt. The Hunter had been an Expendable once but not for long—he'd made sure of that. And now, he thought with a tremor of excitement, now he must find the Trail.

The rubbish dump, however, yielded few clues even to the skilled tracker that the Hunter was. The heat from the decay of the rubbish had melted the snow, and the constant disturbance of the rubbish by rats and gulls had already removed any trace of a Trail. Very well, thought the Hunter. In the absence of a Trail he must search out a Sighting.

The Hunter stood on his vantage point on top of the dump and surveyed the moonlit scene through his narrowed eyes. Behind him rose the steep, dark walls of the Castle, the battlements outlined crisply against the cold, bright starry sky. In front of him lay the undulating landscape of the rich farmland that bordered the far side of the river, and in the distance on the horizon his eyes took in the jagged spine of the Border Mountains. The Hunter gave the snow-covered landscape a long, considered stare but saw nothing of interest to him. He then turned his attention to the more immediate scene below him. He looked down at the broad sweep of the river, his gaze following the flow of the water as it rounded the bend and flowed swiftly on to his right, past the cafe perched on the pontoon, which was floating gently on the high tide, past the little quay with its boats moored up for the night, and on down the broad sweep of the river until it disappeared from view behind Raven's Rock, a jagged outcrop that towered over the river.

The Hunter listened intently for sounds rising up from the water, but all he heard was the silence that the blanketing of snow brings. He scanned the water for clues—perhaps a shadow under the banks, a startled bird, a telltale ripple—but he could see nothing. *Nothing.* It was strangely quiet and still, the dark river silently winding through the bright snowy landscape lit by the shimmer of the full moon. It was, thought the Hunter, a perfect night for a Hunt.

The Hunter stood immobile, tense, waiting for the Sighting to show itself to him.

Watching and waiting . . .

Something caught his eye. A white face at the window of the cafe. A frightened face, a face that *knew* something. The Hunter smiled. He had a Sighting. He was back on the Trail.

THE TRAIL

S*ally saw them coming.*
  She jumped back from the window, straightened her skirts and collected her thoughts. Go for it, girl, she told herself. You can do it. Just put on your Welcoming Landlady face and they won't suspect a thing. Sally took refuge behind the bar and, for the first time ever during cafe hours, she poured herself a tankard of Springo Special and took a large gulp.

Eurgh. She had never liked the stuff. Too many dead rats in the bottom of the barrel for her taste.

As Sally took another mouthful of dead rat, a powerful searchlight beam cut into the cafe and swept over the occupants.

Briefly, it shone straight into Sally's eyes and then, moving on, lit up the pale faces of the Northern Traders. The Traders stopped talking and exchanged worried glances.

A moment later Sally heard the heavy thud of hurried footsteps coming up the gangway. The pontoon rocked as the Pack ran along it, and the cafe shook, its plates and glasses nervously clinking with the movement. Sally put her tankard away, stood up straight and with great difficulty put a welcoming smile on her face.

The door crashed open.

The Hunter strode in. Behind him, in the beam of the searchlight, Sally could see the Pack lined up along the pontoon, pistols at the ready.

"Good evening, sir. What can I get you?" Sally trilled nervously.

The Hunter heard the tremor in her voice with satisfaction. He liked it when they were frightened.

He walked slowly up to the bar, leaned over and stared at Sally intently.

"You can get me some *information*. I know you have it."

"Oh?" Sally tried to sound politely interested. But that wasn't what the Hunter heard. He heard scared and playing for time.

Good, he thought. This one knows something.

"I am in pursuit of a small and dangerous group of terrorists," said the Hunter, carefully watching Sally's face. Sally struggled to keep her Welcoming Landlady face, but for a fraction of a second it slipped, and the briefest of expressions flitted across her features: surprise.

"Surprised to hear your friends described as terrorists, are you?"

"No," said Sally quickly. And then, realizing what she had said, stuttered, "I—I don't mean that. I . . . ."

Sally gave up. The damage was done. How had it happened so easily? It was his eyes, thought Sally, those thin, bright slits of eyes like two searchlights shining into your brain. What a fool she was to think she could outwit a Hunter. Sally's heart was pounding so loudly she was sure the Hunter could hear it.

Which of course he could. That was one of his favorite sounds, the beating heart of cornered prey. He listened for a delightful moment longer and then he said, "You will tell us where they are."

"No," muttered Sally.

The Hunter seemed untroubled by this small act of rebellion. "You will," he told her matter-of-factly.

The Hunter leaned against the bar.

"Nice place you've got here, Sally Mullin. Very pretty. Built of wood, isn't it? Been here a while if I remember right. Good dry seasoned timber by now. Burns exceedingly well, I'm told."

"No . . ." whispered Sally.

"Well, I'll tell you what, then. You just tell me where your friends have gone, and I'll mislay my tinder box . . ."

Sally said nothing. Her mind was racing, but her thoughts made no sense to her. All she could think of was that she had never got the fire buckets refilled after the Washing-up Boy set the tea towels alight.

"Right, then," said the Hunter. "I'll go and tell the boys to get the fire started. I'll lock the doors behind me when I go. We don't want anyone running out and getting hurt, do we?"

"You *can't* . . ." gasped Sally, understanding that the Hunter was not only about to burn down her beloved cafe but intended to burn it down with her inside it. Not to mention the five Northern Traders. Sally glanced at them. They were muttering anxiously among themselves.

The Hunter had said all he'd come to say. It was going pretty much as he had expected, and now was the time to show that he meant business. He turned abruptly and walked toward the door.

Sally stared after him, suddenly angry. How dare he come

into *my* cafe and terrorize *my* customers! And then swagger off to burn us all to cinders? That man, thought Sally, is nothing but a bully. She didn't like bullies.

Sally, impetuous as ever, ran out from behind the bar.

"Wait!" she yelled.

The Hunter smiled. It was working. It always did. Walk away and leave them to think about it for a moment. They always come around. The Hunter stopped but did not turn.

A hard kick on his leg from Sally's sturdy right boot caught the Hunter by surprise.

"Bully," shouted Sally.

"Fool," gasped the Hunter, clutching his leg. "You will regret this, Sally Mullin."

A Senior Pack Guard appeared. "Trouble, sir?" he inquired.

The Hunter was not pleased to be seen hopping about in such an undignified manner. "No," he snapped. "All part of the plan."

"The men have collected the brushwood, sir, and set it under the cafe as you ordered. The tinder is dry and the flints are sparking well, sir."

"Good," said the Hunter grimly.

"Excuse me, sir?" said a heavily accented voice behind him. One of the Northern Traders had left their table and made his way over to the Hunter.

"Yes?" replied the Hunter through gritted teeth, spinning around on one leg to face the man. The Trader stood awkwardly. He was dressed in the dark red tunic of the Hanseatic League, travel-stained and ragged. His straggly blond hair was held in place by a greasy leather band around his forehead, and his face was a pasty white in the glare of the searchlight.

"I believe we have the information you require?" the Trader continued. His voice was slowly searching for the right words in an unfamiliar language, rising as though asking a question.

"Have you now?" replied the Hunter, the pain in his leg leaving him as, at last, the Hunt began to pick up the Trail.

Sally stared at the Northern Trader in horror. How did *he* know anything? Then she realized. He must have seen them from the window.

The Trader avoided Sally's accusing stare. He looked uncomfortable, but he had obviously understood enough of the Hunter's words to also be afraid.

"We believe those you seek have left? In the boat?" the Trader said slowly.

"The boat. Which boat?" snapped the Hunter, back in charge now.

"We do not know your boats here. A small boat, red

sails? A family with a wolf."

"A wolf. Ah, the mutt." The Hunter moved uncomfortably close to the Trader and growled in a low voice, "Which direction? Upstream or downstream? To the mountains or to the Port? Think carefully, my friend, if you and your companions wish to keep cool tonight."

"Downstream. To the Port," muttered the Trader, finding the hot breath of the Hunter unpleasant.

"Right," said the Hunter, satisfied. "I suggest you and your friends leave now while you can."

The other four Traders silently got up and walked over to the fifth Trader, guiltily avoiding Sally's horrified gaze. Swiftly they slipped out into the night, leaving Sally to her fate.

The Hunter gave her a little mocking bow.

"And good night to you too, Madam," he said. "Thank you for your hospitality." The Hunter swept out and slammed the cafe door behind him.

"Nail the door shut!" he shouted angrily. "And the windows. Don't let her escape!"

The Hunter strode off down the gangway. "Get me a fast-pursuit bullet boat," he ordered the Runner waiting at the end of the gangway. "At the quay. *Now!*"

The Hunter reached the riverbank and turned to survey

Sally Mullin's beleaguered cafe. As much as he wanted to see the first lick of the flames before he left, he did not stop. He needed to catch the Trail before it went cold. As he strode down to the quay to await the arrival of the bullet boat, the Hunter smiled a satisfied smile.

No one tried to make a fool of *him* and got away with it.

Behind the smiling Hunter trotted the Apprentice. He was somewhat sulky at having been left outside the cafe in the cold, but he was also very excited. He wrapped his thick cloak around him and hugged himself with anticipation. His dark eyes shone, and his pale cheeks were flushed with the chill night air. This was turning into the Big Adventure his Master had told him it would be. It was the start of his Master's Return. And he was part of it because without him it could not happen. He was Advisor to the Hunter. He was the one who would Oversee the Hunt. The one whose Magykal powers would Save the Day. A brief tremor of doubt crossed the Apprentice's mind at this thought, but he pushed it away. He felt so important it made him want to shout. Or jump about. Or hit someone. But he couldn't. He had to do as his Master told him and follow the Hunter carefully and quietly. But he might just hit the Queenling when he got her—that would show her.

"Stop daydreaming and get in the boat, will you?" the Hunter snapped at him. "Get in the back, out of the way."

The Apprentice did as he was told. He didn't want to admit it, but the Hunter scared him. He stepped carefully into the stern of the boat and squeezed himself into the tiny space in front of the feet of the oarsmen.

The Hunter looked approvingly at the bullet boat. Long, narrow, sleek and as black as the night, it was coated with a polished lacquer that allowed it to slip through the water with the ease of a skater's blade on ice. Powered by ten highly trained oarsmen, it could outrun anything on the water.

On the prow it carried a powerful searchlight and a sturdy tripod on which a pistol could be mounted. The Hunter stepped carefully into the prow and sat on the narrow plank behind the tripod, where he set about quickly and expertly mounting the Assassin's silver pistol onto it. He then took a silver bullet from his pouch, looked at it closely to make sure it was the one he wanted and laid it down in a small tray beside the pistol in readiness. Finally the Hunter took five standard bullets from the boat's bullet box and lined them up beside the silver bullet. He was ready.

"Go!" he said.

The bullet boat pulled smoothly and silently out from the

quay, found the fast current in the middle of the river and disappeared into the night.

But not before the Hunter had glanced behind him and seen the sight he had been waiting for.

A sheet of flame was snaking up into the night.

Sally Mullin's cafe was ablaze.

✠ I 2 ✠
MURIEL

A few miles downriver the sailboat *Muriel* was running
with the wind, and Nicko was in his element. He
stood at the helm of the small crowded boat and guided her
skillfully along the channel that wound down the middle of
the river, where the water flowed swift and deep. The spring
tide was ebbing fast and taking them with it, while the wind
had risen enough to make the water choppy and send *Muriel*
bouncing through the waves.

The full moon rode high in the sky and cast a bright silver
light over the river, lighting their way. The river widened as

it traveled ever onward toward the sea, and as the occupants
of the boat gazed out they noticed that the low-lying riverbanks with their overhanging trees and occasional lonely
cottage appeared increasingly distant. A silence descended
as the passengers began to feel uncomfortably small in such
a large expanse of water. And Marcia began to feel horribly
sick.

Jenna was sitting on the wooden deck, resting against the
hull and holding on to a rope for Nicko. The rope was
attached to the small triangular sail at the prow that tugged
and pulled with the wind, and Jenna was kept busy trying to
keep hold of it. Her fingers felt stiff and numb, but she did not
dare let go. Nicko got very bossy when he was in charge of a
boat, Jenna thought.

The wind felt cold, and even with the thick sweater, big
sheepskin jacket and itchy woolen hat that Silas had found for
her in Sally's clothes cupboard, Jenna shivered in the chill
from the water.

Curled up beside Jenna lay Boy 412. Once Jenna had pulled
him into the boat, Boy 412 had decided that there was nothing
he could do anymore and had given up his struggle against the
Wizards and the weird kids. And when *Muriel* had rounded
Raven's Rock and he could no longer see the Castle, Boy 412

had simply curled up into a ball beside Jenna and fallen fast asleep. Now that *Muriel* had reached rougher waters, his head was thumping against the mast with the movement of the boat, and Jenna gently shifted Boy 412 and placed his head on her lap. She looked down at his thin, pinched face almost hidden beneath his red felt hat and thought that Boy 412 looked a lot happier in his sleep than he did when he was awake. Then her thoughts turned to Sally.

Jenna loved Sally. She loved the way Sally never stopped talking and the way she made things happen. When Sally breezed in to see the Heaps, she brought with her all the excitement of life in the Castle, and Jenna loved it.

"I hope Sally is all right," said Jenna quietly as she listened to the steady creaking and gentle purposeful swish of the little boat speeding through the shining black water.

"So do I, poppet," said Silas, deep in thought.

Since the Castle had disappeared from view, Silas too now had time to think. And, after he had thought about Sarah and the boys and hoped they had reached Galen's tree house in the Forest safely, his thoughts had also turned to Sally, and they made for uncomfortable thinking.

"She'll be fine," said Marcia weakly. She felt sick, and she didn't like it.

"That's just so typical of you, Marcia," snapped Silas. "Now that you're ExtraOrdinary Wizard you just take what you want from someone and don't give them another thought. You just don't live in the real world anymore, do you? Unlike us Ordinary Wizards. We *know* what it's like to be in danger."

"*Muriel's* going well," said Nicko brightly, trying to change the subject. He didn't like it when Silas got upset about Ordinary Wizards. Nicko thought being an Ordinary Wizard was pretty good. He wouldn't fancy it himself—too many books to read and not enough time to go sailing—but he reckoned it was a respectable job. And who would want to be *Extra*Ordinary Wizard anyway? Stuck in that weird Tower for most of the time and never able to go anywhere without people gawking at you. There was no way he would ever want to do *that*.

Marcia sighed. "I imagine the platinum KeepSafe I gave her from my belt will be of some help," she said slowly, gazing studiedly at the distant riverbank.

"You gave Sally one of your belt Charms?" asked Silas, amazed. "Your KeepSafe? Wasn't that a bit risky? You might need it."

"The KeepSafe is there to be used when the Need is Great. Sally is going to join Sarah and Galen. It may be of some use to them too. Now be quiet. I think I'm going to be sick."

An uneasy silence fell.

"*Muriel*'s doing nicely, Nicko. You're a good sailor," said Silas some time later.

"Thanks, Dad," said Nicko, smiling broadly, as he always did when a boat was sailing well. Nicko was guiding *Muriel* expertly through the water, balancing the pull of the tiller against the force of the wind in the sails and sending the little boat singing through the waves.

"Is that the Marram Marshes, Dad?" asked Nicko after a while, pointing to the distant riverbank on his left. He had noticed that the landscape around them was changing. *Muriel* was now sailing down the middle of what was a wide expanse of water, and in the distance Nicko could see a vast stretch of flat low-lying land, dusted with snow and shimmering in the moonlight.

Silas stared out across the water.

"Perhaps you should sail that way a bit, Nicko," suggested Silas, waving his arm in the general direction where Nicko was pointing. "Then we can keep an eye open for the Deppen Ditch. That's the one we need."

Silas hoped he could remember the entrance to the Deppen

Ditch, which was the channel that led to Keeper's Cottage, where Aunt Zelda lived. It had been a long time since he had been to see Aunt Zelda, and the marshland all looked much the same to Silas.

Nicko had just changed course and was heading in the direction of Silas's waving arm when a brilliant beam of light cut through the darkness behind them.

It was the bullet boat's searchlight.

✢ 13 ✢
THE CHASE

Everyone—*except* Boy 412, who was still asleep—stared into the darkness. As they did so the searchlight swept across the distant horizon again, lighting up the broad expanse of the river and the low-lying banks on either side. There was no doubt in anyone's mind what it was.

"It's the Hunter, isn't it, Dad?" whispered Jenna.

Silas knew Jenna was right, but he said, "Well, it could be anything, poppet. Just a boat out fishing . . . or something," he added lamely.

"Of course it's the Hunter. In a fast-pursuit bullet boat,

if I'm not mistaken," snapped Marcia, who had suddenly stopped feeling sick.

Marcia didn't realize it, but she no longer felt sick because *Muriel* had stopped bouncing through the water. In fact, *Muriel* had stopped doing anything at all, except slowly drifting nowhere in particular.

Marcia looked accusingly at Nicko. "Get a move on, Nicko. What have you slowed down for?"

"There's nothing I can do. The wind's dropped," muttered Nicko, worried. He had just turned *Muriel* toward the Marram Marshes only to find that the wind had died. *Muriel* had lost all speed, and her sails were hanging limply.

"Well, we can't just *sit* here," said Marcia, anxiously watching the searchlight coming rapidly closer. "That bullet boat's going to be here in a few minutes."

"Can't you rustle up some wind for us?" Silas asked Marcia, agitated. "I thought you did Element Control on the Advanced Course. Or make us invisible. Come on, Marcia. *Do* something."

"I can't just 'rustle up some wind,' as you put it. There's nowhere near enough time. And you *know* Invisibility is a personal spell. I can't do it for anyone else."

The searchlight swept across the water again. Bigger,

brighter, nearer. And coming toward them *fast*.

"We'll have to use the paddles," said Nicko, who, as skipper, had decided to take charge. "We can paddle over to the marsh and hide there. Come on. *Quick*."

Marcia, Silas and Jenna grabbed a paddle each. Boy 412 woke up with a start as Jenna thumped his head down on the deck in her rush to pick up a paddle. He looked around him unhappily. Why was he still in the boat with all the Wizards? What did they want him for?

Jenna thrust the remaining paddle into his hand.

"Paddle!" she told him. "As fast as you can!" Jenna's tone of voice reminded Boy 412 of his drill teacher. He put his paddle into the water and paddled as fast as he could.

Slowly, far too slowly, *Muriel* crept toward the safety of the Marram Marshes while the bullet boat's searchlight swung backward and forward across the water, mercilessly seeking out its prey.

Jenna stole a look behind her and, to her horror, saw the black shape of the bullet boat. It was like a long repulsive beetle, its five pairs of thin black legs silently slicing through the water to and fro, to and fro, as the highly trained oarsmen pushed themselves and the boat to the limits, gaining fast on *Muriel's* frantically paddling occupants.

Sitting in the prow was the unmistakable shape of the Hunter, tense and ready to pounce. Jenna caught the Hunter's cold, calculating stare and suddenly she felt brave enough to talk to Marcia.

"Marcia," said Jenna, "we're not going to reach the marshes in time. You *must* do something. *Now.*"

Although Marcia looked surprised at being spoken to so directly, she approved. Spoken like a true Princess, she thought.

"Very well," agreed Marcia. "I could try a Fog. I can do that in fifty-three seconds. If it's cold and damp enough."

Muriel's crew was sure that there were no problems with the cold and damp bit. They just hoped they had fifty-three seconds left.

"Everyone stop paddling," instructed Marcia. "Keep still. And quiet. Very quiet." *Muriel*'s crew did as they were told, and in the silence that fell, they heard a new sound in the distance. The rhythmic splash of the bullet boat's oars.

Marcia gingerly stood up, wishing that the floor wouldn't move around so much. Then she leaned against the mast to steady herself, took a deep breath and threw her arms wide, her cloak flying out like a pair of purple wings.

"Murken Wake!" the ExtraOrdinary Wizard whispered as loud as she dared. "Murken Wake and Refuge Make!"

It was a beautiful spell. Jenna watched as thick white clouds gathered themselves together in the bright moonlit sky, quickly obscuring the moon and bringing down a deep chill into the night air. In the darkness all became deathly still as the first delicate tendrils of mist started rising from the black water as far as the eye could see. Faster and faster the tendrils grew, gathering together and growing into thick swathes of Fog, as the mist from the marshes rolled over the water to join them. In the very center, in the eye of the Fog, sat *Muriel*, becalmed and patiently waiting as the mist tumbled, swirled and thickened around her.

Soon *Muriel* was blanketed by a deep white thickness that struck a damp chill into Jenna's bones. Next to her she felt Boy 412 start shivering badly. He was still chilled from his time under the snow.

"Fifty-three seconds precisely," Marcia's voice muttered from out of the Fog. "Not bad."

"*Shhhh*," shushed Silas.

Thick white silence fell in the little boat. Slowly Jenna lifted her hand and placed it in front of her wide-open eyes. She could see nothing but whiteness. But she could hear everything.

She could hear the synchronized splash of ten knife-sharp oars being dipped into the water and out again, in and out, in and out. She could hear the swishing whisper of the bullet boat's prow slicing through the river, and now—now the bullet boat was so close that she could even hear the labored breathing of the oarsmen.

"*Stop!*" the Hunter's voice boomed through the Fog. The splash of the oars ceased and the bullet boat drifted to a halt. Inside the Fog *Muriel*'s occupants held their breath, convinced that the bullet boat was very close indeed. Maybe close enough for them to reach out and touch. Or close enough even for the Hunter to leap onto *Muriel*'s crowded deck. . . .

Jenna felt her heart beating fast and loud, but she made herself breathe slowly, silently, and stay completely still. She knew that although they could not be seen, they could still be heard. Nicko and Marcia were doing the same. Silas was too, with the added interest of having one hand clasped around Maxie's long, damp muzzle to stop him from howling and the other hand slowly and calmly stroking the agitated wolfhound, who had become quite spooked by the Fog.

Jenna could feel Boy 412's constant shivering. She slowly reached out her arm and pulled him close to her to try and warm him up. Boy 412 seemed tense. Jenna could tell he was listening hard to the Hunter's voice.

"We have them!" the Hunter was saying. "This is a Hexed

Fog if ever I saw one. And what do you always find in the middle of a Hexed Fog? One hexing Wizard. And her accomplices." His low, self-satisfied chuckle drifted through the Fog and made Jenna shiver.

"Give . . . yourselves . . . up." The Hunter's disembodied voice enveloped *Muriel*. "The Qu—the Princess has nothing to fear from us. Neither do the rest of you. We are only concerned for your own safety and wish to escort you back to the Castle before you have an unfortunate accident."

Jenna hated the Hunter's oily voice. She hated the way they could not escape it, the way they had to just sit there and listen to his silky smooth lies. She wanted to shout at him. To tell him that *she* was in charge here. That *she* would not listen to his threats. That soon *he* would be sorry. And then she felt Boy 412 take a deep breath, and she knew exactly what he was going to do.

Yell.

Jenna clapped her hand tightly around Boy 412's mouth. He struggled with her and tried to push her away, but she grabbed his arms with her other hand and held them tightly against his sides. Jenna was strong for her size and very quick. Boy 412 was no match for her, thin and weak as he was.

Boy 412 was furious. His last chance to redeem himself had

been thwarted. He could have returned to the Young Army as a hero, having bravely foiled the Wizards' attempt to escape. Instead he had the Princess's grubby little hand shoved over his mouth, which was making him feel sick. *And* she was stronger than him. That wasn't right. He was a boy and she was just a stupid girl. In his anger Boy 412 kicked out and hit the deck with a loud thump. At once Nicko was on him, pinning his legs down and holding him so tightly that he was completely unable to move or make another sound.

But the damage was done. The Hunter was loading his pistol with a silver bullet. Boy 412's angry kick had been all the Hunter needed to pinpoint exactly where they were. He smiled to himself as he turned the pistol on its tripod to face into the Fog. He was indeed pointing it straight at Jenna.

Marcia heard the metallic clicks of the silver bullet being loaded, a sound she had heard once before and never forgotten. She thought fast. She could do a Begird and Preserve, but she understood the Hunter well enough to know that he would merely watch and wait until the spell faded. The only solution, thought Marcia, was a Projection. She just hoped she had enough energy to maintain it.

Marcia closed her eyes and Projected. She Projected an image of *Muriel* and all its occupants sailing out of the Fog at full speed. Like all Projections it was a mirror image, but she hoped that in the darkness, and with Muɾıᴉɐ already sailing away fast, the Hunter would not notice.

"Sir!" came the shout of an oarsman. "They're trying to outrun us, sir!"

The sounds of the pistol being primed ceased. The Hunter swore.

"Follow them, you idiots!" he screamed at the oarsmen.

Slowly the bullet boat pulled away from the Fog.

"Faster!" yelled the Hunter angrily, unable to bear the sight of his prey escaping him for the *third* time that night.

Inside the Fog, Jenna and Nicko grinned. Score: one up for them.

✠ 14 ✠
DEPPEN DITCH

Marcia was snappy. Very snappy.

Keeping two spells on the go was a tough one. Especially since one of them, being a Projection, was a Reverse form of Magyk and, unlike most spells that Marcia used, still had links to the Darke side—the Other side, as Marcia preferred to call it. It took a brave and skillful Wizard to use Reverse Magyk without inviting the Other in. Alther had taught Marcia well, for many of the spells he had learned from DomDaniel did indeed bring in Darke Magyk, and Alther had become adept at blocking it out. Marcia was only too well aware that all the time she was using the

Projection, the Other hovered about them, awaiting its chance to break into the spell.

Which explained why Marcia felt as though her brain had no room left for anything else, certainly not for making the effort to be polite.

"For goodness' sake, get this wretched boat moving, Nicko," snapped Marcia. Nicko looked hurt. There was no need to talk to him like that.

"Someone's got to paddle it, then," muttered Nicko. "And it would help if I could see where we're going."

With some effort, and a consequent increase in snappiness, Marcia cleared a tunnel through the Fog. Silas kept quiet. He knew that Marcia was having to use a huge amount of Magyk energy and skill, and he felt a grudging respect for her. There was no way Silas would ever dare attempt a Projection, let alone keep a massive Fog going at the same time. He had to hand it to her—she was pretty good.

Silas left Marcia to her Magyk and paddled *Muriel* through the thick white cocoon of the Fog tunnel while Nicko carefully steered the boat toward the bright starry sky at the end of the tunnel. Soon Nicko felt the bottom of the boat scraping along rough sand, and *Muriel* bumped up against a thick tuft of sedge grass.

They had reached the safety of the Marram Marshes.

Marcia breathed a sigh of relief and let the Fog disperse. Everyone relaxed, except for Jenna. Jenna, who had not been the only girl in a family of six boys without learning a thing or two, had Boy 412 facedown on the deck in an armlock.

"Let him go, Jen," said Nicko.

"Why?" demanded Jenna.

"He's only a silly boy."

"But he nearly got us all killed. We saved his life when he was buried in the snow and he betrayed us," Jenna said angrily.

Boy 412 was silent. Buried in the snow? Saved his life? All he remembered was falling asleep outside the Wizard Tower and then waking up a prisoner in Marcia's rooms.

"Let him go, Jenna," said Silas. "He doesn't understand what's going on."

"All right," said Jenna, a little reluctantly releasing Boy 412 from the armlock. "But I think he's a *pig*."

Boy 412 sat up slowly, rubbing his arm. He didn't like the way everyone was glaring him. And he didn't like the way the Princess girl called him a pig, especially after she had been so nice to him before. Boy 412 huddled by himself as far away from Jenna as he could get and tried to work things out in his head. It wasn't easy. Nothing made sense. He tried to remember what they told him in the Young Army.

Facts. There are only facts. Good facts. Bad facts. So:

> *Fact One. Kidnapped: BAD.*
>
> *Fact Two. Uniform stolen: BAD.*
>
> *Fact Three. Pushed down rubbish chute: BAD.*
>   *Really BAD.*
>
> *Fact Four. Shoved into cold smelly boat: BAD.*
>
> *Fact Five. Not killed by Wizards (yet): GOOD.*
>
> *Fact Six. Probably going to be killed by Wizards*
>   *soon: BAD.*

Boy 412 counted up the GOODs and the BADs. As usual, the BADs outnumbered the GOODs, which didn't surprise him.

Nicko and Jenna clambered out of *Muriel* and scrambled up the grassy bank beside the small sandy beach on which *Muriel* now lay with her sails hanging loose. Nicko wanted a rest from being in charge of the boat. He took his responsibilities as skipper very seriously, and while he was actually in *Muriel* he felt that if anything went wrong, it was somehow his fault. Jenna was pleased to be on dry land again, or rather slightly damp land—the grass she sat down on had a soggy, squashy feel to it, as though it was growing on a big piece of wet sponge, and it was covered in a light dusting of snow.

With Jenna at a safe distance, Boy 412 dared to look up, and he saw something that made the hair on the back of his neck stand up.

Magyk. Powerful Magyk.

Boy 412 stared at Marcia. Although no one else seemed to have noticed, he could see the haze of Magyk energy that surrounded her. It glowed a shimmering purple, flickering across the surface of her ExtraOrdinary Wizard cloak and giving her dark curly hair a deep purple shine. Marcia's brilliant green eyes glittered as she gazed into infinity, observing a silent film that only she could see. Despite his Young Army anti-Wizard training, Boy 412 found himself awestruck in the presence of Magyk.

The film Marcia was watching was, of course, ꟾɒiɔɿɒM and her six mirror-image crew. They were sailing fast toward the wide mouth of the river and had nearly reached the open sea at the Port. They were, to the Hunter's amazement, reaching incredible speeds for a small sailing boat, and although the bullet boat managed to keep ꟾɒiɔɿɒM in sight, it was having trouble closing the distance enough for the Hunter to fire his silver bullet. The ten oarsmen were also tiring, and the Hunter was quite hoarse from screaming at them to go "faster, fools!"

The Apprentice had sat obediently in the back of the boat for the entire Chase. The angrier the Hunter had become, the less he had dared to say anything at all and the more he had slunk down into his tiny space at the sweaty feet of Oarsman Number Ten. But as time went on Oarsman Number Ten began to mutter extremely rude and interesting comments about the Hunter under his breath, and the Apprentice got a little braver. He gazed out over the water and stared at the speeding lɘiɿuM. The more he looked at lɘiɿuM, the more he knew that something was wrong.

Finally the Apprentice dared to shout out to the Hunter, "Did you know that that boat's name is back to front?"

"Don't try to be clever with *me*, boy."

The Hunter's eyesight was good, but maybe not as good as a ten-and-a-half-year-old boy's, whose hobby was collecting and labeling ants. Not for nothing had the Apprentice spent hours at his Master's Camera Obscura, hidden far away in the Badlands, watching the river. He knew the names and histories of all the boats that sailed there. He knew that the boat they had been chasing *before* the Fog was *Muriel*, built by Rupert Gringe and hired out to catch herring. He also knew that *after* the Fog the boat was called lɘiɿuM, and " lɘiɿuM" was

a mirror image of "Muriel." And he had been an Apprentice
to DomDaniel for long enough to know exactly what that
meant.

ləiɾuM was a Projection, an Apparition, a Phantasm and an
Illusion.

Luckily for the Apprentice, who was just about to inform the
Hunter of this interesting fact, at that very moment back in the
real *Muriel*, Maxie licked Marcia's hand in a friendly, slobbery
wolfhound way. Marcia shuddered at the warm wolfhound spit,
her concentration lapsed for a second, and ləiɾuM briefly disappeared in front of the Hunter's own eyes. The boat quickly
reappeared again, but too late. ləiɾuM had given herself away.

The Hunter screamed in fury and slammed his fist down
on the bullet box. Then he screamed again, this time in pain.
He had broken his fifth metacarpal. His little finger. And it
hurt. Nursing his hand, the Hunter yelled at the oarsmen:
"*Turn around, you fools!*"

The bullet boat stopped, the oarsmen reversed their seats
and wearily started rowing in the opposite direction. The
Hunter found himself in the back of the boat. The Apprentice,
to his delight, was now in the front.

But the bullet boat was not the efficient machine it had
been. The oarsmen were rapidly tiring and were not taking

kindly to having insults screamed at them by an increasingly hysterical would-be murderer. The rhythm of their rowing faltered, and the smooth movement of the bullet boat became uneven and uncomfortable.

The Hunter sat glowering in the back of the boat. He knew that for the *fourth* time that night the Trail had gone cold. The Hunt was turning bad.

The Apprentice, however, was enjoying the turnaround. He sat low at what was now the prow and, rather like Maxie, put his nose in the air and enjoyed the sensation of the night air rushing past him. He also felt relieved that he had been able to do his job. His Master would be proud. He imagined himself back at his Master's side and how he would describe the way *he* had detected a fiendish Projection and saved the day. Perhaps it would stop his Master from being so disappointed in his lack of Magykal talent. He did try, thought the Apprentice, he really did, but somehow he just never quite got it. Whatever *it* was.

It was Jenna who saw the dreaded searchlight coming around a distant bend.

"They're coming back!" she yelled.

Marcia jumped, lost the Projection completely and, far

away at the Port, Muriel and her crew disappeared forever, much to the shock of a lone fisherman on the harbor wall.

"We've got to hide the boat," said Nicko, jumping up and running along the grassy bank, followed by Jenna.

Silas shoved Maxie out of the boat and told him to go and lie down. Then he helped Marcia out, and Boy 412 scrambled after her.

Marcia sat on the grassy bank of Deppen Ditch, determined to keep her purple python shoes dry for as long as she possibly could. Everyone else, including, to Jenna's surprise, Boy 412, waded into the shallow water and pushed *Muriel* clear of the sand so that she was floating again. Then Nicko grabbed a rope and pulled *Muriel* along the Deppen Ditch until she rounded a corner and could no longer be seen from the river. The tide was falling now, and *Muriel* floated low in the Ditch, her short mast hidden by the steeply rising banks.

The sound of the Hunter screaming at the oarsmen drifted across the water, and Marcia stuck her head up over the top of the Ditch to see what was going on. She had never seen anything quite like it. The Hunter was standing very precariously in the back of the bullet boat wildly waving one arm in the air. He kept up a nonstop barrage of insults directed at the oarsmen, who had by now lost all sense of rhythm and were letting the bullet boat zigzag across the water.

"I shouldn't do this," said Marcia. "I really shouldn't. It's petty and vindictive and it demeans the power of Magyk, but I *don't care*."

Jenna, Nicko and Boy 412 rushed to the top of the Ditch to see what Marcia was about to do. As they watched, Marcia pointed her finger at the Hunter and muttered, "Dive!"

For a split second the Hunter felt odd, as though he was about to do something very stupid—which he was. For some reason he could not understand, he raised his arms elegantly above his head and carefully pointed his hands toward the water. Then he slowly bent his knees and dived neatly out of the bullet boat, performing a skillful somersault before he landed perfectly in the freezing cold water.

Reluctantly, and rather unnecessarily slowly, the oarsmen rowed back and helped the gasping Hunter into the boat.

"You really shouldn't have done that, sir," said Oarsman Number Ten. "Not in this weather."

The Hunter could not reply. His teeth chattered so loudly that he could hardly think, let alone speak. His wet clothes clung to him as he shivered violently in the cold night air. Gloomily, he surveyed the marshland where he was sure his quarry had fled but could see no sign of them. Seasoned

Hunter that he was, he knew better than to take to the Marram Marshes on foot in the middle of the night. There was nothing else for it—the Trail was dead and he must return to the Castle.

The bullet boat began its long, cold journey to the Castle while the Hunter huddled in the stern, nursing his broken finger and contemplating the ruins of his Hunt. And his reputation.

"Serves him right," said Marcia. "Horrible little man."

"Not entirely professional," a familiar voice boomed from the bottom of the Ditch, "but completely understandable, my dear. In my younger days I would have been tempted myself."

"Alther!" gasped Marcia, turning a little pink.

MIDNIGHT AT THE BEACH

U ncle Alther!" yelled Jenna happily. She scrambled down the bank and joined Alther, who was standing on the beach staring, puzzled, at a fishing rod he was holding.

"Princess!" Alther beamed and gave her his ghostly hug, which always made Jenna feel as though a warm summer breeze had wafted through her.

"Well, well," said Alther, "I used to come here fishing as a boy, and I seem to have brought the fishing rod too. I hoped I might find you all here."

Jenna laughed. She could not believe that Uncle Alther had ever been a boy.

"Are you coming with us, Uncle Alther?" she asked.

"Sorry, Princess. I can't. You know the rules of Ghosthood:

A Ghost may only tread once more
Where, living, he has trod before.

And, unfortunately, as a boy I never got farther than this beach here. Too many good fish to be had, you see. Now," said Alther changing the subject, "is that a picnic basket I see in the bottom of the boat?"

Lying under a soggy coil of rope was the picnic basket that Sally Mullin had made up for them. Silas heaved it out.

"Oh, my back," he groaned. "What *has* she put in it?" Silas lifted the lid. "Ah, that explains it." He sighed. "Stuffed full of barley cake. Still, it made good ballast, hey?"

"*Dad*," remonstrated Jenna. "Don't be mean. Anyway, we like barley cake, don't we, Nicko?"

Nicko pulled a face, but Boy 412 looked hopeful. *Food*. He was so hungry—he couldn't even remember the last thing he had to eat. Oh, yes, that was it, a bowl of cold, lumpy porridge just before the 6 A.M. roll call that morning. It seemed a lifetime away.

Silas lifted out the other rather squashed items that lay

under the barley cake. A tinder box and dry kindling, a can of
water, some chocolate, sugar and milk. He set about making
a small fire and hung the can of water over it to boil while
everyone clustered around the flickering flames, warming up
their cold hands in between chewing on the thick slabs of
cake.

Even Marcia ignored the barley cake's well-known tendency to glue the teeth together and ate almost a whole slab. Boy
412 gulped down his share and finished off all the bits that
anyone else had left too. Then he lay back on the damp sand
and wondered if he would ever be able to move again. He felt
as though someone had poured concrete into him.

Jenna put her hand in her pocket and took out Petroc
Trelawney. He sat very still and quiet in her hand, Jenna
stroked him gently, and Petroc put out his four stumpy legs
and waved them helplessly in the air. He was lying on his back
like a stranded beetle.

"Oops, wrong way up." Jenna chuckled. She set him the
right way up, and Petroc Trelawney opened his eyes and
blinked slowly.

Jenna stuck a crumb of barley cake on her thumb and
offered it to the pet rock.

Petroc Trelawney blinked again, gave the barley cake some

thought, then nibbled delicately at the cake crumb. Jenna was thrilled.

"He's eaten it!" she exclaimed.

"He would," said Nicko. "Rock cake for a pet rock. Perfect."

But even Petroc Trelawney could not manage more than a large crumb of barley cake. He gazed around him for a few more minutes and then closed his eyes and went back to sleep in the warmth of Jenna's hand.

Soon the water in the can over the fire was boiling. Silas melted the dark chocolate squares into it and added the milk. He mixed it up just the way he liked it, and when it was about to bubble over, he poured in the sugar and stirred.

"The best hot chocolate ever," Nicko pronounced. No one disagreed as the can was passed around and finished all too soon.

While everyone was eating, Alther had been practicing his casting technique with his fishing rod in a preoccupied man-ner, and when he saw that they had finished, he wafted over to the fire. He looked serious.

"Something happened after you left," he said quietly.

Silas felt a weight lurch to the bottom of his stomach, and it wasn't just the barley cake. It was dread.

"What is it, Alther?" asked Silas, horribly sure that he was going to hear that Sarah and the boys had been captured.

Alther knew what Silas was thinking.

"It's not that, Silas," he said. "Sarah and the boys are fine. But it is very bad. DomDaniel has come back to the Castle."

"What?" gasped Marcia. "He *can't* come back. *I'm* the ExtraOrdinary Wizard—I've got the Amulet. And I've left the Tower stuffed full of Wizards—there's enough Magyk in that tower to keep the old has-been buried in the Badlands where he belongs. Are you sure he's back, Alther, and it's not some joke the Supreme Custodian—that revolting little rat— is playing while I'm away?"

"It's no joke, Marcia," Alther said. "I saw him myself. As soon as Muriel had rounded Raven's Rock, he Materialized in the Wizard Tower Courtyard. The whole place crackled with Darke Magyk. Smelled terrible. Sent the Wizards into a blind panic, scurrying here, there and everywhere, like a crowd of ants when you tread on their nest."

"That's disgraceful. What were they thinking of? I don't know, the quality of the average Ordinary Wizard is appalling nowdays," said Marcia, casting a glance in Silas's direction. "And where was Endor? She's meant to be my deputy—don't tell me Endor panicked as well?"

"No. No, she didn't. She came out and confronted him. She put a Bar across the doors to the Tower."

"Oh, thank goodness. The Tower is safe." Marcia sighed with relief.

"No, Marcia, it's not. DomDaniel struck Endor down with a Thunderflash. She's dead." Alther tied a particularly complicated knot in his fishing line. "I'm sorry," he said.

"Dead," Marcia mumbled.

"Then he Removed the Wizards."

"All of them? Where to?"

"They all shot off toward the Badlands—there was nothing they could do. I expect he's got them in one of his Burrows down there."

"Oh, *Alther*."

"Then the Supreme Custodian—that horrible little man—arrives with his retinue, bowing and scraping and practically *drooling* all over his Master. The next thing I know he's escorted DomDaniel into the Wizard Tower and up to . . . er, well, up to your rooms, Marcia."

"My rooms? DomDaniel in *my rooms*?"

"Well, you'll be pleased to know he was in no fit state to appreciate them by the time he got up there, as they had to walk all the way up. There wasn't enough Magyk left to keep the stairs working. Or anything else in the Tower for that matter."

Marcia shook her head in disbelief. "I never thought DomDaniel could do this. *Never.*"

"No, neither did I," said Alther.

"I thought," said Marcia, "that as long as we Wizards could hang on until the Princess was old enough to wear the Crown, we would be all right. Then we could get rid of those Custodians, the Young Army and all the creeping Darkenesse that infests the Castle and makes people's lives so miserable."

"So did I," said Alther, "but I followed DomDaniel up the stairs. He was blathering on to the Supreme Custodian about how he couldn't believe his luck—not only had *you* left the Castle, but you had taken the one obstacle to his return with you."

"Obstacle?"

"Jenna."

Jenna gazed at Alther in dismay. "*Me? An obstacle? Why?*"

Alther stared at the fire, deep in thought. "It seems, Princess, that you have somehow been stopping that awful old Necromancer from coming back to the Castle. Just by being there. And very likely your mother did too. I always wondered why he sent the Assassin for the Queen and not for me."

Jenna shivered. She suddenly felt very afraid. Silas put his arm around her. "That's enough now, Alther. There's no need to frighten us all out of our wits. Frankly, I think you just dropped off to sleep and had a nightmare. You know you get them every now and then. The Custodians are simply a load of thugs that any *decent* ExtraOrdinary Wizard would have seen off years ago."

"I am not going to just sit here and be insulted like this," Marcia spluttered. "You have no idea the things we have tried to get rid of them. No idea at all. It's been all we can do to keep the Wizard Tower going sometimes. And with no help from you, Silas Heap."

"Well, I don't know what the fuss is all about, Marcia. DomDaniel's *dead*," Silas replied.

"No, he's not," said Marcia quietly.

"Don't be silly, Marcia," snapped Silas. "Alther threw him off the top of the Tower forty years ago."

Jenna and Nicko gasped. "Did you really, Uncle Alther?" asked Jenna.

"No!" exclaimed Alther crossly. "I *didn't*. He threw *himself* off."

"Well, whatever," said Silas stubbornly. "He's still dead."

"Not necessarily . . ." said Alther in a low voice, staring

into the fire. The light from the glowing embers cast flickering shadows over everyone except Alther, who floated unhappily through them, absentmindedly trying to undo the knot he had just tied in his fishing line. The fire blazed for a moment and lit up the circle of people around it. Suddenly Jenna spoke.

"What *did* happen on top of the Wizard Tower with DomDaniel, Uncle Alther?" she whispered.

"It's a bit of a scary story, Princess. I don't want to frighten you."

"Oh, go on, tell us," said Nicko. "Jen likes scary stories."

Jenna nodded a little uncertainly.

"Well," said Alther, "it's hard for me to tell it in my own words, but I'll tell you the story as I once heard it spoken around a campfire deep in the Forest. It was a night like this, midnight with a full moon high in the sky, and it was told by an old and wise Wendron Witch Mother to her witches."

And so, beside the fire, Alther Mella changed his form into a large and comfortable-looking woman dressed in green. Speaking in the witch's quiet Forest burr, he began.

"This is where the story begins: on top of a golden Pyramid crowning a tall silver Tower. The Wizard Tower shimmers in the early morning sun and is so high that the crowd of people gathered at its foot appear like ants to the young man who is clambering up the stepped sides of the Pyramid. The young man has looked down at the ants once already and felt sick with the giddy sensation of height. He now keeps his gaze firmly fixed on the figure in front of him—an older but remarkably agile man who, to his great advantage, has no fear of heights. The older man's purple cloak flies out from him in the brisk wind that always plays around the top of the Tower, and to the crowd below he looks like nothing more than a fluttering purple bat creeping up to the point of the Pyramid.

"What, the watchers below ask themselves, is their ExtraOrdinary Wizard doing? And isn't that his Apprentice following him, chasing him even?

"The Apprentice, Alther Mella, now has his Master, DomDaniel, within his grasp. DomDaniel has reached the pinnacle of the Pyramid, a small square platform of hammered gold inlaid with the silver hieroglyphs that Enchant the Tower. DomDaniel stands tall, his thick purple cloak streaming out behind him, his gold and platinum ExtraOrdinary Wizard belt flashing in the sun. He is daring his Apprentice to come closer.

"Alther Mella knows he has no choice. In a brave and terrified leap he lunges at his Master and takes him by surprise.

DomDaniel is knocked off his feet, and his Apprentice dives onto him, grabbing at the gold and lapis lazuli Akhu Amulet that his Master wears around his neck on a thick silver chain.

"Far below, in the courtyard of the Wizard Tower, the people gasp in disbelief as they gaze with squinting eyes into the brightness of the golden Pyramid and watch the Apprentice grapple with his Master. Together they balance on the tiny platform, rolling this way and that as the ExtraOrdinary Wizard tries to break free of Alther Mella's grasp on the Amulet.

"DomDaniel fixes Alther Mella with a baleful glare, his dark green eyes glittering with fury. Alther's bright green eyes meet the stare unflinchingly, and he feels the Amulet loosen. He pulls hard, the chain snaps into a hundred pieces, and the Amulet comes away in his grasp.

"'Take it,' hisses DomDaniel. 'But I will be back for it. I will be back with the seventh of the seventh.'

"One piercing scream rises from below as the crowd sees its ExtraOrdinary Wizard launch himself from the top of the Pyramid and tumble from the Tower. His cloak spreads like a magnificent pair of wings, but it does not slow his long, tumbling fall to earth.

"And then he is gone.

"At the top of the Pyramid his Apprentice clutches the

Akhu Amulet and gazes in shock at what he has seen—his Master enter the Abyss.

"The crowd clusters around the scorched earth which marks the spot where DomDaniel hit the ground. Each has seen something different. One says he changed into a bat and flew away. Another saw a dark horse appear and gallop off into the Forest, and still another saw DomDaniel change into a snake and slither under a rock. But none saw the truth that Alther saw.

"Alther Mella makes his way back down the Pyramid with his eyes closed so that he does not have to see the dizzying drop beneath him. He only opens his eyes when he has crawled through the small hatch into the safety of the Library, which is housed inside the golden Pyramid. And then, with a sense of dread, he sees what has happened. His plain green woolen Apprentice Wizard robes have changed to a heavy purple silk. The simple leather belt that he wears around his tunic has become remarkably weighty; it is now made of gold with the intricate platinum inlay of runes and charms that protect and empower the ExtraOrdinary Wizard that Alther has, to his amazement, become.

"Alther gazes at the Amulet that he holds in his trembling hand. It is a small round stone of ultramarine lapis lazuli shot through with streaks of gold and carved with an enchanted dragon. The stone lies heavily in his palm, bound with a band of gold pinched together at the top to form a loop. From this loop hangs a broken silver link, snapped when Alther ripped the Amulet from its silver chain.

"After a moment's thought Alther bends down and takes out the leather lace from one of his boots. He threads the Amulet onto it and, as all ExtraOrdinary Wizards have done before him, hangs it around his neck. And then, with his long wispy brown hair still awry from his fight, his face pale and anxious, his green eyes wide with awe, Alther makes the long journey down through the Tower to face the waiting, murmuring crowd outside.

"When Alther stumbles out through the huge, solid silver doors that guard the entrance to the Wizard Tower, he is greeted by a gasp. But nothing more is said, for there is no arguing with the presence of a new ExtraOrdinary Wizard. Amid a few quiet mutterings the crowd disperses, although one voice calls out.

"'As you have gained it, so will you lose it.'

"Alther sighs. He knows this is true.

"As he makes his lonely way back into the Tower to begin the work of undoing DomDaniel's Darkenesse, in a small room not so very far away a baby boy is born to a poor Wizard family.

"He is their seventh son, and his name is Silas Heap."

There was a long silence around the fire while Alther slowly regained his own form. Silas shivered. He had never heard the story told like that before.

"That's amazing, Alther," he said in a hoarse whisper. "I had no idea. H-how did the Witch Mother know so much?"

"She was watching in the crowd," said Alther. "She came to see me later that day to congratulate me on becoming ExtraOrdinary Wizard, and I told her my side of the story. If you want the truth to be known then all you need to do is tell the Witch Mother. She will tell everyone else. Of course, whether they believe it or not is another matter."

Jenna was thinking hard. "But why, Uncle Alther, were you chasing DomDaniel?"

"Ah, good question. I didn't tell the Witch Mother that. There are some Darke matters that should not be spoken of lightly. But you should know, so I will tell you. You see, that morning, like every morning, I had been tidying up the Pyramid Library. One of the tasks of an Apprentice is to keep the Library organized, and I took my duties seriously, even if they *were* for such an unpleasant Master. Anyway, that particular morning I had found a strange Incantation in DomDaniel's handwriting tucked into one of the books. I had seen one lying around before and hadn't been able to read the writing, but as I studied this one, an idea occurred to me. I held the Incantation up to the looking glass and discovered I was right: it was written in mirror writing. I began to get a bad feeling about it then, because I knew that it must be a Reverse Incantation, using Magyk from the Darke side—or the Other side, as I prefer to call it, as it is not always Darke Magyk that the Other side puts to use. Anyway, I had to know the truth about DomDaniel and what he was doing, so I decided to risk reading the Incantation. I had just started when something terrible happened."

"What?" whispered Jenna.

"A Spectre Appeared behind me. Well, at least I could see it in the looking glass, but when I turned around it wasn't there. But I could feel it. I could feel it put its hand on my shoulder, and then—I heard it. I heard its empty voice speaking to me. It told me that my time had come. That it had come to collect me *as arranged*."

Alther shivered at the memory and raised his hand to his left shoulder as the Spectre had done. It still ached with cold, as it had ever since that morning.

Everyone else shivered too and drew closer around the fire.

"I told the Spectre that I was not ready. Not yet. You see I knew enough about the Other side to know you must never refuse them. But they are willing to wait. Time is nothing to them. They have nothing else to do *but* wait. The Spectre told me it would return for me the next day and that I had better be ready then, and it faded away. After it went, I made myself read the Reverse words, and I saw that DomDaniel had offered me up as part of a bargain with the Other side, to be collected at the time I read the Incantation. And then I knew for sure he was using Reverse Magyk—the mirror image of Magyk, the kind that uses people up—and I had fallen into his trap."

The fire on the beach began to die down, and everyone clustered around it, huddling together in the fading glow as Alther continued his story.

"Suddenly DomDaniel came in and saw me reading the Incantation. And that I was still there—I had not been Taken. He knew that his plan was discovered and he ran. He scuttled up the Library stepladder like a spider, ran along the top of the shelves and squeezed through the trapdoor that led outside of the Pyramid. He laughed at me and taunted me to follow him if I dared. You see, he knew I was terrified of heights. But I had no choice but to follow him. So I did."

Everyone was silent. No one, not even Marcia, had heard the full story of the Spectre before then.

Jenna broke the silence. "That's horrible." She shuddered. "So did the Spectre come back for you, Uncle Alther?"

"No, Princess. With some help I devised an Anti-Hex Formula. It was powerless after that." Alther sat in thought for a while, and then he said, "I just want you all to know that I am not proud of what I did at the top of the Wizard Tower— even though I did *not* push DomDaniel off. You know, it is a terrible thing for an Apprentice to supplant his Master."

"But you had to do it, Uncle Alther. Didn't you?" said Jenna.

"Yes, I did," said Alther quietly. "And we will have to do it again."

"We shall do it tonight," declared Marcia. "I shall go right back and throw that evil man out of the Tower. He'll soon learn that he doesn't mess with the ExtraOrdinaryWizard." She got up purposefully and wrapped her purple cloak around her, ready to go.

Alther leapt into the air and put a ghostly hand on Marcia's arm. "*No. No, Marcia.*"

"But, Alther—" Marcia protested.

"Marcia, there are no Wizards left to protect you at the Tower, and I hear you gave your KeepSafe to Sally Mullin. I beg you not to go back. It is too dangerous. You must get the Princess to safety. And keep her safe. I shall go back to the Castle and do what I can."

Marcia sank back down onto the wet sand. She knew Alther was right. The last flames of the fire spluttered out as large wet flakes of snow began to fall and darkness closed in on them. Alther put his ghostly fishing rod down on the sand and floated above the Deppen Ditch. He gazed across the marshlands that stretched far into the distance. They were a peaceful sight in the moonlight, broad wetlands dusted with snow and dotted with little islands here and there as far as he could see.

"Canoes," said Alther, floating back down. "When I was a boy that's how the marsh folk got around. And that's what you're going to need too."

"You can do that, Silas," said Marcia dismally. "I'm far too tired to go messing about with boats."

Silas got to his feet. "Come on then, Nicko," he said. "We'll go and Transmute *Muriel* into some canoes."

Muriel was still floating patiently in Deppen Ditch, just around the bend, out of sight of the river. Nicko felt sad to see their faithful boat go but he knew the Rules of Magyk, and so he knew only too well that in a spell, matter can neither be created nor destroyed. *Muriel* would not really be gone but, Nicko hoped, rearranged into a set of smart canoes.

"Can I have a fast one, Dad?" asked Nicko as Silas stared at *Muriel* and tried to think of a suitable spell.

"I don't know about 'fast,' Nicko. I shall just be happy if it floats. Now, let me think. I suppose one canoe each would be good. Here goes. Convert to Five! Oh, bother."

Five very small *Muriel*s bobbed up and down in front of them.

"Dad," complained Nicko, "you're not doing it right."

"Wait a minute, Nicko. I'm thinking. That's it—Canoe Renew!"

"*Dad!*"

One enormous canoe sat wedged into the banks of the Ditch.

"Now, let's be logical about this," Silas muttered to himself.

"Why don't you just ask for five canoes, Dad?" suggested Nicko.

"Good idea, Nicko. We'll make a Wizard of you yet. I Choose Canoes for Five to Use!"

The spell fizzled out before it really got going, and Silas

ended up with just two canoes and a forlorn pile of *Muriel*-colored timbers and rope.

"Only two, Dad?" said Nicko, disappointed not to be getting his own canoe.

"They'll have to do," said Silas. "You can't change matter more than three times without it getting fragile."

In fact, Silas was just pleased that he had ended up with any canoes at all.

Soon Jenna, Nicko and Boy 412 were sitting in what Nicko had named the *Muriel One* canoe, and Silas and Marcia were squashed together in the *Muriel Two*. Silas insisted on sitting in the front because, "I know the way, Marcia. It makes sense."

Marcia snorted dubiously, but she was far too tired to fuss.

"Go on, Maxie," Silas told the wolfhound. "Go and sit with Nicko."

But Maxie had other ideas. Maxie's purpose in life was to stay by his master, and stay by his master he would. He bounded onto Silas's lap, and the canoe tilted dangerously.

"Can't you control that animal?" demanded Marcia, who was dismayed to find herself horribly close to the water again.

"Of course I can. He does exactly what I tell him, don't you, Maxie?"

Nicko made a spluttering sound.

"Go sit at the back, Maxie," Silas told the wolfhound sternly. Looking crestfallen, Maxie bounded over Marcia to the back of the canoe and settled himself down behind her.

"He's not sitting behind *me*," said Marcia.

"Well he can't sit by me. I have to concentrate on where we're going," Silas told her.

"And it's high time you were going too," said Alther, hovering anxiously. "Before the snow really sets in. I just wish I could come with you."

Alther floated up and watched them set off, paddling along the Deppen Ditch, which was now slowly filling as the tide came back in and would take them deep into the Marram Marshes. Jenna, Nicko and Boy 412's canoe led the way, with Silas, Marcia and Maxie following them.

Maxie sat bolt upright behind Marcia and breathed excited dog breath onto the back of her neck. He sniffed the new, damp marshland smells and listened to the scrabbling sounds made by assorted small animals as they scuttled out of the way of the canoes. Every now and then his excitement overwhelmed him, and he dribbled happily into Marcia's hair.

Soon Jenna reached a narrow channel running off the Ditch. She stopped.

"Do we go down here, Dad?" she called back to Silas.

Silas looked confused. He didn't remember this bit at all. Just as he was wondering whether to say yes or no, his thoughts were interrupted by a piercing shriek from Jenna.

A slimy mud-brown hand with webbed fingers and broad black claws had reached out of the water and grabbed the end of her canoe.

↢ 16 ↣
THE BOGGART

The slimy brown hand fumbled along the side of the canoe, making its way toward Jenna. Then it grabbed hold of her paddle. Jenna wrested the paddle away and was about to hit the slimy brown thing with it—*hard*—when a voice said, "Oi. No need fer that."

A seallike creature covered in slippery brown fur pulled itself up so that its head was just out of the water. Two bright black-button eyes stared at Jenna, who had her paddle still poised in midair.

"Wish you'd put that down. Could hurt someone. So where you *bin*, then?" the creature asked grumpily in a deep, gurgling voice with a broad marshland drawl. "I bin waitin' for hours. Freezin' in here. How'd *you* like it? Stuck in a ditch. Just *waitin'*."

All Jenna could manage in reply was a small squeak; her voice seemed to have stopped working.

"What is it, Jen?" asked Nicko, who was sitting behind Boy 412, just to make sure he didn't do anything stupid, and couldn't see the creature.

"Th—this . . ." Jenna pointed at the creature, who looked offended.

"What you mean *this*?" he asked. "You mean me? You mean *Boggart*?"

"Boggart? No. I didn't say that," muttered Jenna.

"Well I did. Boggart. That's me. I'm Boggart. Boggart, the Boggart. Good name, innit?"

"Lovely," said Jenna politely.

"What's going on?" asked Silas, catching up with them. "Stoppit, Maxie. *Stoppit* I say!"

Maxie had caught sight of the Boggart and was barking frantically. The Boggart took one look at Maxie and disappeared back under the water. Since the notorious Boggart

Hunts many years ago in which Maxie's ancestors had taken part so effectively, the Marram Marsh Boggart had become a rare creature. With a long memory.

The Boggart reappeared at a safe distance. "You're not bringin' *that*?" he said, looking balefully at Maxie. "She didunt say nothin' 'bout one a *them*."

"Do I hear a Boggart?" asked Silas.

"Yeah," said the Boggart.

"Zelda's Boggart?"

"Yeah," said the Boggart.

"Has she sent you to find us?"

"Yeah," said the Boggart.

"Good," said Silas, very relieved. "We'll follow you, then."

"Yeah," said the Boggart, and he swam off along Deppen Ditch and took the next turning but one.

The next turning but one was much narrower than the Deppen Ditch and wound its snakelike way deep into the moonlit, snow-covered marshes. The snow fell steadily and all was quiet and still, apart from the gurgles and splashes of the Boggart as he swam in front of the canoes, every now and then sticking his head out of the dark water and calling out, "You *followin*'?"

"I don't know what else he thinks we *can* do," Jenna said to

Nicko as they paddled the canoe along the increasingly narrow ditch. "It's not as if there's anywhere else to go."

But the Boggart took his duties seriously and kept going
with the same question until they reached a small marsh pool
with several overgrown channels leading off it.

"Best wait for the others," said the Boggart. "Don't want
'em gettin' lost."

Jenna glanced back to see where Marcia and Silas had got to.
They were far behind now, as Silas was the only one paddling.
Marcia had given up and had both hands clamped firmly to the
top of her head. Behind her the long and pointy snout of an
Abyssinian wolfhound loftily surveyed the scene before him
and let drop the occasional long strand of glistening dribble.
Straight onto Marcia's head.

As Silas propelled the canoe into the pool and wearily laid
his paddle down, Marcia declared, "I am *not* sitting in front of
that animal one moment longer. There's dog dribble all over
my hair. It's disgusting. I'm getting out. I'd rather walk."

"You don't wanter be doin' that, Yer Majesty," came the
Boggart's voice from out of the water beside Marcia. He gazed
up at Marcia, his bright black eyes blinking through his brown
fur, amazed by her ExtraOrdinary Wizard belt that glinted in
the moonlight. Although he was a creature of the marsh mud,

the Boggart loved bright and shiny things. And he had never seen such a bright and shiny thing as Marcia's gold and platinum belt.

"You don't wanter be walkin' round 'ere, Yer Majesty," the Boggart told her respectfully. "You'll start followin' the Marshfire, and it'll lead you into the Quake Ooze before you know it. There's many as has followed the Marshfire and there's none as has returned."

A rumbling growl was coming from deep down in Maxie's throat. The fur on the back of his neck stood up, and suddenly, obeying an old and compelling wolfhound instinct, Maxie leaped into the water after the Boggart.

"Maxie! *Maxie!* Oh, you *stupid* dog," yelled Silas.

The water in the pool was freezing. Maxie yelped and frantically dog-paddled back to Silas's and Marcia's canoe.

Marcia shoved him away.

"That dog is *not* getting back in here," she announced.

"Marcia, he'll freeze," protested Silas.

"I don't *care*."

"Here, Maxie. C'mon boy," said Nicko. He grabbed Maxie's neckerchief and, with Jenna's help, hauled the dog into their canoe. The canoe tipped dangerously, but Boy 412, who had no desire to end up in the water like Maxie, steadied it by grabbing hold of a tree root.

Maxie stood shivering for a moment, then he did what any wet dog has to do: he shook himself.

"*Maxie!*" gasped Nicko and Jenna.

Boy 412 said nothing. He didn't like dogs at all. The only dogs he had ever known were the vicious Custodian Guard Dogs, and although he could see that Maxie looked nothing like them, he still expected him to bite at any moment. And so when Maxie settled down, laid his head on Boy 412's lap and went to sleep, it was just another very bad moment in Boy 412's worst day ever. But Maxie was happy. Boy 412's sheepskin jacket was warm and comfortable, and the wolfhound spent the rest of the journey dreaming that he was back at home curled up in front of the fire with all the other Heaps.

But the Boggart had gone.

"Boggart? Where are you, Mr. Boggart?" Jenna called out politely.

There was no reply. Just the deep silence that comes to the marshes when a blanket of snow covers the bogs and quags, silences their gurgles and gloops and sends all the slimy creatures back into the stillness of the mud.

"Now we've lost that nice Boggart because of your stupid

animal," Marcia told Silas crossly. "I don't know *why* you had to bring him."

Silas sighed. Sharing a canoe with Marcia Overstrand was not something he had ever imagined he would have to do. But if he had, in a mad moment, ever imagined it, this was exactly how it would have been.

Silas scanned the horizon in the hope that he might be able to see Keeper's Cottage, where Aunt Zelda lived. The cottage stood on Draggen Island, one of the many islands in the marsh, which became true islands only when the marsh-land flooded. But all Silas could see was white flatness stretching out before him in all directions. To make matters worse, he could see the marsh mist beginning to rise up and drift across the water, and he knew that if the mist came in they would never see Keeper's Cottage, however close they might be to it.

Then he remembered that the cottage was Enchanted. Which meant that no one could see it anyway.

If they ever needed the Boggart, it was now.

"I can see a light!" said Jenna, suddenly. "It must be Aunt Zelda coming to look for us. Look, over there!"

All eyes followed Jenna's pointing finger.

A flickering light was jumping over the marshes, as if

bounding from tussock to tussock.

"She's coming toward us," said Jenna, excited.

"No, she's not," Nicko said. "Look, she's going away."

"Perhaps we ought to go and meet her," said Silas.

Marcia was not convinced. "How can you be sure it's Zelda?" she said. "It could be anyone. Any*thing*."

Everyone fell silent at the thought of a *thing* with a light coming toward them, until Silas said, "It *is* Zelda. Look, I can see her."

"No, you can't," said Marcia. "It's *Marshfire*, like that very intelligent Boggart said."

"Marcia, I know Zelda when I see her, and I can see her now. She's carrying a light. She's come all this way to find us and we are just *sitting* here. I'm going to meet her."

"They say that fools see what they want to see in Marshfire," said Marcia tartly, "and you've just proved that saying true, Silas."

Silas made to get out of the canoe, and Marcia grabbed his cloak.

"*Sit!*" she said as though she was talking to Maxie.

But Silas pulled away, half in a dream, drawn to the flickering light and the shadow of Aunt Zelda that appeared and disappeared through the rising mist. Sometimes she was tantalizingly near, about to find them all and lead them to a warm fire and a soft bed, sometimes fading away sorrowfully and inviting them to follow and be with her. But Silas could no longer bear to be away from the light. He climbed out of the canoe and stumbled off toward the flickering glow.

"Dad!" yelled Jenna. "Can we come too?"

"*No*, you may not," said Marcia firmly. "And I'm going to have to bring the silly old fool back."

Marcia was just drawing breath for the Boomerang Spell when Silas tripped and fell headlong onto the boggy ground. As he lay winded, Silas felt the marsh beneath him begin to shift as though living things were stirring in the depths of the mud. And when he tried to get up, Silas found that he could not. It was as if he were glued to the ground. In his Marshfire daze, Silas was confused about why he seemed unable to move. He tried to lift his head to see what was happening but was unable to. It was then that he realized the awful truth: *something was pulling at his hair.*

Silas raised his hands to his head, and to his horror, he could feel little bony fingers in his hair, winding and knotting his long straggling curls around them and pulling, tugging him down into the bog. Desperately Silas struggled to get free, but the more he struggled, the more the fingers tangled themselves up in his hair. Slowly and steadily they pulled Silas down until the mud covered his eyes and soon, very soon, would cover his nose.

Marcia could see what was happening, but she knew better than to run to Silas's aid.

"Dad!" yelled Jenna, getting out of the canoe. "I'll help you, Dad."

"No!" Marcia told her. "No. That's how the Marshfire works. The bog will drag you down too."

"But—but we can't just watch Dad *drown*," cried Jenna.

Suddenly a squat brown shape heaved itself out of the water, scrambled up the bank and, leaping expertly from tussock to tussock, ran toward Silas.

"What you doin' in the Quake Ooze, sir?" said the Boggart crossly.

"Whaaa?" mumbled Silas whose ears were full of mud and could hear only the shrieking and wailing of the creatures in the bog beneath him. The bony fingers continued their pulling and twisting, and Silas was beginning to feel the painful cuts of razor-sharp teeth nipping at his head. He struggled frantically, but each struggle pulled him farther down into the Ooze and set off another wave of screeching.

Jenna and Nicko watched Silas slowly sinking into the

Ooze with horror. Why didn't the Boggart *do* something? *Now*, before Silas disappeared forever. Suddenly Jenna could stand it no longer and sprang up again from the canoe, and Nicko went to follow her. Boy 412, who had heard all about Marshfire from the only survivor of a platoon of Young Army boys who had gotten lost in the Quake Ooze a few years earlier, grabbed hold of Jenna and tried to pull her back into the canoe. Angrily, she pushed him away.

The sudden movement caught the Boggart's attention. "*Stay there, miss,*" he said urgently. Boy 412 gave another hefty tug on Jenna's sheepskin jacket, and she sat down in the canoe with a bump. Maxie whined.

The Boggart's bright black eyes were worried. He knew exactly who the knotting, twisting fingers belonged to, and he knew they were trouble.

"Blinkin' Brownies!" said the Boggart. "Nasty little articles. Try a taste of Boggart Breath, you spiteful creatures." The Boggart leaned over Silas, took a very deep breath and breathed out over the tugging fingers. From deep inside the bog Silas heard a teeth-shattering screech as though someone was scraping fingernails down a blackboard, then the snarling fingers slipped from his hair, and the bog moved as he felt the creatures below shift away.

Silas was free.

The Boggart helped him sit up and rubbed the mud from his eyes.

"I told you Marshfire will lead you to the Quake Ooze. An' it did, didunt it?" remonstrated the Boggart.

Silas said nothing. He was quite overcome by the pungent smell of Boggart Breath still in his hair.

"Yer all right now, sir," the Boggart told him. "But it were close. I don't mind telling you that. Haven't had to *breathe* on a Brownie since they ransacked the cottage. Ah, Boggart Breath is a wonderful thing. Some may not like it much, but I always says to 'em, 'You'd think different if you was got by the Quake Ooze Brownies.'"

"Oh. Ah. Quite. Thank you, Boggart. Thank you very much," mumbled Silas, still dazed.

The Boggart carefully led him back to the canoe.

"You'd best go in the front, Yer Majesty," the Boggart said to Marcia. "He's in no fit state ter drive one a these things."

Marcia helped the Boggart get Silas into the canoe, and then the Boggart slipped into the water.

"I'll take you to Miss Zelda's, but mind you keep that animal out me way," he said, glaring at Maxie. "Brought me out in a nasty rash that growlin' did. I is covered in lumps now.

Here feel this." The Boggart offered his large round tummy for Marcia to feel.

"It's very kind of you, but no thank you, not just now," said Marcia faintly.

"Another time, then."

"Indeed."

"Right, then." The Boggart swam toward a small channel that no one had even noticed before.

"Now, you *followin'*?" he asked, not for the last time.

ALTHER ALONE

While the Boggart and the canoes were winding their long and complicated way through the marshes, Alther was following the route his old boat, *Molly*, used to take back to the Castle.

Alther was flying the way he loved to fly, low and very fast, and it was not long before he overtook the bullet boat. It was a sorry sight. Ten oarsmen were wearily pulling on the oars as the boat crept slowly back up the river. Sitting in the stern of the boat was the Hunter, hunched, shivering and silently pondering his fate, while in the prow the Apprentice, to the Hunter's extreme irritation, fidgeted about, occasionally kicking the side of the boat out of boredom and in an effort to get some feeling back into his toes.

Alther flew unseen over the boat, for he Appeared only to those he chose, and continued his journey. Above him the clear sky was clouding over with heavy snow clouds, and the moon had disappeared, plunging the bright snow-covered riverbanks into darkness. As Alther drew nearer to the Castle, fat snowflakes began to drift lazily down from the sky, and as he approached the final bend in the river that would take him around Raven's Rock, the air became suddenly thick with snow.

Alther slowed right down, for even a ghost can find it hard to see where he's going in a blizzard, and carefully flew on toward the Castle. Soon, through the white wall of snow, Alther could see the glowing red embers that were all that remained of Sally Mullin's Tea and Ale House. The snow sizzled and spat as it landed on the charred pontoon, and as Alther lingered for a moment over the remains of Sally's pride and joy, he hoped that somewhere on the cold river the Hunter was enjoying the blizzard.

Alther flew up the rubbish dump, past the discarded rat door and made a steep ascent over the Castle wall. He was surprised how peaceful and quiet the Castle was. He had somehow expected the upheavals of the evening to show, but it was past midnight by now and a fresh blanket of snow covered the deserted courtyards and old stone buildings. Alther skirted around the Palace and headed along the broad avenue known as Wizard Way that led to the Wizard Tower. He began to feel nervous. What would he find?

Drifting up the outside of the Tower, he soon spotted the small arched window at the top that he had been looking for. He melted himself through the window and found himself standing outside Marcia's front door, or so it had been a few hours earlier. Alther did the ghost equivalent of taking a deep breath and composed himself. Then he carefully Discomposed himself just enough to pass through the solid purple planks and thick silver hinges of the door and expertly Rearranged himself on the other side. Perfect. He was back in Marcia's rooms.

And so was the Darke Wizard, the Necromancer, DomDaniel.

DomDaniel was asleep on Marcia's sofa. He lay on his back with his black robes wrapped around him and his short, black, cylindrical hat pulled down over his eyes while his head rested on Boy 412's pillows. DomDaniel's mouth was wide open and he was snoring loudly. It was not a pretty sight.

Alther stared at DomDaniel, finding it strange to see his old Master again in the very same place where they had spent so many years together. Alther did not remember those years with any fondness even though he had learned all, and much more than he had wanted to know, about Magyk. DomDaniel had been an arrogant and unpleasant ExtraOrdinary Wizard, completely uninterested in the Castle and the people there who needed his help, pursuing only his desire for extreme power and eternal youth. Or rather, since DomDaniel had taken a while to work it out, eternal middle age.

The DomDaniel who lay snoring in front of Alther looked, at first glance, much the same as he had remembered him from all those years ago, but as Alther scrutinized him more closely he saw that all was not unchanged. There was a gray tinge to the Necromancer's skin that spoke of years spent underground in the company of Shades and Shadows. An aura of the Other side still clung to him and filled the room with the smell of overripe mold and damp earth. As Alther watched, a thin line of dribble slowly made its way out of the corner of DomDaniel's mouth and wandered down his chin, where it dripped onto his black cloak.

To the accompaniment of DomDaniel's snores, Alther sur-veyed the room. It looked remarkably unchanged, as though

Marcia was likely to walk in at any moment, sit down and tell him about her day, as she always did. But then Alther noticed the large scorch mark where the Thunderflash had struck down the Assassin. A charred black Assassin-shaped hole was burned into Marcia's treasured silk carpet.

So it really *had* happened, thought Alther.

The ghost wafted over to the hatch on the rubbish chute, which was still gaping open, and peered into the chill blackness. He shivered and reflected on the terrifying journey they all must have had. And then, because Alther wanted to do *something*, however small it might be, he stepped over the boundary between the ghostly and the living world. He Caused something to happen.

He slammed the hatch closed.

Bang!

DomDaniel woke up with a start. He sat bolt upright and stared around him, momentarily wondering where he was. Soon, with a little sigh of satisfaction, he remembered. He was back where he belonged. Back in the rooms of the ExtraOrdinary Wizard. Back at the top of the Tower. Back with a vengeance. DomDaniel looked about him, expecting to see his Apprentice, who should have returned hours ago with the news at last of the end of the Princess and that awful

woman, Marcia Overstrand, not to mention a couple of the
Heaps thrown into the bargain. The fewer of *them* remaining
the better, thought DomDaniel. He shivered in the chill air of
the night and clicked his fingers impatiently to rekindle the
fire in the grate. It flared up and, *pouf!* Alther blew it out.
Then he wafted the smoke out from the chimney and set
DomDaniel coughing.

The old Necromancer may be here, thought Alther grimly,
and there may be nothing I can do about *that*, but he's not
going to enjoy it. Not if I can help it.

It was well into the early hours of the morning, after
DomDaniel had gone upstairs to bed and had had consider-
able trouble sleeping due to the fact that the sheets seemed to
be intent on strangling him, when the Apprentice returned.
The boy was white with tiredness and cold, his green robes
were caked in snow and he trembled as the Guardsman who
had escorted him to the door made a quick exit and left him
alone to face his Master.

DomDaniel was in a foul temper as the door let the
Apprentice in.

"I hope," DomDaniel told the trembling boy, "that you
have some *interesting* news for me."

Alther hovered around the boy, who was almost unable to speak from exhaustion. He felt sorry for the boy—it was not his fault that he was Apprenticed to DomDaniel. Alther blew on the fire and got it going again. The boy saw the flames jump in the grate and made to move over to the warmth.

"Where are you going?" thundered DomDaniel.

"I—I'm cold, sir."

"You're not going near that fire until you tell me what happened. Are they *dispatched*?"

The boy looked puzzled. "I—I told him it was a Projection," he mumbled.

"What *are* you on about, boy? *What* was a Projection?"

"Their boat."

"Well, you managed *that* I suppose. Simple enough. But are they dispatched? *Dead? Yes or no?*" DomDaniel's voice rose in exasperation. He had already guessed the answer, but he had to hear it.

"No," whispered the boy, looking terrified, his sodden robes dripping on the floor as the snow began to melt in the faint heat that Alther's fire was giving off.

DomDaniel cast a withering look toward the boy.

"You are nothing but a disappointment. I go to endless trouble to rescue you from a *disgrace* of a family. I give you an education most boys can only *dream* of. And what do you do? Act like a *complete* fool! I just do not understand it. A boy like you should have found that rabble in *no time*. And all you do is come back with some story about Projections and—and *drip all over the floor!*"

DomDaniel decided that if *he* was awake, he didn't see why the Supreme Custodian should not be awake too. And as for the Hunter, he'd be *very* interested in what he had to say for himself. DomDaniel strode out, slamming the door behind him, and set off down the static silver stairs, clattering past endless dark floors left empty and echoing by the exodus of all the Ordinary Wizards earlier that evening.

The Wizard Tower was chill and gloomy with the absence of Magyk. A cold wind moaned as it was drawn up as if through a huge chimney, and doors banged mournfully in the empty rooms. As DomDaniel descended, becoming quite dizzy from the never-ending spirals of the stairs, he noted all the changes with approval. This was how the Tower was going to be from now on. A place for serious Darke Magyk. None of those irritating Ordinary Wizards prancing around with their pathetic little spells. No more namby-pamby incense and plinky-plonky happy sounds floating in the air, and certainly no more frivolous colors and lights. *His* Magyk would be used for greater things. Except he might fix the stairs.

DomDaniel eventually emerged into the dark and silent hall. The silver doors to the Tower hung forlornly open. Snow had blown in and covered the motionless floor which was now a dull gray stone. He swept through the doors and strode across the courtyard.

As DomDaniel stamped angrily through the snow and made his way along Wizard Way to the Palace, he began to wish he had thought to change out of his sleeping robes and slippers before he had stormed out. He arrived at the Palace Gate a somewhat soggy and unprepossessing figure, and the lone Palace Guard refused to let him in.

DomDaniel struck the Guard down with a Thunderflash and strode in. Very soon the Supreme Custodian was roused from his bed for the second night running.

Back at the Tower, the Apprentice had stumbled to the sofa and fallen into a cold and unhappy sleep. Alther took pity on him and kept the fire going. While the boy slept, the ghost also took the opportunity of Causing a few more changes. He loosened the heavy canopy above the bed so that it was hanging only by a thread. He took the wicks out of all the candles. He added a murky green color to the water tanks and installed a large, aggressive family of cockroaches in the kitchen. He put an irritable rat under the floorboards and loosened all the joints of the most comfortable chairs. And then, as an after-thought, he exchanged DomDaniel's stiff black cylindrical hat, which lay abandoned on the bed, for one just a little bigger.

As dawn broke, Alther left the Apprentice sleeping and made his way out to the Forest, where he followed the path he had once taken with Silas on a visit to Sarah and Galen many years ago.

✢ 18 ✢
KEEPER'S COTTAGE

It *was the silence that* woke Jenna in Keeper's Cottage the next morning. After ten years of waking every day to the busy sounds of The Ramblings, not to mention the riot and hubbub of the six Heap boys, the silence was deafening. Jenna opened her eyes, and for a moment thought that she was still dreaming. Where was she? Why wasn't she at home in her cupboard? Why were just Jo-Jo and Nicko here? Where were all her other brothers?

And then she remembered.

Jenna sat up quietly so as not to wake the boys who were lying beside her by the glowing embers of the fire downstairs in Aunt Zelda's cottage. She wrapped her quilt around her as, despite the fire, the air in the cottage had a damp chill to it. And then, hesitantly, she raised a hand to her head.

So it *was* true. The gold circlet was still there. She was still a Princess. It hadn't been just for her birthday.

All through the previous day, Jenna had had that feeling of unreality that she always got on her birthday. A feeling that the day was somehow part of another world, another time, and that anything that happened on her birthday was not real. And it was that feeling that had carried Jenna through the amazing events of her tenth birthday, a feeling that, whatever happened, it would all be back to normal the next day, so it didn't really matter.

But it wasn't. And it did.

Jenna hugged herself to keep warm and considered the matter. She was a *Princess*.

Jenna and her best friend, Bo, had often discussed together the fact that they were in fact long-lost Princess sisters, separated at birth, whom fate had thrown together in the form of a shared desk in Class 6 of East Side Third School. Jenna had almost believed this; it had seemed so right somehow.

Although, when she went around to Bo's rooms to play, Jenna didn't see how Bo could really belong to another family. Bo looked so much like her mother, thought Jenna, with her bright red hair and masses of freckles, that she *had* to be her daughter. But Bo had been scathing about this when Jenna had pointed it out, so she didn't mention it again.

Even so, it hadn't stopped Jenna wondering why she looked so unlike her own mother. And father. And brothers. Why was she the only one with dark hair? Why didn't she have green eyes? Jenna had desperately wanted her eyes to turn green. In fact, up until the previous day, she had still hoped that they might.

She had longed for the excitement of Sarah saying to her, as she watched her do with all the boys, "You know, I *do* think your eyes are beginning to turn. I can definitely see a bit of green in them today." And then: "You *are* growing up fast. Your eyes are nearly as green as your father's."

But when Jenna demanded to be told about *her* eyes, and why they weren't green yet like her brothers', Sarah would only say, "But you're our little *girl*, Jenna. You're special. You have beautiful eyes."

But that didn't fool Jenna. She knew that girls could have green Wizard eyes too. Just look at Miranda Bott down the corridor, whose grandfather ran the Wizard secondhand cloak shop. Miranda had green eyes, and it was only her *grandfather* who was a Wizard. So why didn't *she*?

Jenna felt upset thinking about Sarah. She wondered when she would see her again. She even wondered if Sarah would still want to be her mother, now that everything had changed.

Jenna shook herself and told herself not to be silly. She stood up, keeping her quilt around her, and picked her way over the two sleeping boys. She paused to glance at Boy 412 and wondered why she had thought he was Jo-Jo. It must have been a trick of the light, she decided.

The inside of the cottage was still dark apart from the dull glow cast by the fire, but Jenna had become accustomed to the gloom, and she began to wander around, trailing her quilt along the floor and slowly taking in her new surroundings.

The cottage was not big. There was one room downstairs; at one end was a huge open fireplace with a pile of gently smoldering logs still glowing on the hot stone hearth. Nicko and Boy 412 were fast asleep on the rug in front of the fire, each wrapped warmly in one of Aunt Zelda's patchwork quilts. In the middle of the room was a flight of narrow stairs with a cupboard underneath, with the words UNSTABLE POTIONS AND PARTIKU-LAR POISONS written in flowing golden letters on the firmly closed door. She peered up the narrow stairs that led up to a large darkened room where Aunt Zelda, Marcia and Silas were still sleeping. And of course Maxie, whose snores and snuffles drifted down to Jenna. Or were they Silas's snores and Maxie's snuffles? When they were asleep, master and wolfhound sounded remarkably similar.

Downstairs the ceilings were low and showed the rough-hewn beams that the cottage was built from. All manner of things were hung from these beams: boat paddles, hats, bags of shells, spades, hoes, sacks of potatoes, shoes, ribbons, brooms, bundles of reeds, willow knots and of course hundreds of bunches of the herbs that Aunt Zelda either grew herself or bought at the Magyk Market, which was held every year and a day down at the Port. As a White Witch, Aunt Zelda used herbs for charms and potions as well as medicine, and you'd be lucky to be able to tell Aunt Zelda anything about a herb that she did not know already.

Jenna gazed around her, loving the feeling of being the only one awake, free to wander undisturbed for a while. As she walked about, she thought how strange it was to be in a cottage with four walls all of its very own that were not joined to anyone else's walls. It was so different from the hurly-burly of The Ramblings, but she already felt at home. Jenna carried on with her exploration, noticing the old but comfortable chairs, the well-scrubbed table that did not look as though it was about to roll over and die at any minute and, most strikingly, the newly swept stone floor that was *empty*. There was *nothing* on it apart from some worn rugs and, by the door, a pair of Aunt Zelda's boots.

She peeked into the little built-on kitchen, with its large sink, some neat and tidy pots and pans and a small table, but it was far too cold to linger in. Then she wandered over to the end of the room where shelves of potion bottles and jars lined the walls, reminding her of home. There were some that she recognized and remembered Sarah using. Frog Fusions, Marvel Mixture and Basic Brew were all familiar names to Jenna. And then, just like home, surrounding a small desk covered with neat piles of pens, papers and notebooks, there were teetering piles of Magyk books reaching up to the ceiling. There were so many that they covered almost an entire wall, but unlike home, they did not cover the floor as well.

The dawn light was beginning to creep through the frost-covered windows, and Jenna decided to take a look outside. She tiptoed over to the big wooden door and very slowly drew back the huge, well-oiled bolt. Then she carefully pulled the door open, hoping that it wouldn't creak. It didn't, because

Aunt Zelda, like all witches, was very particular about doors.
A creaking door in the house of a White Witch was a bad
sign, a sign of misplaced Magyk and ill-founded spells.

Jenna slipped quietly outside and sat on the doorstep with
her quilt wrapped around her and her warm breath turning to
white clouds in the chill dawn air. The marsh mist was heavy
and low. It hugged the ground and swirled over the surface of
the water and around a small wooden bridge that crossed a
broad channel to the marsh on the other side. The water was
brimming up over the banks of the channel, which was known
as the Mott, and ran all the way around Aunt Zelda's island
like a moat. The water was dark and so flat that it looked as
though a thin skin was stretched over its surface, and yet,
as Jenna gazed at it she could see that the water was slowly
creeping over the edges of the banks and wandering onto the
island.

For years Jenna had watched the tides come and go, and
she knew the tide that morning was a high spring tide after the
full moon the night before, and she also knew that soon it
would start to creep out again, just as it did in the river outside her little window at home, until it was as low as it had
been high, leaving the mud and sand for the waterbirds to dip
into with their long, curved beaks.

The pale white disk of the winter sun rose slowly through the thick blanket of mist, and around Jenna the silence began to change into the dawn sounds of stirring animals. A fussy clucking noise made Jenna jump in surprise and glance over to where the sound was coming from. To her amazement, Jenna could see the shape of a fishing boat looming through the mist.

For Jenna, who had seen more new and strange things in the last twenty-four hours than she had ever dreamed possible, a fishing boat crewed by chickens was not as much a surprise as it might have been. She just sat on the doorstep and waited for the boat to pass by. After a few minutes the boat appeared not to have moved, and she wondered if it had run aground on the island. A few minutes after that, when the mist had cleared a little more, she realized what it was: the fishing boat was a chicken house. Stepping delicately down the gangplank were a dozen hens, busily beginning the work of the day. Pecking and scratching, scratching and pecking.

Things, thought Jenna, are not always what they seem.

A thin, reedy birdcall drifted through the mist, and some muffled splashes were coming from the water, which sounded as though they belonged to small and, Jenna hoped, furry animals. It crossed her mind that they might be made by water snakes or eels, but she decided not to think about that. Jenna leaned back against the door post and breathed in the fresh, slightly salty marsh air. It was perfect. Peace and quiet.

"Boo!" said Nicko. "Got you, Jen!"

"Nicko," protested Jenna. "You're so noisy. Shhh."

Nicko settled himself down on the doorstep next to Jenna and grabbed some of her quilt to wrap himself in.

"Please," Jenna told him.

"What?"

"Please, Jenna, may I share your quilt? Yes, you may, Nicko. Oh, thank you very much, Jenna, that's very kind of you. Don't mention it, Nicko."

"All right, then, I won't." Nicko grinned. "And I suppose I have to curtsy to you now you're Miss High and Mighty."

"Boys don't curtsy." Jenna laughed. "You have to bow."

Nicko leaped to his feet and, doffing an imaginary hat with a sweep of his arm, bowed an exaggerated bow. Jenna clapped.

"Very good. You can do that every morning." She laughed again.

"Thank you, Your Majesty," said Nicko gravely, stuffing his imaginary hat back on his head.

"I wonder where the Boggart is?" said Jenna a little sleepily.

Nicko yawned. "Probably at the bottom of some mud pool somewhere. I don't suppose he's tucked up in bed."

"He'd hate it, wouldn't he? Too dry and clean."

"Well," said Nicko, "*I'm* going back to bed. I need more than two hours sleep, even if you don't." He extricated himself from Jenna's quilt and wandered back inside to his own, which lay in a crumpled heap by the fire. Jenna realized that she still felt tired too. Her eyelids were beginning to get that prickly feeling that told her she had not slept long enough, and she was getting cold. She stood up, gathered her quilt around her, slipped back into the half-light of the cottage and very quietly closed the door behind her.

✣ 19 ✣
AUNT ZELDA

ood morning, everyone!" Aunt Zelda's cheery voice called
out to the pile of quilts and their inhabitants by the fire.
Boy 412 woke up in a panic, expecting to have to tumble
out of his Young Army bed and line up outside in thirty seconds
flat for roll call. He stared uncomprehendingly at Aunt Zelda,
who looked nothing like his usual morning tormenter, the
shaven-headed Chief Cadet, who took great pleasure in chuck-
ing buckets of icy water over anyone who didn't jump out of

bed immediately. The last time that had happened to Boy 412, he had had to sleep in a cold, wet bed for days before it dried out. Boy 412 leaped to his feet with a terrified look on his face but relaxed a little when he noticed that Aunt Zelda did not actually have a bucket of icy water in her hand. Rather, she was carrying a tray laden with mugs of hot milk and a huge pile of hot buttered toast.

"Now, young man," said Aunt Zelda, "there's no rush. Just snuggle yourself back down and drink this while it's still hot." She offered a mug of milk and the biggest slice of toast to Boy 412, who looked, she thought, like he could do with fattening up.

Boy 412 sat back down, wrapped his quilt around him and somewhat warily drank the hot milk and ate his buttered toast. In between sips of milk and mouthfuls of toast he glanced around him, his dark gray eyes wide with apprehension.

Aunt Zelda settled herself down on an old chair beside the fire and threw a few logs onto the embers. Soon the fire was blazing, and Aunt Zelda sat contentedly warming her hands by the flames. Boy 412 glanced at Aunt Zelda whenever he thought she wouldn't notice. Of course she did notice, but she was used to looking after frightened and injured creatures, and she saw Boy 412 as no different from the assortment of marsh animals that she regularly nursed back to health. In fact, he particularly reminded her of a small and very frightened rabbit she had rescued from the clutches of a Marsh Lynx not long ago. The Lynx had been taunting the rabbit for hours, nipping its ears and throwing it about, enjoying the rabbit's frozen terror before it would eventually decide to break its neck. When, in an overenthusiastic throw, the Lynx had hurled the terrified animal into her path, Aunt Zelda had snatched the rabbit up, stuffed it into the large bag she always took out with her and gone straight home, leaving the Lynx wandering around for hours searching for its lost prey.

That rabbit had spent days sitting by the fire looking at her in just the same way that Boy 412 was now. Aunt Zelda reflected as she busied herself with the fire, careful not to frighten Boy 412 by looking at him for very long, the rabbit had recovered, and she was sure Boy 412 would too.

Boy 412's sidelong glances took in Aunt Zelda's frizzy gray hair, rosy cheeks, comfortable smile and friendly witch's brilliant blue eyes. He needed quite a few glances to take in her large patchwork dress, which made it hard to tell exactly what shape she might be, especially when she was sitting down. It gave Boy 412 the impression that Aunt Zelda had walked into a large patchwork tent and had just, that very minute, poked her head out of the top to see what was going on. Briefly, a smile flickered at the corner of his mouth at the thought.

Aunt Zelda noticed the hint of a smile and was pleased. She had never in her life seen such a pinched and frightened-looking child, and it upset her to think about what could have made Boy 412 become that way. She had heard talk about the Young Army in her occasional visits to the Port, but she had never really believed all the terrible stories she had heard. Surely no one could treat children in such a way? But now she began to wonder whether there was more truth in them than she had realized.

Aunt Zelda smiled at Boy 412; then with a comfortable groan she heaved herself out of the chair and pottered off to fetch some more hot milk.

While she was gone Nicko and Jenna woke up. Boy 412 stared at them and moved away a little, remembering only too well Jenna's armlock of the night before. But Jenna just smiled sleepily at him and said, "Did you sleep well?"

Boy 412 nodded and stared at his almost empty mug of milk.

Nicko sat up, grunted a hello in Jenna and Boy 412's direction, grabbed a slice of toast and was surprised to find how hungry he was. Aunt Zelda arrived back at the fireside carrying a jug of hot milk.

"Nicko!" Aunt Zelda smiled. "Well, you've changed a bit since I last saw you, that's for sure. You were just a little baby then. Those were the days when I used to visit your ma and pa in The Ramblings. Happy days."

Aunt Zelda sighed and passed Nicko his hot milk.

"And our Jenna!"—Aunt Zelda smiled a broad smile at her—"I always wanted to come and see you, but things became very difficult after the . . . well, after a while. But Silas has been making up for lost time and telling me *all* about you."

Jenna smiled a little shyly, glad that Aunt Zelda had said "our." She took the mug of hot milk that Aunt Zelda offered her and sat sleepily looking at the fire.

A contented silence fell for a while, broken only by the sound of Silas and Maxie still snoring upstairs and toast being munched downstairs. Jenna, who was leaning against the wall by the fire, thought she could hear a faint sound of meowing from inside the wall, but as that was obviously impossible, she decided it must be coming from outside and ignored it. But the meowing continued. It became steadily louder and, thought Jenna, crosser. She put her ear to the wall and heard the distinctive sounds of an angry cat.

"There's a cat in the wall . . ." said Jenna.

"Go on," said Nicko. "I don't know that one."

"It's not a joke. There *is* a cat in the wall. I can hear it."

Aunt Zelda jumped up.

"Oh, *my*. I completely forgot about Bert! Jenna love, could you just open Bert's door for her, please?" Jenna looked confused.

Aunt Zelda pointed to a small wooden door set into the bottom of the wall beside Jenna. Jenna tugged at the little door. It flew open, and out waddled an angry duck.

"I'm so sorry, Bert darling," apologized Aunt Zelda. "Have you been waiting for ages?"

Bert waddled unsteadily over the heap of quilts and sat herself down by the fire. The duck was cross. It very deliberately turned her back on Aunt Zelda and ruffled its feathers. Aunt Zelda leaned over and stroked her.

"Let me introduce you to my cat, Bert," she said.

Three pairs of bewildered eyes stared at Aunt Zelda. Nicko inhaled his milk and started choking. Boy 412 looked disappointed. He was just starting to like Aunt Zelda and now it turned out she was as mad as the rest of them.

"But Bert's a duck," said Jenna. She was thinking that someone had to say it, and they had better say it straight away before they all got into the let's-pretend-the-duck's-a-cat-just-to-humor-Aunt-Zelda thing.

"Ah, yes. Well, of course she *is* a duck at the moment. In fact, she has been a duck for a while now, haven't you, Bert?"

Bert gave a small meow.

"You see, ducks can fly and swim and that is a great advantage in the marshes. And I have yet to meet a cat who enjoys getting her feet wet, and Bert was no exception. So she decided to become a duck and enjoy the water. And you do, don't you, Bert?"

There was no answer. Like the cat she really was, Bert had fallen asleep by the fire.

Jenna tentatively stroked the duck's feathers, wondering if they felt like cat fur, but they were soft and smooth and felt entirely like duck feathers.

"Hello, Bert," whispered Jenna.

Nicko and Boy 412 said nothing. Neither of them was about to start talking to a *duck*.

"Poor old Bert," said Aunt Zelda. "She often gets stuck outside. But ever since the Quake Ooze Brownies got in through the cat tunnel I've tried to keep the cat door CharmLocked. You have no idea what a shock it was to come downstairs that morning and find the place heaving with those nasty little creatures, like a sea of mud they were, swarming up the walls and poking their long bony fingers into everything and staring at me with those little red eyes. They ate everything they could and messed up anything else they couldn't. And then, of course, as soon as they saw me they started all that high-pitched screaming." Aunt Zelda shuddered. "It set my teeth on edge for weeks. If it hadn't been for Boggart, I don't know what I would have done. I spent weeks cleaning the mud off the books, not to mention making up all my potions again. Talking of mud, would anyone like a dip in the hot spring?"

A little later, Jenna and Nicko felt a lot cleaner after Aunt Zelda had shown them where the hot spring bubbled up into the little bath hut in the backyard. Boy 412 had refused to have anything to do with it and had stayed huddled by the fire, his red hat crammed down over his ears and his sailor's sheepskin jacket still wrapped around him. Boy 412 felt as if the cold of the previous day was still deep in his bones, and he thought he would never again feel warm. Aunt Zelda let him sit by the fire for a while, but when Jenna and Nicko decided to go out and explore the island she shooed Boy 412 out with them.

"Here, take this," Aunt Zelda said, handing Nicko a lantern. Nicko gave Aunt Zelda a quizzical look. What were they going to need a lantern for at midday?

"Haar," said Aunt Zelda.

"Ha?" asked Nicko.

"Haar. Because of the haar, the salt marsh mist that rolls in from the sea," explained Aunt Zelda. "Look, we're surrounded by it today." She waved her hand around in a grand sweep. "On a clear day you can see the Port from where we're standing. The haar's lying low today, and we're high enough to be above it, but if it rises it'll come over us too. *Then* you'll need the lantern."

So Nicko took the lantern and, surrounded by the haar, which lay like an undulating white blanket over the marshes below, they set off to explore the island while Aunt Zelda, Silas and Marcia sat inside talking earnestly by the fireside.

Jenna led the way, closely followed by Nicko, while Boy 412 lagged behind, shivering every now and then and wishing he was back by the fire. The snow had melted in the warmer, damper marsh climate, and the ground was damp and soggy. Jenna took a path that led them down to the banks of the Mott. The tide had dropped and the water had all but disappeared, leaving marsh mud behind it, which was covered with hundreds of bird footprints and a few zigzag water snake trails.

Draggen Island itself was about a quarter of a mile long and looked as if someone had cut a huge green egg in half length-ways and plopped it down on top of the marsh. A footpath ran all the way around it along the bank of the Mott, and Jenna set off along the path, breathing in the cold salt air rolling in from the haar. Jenna liked the haar surrounding them. It made her feel safe at last—no one could find them now.

Apart from the boat-dwelling chickens, which Jenna and Nicko had seen earlier that morning, they found a nanny goat tethered in the middle of some long grass. They also found a colony of rabbits living in a burrow bank that Aunt Zelda had fenced off to keep the rabbits out of the winter cabbage patch.

The well-worn path took them past the burrows, through a lot of cabbages and wound down to a low-lying patch of mud and suspiciously bright green grass.

"Do you reckon there might be some of those Brownies in there?" Jenna whispered to Nicko, hanging back a little.

Some bubbles floated to the surface of the mud, and there was a loud sucking noise as if someone was trying to pull a stuck boot from out of the mire. Jenna jumped back in alarm as the mud bubbled and heaved.

"Not if I've got anything ter do with it, there won't be." The broad brown face of the Boggart pushed its way to the surface. He blinked the Ooze away from his round black eyes and regarded them with a bleary gaze.

"Mornin'," he said slowly.

"Good morning, Mr. Boggart," said Jenna.

"Just Boggart'll do, ta."

"Is this where you live? I hope we're not disturbing you?" Jenna said politely.

"Well you *is* disturbing me, as a matter of fact. I sleeps in the day, see." The Boggart blinked again and began to sink back into the mud. "But you's not ter know that. Just don't mention them Brownies as it wakes me up, see. Just hearin' the name gets me all wide awake."

"I'm sorry," said Jenna. "We'll go away and leave you in peace."

"Yeah," agreed the Boggart, and he disappeared back into the mud.

Jenna, Nicko and Boy 412 tiptoed back up the path.

"He was cross, wasn't he?" said Jenna.

"No," said Nicko. "I reckon he's always like that. He's okay."

"I hope so," said Jenna.

They carried on walking around the island until they reached the blunt end of the green "egg." This consisted of a large grassy mound covered with a scattering of small, prickly round bushes. They wandered across the mound and stopped for a while, watching the haar swirling below them.

Jenna and Nicko had been silent in case they should wake the Boggart up again, but as they stood on top of the mound Jenna said, "Don't you think there's a funny feeling under your feet?"

"My boots *are* a bit uncomfortable," said Nicko, "now you mention it. I think they're still wet."

"No. I mean the ground under your feet. It feels kind of . . . er . . ."

"Hollow," supplied Nicko.

"Yes, that's it. Hollow." Jenna stamped her foot down hard. The ground was firm enough, but there was something about it that felt different.

"Must be all those rabbit burrows," said Nicko.

They wandered off down the mound and headed toward a large duck pond with a wooden duck house beside it. A few ducks noticed them and began to waddle over the grass in the hope that they might have brought some bread with them.

"Hey, where's he gone?" Jenna suddenly said, looking around for Boy 412.

"He's probably gone back to the cottage," said Nicko. "I don't think he likes being with us much."

"No, I don't think he does—but aren't we meant to be

looking after him? I mean, he might have fallen into the
Boggart patch, or the ditch or a *Brownie* might have got him."

"*Shhh*. You'll wake the Boggart up again."

"Well, a Brownie *might* have got him. We ought to try and
find him."

"I suppose," said Nicko doubtfully, "that Aunt Zelda will
be upset if we lose him."

"Well, I will too," said Jenna.

"You don't *like* him, do you?" asked Nicko. "Not after the
little twerp nearly got us killed?"

"He didn't mean to," said Jenna. "I can see that now. He
was as scared as we were. And just think, he's probably been
in the Young Army all his life and never had a mum or dad.
Not like us. I mean you," Jenna corrected herself.

"You *have* had a mum and dad. Still have. Silly," said Nicko.
"All right, we'll go and look for the kid if you really want to."

Jenna looked around, wondering where to start, and realized she could no longer see the cottage. In fact she could no
longer see much at all except for Nicko, and that was only
because his lantern gave off a low red light.

The haar had risen.

✥ 20 ✥
BOY 412

Boy 412 *had fallen down a hole.* He hadn't meant to, and he had no idea how it had happened, but there he was, at the bottom of a hole.

Just before he had fallen down the hole, Boy 412 had become decidedly fed up with trailing around after the Princess-girl and the Wizard-boy. They didn't seem to want him with them, and he felt cold and bored. So he had decided to slip off back to the cottage and hoped that he might get Aunt Zelda to himself for a while.

And then the haar had come in.

If nothing else, the Young Army training had prepared him for something like this. Many times, in the middle of a foggy night, his platoon of boys had been taken out into the Forest and left to find their own way back. Not all of them did, of course. There was always one unlucky boy who fell foul of a hungry wolverine or was left lingering in a trap set by one of the Wendron Witches, but Boy 412 had been lucky, and he knew how to keep quiet and move fast through the night fog. And so, quiet as the haar itself, Boy 412 had started to make his way back to the cottage. At some point he had actually passed so close to Nicko and Jenna that they could have put their hands out and touched him, but he had slipped by them noiselessly, enjoying his freedom and the feeling of independence.

After a while Boy 412 reached the large grassy mound at the end of the island. This confused him because he was sure he had already walked across it, and by now he should have been nearly back at the cottage. Maybe this was a different grassy mound? Maybe there was one at the other end of the island too? He began to wonder if he might be lost. It occurred to him that it would be possible to walk endlessly around and around the island and *never* get to the cottage. Preoccupied with his thoughts, Boy 412 lost his footing and fell headlong into a small, and unpleasantly prickly, bush. And that was when it had happened. One moment the bush was there, and the next moment Boy 412 had crashed through it and was falling into darkness.

His yell of surprise was lost on the thick damp air of the haar, and he landed with a heavy thud on his back. Winded, Boy 412 lay still for a moment, wondering if he had broken any bones. No, he thought as he sat up slowly, nothing seemed to hurt too much. He was lucky. He had landed on what felt like sand, and it had cushioned his fall. Boy 412 stood up and promptly hit his head on a low rock above him. That *did* hurt.

Holding the top of his head with one hand, Boy 412 stretched up his other hand and tried to feel for the hole he had fallen through, but the rock sloped smoothly upward and gave him no clues, no handholds or footholds. Nothing but silk-smooth, ice-cold rock.

It was also pitch-black. No chink of light shone from above, and however much Boy 412 stared into the darkness hoping his eyes would get used to it, they didn't. It was as though he was blind.

Boy 412 dropped to his hands and knees and began to feel about him on the sandy floor. He had a wild thought that maybe he could dig his way out, but as his fingers scrabbled the sand away he soon hit a smooth stone floor, so smooth and cold that Boy 412 wondered if it might be marble. He had seen marble a few times when he had stood guard at the Palace, but he couldn't imagine what it might be doing out here in the Marram Marshes in the middle of nowhere.

Boy 412 sat down on the sandy floor and nervously ran his hands through the sand, trying to think what to do next. He was wondering if maybe his luck had finally run out when his fingers brushed against something metallic. At first Boy 412's spirits rose—maybe this was what he had been looking for, a hidden lock or a secret handle—but as his fingers closed around the metal object his heart sank. All he had found was a ring. Boy 412 lifted the ring, cradled it in his palm and stared at it, although in the pitch blackness he could see nothing.

"I wish I had a light," Boy 412 muttered to himself, trying to see the ring and holding his eyes as wide as they would go, as if it might make a difference. The ring sat in his palm, and after hundreds of years lying alone in a chill dark place under the ground, it slowly warmed up in the small human hand that held it for the first time since it had been lost so long ago.

As Boy 412 sat with the ring, he began to relax. He realized that he was not afraid of the dark, that he felt quite safe, safer in fact than he had felt for years. He was miles away from his tormentors in the Young Army, and he knew that they would never be able to find him here. Boy 412 smiled and leaned back against the wall. He would find a way out, that was for sure.

Boy 412 decided to see if the ring would fit. It was far too big for any of his skinny fingers, so he slipped it onto his right index finger, the biggest finger that he had. Boy 412 turned it around and around, enjoying the feeling of warmth, even heat, which was coming from it. Very soon Boy 412 became aware of a strange sensation. The ring, which felt as if it had come alive, was tightening around his index finger; it now fitted perfectly. Not only that, but it was giving off a faint golden glow.

Boy 412 gazed at the ring in delight, seeing his find for the first time. It was like no ring he had ever seen before. Curled around his finger was a gold dragon, its tail clasped in its mouth. Its emerald-green eyes glinted at him, and Boy 412 had the strangest feeling of being looked at by the dragon itself. Excited, he stood up, holding his right hand out in front of him with his very own ring, his dragon ring, now glowing as brightly as if it were a lantern.

Boy 412 looked around him in the golden light of the ring. He realized that he was at the end of a tunnel. In front of him, sloping down even deeper into the ground, was a narrow, high-sided passageway cut neatly from the rock. Holding his hand high above his head, Boy 412 stared upward into the blackness through which he had fallen, but could see no way of climbing back up. He reluctantly decided that the only thing he could do was follow the tunnel and hope it would lead him to another way out.

And so, holding out the ring, Boy 412 set off. The tunnel's sandy floor followed a steady downward slope. It twisted and turned this way and that, leading him into dead ends and at times taking him around in circles, until Boy 412 lost all sense of direction and became almost dizzy with confusion. It was as if the person who had built the tunnel was deliberately trying to confuse him. And succeeding.

And that, reckoned Boy 412, was why he fell down the steps.

At the foot of the steps Boy 412 caught his breath. He was all right, he told himself. He hadn't fallen far. But something was missing—*his ring was gone*. For the first time since he had been in the tunnel, Boy 412 felt scared. The ring had not only given him light; it had kept him company. It had also, Boy 412 realized as he shivered in the chill, made him feel warm. He looked about him, eyes wide open in the pitch blackness, desperately looking for that faint golden glow.

He could see nothing but black. *Nothing*. Boy 412 felt

desolate. As desolate as he had felt when his best friend, Boy 409, had fallen overboard in a night raid and they had not been allowed to stop to pick him up. Boy 412 put his head in his hands. He felt like giving up.

And then he heard the singing.

A soft, thin, beautiful sound drifted over to him, calling him toward it. On his hands and knees, because he did not want to fall down any more steps just then, Boy 412 inched his way toward the sound, feeling along the cold marble floor as he did so. Steadily, he crawled toward it and the singing became softer and less urgent, until it became strangely muffled, and Boy 412 realized he had his hand over the ring.

He had found it. Or rather, the ring had found him. Grinning happily, Boy 412 slipped the dragon ring back onto his finger, and the darkness around him faded away.

It was easy after that. The ring guided Boy 412 along the tunnel, which had opened out to become wide and straight and now had white marble walls richly decorated with hundreds of simple pictures in bright blues, yellow and reds. But Boy 412 paid little attention to the pictures. By now all he really wanted to do was find his way out. And so he kept going until he found what he was hoping to find, a flight of steps that at last led upward. With a feeling of relief, Boy 412 climbed the steps and found himself walking up a steep sandy slope that soon came to a dead end.

At last, in the light of the ring, Boy 412 saw his exit. An old ladder was propped up against a wall and above it was a wooden trapdoor. Boy 412 climbed the ladder, reached over and gave the trapdoor a push. To his relief it moved. He pushed a little harder, the trapdoor opened and Boy 412 peered out. It was still dark but a change in the air told Boy 412 that he was now aboveground, and as he waited, trying to get his bearings, he noticed a narrow strip of light along the floor. Boy 412 breathed a sigh of relief. He knew where he was. He was in Aunt Zelda's Unstable Potions and Partikular Poisons cupboard. Silently Boy 412 pulled himself up through the trapdoor, closed it and replaced the rug that covered it. Then he gingerly opened the cupboard door and peered out to see if anyone was around.

In the kitchen Aunt Zelda was making up a new potion. As Boy 412 crept past the door she glanced up, but, seemingly preoccupied by her work, she said nothing. Boy 412 slipped by and headed for the fireside. Suddenly Boy 412 felt very tired. He took off the dragon ring and tucked it safely into the pocket he had discovered inside his red hat, then he lay himself down next to Bert on the rug in front of the fire and fell fast asleep.

He was so deeply asleep that he didn't hear Marcia come downstairs and Command Aunt Zelda's tallest and most wobbly pile of Magyk books to lift themselves up. He certainly didn't hear the soft swish of a large and very ancient book, *The Undoing of the Darkenesse*, pulling itself out from the bottom of the swaying pile and flying over to the most comfortable chair by the fire. Nor did he hear the rustle of its pages as the book obediently opened and found the exact page that Marcia wanted to see.

Boy 412 didn't even hear Marcia squeal as, on her way to the chair, she nearly trod on him, stepped back and trod on Bert instead. But, deep in his sleep, Boy 412 had a strange dream about a flock of angry ducks and cats who chased him out of a tunnel and then carried him into the sky and taught him how to fly.

Far away in his dream, Boy 412 smiled. He was free.

✢ 21 ✢
RATTUS RATTUS

H ow did you get back so fast?" Jenna asked Boy 412.

It had taken Nicko and Jenna all afternoon to find their way back through the haar to the cottage. While Nicko had spent the time they were lost deciding which were his top-ten best boats and then, as he became hungrier, imagining what his all-time favorite supper would be, Jenna had spent most of the time worrying about what had happened to Boy 412 and deciding she was going to be much nicer to him from now on. That was if he hadn't already fallen into the Mott and drowned.

So when Jenna at last got back to the cottage cold and wet, with the haar still clinging to her clothes, and found Boy 412 sitting perkily on the sofa next to Aunt Zelda, looking almost pleased with himself, she did not feel quite as irritated as Nicko did. Nicko just grunted and went off to soak himself in the hot spring. Jenna let Aunt Zelda rub her hair dry for her, and then she sat down next to Boy 412 and asked him her question, "How did you get back so fast?"

Boy 412 looked at her sheepishly but said nothing. Jenna tried again.

"I was scared you had fallen in the Mott."

Boy 412 looked a little surprised at this. He didn't expect the Princess-girl to care whether he had fallen into the Mott, or even down a hole for that matter.

"I'm glad you got back safely," Jenna persisted. "It took me and Nicko ages. We kept getting lost."

Boy 412 smiled. He almost wanted to tell Jenna about what had happened to him and show her his ring, but years of having to keep things to himself had taught him to be careful. The only person he had ever shared secrets with had been Boy 409, and although there was something nice about Jenna that did remind him of Boy 409, she was a Princess, and even worse, a *girl*. So he said nothing.

Jenna noticed the smile and felt pleased. She was about to try another question when, in a voice that made the potion bottles rattle, Aunt Zelda yelled, "Message Rat!"

Marcia, who had taken over Aunt Zelda's desk at the far end of the room, got up quickly and, to Jenna's surprise, grabbed her by the hand and hauled her off the sofa.

"Hey!" protested Jenna. Marcia took no notice. She headed up the stairs, pulling Jenna along behind her. Halfway up they collided with Silas and Maxie, who were rushing down to see the Message Rat.

"That dog should not be allowed upstairs," snapped Marcia as she tried to squeeze past Maxie without getting any dog-dribble trails on her cloak.

Maxie slobbered excitedly on Marcia's hand and rushed down after Silas, one of his large paws treading heavily on Marcia's foot. Maxie paid very little attention to Marcia. He didn't bother to get out of her way or take any notice of what she said because, in his wolfhound way of looking at the world, Silas was Top Dog and Marcia was right at the bottom of the pile.

Happily for Marcia, these finer points of Maxie's inner life had passed her by, and she pushed past the wolfhound and strode upstairs, trailing Jenna in her wake, out of the way of the Message Rat.

"Wha-what did you do that for?" asked Jenna, getting her breath back as they reached the attic room.

"The Message Rat," said Marcia, a little puffed. "We don't know what kind of rat it is. It might not be a Chartered Confidential Rat."

"A *what* rat?" asked Jenna, puzzled.

"Well," whispered Marcia, sitting down on Aunt Zelda's narrow bed, which was covered with an assortment of patchwork blankets that were the result of many long, solitary evenings by the fireside. She patted the space beside her, and Jenna sat down too.

"Do you know about Message Rats?" asked Marcia in a low voice.

"I think so," said Jenna uncertainly, "but we never got one at home. Ever. I thought you had to be really important to get a Message Rat."

"No," said Marcia, "anyone can get one. Or send one."

"Maybe Mum sent it," said Jenna in a hopeful voice.

"Maybe," said Marcia, "and maybe not. We need to know if it is a Confidential Rat before we can trust it. A Confidential Rat will always tell the truth and keep all secrets at all times. It is also extremely expensive."

Jenna thought gloomily that in that case Sarah could never have sent the rat.

"So we'll just have to wait and see," said Marcia. "And meanwhile you and I will wait up here just in case it's a spy rat come to see where the ExtraOrdinary Wizard is hiding with the Princess."

Jenna nodded slowly. It was that word again. Princess. It still took her by surprise. She couldn't quite believe that that was who she really was. But she sat quietly next to Marcia, gazing around the attic room.

The room felt surprisingly large and airy. It had a sloping ceiling in which was set a small window that looked out far across the snow-covered marshes. Huge sturdy beams supported the roof. Below the beams hung an assortment of what looked like large patchwork tents, until Jenna realized that they must be Aunt Zelda's dresses. There were three beds in the room. Jenna guessed from the patchwork covers that they were sitting on Aunt Zelda's bed, and the one tucked away low in an alcove by the stairs and covered in dog hair was likely to belong to Silas. In the far corner was a large bed built into the wall. It reminded Jenna of her own box bed at home and gave her a sharp pang of homesickness when she looked at it. She guessed that it was Marcia's, for beside the bed was her book, *The Undoing of the Darkenesse*, a fine onyx pen and a pile of the best quality vellum covered in Magykal signs and symbols.

Marcia followed her gaze.

"Come on, you can try out my pen. You'll like that. It writes in any color you ask it to—if it's in a good mood."

While Jenna was upstairs trying out Marcia's pen, which was being somewhat contrary by insisting on writing every other letter in lurid green, Silas was downstairs trying to restrain an excitable Maxie, who had caught sight of the Message Rat.

"Nicko," said Silas distractedly, having spotted his damp-looking son just coming in from the hot spring. "Hang on to Maxie and keep him away from the rat, would you?" Nicko and Maxie bounded onto the sofa, and with equal speed, Boy 412 shot off.

"Now, where's that rat?" asked Silas.

A large brown rat was sitting outside the window, tapping on the glass. Aunt Zelda opened the window, and the rat hopped in and looked around the room with his quick, bright eyes.

"Squeeke, Rat!" said Silas in Magyk.

The rat looked at him impatiently.

"Speeke, Rat!"

The rat crossed his arms and waited. He gave Silas a withering look.

"Um . . . sorry. It's been ages since I've had a Message Rat," Silas excused himself. "Oh, *that's* it . . . Speeke, Rattus Rattus."

"Right-ho," sighed the rat. "Got there in the end." He drew himself up and said, "First I have to ask. Is there anyone here answering to the name of Silas Heap?" The rat stared straight at Silas.

"Yes, me," said Silas.

"Thought so," said the rat. "Fits the description." He gave a small, important-sounding cough, stood up straight and clasped his front paws behind his back.

"I am come here to deliver a message to Silas Heap. The message is sent today at eight o'clock this morning from one Sarah Heap residing in the house of Galen.

"Message begins:

> Hello, Silas love. And Jenna piglet and Nicko angel.
> I have sent the rat to Zelda's in the hope that he
> finds you safe and well. Sally told us that the Hunter
> was after you, and I couldn't sleep all night for

thinking about it. That man has such a terrible rep-
utation. I was at my wits' end by the morning and
was convinced you had all been caught (although
Galen told me she knew you were safe), but dear
Alther came to see us as soon as it was light and told
us the wonderful news that you had escaped. He said
he last saw you setting off into the Marram Marshes.
He wished he could have come with you.

Silas, something has happened. Simon disap-
peared on our way here. We were on the riverside
path that leads into Galen's part of the Forest when
I realized that he had gone. I just don't know what
can have happened to him. We didn't see any
Guards, and no one saw or heard him go. Silas, I
am so afraid he has fallen into one of those traps that
those awful witches set. We are going out to search
for him today.

The Guards set fire to Sally's cafe and she only
just managed to escape. She is not sure how she did
it, but she arrived here safely this morning and asked
me to tell Marcia that she is very grateful for the
KeepSafe she gave her. In fact, we all are. It was
very generous of Marcia.

Silas, please send the rat back and let me know
how you are.

All our love and thoughts go to you all.

Your loving Sarah

"Message ends."

Exhausted, the rat slumped down on the windowsill.

"I could murder a cup of tea," he said.

Silas was very agitated.

"I shall have to go back," he said, "and look for Simon. Who knows what might have happened?"

Aunt Zelda tried to calm him down. She brought out two mugs of hot sweet tea and gave one to the rat and one to Silas. The rat downed his mug in one go while Silas sat gloomily nursing his.

"Simon's really tough, Dad," said Nicko. "He'll be all right. I expect he just got lost. He'll be back with Mum by now."

Silas was not convinced.

Aunt Zelda decided the only sensible thing to do was to have supper. Aunt Zelda's suppers usually took people's minds off their problems. She was a hospitable cook who liked to have as many people around her table as she could, and although her guests always enjoyed the conversation, the food could be more of a challenge. The most frequent description was "interesting," as in, "That bread and cabbage bake was very . . . interesting, Zelda. I never would have thought of that myself," or, "Well, I must say that strawberry jam is such an . . . interesting sauce for sliced eel."

Silas was put to work laying the table to take his mind off things, and the Message Rat was invited to supper.

Aunt Zelda served frog and rabbit casserole with twice-boiled turnip heads followed by cherry and parsnip delight. Boy 412 tucked into it with great enthusiasm, as it was a wonderful improvement on the Young Army food, and he even had second and third helpings, much to Aunt Zelda's delight. No one had ever asked her for second helpings before, let alone *third*.

Nicko was pleased that Boy 412 was eating so much, as it meant that Aunt Zelda did not notice the frog lumps that he had lined up and hidden under his knife. Or if she did, it didn't bother her too much. Nicko also managed to feed the complete rabbit ear that he had found on his plate to Maxie, much to his relief and Maxie's delight.

Marcia had called down, excusing herself and Jenna from supper on account of the presence of the Message Rat. Silas thought it was a feeble excuse and suspected her of secretly doing a few gourmet food spells on the side.

Despite—or maybe because of—Marcia's absence, supper was an enjoyable affair. The Message Rat was good company. Silas had not bothered to undo the Speeke, Rattus Rattus command, and so the talkative rat held forth on any topic that caught his imagination, which ranged from the problem with young rats today to the rat sausage scandal in the Guards' canteen that had upset the entire rat community, not to mention the Guards.

As the meal drew to a close, Aunt Zelda asked Silas if he was going to send the Message Rat back to Sarah that night.

The rat looked apprehensive. Although he was a big rat and could, as he was fond of telling everyone, "take care of myself," Marram Marshes at night was not his favorite place. The suckers on a large Water Nixie could spell the end for a rat, and neither Brownies nor Boggarts were the rat's first choice of companions. The Brownies would drag a rat down into the Ooze just for fun, and a hungry Boggart would happily boil up a rat stew for its baby Boggarts, who were, in the Message Rat's opinion, voracious little pests.

(The Boggart of course had not joined them for supper. He never did. He preferred to eat the boiled cabbage sandwiches that Aunt Zelda made for him in the comfort of his own mud patch. He himself had not eaten rat for a long time. He didn't like the taste much, and the little bones got stuck between his teeth.)

"I was thinking," said Silas slowly, "that it might be better to send the rat back in the morning. He's come a long way, and he ought to get some sleep."

The rat look pleased.

"Quite right, sir. Very wise," he said. "Many a message is lost for want of a good rest. And a good supper. And may I say that was an exceptionally . . . interesting supper, Madam." He bowed his head in Aunt Zelda's direction.

"My pleasure." Aunt Zelda smiled.

"*Is that rat a Confidential Rat?*" asked the pepper pot in Marcia's voice. Everyone jumped.

"You might give us a bit of warning if you're going to start throwing your voice around," complained Silas. "I nearly inhaled my parsnip delight."

"*Well, is it?*" the pepper pot persisted.

"Are you?" Silas asked the rat, who was staring at the pepper pot and for once seemed lost for words. "Are you a Confidential Rat or not?"

"Yes," said the rat, unsure whether to answer Silas or the pepper pot. He went for the pepper pot. "I am indeed, Miss

Pot. I am a Chartered Confidential Long-Distance Rat. At your service."

"Good. I'm coming down."

Marcia came down the stairs two at a time and strode across the room, book in hand, her silk robes sweeping over the floor and sending a pile of potion jars flying. Jenna followed her quickly, eager to at last see a Message Rat for herself.

"It's so *small* in here," complained Marcia, irritably brushing Aunt Zelda's best multicolored Brilliant Blends off her cloak. "I really don't know how you manage, Zelda."

"I seemed to manage quite well before you arrived," Aunt Zelda muttered under her breath as Marcia sat down at the table beside the Message Rat. The rat went pale underneath his brown fur. Never in his wildest dreams had he expected to meet the ExtraOrdinary Wizard. He bowed low, far too low, and overbalanced into the remains of the cherry and parsnip delight.

"I want *you* to go back with the rat, Silas," announced Marcia.

"What?" said Silas. "*Now?*"

"I am not certified for passengers, Your Honor," the rat addressed Marcia hesitantly. "In fact, Your Most Graciousness, and I do say this with the greatest of respect—"

"UnSpeeke, Rattus Rattus," snapped Marcia.

The Message Rat opened and closed his mouth silently for a few more words until he realized that nothing was coming out. Then he sat down, reluctantly licking the cherry and parsnip delight off his paws, and waited. The rat had no choice but to wait, for a Message Rat may leave only with a reply or a refusal to reply. And so far the Message Rat had been given neither, so, like the true professional he was, he sat patiently and gloomily remembered his wife's words to him that morning when he had told her he was doing a job for a Wizard.

"Stanley," his wife, Dawnie, had said, wagging her finger at him, "if I was you, I wouldn't have nothing to do with them Wizards. Remember Elli's husband, who ended up bewitched by that small fat Wizard up at the Tower and got trapped in the hot pot? He didn't come back for two weeks and then he was in a terrible state. Don't go, Stanley. Please."

But Stanley had been secretly flattered that the Rat Office had asked him to go on an outside job, particularly for a Wizard, and was glad for a change from his previous job. He had spent the last week taking messages between two sisters who were having an argument. The messages had become increasingly short and distinctly ruder until his previous day's work had consisted of running from one sister to another and actually saying nothing at all, because each wished to tell the other that she was no longer speaking to her. He had been extremely relieved when their mother, horrified by the huge bill she had suddenly received from the Rat Office, had canceled the job.

And so Stanley had quite happily told his wife that, if he was needed, he must go. "I am after all," he told her, "one of the few Confidential Long-Distance Rats in the Castle."

"And one of the silliest," his wife had retorted.

And so Stanley sat on the table among the remains of the oddest supper he had ever eaten and listened to the surprisingly grumpy ExtraOrdinary Wizard telling the Ordinary Wizard what to do. Marcia thumped her book down on the table, rattling the plates.

"I have been going through Zelda's *The Undoing of the Darkenesse*. I only wish I had had a copy back at Wizard Tower. It's invaluable." Marcia tapped the book approvingly. The book misunderstood her. It suddenly left the table and flew back to its place in Aunt Zelda's book pile, much to Marcia's irritation.

"Silas," said Marcia, "I want you to go and get my KeepSafe back from Sally. We need it here."

"All right," said Silas.

"You *must* go, Silas," said Marcia. "Our safety may depend upon it. Without it I have less power than I thought."

"Yes, yes. *All right*, Marcia," said Silas impatiently, preoccupied with his thoughts about Simon.

"In fact, as ExtraOrdinary Wizard, I am *ordering* you to go,"
Marcia persisted.

"Yes! Marcia, I said *yes*. I'm *going*. I was going anyway," said
Silas, exasperated. "Simon has disappeared. I am going to look
for him."

"Good," said Marcia, paying little attention, as ever, to
what Silas was saying. "Now, where's that rat?"

The rat, still unable to speak, raised his paw.

"Your message is this Wizard, returned to sender. Do you
understand?"

Stanley nodded uncertainly. He wanted to tell the
ExtraOrdinary Wizard that this was against Rat Office regu-
lations. They did not deal in packages, human or otherwise.
He sighed. How right his wife had been.

"You will convey this Wizard safely and properly by appropriate means to the return address. Understood?"

Stanley nodded unhappily. Appropriate means? He supposed
that meant that Silas wasn't going to be able to swim the river.
Or hitch a lift in the baggage of a passing peddler. Great.

Silas came to the rat's rescue.

"I do not need to be booked in like a parcel, thank you,

Marcia," he said. "I will take a canoe, and the rat can come with me and show me the way."

"Very well," said Marcia, "but I want confirmation of order. Speeke, Rattus Rattus."

"Yes," said the rat weakly. "Order confirmed."

Silas and the Message Rat left early the next morning, just after sunrise, taking the *Muriel One* canoe. The haar had dis-appeared overnight, and the winter sun cast long shadows over the marshes in the gray early morning light.

Jenna, Nicko and Maxie had got up early to wave Silas off and give him messages for Sarah and the boys. The air was cold and frosty, and their breath hung in white clouds. Silas wrapped his heavy blue woolen cloak around him and pulled up his hood, while the Message Rat stood beside him shiver-ing a little, and not entirely with the cold.

The rat could hear horrible choking noises from Maxie close behind him as Nicko kept a tight grip on the wolf-hound's neckerchief, and, as if that wasn't enough, he had just caught sight of the Boggart.

"Ah, Boggart." Aunt Zelda smiled. "Thank you very much, Boggart dear, for staying up. Here's some sandwiches to keep you going. I'll put them in the canoe. There's some for you and the rat too, Silas."

"Oh. Well, thank you, Zelda. What kind of sandwiches would they be, exactly?"

"Best boiled cabbage."

"Ah. Well, that's most . . . thoughtful." Silas was glad he had smuggled some bread and cheese in his sleeve.

The Boggart was floating grumpily in the Mott and was not completely placated by the mention of cabbage sandwiches. He did not like being out in the daylight, even in the middle of winter. It made his weak Boggart eyes ache, and the sunlight burned his ears if he was not careful.

The Message Rat sat unhappily on the bank of the Mott, caught between dog breath behind him and Boggart Breath in front of him.

"Right," said Silas to the rat. "In you get. I expect you'll want to sit at the front. Maxie always does."

"I am *not* a dog," sniffed Stanley, "and I *don't* travel with Boggarts."

"This Boggart is a safe Boggart," Aunt Zelda told him.

"There's no such thing as a safe Boggart," muttered Stanley. Catching a glimpse of Marcia coming out of the cottage to wave Silas off, he said no more, but jumped smartly into the canoe and hid under the seat.

"Be careful, Dad," Jenna told Silas, hugging him tightly.

Nicko hugged Silas too. "Find Simon, Dad. And don't forget to stay by the edge of the river if the tide's against you. The tide always flows faster in the middle."

"I won't forget." Silas smiled. "Look after each other, both of you. And Maxie."

"Bye, Dad!"

Maxie whined and yelped as he saw, to his dismay, that Silas really *was* leaving him.

"Bye!" Silas waved as he unsteadily steered the canoe along the Mott to the familiar Boggart inquiry: "You followin'?"

Jenna and Nicko watched the canoe make its way slowly along the winding ditches and out into the wide expanse of the Marram Marshes until they could no longer make out Silas's blue hood.

"I hope Dad'll be all right," said Jenna quietly. "He's not very good at finding places."

"The Message Rat will make sure he gets there," said Nicko. "He knows he'll have some explaining to do to Marcia if he doesn't."

Deep in the Marram Marshes the Message Rat sat in the canoe surveying the first package he had ever had to deliver. He had

decided not to mention it to Dawnie, or to the rats at the Rat
Office; it was all, he sighed to himself, highly irregular.

But after a while, as Silas took them slowly and somewhat
erratically through the twisting channels of the marsh, Stanley
began to see that this was not such a bad way to travel. He did
after all have a ride all the way to his destination. And all he
had to do was sit there, tell a few stories and enjoy the ride
while Silas did all the work.

And that, as Silas said good-bye to the Boggart at the end
of Deppen Ditch and started paddling up the river on his way
to the Forest, is exactly what the Message Rat did.

✛ 2 2 ✛

MAGYK

That evening the east wind blew in across the marshes.

Aunt Zelda closed the wooden shutters on the windows and CharmLocked the door to the cat tunnel, making sure that Bert was safely indoors first. Then she walked around the cottage, lighting the lamps and placing storm candles at the windows to keep the wind at bay. She was looking forward to a quiet time at her desk updating her potion list.

But Marcia had got there first. She was leafing through some small Magyk books and busily making notes. Every now and then she tried out a quick spell to see if it still worked, and there would be a small popping noise and a peculiar-smelling puff of smoke. Aunt Zelda was not pleased to see what Marcia had done to the desk either. Marcia had given the desk duck feet to stop it from wobbling and a pair of arms to help with organizing the paperwork.

"When you've quite finished, Marcia, I'd like my desk back," said Aunt Zelda irritably.

"All yours, Zelda," Marcia said cheerily. She picked up a small square book and took it over to the fireside with her, leaving a pile of mess on the desk. Aunt Zelda swept the mess onto the floor before the arms could grab it and sat herself down with a sigh.

Marcia joined Jenna, Nicko and Boy 412 by the fire. She sat down next to them and opened the book, which Jenna could see was called:

Safety Spelles and Unharm Charms
For the Use of the Beginner and Those of Simple Mind
Compiled and Guaranteed by the Wizard Assurance League

"*Simple Mind?*" said Jenna. "That's a bit rude, isn't it?"

"Pay no attention to that," said Marcia. "It's very old-fashioned. But the old ones are often the best. Nice and simple, before every Wizard tried to get their own name on spells just by tinkering with them a little, which is when you get trouble. I remember I found what seemed like an easy Fetch Spell once. Latest edition with lots of brand-new unused Charms, which I suppose should have warned me. When I got it to Fetch my python shoes, it Fetched the wretched python as well. Not exactly what you want to see first thing in the morning."

Marcia was busy leafing through the book.

"There's an easy version of Cause Yourself to be Unseen somewhere here. I found it yesterday . . . Ah, yes, here it is."

Jenna peered over Marcia's shoulder at the yellowed page that Marcia had open. Like all Magyk books, each page had a different spell or incantation on it, and in the older books these would be carefully written by hand in various strange colored inks. Underneath each spell the page was folded back on itself to form a pocket in which the Charms were placed. The Charm contained the Magyk imprint of the spell. It was often a piece of parchment, although it could be anything. Marcia had seen Charms written on bits of silk, wood, shells and even toast, although that one had not worked properly, as mice had nibbled the ending.

And so this was how a Magyk book worked: the first

Wizard to create the spell wrote down the words and instructions on whatever he or she had at hand. It was best to write it
down at once, as Wizards are notoriously forgetful creatures,
and also the Magyk will fade if not captured quickly. So possibly, if the Wizard were in the middle of having breakfast when
he or she thought of the spell, they might just use a piece of
(preferably unbuttered) toast. This was the Charm. The number of Charms made would depend on how many times the
Wizard wrote down the spell. Or on how many pieces of toast
were made for breakfast.

When a Wizard had collected enough spells together, he or
she would usually bind them into a book for safekeeping;
although, many Magyk books were collections of older books
that had fallen apart and been remixed in various forms. A full
Magyk book with all its Charms still in their pockets was a rare
treasure. It was far more common to find a virtually empty book
with only one or two of the less popular Charms still in place.

Some Wizards only made one or two Charms for their
more complicated spells, and these were very hard to find,
although most Charms could be found in the Pyramid Library
back at the Wizard Tower. Marcia missed her library more
than anything else in the Tower, but she had been surprised
and very pleased with Aunt Zelda's collection of Magyk books.

"Here you are," said Marcia, passing the book to Jenna. "Why don't you take out a Charm?"

Jenna took the small and surprisingly heavy book. It was open at a grubby and much-thumbed page that was written in faded purple ink and large neat writing, which was easy to read.

The words said:

Cause Yourself to be Unseen
a Valued and Esteem'd Spelle
for all those Persons who might wishe
(for Reasons only Pertaining to their
Owne or Others' safekeeping)
to be Missed by those who may cause
them Harme

Jenna read the words with a feeling of apprehension, not wanting to think about who may cause her harm, and then felt inside the thick paper pocket that held the Charms. Inside the pocket were what felt like a lot of smooth, flat counters. Jenna's fingers closed around one of the counters and drew out a small oval piece of polished ebony.

"Very nice," said Marcia approvingly. "Black as the night.

Just right. Can you see the words on the Charm?"

Jenna screwed up her eyes in an effort to see what was written on the sliver of ebony. The words were tiny, written in an old-fashioned script in a faded golden ink. Marcia fished a large flat magnifying glass from her belt, which she unfolded and passed to Jenna.

"See if that helps," she said.

Jenna slowly passed the glass over the golden letters, and as they jumped into view she read them out:

Let me Fade into the Aire
Let all against me know not Where
Let them that Seeke me pass me by
Let Harme not reach me from their Eye.

"Nice and simple," said Marcia. "Not too hard to remember if things get a bit tricky. Some spells are all well and good, but try and remember them in a crisis and it's not so easy. Now you need to Imprint the spell."

"Do what?" asked Jenna.

"Hold the Charm close to you and say the words of the spell as you hold it. You need to remember the *exact* words. And as you say the words you have to imagine the spell actually happening—that's the really important part."

It wasn't as easy as Jenna expected, particularly with Nicko and Boy 412 watching her. If she remembered the words right, she forgot to imagine the Fade into the Aire bit, and if she thought too much about Fade into the Aire, she forgot the words.

"Have another go," Marcia encouraged her after Jenna had, to her exasperation, got everything right except one little word. "Everyone thinks spells are easy, but they're not. But you're nearly there."

Jenna took a deep breath. "Stop *looking* at me," she told Nicko and Boy 412.

They grinned and pointedly stared at Bert instead. Bert shifted uncomfortably in her sleep. She always knew when someone was looking at her.

So Nicko and Boy 412 missed Jenna's first Disappearance. Marcia clapped her hands. "You did it!" she said.

"Did I? *Have* I?" Jenna's voice came from out of the air.

"Hey, Jen, where are you?" asked Nicko, laughing.

Marcia looked at her timepiece. "Now don't forget, the first time you do a spell it doesn't last very long. You'll Reappear in a minute or so. After that it should last as long as you want it to."

Boy 412 watched Jenna's blurred shape slowly Materialize out of the flickering shadows cast by Aunt Zelda's candles. He stared openmouthed. *He* wanted to do that.

"Nicko," said Marcia, "your turn."

Boy 412 felt cross with himself. What had made him think Marcia would ask *him*? Of course she wouldn't. He didn't belong. He was just a Young Army Expendable.

"I've got my own Disappear, thanks," said Nicko. "Don't want to get it muddled up with this one."

Nicko had a workmanlike approach to Magyk. He had no intention of becoming a Wizard, even though he was from a Magykal family and had been taught Basyk Magyk. Nicko didn't see why he needed more than one of each kind of spell. Why clog your brain up with all that stuff? He reckoned he already had all the spells in his head that he would ever need. He'd rather use his brain space for useful things like tide times and sail rigging.

"Very well," said Marcia, who knew better than to try and make Nicko do anything he wasn't interested in, "but just remember that only those within the same Unseen can see each other. If you have a different one, Nicko, you will not be visible to anyone who has a different spell, even if they too are Unseen. All right?"

Nicko nodded vaguely. He didn't really see why it mattered.

"Now, then"—Marcia turned to Boy 412—"it's your turn."

Boy 412 went pink. He stared at his feet. *She had asked him.* More than anything he wanted to try the spell, but he hated the way everyone was looking at him, and he was sure he was going to look stupid if he tried it.

"You really should have a go," said Marcia. "I want you *all* to be able to do this."

Boy 412 looked up, surprised. Did Marcia mean he was just as important as the two other kids? The two who *belonged?*

Aunt Zelda's voice came from the other end of the room. "Of *course* he'll have a go."

Boy 412 stood up awkwardly. Marcia fished out another Charm from the book and gave it to him. "Now you Imprint it," she told him.

Boy 412 held the Charm in his hand. Jenna and Nicko looked at him, curious to see what he would do now that it was his turn.

"Say the words," Marcia prompted gently. Boy 412 said nothing, but the words to the spell whizzed around his brain and filled his head with a strange buzzing sensation. Underneath his red beanie hat, the stubbly hairs on the back of his head stood up. He could feel the Magyk tingling through his hand.

"He's gone!" gasped Jenna.

Nicko gave a low whistle of admiration. "He doesn't hang about, does he?"

Boy 412 felt cross. There was no need to make fun of him. And why was Marcia giving him such a weird look? Had he done something wrong?

"Come back now," Marcia said very quietly. Something in Marcia's voice made Boy 412 a little scared. What had happened?

Then an amazing thought crossed Boy 412's mind. Very quietly he stepped over Bert, slipped past Jenna without touching her and wandered into the middle of the room. No one watched him go. They were all still staring at the space where he had just been standing.

A thrill of excitement ran through Boy 412. He could *do* it. He could do Magyk. He could Fade into the Aire! No one could see him. He was *free!*

Boy 412 gave a small hop of excitement. No one noticed. He put his arms in the air and waved them above his head. No one noticed. He put his thumbs in his ears and waggled his fingers. No one noticed. Then, silently, he skipped over to blow out a storm candle, caught his foot under a rug and crashed to the floor.

"*There* you are," said Marcia crossly.

And there he was, sitting on the floor nursing a bruised knee and slowly Appearing to his impressed audience.

"You're *good*," said Jenna. "How did you do that so easily?"

Boy 412 shook his head. He had no idea how he had done it. It had just happened. But it felt great.

Marcia was in a strange mood. Boy 412 thought she would be pleased with him, but she seemed to be anything but.

"You shouldn't Imprint a spell so fast. It can be dangerous. You might not have been able to come back properly."

What Marcia didn't say to Boy 412 was that she had never seen a first-timer master a spell so quickly. It unsettled her. And she felt even more unsettled when Boy 412 gave her back the Charm and she felt a buzz of Magyk, like a small click of static electricity, jump from his hand.

"No," she said, giving it back to him, "you keep the Charm. And Jenna too. It's best for beginners to keep the Charms for spells they might want to use."

Boy 412 put the Charm in his trouser pocket. He felt confused. His head still swam with the excitement of the Magyk, and he knew he had done the spell perfectly. So why was Marcia cross? What had he done wrong? Maybe the Young Army was right. Maybe the ExtraOrdinary Wizard really was crazy—what was it they used to chant every morning in the Young Army before they went off to guard the Wizard Tower and spy on the comings and goings of all the Wizards, particularly the ExtraOrdinary Wizard?

> *Crazy as a cuttlefish,*
> *Nasty as a RAT,*
> *Put her in a pie dish,*
> *Give her to the CAT!*

But the rhyme didn't make Boy 412 laugh anymore, and it didn't seem to have much to do with Marcia at all. In fact, the more he thought about the Young Army, the more Boy 412 realized the truth.

The *Young Army* was crazy.

Marcia was Magyk.

✠ 2 3 ✠
WINGS

Thatnight*the easterly wind* blew up into a gale. It rattled the shutters, shook the doors and unsettled the whole cottage. Every now and then a great gust of wind howled around the cottage, blowing the smoke back down the chimney and leaving the three occupants of the fireside quilts choking and spluttering.

Upstairs, Maxie had refused to leave his master's bed and was snoring as loudly as ever, much to the irritation of Marcia and Aunt Zelda, neither of whom could sleep.

Aunt Zelda got up quietly and peered out of the window as she always did on stormy nights, ever since her younger brother Theo, a Shape-Shifter like her older brother, Benjamin Heap, had decided he had had enough of living his life below the clouds. Theo wanted to soar up through them into the sunlight forever. One winter's day he had come to say good-bye to his sister, and at dawn the next day she had sat by the Mott and watched as he Shifted for the last time into his chosen Shape, a storm petrel. The last Aunt Zelda had seen of Theo was the powerful bird heading out over the Marram Marshes toward the sea. As she watched the bird go, she knew that she was unlikely to ever see her brother again, for storm petrels spend their lives flying over the oceans and rarely return to land, unless blown in by a storm. Aunt Zelda sighed and tip-toed back to bed.

Marcia had stuffed her pillow over her head in an effort to drown out the dog snores and the high-pitched howl of the wind as it swept over the marshes and, finding the cottage in its way, tried to batter its way through and out the other side. But it wasn't just the noise that kept her awake. There was something else on her mind. Something she had seen that evening had given her some hope for the future. A future back at the Castle, free from Darke Magyk. She lay awake planning her next move.

Downstairs, Boy 412 couldn't sleep at all. Ever since he had done the spell he felt odd, as if a swarm of bees was buzzing inside his head. He imagined little bits of Magyk left behind from the spell, spinning around and around. He wondered why Jenna, who was now sleeping soundly, wasn't awake. Why wasn't her head buzzing too? He slipped his ring on, and the golden glow lit up the room, giving Boy 412 an idea. It must be the ring. That was why his head was buzzing, and that was why he could do the spell so easily. He had found a Magyk ring.

Boy 412 started thinking about what had happened after he had done the spell. How he had sat with Jenna looking through the spell book until Marcia had noticed and made them put it away, saying that she didn't want any more fooling around, thank you very much. Then, later in the evening, when no one else was about, Marcia had cornered him and told him she wanted to talk to him the next day. By himself. To Boy 412's way of thinking, that could only mean trouble.

Boy 412 felt unhappy. He couldn't think straight, so he decided to make a list. The Young Army Facts List. It had always worked before.

Fact One. No early morning roll call:
      GOOD.
Fact Two. Much better food: GOOD.
Fact Three. Aunt Zelda nice: GOOD.
Fact Four. Princess-girl friendly: GOOD.
Fact Five. Have Magyk *ring:* GOOD.
Fact Six. ExtraOrdinary Wizard cross: BAD.

Boy 412 was surprised. Never before in his life had the GOOD outnumbered the BAD. But somehow that made the one BAD even worse. Because, for the first time, Boy 412 felt he had something to lose. Eventually he fell into an uneasy sleep and woke early with the dawn.

The next morning the east wind had died down, and there was a general air of expectation in the cottage.

Aunt Zelda was out at dawn checking for storm petrels blown in after the windy night. There weren't any, which was what she expected, although she always hoped otherwise.

Marcia was expecting Silas back with her KeepSafe.

Jenna and Nicko were expecting a message from Silas.

Maxie was expecting his breakfast.

Boy 412 was expecting trouble.

"Don't you want your porridge chunks?" Aunt Zelda asked Boy 412 at breakfast. "You had two helpings yesterday, and you've hardly touched them today."

Boy 412 shook his head.

Aunt Zelda looked concerned. "You're looking a bit peaky," she said. "Are you feeling all right?"

Boy 412 nodded, even though he wasn't.

After breakfast, while Boy 412 was carefully folding his quilt as neatly as he had always folded his Army blankets every morning of his life, Jenna asked him if he wanted to come out in the *Muriel Two* with her and Nicko to watch for the Message Rat coming back. He shook his head. Jenna wasn't surprised. She knew Boy 412 did not like boats.

"See you later, then," she called out cheerily as she ran off to join Nicko in the canoe.

Boy 412 watched Nicko steer the canoe out along the Mott and into the marshes. The marshland looked bleak and cold that morning, as though the night's east wind had rubbed it raw. He was glad he was staying in the cottage by the warm fire.

"Ah, there you are," said Marcia behind him. Boy 412 jumped. "I'd like a word with you."

Boy 412's heart sank. Well, that was it, he thought. She's

going to send me away. Back to the Young Army. He should have realized it was all too good to last.

Marcia noticed how pale Boy 412 had suddenly become.

"Are you all right?" she asked him. "Was it the pig-foot pie last night? I found it a bit indigestible myself. Didn't get much sleep either, especially with that awful east wind. And speaking of wind, I don't see why that disgusting dog can't sleep somewhere else."

Boy 412 smiled. He for one was glad that Maxie slept upstairs.

"I thought you might like to show me the island," Marcia continued. "I expect you already know your way around."

Boy 412 looked at Marcia in alarm. What did she suspect? Did she know he'd found the tunnel?

"Don't look so worried." Marcia smiled. "Come on, why don't you show me the Boggart patch? I've never seen where a Boggart lives."

Regretfully leaving the warmth of the cottage behind, Boy 412 set off with Marcia to the Boggart patch.

Together they made a strange pair: Boy 412, ex–Young Army Expendable, a small, slight figure even in his bulky sheepskin jacket and baggy rolled-up sailor's trousers, was made instantly visible by his bright red hat, which so far

he had refused to take off, even for Aunt Zelda. Towering
above him, Marcia Overstrand, ExtraOrdinary Wizard, strode
along at a brisk pace, which Boy 412 had to occasionally
break into a trot to keep up with. Her gold and platinum
belt flashed in the weak winter sunlight, and her heavy
silk and fur robes flowed out behind her in a rich purple
stream.

They soon arrived at the Boggart patch.

"Is that *it*?" asked Marcia, a little shocked at how any creature could live in such a cold and muddy place.

Boy 412 nodded, proud that he could show Marcia something she didn't already know.

"Well, well," said Marcia. "You learn something every day.
And yesterday," she said, looking Boy 412 in the eye before
he had a chance to look away. "Yesterday I learned something
too. Something very interesting."

Boy 412 shuffled his feet uneasily and looked away. He
didn't like the sound of this.

"I learned," said Marcia in a low voice, "that you have a natural Magykal gift. You did that spell as easily as if you had been
studying Magyk for years. But you've never been near a spell
in your life, have you?"

Boy 412 shook his head and looked at his feet. He still felt as though he had done something wrong.

"Quite," said Marcia. "I didn't think so. I suppose you have been in the Young Army since you were, what . . . two and a half? That's when they usually take them."

Boy 412 had no idea how long he had been in the Young Army. He could remember nothing else in his life, so he supposed Marcia was right. He nodded again.

"Well, we all know that the Young Army is the last place you'd come up against any Magyk. And yet somehow you have your own Magykal energy. It gave me quite a shock when you handed me the Charm last night."

Marcia took something small and shiny from a pocket in her belt and placed it in Boy 412's hand. Boy 412 looked down and saw a tiny pair of silver wings nestling in his grubby palm. The wings shimmered in the light and looked to Boy 412 as though they might fly away at any moment. He peered closer and saw some minute letters set into each wing in a fine gold inlay. Boy 412 knew what that meant. He was holding a Charm, but this time it wasn't just a piece of wood—it was a beautiful jewel.

"Some Charms for higher Magyk can be very beautiful," said Marcia. "They're not all pieces of soggy toast. I remember when Alther first showed this one to me. I thought it was one of the most simple and beautiful Charms I had ever seen. And I still do."

Boy 412 gazed at the wings. On one beautiful silver wing were the words FLY FREE, and on the other wing were the words WITH ME.

Fly Free With Me, Boy 412 said to himself, loving how the words sounded inside his head. And then . . .

He couldn't help it.

He didn't really know he was doing it.

He just said the words to himself, his flying dream came into his head and . . .

"I knew you would do it!" exclaimed Marcia excitedly. "I just *knew* it!"

Boy 412 wondered what she meant. Until he realized that he seemed to be the same height as Marcia. Or even taller— in fact, he was floating above her. Boy 412 looked down in surprise, expecting Marcia to tell him off like she had done the evening before, to tell him to stop fooling around and come back down *this minute*, but to his relief she had a huge smile on her face and her green eyes flashed with excitement.

"It's amazing!" Marcia shielded her eyes against the morning sun as she squinted up to look at Boy 412 floating over the Boggart patch. "This is advanced Magyk. This is stuff you don't do for years. I just don't *believe* it."

Which was probably the wrong thing to say, because Boy 412 didn't believe it either. Not really.

There was a huge splash as he landed in the middle of the Boggart patch.

"Oi! Can't a poor Boggart have no peace?" An indignant pair of black-button eyes blinked reproachfully out of the mud.

"Aaah . . . " gasped Boy 412, struggling to the surface and grabbing hold of the Boggart.

"I bin awake all yesterday," the Boggart complained as he pulled the spluttering boy toward the edge of the mud patch. "Went all the way ter the river, sun in me eyes, rat yammering in me ear"—the Boggart pushed Boy 412 up onto the bank beside the mud patch—"an all I hope fer is a bit a sleep the next day. Don't want no visitors. Just want ter sleep. Got it? You all right, lad?"

Boy 412 nodded, still spluttering.

Marcia had knelt down and was wiping Boy 412's face with a rather fine purple silk handkerchief. The short-sighted Boggart looked taken aback.

"Oh, mornin', Yer Majesty," said the Boggart respectfully. "Didunt see you there."

"Good Morning, Boggart. I'm so sorry we disturbed you. Thank you very much for your help. We'll be off now and leave you in peace."

"Think nothin' of it. Bin a pleasure."

With that the Boggart sank to the bottom of the mud patch, leaving nothing more than a few bubbles on the surface.

Marcia and Boy 412 slowly made their way back to the cottage. Marcia decided to ignore the fact that Boy 412 was covered from head to toe in mud. There was something she wanted to ask him. She had made up her mind, and she didn't want to wait.

"I wonder," she said, "if you would consider being my Apprentice?"

Boy 412 stopped in his tracks and stared at Marcia, the whites of his eyes shining out from his mud-covered face. *What* had she said?

"You would be my first one. I have never found anyone suitable before."

Boy 412 just stared at Marcia in disbelief.

"What I mean is," said Marcia, trying to explain, "that I have never found anyone with any Magykal spark before now, but you have it. I don't know why you have it or how you got

it, but you do. And with your power and mine together I think
we can dispel the Darke, the Other side. Maybe forever. What
do you say? Will you be my Apprentice?"

Boy 412 was shocked. How could he *possibly* help Marcia,
the ExtraOrdinary Wizard? She had it all wrong. He was a
fraud—it was the dragon ring that was Magykal, not him. As
much as he longed to say yes, he couldn't.

Boy 412 shook his head.

"No?" Marcia sounded shocked. "Do you mean *no*?"

Boy 412 nodded slowly.

"No . . ." Marcia was, for once, lost for words. It had never
occurred to her that Boy 412 would turn her down. No one
ever turned down the chance to be Apprenticed to the
ExtraOrdinary Wizard. Apart from that idiot Silas, of course.

"You do realize what you are saying?" she asked.

Boy 412 did not respond. He felt wretched. He had managed to do something wrong again.

"I am asking you to think about it," said Marcia in a more
gentle voice. She had noticed how scared Boy 412 was looking. "It is an important decision for us both—and for the
Castle. I hope you will change your mind."

Boy 412 didn't see how he *could* change his mind. He held
the Charm out for Marcia to take back. It shone clean and

bright in the middle of Boy 412's muddy paw.

This time it was Marcia who shook her head.

"It is a token of my offer to you, and my offer is still there. Alther gave it to me when he asked me to be his Apprentice. Of course I said yes straight away, but I can see that it's different for you. You need time to think about it. I'd like you to keep the Charm while you think things over."

Marcia decided to change the subject. "Now," she said briskly, "how good are you at catching bugs?"

Boy 412 was very good at catching bugs. He had had numerous pet bugs over the years. Stag, who was a stag beetle, Milly, a millipede, and Ernie, who was a large earwig, had been his particular favorites, but he had also kept a large black house spider with hairy legs, who went by the name of Seven-Leg Joe. Seven-Leg Joe lived in the hole in the wall above his bed. That was until Boy 412 suspected Joe of eating Ernie, and probably Ernie's entire family too. After that Joe found himself living under the bed of the Chief Cadet, who was terrified of spiders.

Marcia was very pleased at their total bug haul. Fifty-seven assorted bugs would do nicely and was about as many bugs as Boy 412 could carry.

"We'll get the Preserve Pots out when we get back and

have these in them in no time," said Marcia.

Boy 412 gulped. So that's what they were for: bug jam.

As he followed Marcia back to the cottage, Boy 412 hoped that the tickly feeling going up his arm was not anything with too many legs.

✛ 24 ✛
SHIELD BUGS

A truly horrible smell of boiled rat and rotten fish was waft-
ing out of the cottage as Jenna and Nicko paddled the
Muriel Two back along the Mott after a long day on the marsh
and no sign at all of the Message Rat.

"You don't think that rat got here before us and Aunt Zelda's
boiling it up for supper, do you?" Nicko laughed as they tied up
the canoe and wondered whether it was wise to venture indoors.

"Oh, *don't*, Nicko. I liked the Message Rat. I hope Dad
sends him back soon."

Keeping their hands clamped firmly over their noses, Jenna and Nicko walked up the path to the cottage. With some trepidation, Jenna pushed open the door.

"Eurgh!"

The smell was even worse inside. Added to the powerful aromas of boiled rat and rotten fish was a definite whiff of old cat poo.

"Come in, dears. We're just cooking." Aunt Zelda's voice came from the kitchen, where, Jenna now realized, the awful smell was coming from.

If this was supper, thought Nicko, he'd rather eat his socks.

"You're just in time," said Aunt Zelda cheerily.

"Oh, great," said Nicko, wondering if Aunt Zelda had any sense of smell at all or whether countless years of boiling cabbage had killed it off.

Jenna and Nicko reluctantly approached the kitchen, wondering what kind of supper could possibly smell so bad.

To their surprise and relief, it wasn't supper. And it wasn't even Aunt Zelda doing the cooking. It was Boy 412.

Boy 412 looked very odd. He was wearing an ill-fitting multicolored knitted suit, consisting of a baggy patchwork sweater and some very droopy knitted shorts. But his red beanie hat was still crammed firmly onto his head and was

steaming gently dry in the heat of the kitchen, while the rest
of his clothes dried by the fire.

Aunt Zelda had at last won the battle of the bath, due only
to the fact that Boy 412 was so uncomfortable when he had
arrived back covered with sticky black mud from the Boggart
patch that he was actually quite glad to disappear into the bath
hut and soak it off. But he wouldn't let his red hat go. Aunt
Zelda had lost that one. Still, she was pleased to get his
clothes clean at last and thought he looked very sweet in
Silas's old knitted suit, which he had worn as a boy. Boy 412
thought he looked very stupid and avoided looking at Jenna as
she came in.

He concentrated hard on stirring the reeking glop, still not
completely convinced that Aunt Zelda was *not* making bug
jam, especially as she was sitting at the kitchen table with a
pile of empty jam jars in front of her. She was busy unscrew-
ing the lids and passing the jars to Marcia, who sat across the
table taking out Charms from a very thick spell book titled:

Shield Bug Preserves

500 Charms

Each Guaranteed Identical and 100% Effective

Ideal for the Safety-Conscious Wizard of Today

"Come and sit down," said Aunt Zelda, clearing a space at the table for them. "We're making up Preserve Pots. Marcia's doing the Charms, and you can do the bugs if you like."

Jenna and Nicko sat down at the table, taking care to breathe only through their mouths. The smell was coming from the pan of bright green gloop that Boy 412 was slowly stirring with great concentration and care.

"Here you are. Here're the bugs." Aunt Zelda pushed a large bowl over to Jenna and Nicko. Jenna peeked in. The bowl was crawling with bugs of all possible shapes and sizes.

"Yuk." Jenna shuddered; she didn't like creepy-crawlies at all. Nicko wasn't exactly pleased either. Ever since Edd and Erik had dropped a millipede down his neck when he was little he had avoided anything that scuttled or crawled.

But Aunt Zelda took no notice. "Nonsense, they're just tiny creatures with lots of little legs. And they're much more scared of you than you are of them. Now, first Marcia will pass around the Charm. We each hold the Charm so that the bug will Imprint us and recognize us when it's released, then she'll put the Charm in a jar. You two can add a bug and pass it to, er, Boy 412. He'll top the jar with the Preserve, and I'll screw the lids back on nice and tight. That way we'll get this done in no time."

And that's what they did, except Jenna ended up screwing on the jar lids after the first bug ran up her arm and was only dislodged by her jumping up and down and screaming loudly.

It was a relief when they were on the last jar. Aunt Zelda unscrewed the lid and passed it to Marcia, who turned the page of the spell book and took out yet another small shield-shaped Charm. She passed the Charm around so that each of them held it for a moment, then dropped it into the jam jar and passed the jar to Nicko. Nicko wasn't looking forward to this one. At the bottom of the bowl lurked the last bug, a large red millipede, just like the one that had gone down the back of his neck all those years ago. It was running frantically around and around the bowl looking for somewhere to hide. If it hadn't made Nicko shudder quite so much, he might have felt sorry for it, but all Nicko could think was that he had to *pick it up*. Marcia was waiting with the Charm already in the jar. Boy 412 was poised with the last disgusting ladleful of Preserve gloop, and everyone was *waiting*.

Nicko took a deep breath, closed his eyes and plunged his hand into the bowl. The millipede saw him coming and ran to the opposite side. Nicko felt around the bowl, but the milli-pede was too quick for him. It scuttled this way and that, until it spotted the shelter of Nicko's dangling sleeve and ran for it.

"You've got it!" said Marcia. "It's on your sleeve. Quick, in the jar." Not daring to look, Nicko frantically shook his sleeve over the jar and knocked it over. The Charm skittered across the table, fell onto the floor and Disappeared.

"Bother," said Marcia. "These are a bit unstable." She fished out another Charm and quickly dropped it into the jar, forgetting to Imprint it.

"Hurry up, do," said Marcia irritably. "The Preserve is wearing off fast. Come *on*."

She reached over and deftly flicked the millipede off Nicko's sleeve, straight into the jar. It was quickly covered in sticky green Preserve by Boy 412. Jenna screwed the lid on tight, plonked the jar down on the table with a flourish, and everyone watched the last Preserve Pot transform.

The millipede lay in the Preserve Pot in a state of shock. It had been asleep under its favorite rock when Something Huge with a Red Head had picked up the rock and lifted it into Space. The worst was yet to come: the millipede, who was a solitary creature, had been thrown into a pile of noisy, dirty and downright *rude* bugs who jostled it and pushed it and even tried to *bite its legs*. The millipede didn't like anything messing with its legs. It had a lot of legs, and each one needed to be kept in perfect working order; otherwise the millipede was in

trouble. One dodgy leg and that was it—a bug could be forever running around in circles. So the millipede had headed
for the bottom of the pile of low-life bugs and sulked, until it
suddenly realized that all the bugs had gone and there *was*
nowhere to hide. Every millipede knew that *nowhere to hide*
meant the end of the world, and now the millipede knew that
that was indeed true because sure enough, here it was, floating in a thick green goo and something *terrible* was happening
to it. One by one it was *losing its legs*.

Not only that, but now its long, sleek body was getting
shorter and fatter, and the millipede was now shaped like a
stubby triangle with a little pointy head. On its back it had a
stout pair of armored green wings, and its front was covered
in heavy green scales. And if that wasn't bad enough, the millipede now had *only four legs*. Four thick green legs. If you
could call them legs. They certainly weren't what it would call
legs. There were two at the top and two at the bottom. The
top two legs were shorter than the two bottom legs. They had
five pointy things on the ends of each of them, which the millipede could move about, and one of the top legs was holding
a small sharp metal stick. The bottom two legs had big flat
green things on the ends of them, and each one of those had
five more little pointy green things on it. It was a complete

disaster. How could anything live with only four fat legs ending in pointy bits? What kind of creature was *that*?

That kind of creature, although the millipede didn't know it, was a Shield Bug.

The ex-millipede, now a completed Shield Bug, lay suspended in the thick green Preserve. The bug moved slowly, as if testing out its new shape. It wore a surprised expression as it stared out at the world through its green haze, waiting for the moment when it would be released.

"The perfect Shield Bug," said Marcia proudly, holding up the jam jar to the light and admiring the ex-millipede. "That's the best one we've done. Well done, everyone."

Soon, the fifty-seven jam jars were lined up along the windowsills, guarding the cottage. They were an eerie sight, their bright green occupants dreamily floating in the green goo, sleeping the time away until someone unscrewed the lids of their jars and released them. When Jenna asked Marcia what happened when you unscrewed the lid, Marcia told her that the Shield Bug would leap out and defend you until its last breath, or until you managed to catch it and put it back in the jar, which did not usually happen. A released Shield Bug had no intention of getting back into any jar ever again.

While Aunt Zelda and Marcia cleared up the pots and

pans, Jenna sat by the door, listening to the clatter from the kitchen. As the twilight fell, she watched the fifty-seven little pools of green light reflected onto the pale stone floor, and saw in each one a small shadow slowly moving, waiting for its moment of freedom to arrive.

✢ 25 ✢
THE WENDRON WITCH

By midnight everyone in the cottage was asleep except Marcia. The east wind had blown in again, this time bringing snow with it. All along the windowsills the Preserve Pots clinked mournfully as the creatures in them shifted about, disturbed by the snowstorm blowing outside.

Marcia was sitting at Aunt Zelda's desk with one small flickering candle so as not to wake the sleepers by the fireside. She was deep into her book, *The Undoing of the Darkenesse.*

Outside, floating just below the surface of the Mott to

stay out of the snow, the Boggart kept a lonely midnight watch.

Far away in the Forest, Silas too kept a lonely midnight vigil in the middle of the snowfall, which was heavy enough to find its way down through the tangled bare branches of the trees. He was standing, shivering a little, under a tall and sturdy elm tree, waiting for the arrival of Morwenna Mould.

Morwenna Mould and Silas went back a long way. Silas had been a young Apprentice out on a night errand for Alther in the Forest when he had heard the bloodcurdling sounds of a baying pack of wolverines. He knew what that meant: they had found their prey for the night and were closing in for the kill. Silas pitied the poor animal. He knew only too well how terrifying it was to be surrounded by a circle of glinting yellow wolverine eyes. It had happened to him once, and he had never forgotten it but, being a Wizard, he was lucky. He had done a quick Freeze and hurried away.

However, that night on his errand, Silas heard a faint voice in his head. *Help me . . .*

Alther had taught him to take notice of such things, and so Silas followed where the voice led him and found himself on the outside of a wolverine circle. On the inside was a young witch. Frozen.

At first Silas had thought that the young witch was simply
frozen with fear. She stood in the middle of the circle, eyes
wide with terror, her hair tangled from running through the
Forest to escape the wolverine pack and her heavy black cloak
clutched tightly to her.

It took Silas a few moments to realize that, in her panic, the
young witch had Frozen herself rather than the wolverines,
leaving them the easiest supper the pack had had since the last
Young Army Do-or-Die night exercise. As Silas watched, the
wolverines began to close in for the kill. Slowly and deliberately, enjoying the prospect of a good feed, they circled the
young witch, drawing in ever closer. Silas waited until he had
all the wolverines in his sight, then quickly he Froze the entire
pack. Unsure how to UnDo a witch spell, Silas lifted up the
witch, who was luckily one of the smaller and lighter
Wendron Witches, and carried her to safety. Then he waited
with her all through the night while the Freeze wore off.

Morwenna Mould had never forgotten what Silas had done
for her. From then on, whenever he ventured into the Forest,
Silas knew he had the Wendron Witches on his side. And he
also knew that Morwenna Mould would be there to help him
if he needed it. All he had to do was to wait beside her tree at

midnight. And that is what, after all those years, he was doing.

"Well, I do believe it is my dear brave Wizard. Silas Heap, what brings you here tonight of all nights, on our MidWinter Eve?" A quiet voice, spoken with a soft Forest burr like the rustling of the leaves on the trees, came out of the dark.

"Morwenna, is that you?" asked Silas, a little flustered, jumping to his feet and looking around him.

"It surely is," said Morwenna, appearing out of the night and surrounded by a flurry of snowflakes. Her black fur cloak was dusted with snow, as was her long dark hair, which was held in place by the traditional green leather Wendron Witch headband. Her bright blue eyes flashed in the dark the way that all witches' eyes do; they had been watching Silas standing under the elm tree for some time before Morwenna had decided it was safe to appear.

"Hello, Morwenna," said Silas, suddenly shy. "You haven't changed a bit." Actually Morwenna had changed quite a lot. There was a good deal more of her since the last time Silas had seen her. He would certainly no longer be able to pick her up and carry her out of a slavering circle of wolverines.

"Neither have you, Silas Heap. I see you've still got your crazy straw hair and those lovely deep-green eyes. What can I do for you? I have waited a long time to repay your favor. A

Wendron Witch never forgets."

Silas felt very nervous. He wasn't sure why, but it was something to do with Morwenna looming up close to him. He hoped he'd done the right thing by meeting her.

"I, er . . . You remember my eldest son, Simon?"

"Well, Silas, I remember you had a baby boy called Simon. You told me all about him while I was DeFrosting. He was having trouble with his teeth I remember. And you were not getting much sleep. How are his teeth now?"

"Teeth? Oh, fine, as far as I know. He's eighteen years old now, Morwenna. And two nights ago he disappeared in the Forest."

"Ah. That's not good. There are Things abroad in the Forest now. Things have come out of the Castle. Things we have not seen before. It is not good for a boy to be out among them. Nor a Wizard, Silas Heap." Morwenna placed her hand on Silas's arm. He jumped.

Morwenna lowered her voice to a husky whisper. "We witches are *sensitive*, Silas."

Silas managed nothing more than a small squeak in reply. Morwenna really was quite overpowering. He had forgotten how Forceful a real grown-up Wendron Witch actually was.

"We know that a terrible Darkenesse has come into the

hub of the Castle. Into the Wizard Tower no less. It may have
Taken your boy."

"I had hoped you might have seen him," said Silas dismally.

"No," said Morwenna. "But I will look out for him. If I find
him, I will return him to you safe, have no fear."

"Thank you, Morwenna," said Silas gratefully.

"It is nothing, Silas, compared with what you did for me. I
am very grateful to be here to help you. If I can."

"If—if you have any news, you can find us at Galen's tree
house. I am staying there with Sarah and the boys."

"You have *more* boys?"

"Er, yes. Five more. We had seven altogether, but . . ."

"Seven. A gift. A seventh son of the seventh son. Magykal
indeed."

"He died."

"Ah. I am sorry, Silas. A great loss. To us all. We could do
with him now."

"Yes."

"I will leave you for now, Silas. I will take the tree house and
all who are in her under our protection, for what it may be
worth with the encroaching Darkenesse. And tomorrow, all in
the tree house are invited to join us for our MidWinter Feast."

Silas was touched.

"Thank you, Morwenna. That is very kind."

"Until the next time, Silas. I bid you good speed and a joy-ful Feast Day tomorrow." With that the Wendron Witch dis-appeared back into the Forest, leaving Silas standing alone under the tall elm tree.

"Good-bye, Morwenna," he whispered into the darkness and hurried off through the snow, back to the tree house where Sarah and Galen were waiting to hear what had happened.

By the next morning Silas had decided that Morwenna was right. Simon must have been Taken into the Castle. Something told him that Simon was there.

Sarah was not convinced.

"I don't see why you are taking so much notice of that *witch*, Silas. It's not as though she knows anything for sure. Suppose Simon's in the Forest and *you* end up being Taken. What then?"

But Silas would not be swayed. He Changed his robes to the short gray hooded tunic of a worker, said good-bye to Sarah and the boys and climbed down from the tree house. The smell of cooking from the Wendron Witches' Mid-Winter Feast almost persuaded Silas to stay, but he resolutely set off in search of Simon.

"Silas!" Sally called after him as he reached the Forest floor. "Catch!"

Sally threw down the KeepSafe Marcia had given her.

Silas caught it. "Thank you, Sally."

Sarah watched as Silas pulled his hood down over his eyes and set off through the Forest toward the Castle, his parting words thrown over his shoulder, "Don't worry. I'll be back soon. With Simon."

But she did.

And he wasn't.

✢ 26 ✢
MidWinter Feast Day

No, *thank you, Galen.* I'm not going to those witches'
MidWinter Feast. We Wizards don't celebrate it,"
Sarah told Galen after Silas had left that morning.

"Well, I shall go," said Galen, "and I think we all should
go. You don't turn down a Wendron Witch invitation lightly,
Sarah. It's an honor to be asked. In fact, I can't imagine how
Silas managed to get us all an invitation."

"Humph" was Sarah's only response.

But as the afternoon wore on and the delicious smell of roast wolverine drifted through the Forest and up to the tree house, the boys became very restless. Galen only ate vegetables, roots and nuts, which was, as Erik had pointed out in a loud voice after their first meal with Galen, exactly what they fed the rabbits at home.

The snow was falling heavily through the trees as Galen opened the tree house trapdoor. Using a clever pulley system she had devised herself, she pulled down the long wooden ladder so that it was resting on the blanket of snow that now covered the ground. The tree house itself was built on a series of platforms running across three ancient oak trees and had been part of the oaks ever since they had reached their full height, many hundreds of years ago. A higgledy-piggledy collection of huts had been put up on the platform over the years. They were covered with ivy and blended in with the trees so well that they were invisible from the floor of the Forest.

Sam, Edd and Erik, and Jo-Jo were sharing the guest hut at the very top of the middle tree and had their own rope down to the Forest. While the boys fought over who was going down the rope first, Galen, Sarah and Sally made a more sedate exit down the main ladder.

Galen had dressed up for the MidWinter Feast. She had

been asked to one many years ago, after she had healed a witch's child, and she knew it was quite an occasion. Galen was a small woman, somewhat weather-beaten after years of outdoor living in the Forest. She had cropped tousled red hair, laughing brown eyes and generally wore a simple short green tunic, leggings and a cloak. But today she wore her MidWinter Feast dress.

"Goodness, Galen, you've gone to a lot of trouble," said Sarah, slightly disapprovingly. "I haven't seen that dress before. It's . . . quite something."

Galen didn't get out much, but when she did, she really dressed up for it. Her dress looked as though it was made from hundreds of multicolored leaves all sewn together and tied in the middle with a brilliant green sash.

"Oh, thank you," said Galen, "I made it myself."

"I thought you had," said Sarah.

Sally Mullin pushed the ladder back up through the trap-door, and the party set off through the Forest, following the delicious smell of roasting wolverine.

Galen led them through the Forest paths, which were covered with a thick fall of new snow and crisscrossed with all shapes and sizes of animal tracks. After a long trudge through a maze of tracks, ditches and gullies, they came to what had once been a slate quarry for the Castle. This was now where the Wendron Witches' Moots took place.

Thirty-nine witches, all dressed in their red MidWinter Feast robes, were gathered around a roaring fire down in the middle of the quarry. The ground was strewn with freshly cut greenery dusted by the snow that fell softly around them, much of it melting and sizzling in the heat of the fire. There was a heady smell of spicy food in the air: spits were turning, wolverines were roasting, rabbits were stewing in bubbling cauldrons and squirrels were baking in underground ovens. A long table was piled high with all kinds of sweet and spicy foods. The Witches had bartered for these treats with the Northern Traders and had saved them for this, the most important day of the year. The boys' eyes opened wide with amazement. They had never seen so much food all in one place in their whole lives. Even Sarah had to admit to herself that it was impressive.

Morwenna Mould spotted them hovering uncertainly at the entrance to the quarry. She gathered up her red fur robes and swept over to greet them.

"Welcome to you all. Please join us."

The assembled witches parted respectfully to allow Morwenna, the Witch Mother, to escort her somewhat overawed guests to the best places by the fire.

"I am so glad to meet you at last, Sarah." Morwenna smiled. "I feel as if I know you already. Silas told me so much about you the night he saved me."

"Did he?" asked Sarah.

"Oh, yes. He talked of you and the baby the whole night long."

"Really?"

Morwenna put her arm around Sarah's shoulder. "We are all looking for your boy. I am sure all will be well in the end. And with your other three who are away from you now. All will be well there too."

"My other three?" asked Sarah.

"Your other three children."

Sarah did a hurried count. Sometimes even she could not remember how many there were.

"Two," she said, "my other two."

The MidWinter Feast carried on far into the night, and after a good deal of Witches' Brew Sarah completely forgot her worries about Simon and Silas. Unfortunately they all came back to her the next morning, along with a very bad headache.

Silas's MidWinter Feast Day was altogether more subdued.

He took the riverside track that ran along the outside of

the Forest and then skirted around the Castle walls, and blown along by chill flurries of snow, he headed for the North Gate. He wanted to get to familiar territory before he decided what he was going to do. Silas pulled his gray hood right down over his green Wizard eyes, took a deep breath and walked across the snow-covered drawbridge, which led to the North Gate.

Gringe was on duty at the gatehouse, and he was in a bad temper. Things were not happy in the Gringe household just then, and Gringe had been pondering his domestic problems all morning.

"Oi, you," grunted Gringe, stamping his feet in the cold snow, "get a move on. You're late for the compulsory street cleaning."

Silas hurried by.

"Not so fast!" barked Gringe. "That'll be one groat from you."

Silas scrabbled around in his pocket and fished out a groat, sticky with some of Aunt Zelda's cherry and parsnip delight, which he had shoved into his pocket to avoid eating. Gringe took the groat and sniffed it suspiciously, then he rubbed it on his jerkin and put it to one side. Mrs. Gringe had the delightful task of washing any sticky money each night, so he added it to her pile and let Silas pass.

"'Ere, don't I know you from somewhere?" Gringe called out as Silas rushed by.

Silas shook his head.

"Morris dancing?"

Silas shook his head again and kept walking.

"Lute lessons?"

"No!" Silas slipped into the shadows and disappeared down an alleyway.

"I *do* know 'im," muttered Gringe to himself. "And 'e ain't no worker neither. Not with them green eyes shinin' out like a couple o' caterpillars in a coal bucket." Gringe thought for a few moments. "That's Silas 'eap! 'E's got a nerve comin' 'ere. I'll soon sort 'im out."

It was not long before Gringe found a passing Guard, and soon the Supreme Custodian had been informed of Silas's return to the Castle. But try as he might, he could not find him. Marcia's KeepSafe was doing its job well.

Silas, meanwhile, had scurried off into the old Ramblings, gratefully getting out of the way of both Gringe and the snow. He knew where he was going; he wasn't sure why, but he wanted to see his old place once again. Silas slipped down the familiar dark corridors. He was glad of his disguise, for no one paid any attention to a lowly worker, but Silas had not realized how little respect they were given. No one stood by to let him pass. People pushed him out of the way, allowed doors to slam in his face, and twice he was roughly told he should be out cleaning the streets. Maybe, thought Silas, being just an Ordinary Wizard was not so bad after all.

The door to the Heap room hung open forlornly. It appeared not to recognize Silas as he tiptoed into the room in which he had spent much of the last twenty-five years of his life. Silas sat down on his favorite homemade chair and surveyed the room sadly, lost in his thoughts. It looked strangely small now that it was empty of children, noise and Sarah presiding over the comings and goings of the days. It also looked embarrassingly dirty, even to Silas, who had never minded a bit of dirt here and there.

"They lived in a tip, didn't they? Dirty Wizards. Never did have no time for them meself," said a rough voice. Silas spun around to see a burly man standing in the doorway. Behind him Silas could see a large wooden cart in the corridor.

"Didn't think they'd send anyone along to 'elp. Good thing they did. It 'ud take all day on me own. Right, cart's outside. It's all to go to the dump. Magyk books to be burned. Got that?"

"*What?*"

"Gawd. They sent me a daft one 'ere. Junk. Cart. Dump. It ain't exactly *Alchemy*. Now give us that heap a wood you're parked on and let's get goin'."

Silas got up from his chair as if in a dream and handed it to the removal man, who took it and hurled it into the cart. The chair shattered and lay in pieces at the bottom of it. Before long it was underneath a huge pile of the Heaps' lifetime accumulation of possessions and the cart was full to overflowing.

"Right, then," said the removal man. "I'll get this down to the dump before it closes while you put them Magyk books outside. The firemen will collect 'em tomorrow on their rounds."

He handed Silas a large broom. "I'll leave yer to sweep up all that disgustin' dog hair and what-have-yer. Then you can get off 'ome. You look a bit done in. Not used to 'ard work, eh!" The removal man chuckled and thumped Silas on the back in what was meant to be a friendly manner. Silas coughed and smiled wanly.

"Don't forget them Magyk books" was the man's parting advice as he trundled the teetering cart off down the corridor on its journey to the Riverside Amenity Rubbish Dump.

In a daze, Silas swept up twenty-five years' worth of dust,

dog hair and dirt into a neat pile. Then he gazed regretfully at
his Magyk books.

"I'll give you a hand if you like," Alther's voice said next
to him. The ghost put his arm around Silas's shoulder.

"Oh. Hello, Alther," said Silas gloomily. "What a day."

"Yes, it's not good. I'm very sorry, Silas."

"All . . . gone," mumbled Silas, "and now the books too.
We had some good ones there. A lot of rare Charms . . . all
going up in flames."

"Not necessarily," said Alther. "They'd fit nicely into
your bedroom in the roof. I'll help you with the Remove Spell
if you like."

Silas brightened a little.

"Just remind me how it goes, Alther, then I can do it. I'm
sure I can."

Silas's Remove worked well. The books lined up neatly,
the trapdoor flew open, and book by book they flew up
through it and stacked up in Silas and Sarah's old bedroom.
One or two of the more contrary books headed out the door
and were halfway down the corridor before Silas managed to
Call them back, but by the end of the spell all the Magyk
books were safely in the roof and Silas had even Disguised the
trapdoor. Now no one could possibly guess what was there.

And so Silas walked out of his empty, echoing room for the last time and took off down Corridor 223. Alther floated along with him.

"Come and sit with us for a while," Alther offered, "down at the Hole in the Wall."

"Where?"

"I only recently discovered it myself. One of the Ancients showed me. It's an old tavern inside the Castle walls. Got bricked up years ago by one of the Queens who disapproved of beer. Seems as long as you've walked the Castle walls—and who hasn't?—a ghost can get in, so it's packed. It's got a great atmosphere—might cheer you up."

"I don't know if I really fancy it, thanks all the same, Alther. Isn't that the one where they bricked up the nun?"

"Oh, she's great fun, is Sister Bernadette. Loves a pint of beer. Life and soul of the party. So to speak. Anyway, I've got some news of Simon that I think you should hear."

"Simon! Is he all right? Where *is* he?" asked Silas.

"He's here, Silas. In the Castle. Come along to the Hole in the Wall. There's someone you need to talk to."

The Hole in the Wall Tavern was buzzing.

✳　✳　✳

Alther had led Silas to a tumbledown pile of stones heaped up against the Castle wall just along from the North Gate. He had shown him a small gap in the wall hidden behind the pile of rubble, and Silas had barely managed to squeeze through. Once through he had found himself in another world.

The Hole in the Wall was an ancient tavern built inside the wide Castle wall. When Marcia had taken her shortcut to the North Side those few days ago, part of her journey had taken her over the roof of the tavern, but she had been unaware of the motley collection of ghosts talking the long years away right beneath her feet.

It took Silas a few minutes for his eyes to adjust from the brightness of the snow to the dull glow of the lamps that flickered along the walls. But as they did he became aware of a most amazing collection of ghosts. They were gathered around long trestle tables, standing together in small groups beside the ghostly fire or just sitting in solitary contemplation in a quiet corner. There was a large contingent of ExtraOrdinary Wizards, their purple cloaks and robes spanning the different styles fashionable through the centuries. There were knights in full armor, pages in extravagant liveries, women with wimples, young Queens with rich silk dresses and older Queens in black, all enjoying one another's company.

Alther led Silas through the crowd. Silas did his best not to walk through any of them, but once or twice he felt a cold breeze as he passed through a ghost. No one seemed to mind—some nodded to him in a friendly manner and others were too intent on their endless conversation to notice him—and Silas got the impression that any friend of Alther's was a welcome guest in The Hole in the Wall.

The ghostly landlord of the tavern had long ago given up hovering by the beer barrels, for the ghosts all nursed the same tankard of beer that they had been given when they first arrived, and some tankards had lasted for many hundreds of years. Alther bade a cheery hello to the landlord, who was deep in conversation with three ExtraOrdinary Wizards and an old tramp who had long ago fallen asleep under one of the tables and never woken up again. Then he steered Silas over to a quiet corner where a plump figure in a nun's habit was sitting waiting for them.

"May I introduce Sister Bernadette," said Alther. "Sister Bernadette, this is Silas Heap—the one I was telling you about. He is the boy's father."

Despite Sister Bernadette's bright smile Silas felt a sense of foreboding.

The round-faced nun turned her twinkling eyes to Silas and

said in a soft lilting voice, "He's quite a lad, your boy, isn't he? He knows what he wants, and isn't afraid of going out to get it."

"Well, I suppose so. He certainly wants to be a Wizard, I know that. He wants an Apprenticeship, but of course with the ways things are now . . ."

"Ah, to be sure it's not a good time to be a young and hopeful Wizard," agreed the nun, "but that's not why he came back to the Castle, you know."

"So he *has* come back. Oh, that's a relief. I thought he had been captured. Or—or *killed*."

Alther put his hand on Silas's shoulder. "Unfortunately Silas, he was captured yesterday. Sister Bernadette was there. She will tell you."

Silas put his head in his hands and groaned.

"How?" he asked. "What happened?"

"Well, now," said the nun, "it would seem that young Simon had a girlfriend."

"Did he?"

"Yes indeed. Lucy Gringe is her name."

"Not Gringe the Gatekeeper's daughter? Oh, *no*."

"I'm sure she's a nice lass, Silas," remonstrated Sister Bernadette.

"Well, I hope she's nothing like her father, that's all I can say. *Lucy Gringe.* Oh, goodness."

"Well now, Silas, it seems Simon took himself back to the Castle for a pressing reason. He and Lucy had a secret appointment at the chapel. To be married. So romantic." The nun smiled dreamily.

"*Married?* I don't *believe* it. I'm related to the ghastly Gringe." Silas looked whiter than some of the occupants of the tavern.

"No, Silas, you are not," said Sister Bernadette disapprovingly. "Because unfortunately young Simon and Lucy did not actually get married."

"*Unfortunately?*"

"Gringe found out and tipped off the Custodian Guards. He no more wanted his daughter to marry a Heap than you wanted Simon to marry a Gringe. The Guards stormed the chapel, sent the distraught lass home and took Simon away." The nun sighed. "So cruel, so cruel."

"Where have they taken him?" Silas asked quietly.

"Well, now, Silas," said Sister Bernadette in her soft voice, "I was in the chapel myself for the wedding. I love a wedding. And the Guard that had hold of Simon walked right through me, and so I knew what he was thinking just at that moment. He was thinking that he was to take your boy to the Courthouse. To the Supreme Custodian no less. I am so sorry to be telling you this, Silas." The nun put her ghostly hand on Silas's arm. It was a warm touch but held little comfort for Silas.

This was the news Silas had been dreading. Simon was in the hands of the Supreme Custodian—how was he to break the terrible news to Sarah? Silas spent the rest of the day in The Hole in the Wall waiting, while Alther sent out as many ghosts as he could to the Courthouse to search for Simon and find out what was happening to him.

None of them had any luck. It was as if Simon had vanished.

✢✦ 27 ✦✢
STANLEY'S JOURNEY

On *MidWinter Feast Day, Stanley* was woken by his wife. He had an urgent message from the Rat Office.

"I don't know why they can't at least let you have *today* off," his wife complained. "It's work, work, work with you, Stanley. We need a holiday."

"Dawnie dear," said Stanley patiently. "If I don't do the work, we don't get the holiday. It's as simple as that. Did they say what they wanted me for?"

"Didn't ask." Dawnie shrugged grumpily. "I expect it's those no-good Wizards again."

"They're not so bad. Even the ExtraOrdinary Wiz—oops."

"Oh, is *that* where you've been?"

"No."

"Yes, it is. You can't hide anything from me, even if you are a Confidential. Well, let me give you one piece of advice, Stanley."

"Only one?"

"Don't get involved with Wizards, Stanley. They are *trouble*. Trust me, I know. The last one, that Marcia woman, you know what she did? She stole some poor Wizard family's only daughter and ran off with her. No one knows why. And now the rest of the family—what was their name? Oh that's it, Heap—well, they've all upped and gone looking for her. Of course the one good thing is we've got a nice new ExtraOrdinary out of it, but goodness knows he's got enough on his plate sorting out the mess the last one left, so we won't be seeing *him* for a while. And isn't it awful about all those poor homeless rats?"

"What poor homeless rats?" said Stanley wearily, itching to get off to the Rat Office and see what his next job was.

"All the ones from Sally Mullin's Tea and Ale House. You know the night we got the new ExtraOrdinary? Well, Sally Mullin left some of that ghastly barley cake in the oven for too

long and burned the whole place down. There're *thirty* rat families homeless now. Terrible thing in this weather."

"Yes, terrible. Well, I'll be off now, dear. I'll see you when I
get back." Stanley hurried off to the Rat Office.

The Rat Office was at the top of the East Gate Lookout
Tower. Stanley took the quick route, running along the top
of the Castle wall, over The Hole in the Wall Tavern, which
even Stanley did not know existed. The rat quickly reached
the Lookout Tower and scurried into a large drainpipe that
ran up the side. Soon he emerged at the top, jumped onto the
parapet and knocked on the door of a small hut bearing the
words:

OFFICIAL RAT OFFICE

MESSAGE RATS ONLY

CUSTOMER OFFICE ON GROUND FLOOR

BY RUBBISH BINS

"Enter!" called a voice that Stanley did not recognize.
Stanley tiptoed in. He didn't like the sound of the voice at all.

Stanley didn't care much for the look of the rat who owned
the voice either. An unfamiliar large black rat sat behind the

message desk. His long pink tail was looped over the desk and flicked impatiently as Stanley took in his new boss.

"You the Confidential I sent for?" barked the black rat.

"That's right," said Stanley, a little uncertainly.

"That's right, *sir*, to you," the black rat told him.

"Oh," said Stanley, taken aback.

"Oh, *sir*," corrected the black rat. "Right, Rat 101—"

"Rat 101?"

"Rat 101, *sir*. I demand some respect around here, Rat 101, and I intend to get it. We start with numbers. Each Message Rat is to be known by number only. A numbered rat is an efficient rat where I come from."

"Where *do* you come from?" ventured Stanley.

"*Sir*. Never you mind," barked the black rat. "Now, I have a job for you, 101." The black rat fished out a piece of paper from the basket that he had winched up from the Customer Office below. It was a message order, and Stanley noticed that it was written on headed note paper from the Palace of the Custodians. And it was signed by the Supreme Custodian no less.

But for some reason that Stanley did not understand, the actual message he was to deliver was not from the Supreme Custodian, but from Silas Heap. And it was to be delivered to Marcia Overstrand.

"Oh, bother," said Stanley, his heart sinking. Another trip across the Marram Marshes dodging that Marsh Python was not what he had hoped for.

"Oh, bother, *sir*," corrected the black rat. "The acceptance of this job is not optional," he barked. "And one last thing, Rat 101. Confidential status withdrawn."

"*What?* You can't do that!"

"*Sir.* You can't do that, *sir.* Can do it. Have, in fact, *done* it." The black rat allowed a smug smile to drift past his whiskers.

"But I've got all my exams, and I've only just done my Higher Confidentials. *And* I came top—"

"*And I came top, sir.* Too bad. Confidential status revoked. End of story. Dismissed."

"But—but—" spluttered Stanley.

"Now *push off*," snapped the black rat, his tail flicking angrily.

Stanley pushed off.

Downstairs, Stanley dropped the paperwork off at the Customer Office as usual. The Office Rat scrutinized the message sheet and poked a stubby paw at Marcia's name.

"Know where to find her, do you?" he inquired.

"Of course," said Stanley.

"Good. That's what we like to hear," said the rat.

"Weird," muttered Stanley to himself. He didn't much like

the new staff at the Rat Office, and he wondered what had happened to the nice old rats who used to run it.

It was a long and perilous journey that Stanley undertook that MidWinter Feast Day.

First he hitched a lift on a small barge taking wood down to the Port. Unfortunately for Stanley, the barge skipper believed in keeping the ship's cat lean and mean, and mean it certainly was. Stanley spent the journey desperately trying to avoid the cat, which was an extremely large orange animal with big yellow fangs and very bad breath. His luck ran out just before Deppen Ditch when he was cornered by the cat and a burly sailor wielding a large plank, and Stanley was forced to make an early exit from the barge.

The river water was freezing, and the tide was running fast, sweeping Stanley downstream as he struggled to keep his head above water in the tide race. It was not until Stanley had reached the Port that he was finally able to struggle ashore at the harbor.

Stanley lay on the bottom of the harbor steps, looking like nothing more than a limp piece of wet fur. He was too exhausted to go any farther. Voices drifted past above him on the harbor wall.

"Ooh, Ma, look! There's a dead rat on those steps. Can I take it home and boil it up for its skeleton?"

"No, Petunia, you can't."

"But I haven't got a rat skeleton, Ma."

"And you're not having one either. Come on."

Stanley thought to himself that if Petunia had taken him home he wouldn't have objected to a nice soak in a pan of boiling water. At least it would have warmed him up a bit.

When he did finally stagger to his feet and drag himself up the harbor steps, he knew he had to get warm and find food before he could carry on his journey. And so he followed his nose to a bakery and sneaked inside, where he lay shivering beside the ovens, slowly warming through. A scream from the baker's wife and a hefty swipe with a broom eventually sent him on his way, but not before he had managed to eat most of a jam doughnut and nibble holes through at least three loaves of bread and a custard tart.

Feeling much refreshed, Stanley set about looking for a lift to Marram Marshes. It was not easy. Although most people in the Port did not celebrate the MidWinter Feast Day, many of the inhabitants had taken it as an excuse to eat a big lunch and fall asleep for most of the afternoon. The Port was almost deserted. The cold northerly wind that was bringing in flurries of snow kept anyone off the streets who did not have to be there, and Stanley began to wonder if he was going to find anyone foolish enough to be traveling out to the Marshes.

And then he found Mad Jack and his donkey cart.

Mad Jack lived in a hovel on the edge of Marram Marshes. He made his living by cutting reeds to thatch the roofs of the Port houses. He had just made his last delivery of the day and was on his way home when he saw Stanley hanging about by some rubbish bins, shivering in the chill wind. Mad Jack's spirits rose. He loved rats and longed for the day when someone would send him a message by Message Rat, but it wasn't the message that Mad Jack really longed for—it was the rat.

Mad Jack stopped the donkey cart by the bins.

"'Ere, Ratty, need a lift? Got a nice warm cart goin' to the edge of the Marshes."

Stanley thought he was hearing things. Wishful thinking, Stanley, he told himself sternly. Stop it.

Mad Jack peered down from the cart and smiled his best gap-toothed smile at the rat.

"Well, don't be shy, boy. Hop in."

Stanley hesitated only for a moment before he hopped in.

"Come and sit up by me, Ratty." Mad Jack chuckled. "'Ere, you get this blanket wrapped around ya. Keep them winter chills out yer fur, that will."

Mad Jack wrapped Stanley up in a blanket that smelled strongly of donkey and geed up the cart. The donkey put its long ears back and plodded off through the flurries of snow, taking the route it knew so well back along the causeway to the hovel that it shared with Mad Jack. By the time they arrived, Stanley felt warm again and very grateful to Jack.

"'Ere we are. 'Ome at last," said Jack cheerfully as he unharnessed the donkey and led the animal inside the hovel. Stanley stayed in the cart, reluctant to leave the warmth of the blanket but knowing that he must.

"Yer welcome to come in and stay a while," Mad Jack offered. "I likes to 'ave a rat around the place. Brightens things up a bit. Bit a company. Know what I mean?"

Stanley very regretfully shook his head. He had a message to deliver, and he was a true professional, even if they had withdrawn his Confidential status.

"Ah, well, I expect yer one a them." Here Mad Jack lowered his voice and looked about him as if to check there was no one listening. "I expect yer one a them *Message Rats*. I know most folk don't believe in 'em, but I do. Bin a pleasure to meet you." Mad Jack knelt down and offered Stanley his hand to shake, and Stanley could not resist offering Mad Jack his paw in return. Mad Jack took it.

"You is, isn't you? You *is* a Message Rat," he whispered.

Stanley nodded. The next thing he knew Mad Jack had his right paw in a vicelike grip and had thrown the donkey blanket over him, bundled him up so tightly that he could not even try to struggle and had taken him into the hovel.

There was a loud clang, and Stanley was dropped into a waiting cage. The door was firmly closed and padlocked. Mad Jack giggled, put the key into his pocket and sat back, surveying his captive with delight.

Stanley rattled the bars of the cage in fury. Fury with himself rather than with Mad Jack. How *could* he have been so stupid? How could he forget his training: A Message Rat *always* travels undetected. A Message Rat *never* makes himself known to strangers.

"Ah, Ratty, what good times we'll have," said Mad Jack. "Just you and me, Ratty. We'll go out cuttin' them reeds together, and if you're good we'll go to the circus when it comes to town and see the clowns. I love them clowns, Ratty. We'll have a good life together. Yes, we will. Oh, yes." He chuckled happily to himself and fetched two withered apples from a sack hanging from the ceiling. He fed one apple to the donkey and then opened his pocketknife and carefully divided the second apple in half, giving the larger half to Stanley, who refused to touch it.

"You'll eat it soon enough, Ratty," said Mad Jack with his mouth full, spraying apple spit all over Stanley. "There ain't no other food comin' your way until this snow stops. An' that'll be a while. The wind's shifted to the north—the Big Freeze is comin' now. Always 'appens round about MidWinter Feast Day. Sure as eggs is eggs, and rats is rats."

Mad Jack cackled to himself at his joke, then he wrapped himself up in the donkey-smelling blanket that had been Stanley's undoing and fell fast asleep.

Stanley kicked the bars of his cage and wondered how thin he would have to get before he could squeeze out.

Stanley sighed. Very thin indeed was the answer.

⊬ 28 ⊬

THE BIG FREEZE

The remains of the *MidWinter Feast* of stewed cabbage, braised eel heads and spicy onions lay abandoned on the table as Aunt Zelda tried to coax some life into the spluttering fire at Keeper's Cottage. The inside of the windows were glazing over with ice, and the temperature in the cottage was plummeting, but still Aunt Zelda could not get the fire going. Bert swallowed her pride and snuggled up to Maxie to keep warm. Everyone else sat wrapped in their quilts, staring at the struggling fire.

"Why don't you let me have a go at that fire, Zelda?"

Marcia asked crossly. "I don't see why we have to sit here and freeze when all I have to do is this." Marcia clicked her fingers and the fire blazed up in the grate.

"You know I don't agree with Interfering with the elements, Marcia," said Aunt Zelda sternly. "You Wizards have no respect for Mother Nature."

"Not when Mother Nature is turning my feet into blocks of ice," Marcia grumbled.

"Well, if you wore some sensible boots like I do instead of prancing around in little purple snakey things, your feet would be fine," Aunt Zelda observed.

Marcia ignored her. She sat warming her purple snakey feet by the blazing fire and noted with some satisfaction that Aunt Zelda had made no attempt to return the fire to Mother Nature's spluttering state.

Outside the cottage, the North Wind howled mournfully. The snow flurries from earlier in the day had thickened, and now the wind brought with it a thick, swirling blizzard that blew in over the Marram Marshes and began to cover the land with deep drifts of snow. As the night wore on and Marcia's fire at last began to warm them up, the noise of the wind became muffled by the snowdrifts piling up outside. Soon the inside of the cottage had become full of a soft, snowy silence.

The fire burned steadily in the grate, and one by one they all followed Maxie's example and fell asleep.

Having successfully buried the cottage up to its roof in snow, the Big Freeze continued its journey. Out over the marshes it traveled, covering the brackish marsh water with a thick white layer of ice, freezing the bogs and quags and sending the marsh creatures burrowing down into the depths of the mires where the frost could not reach. It swept up the river and spread across the land on either side, burying cow barns and cottages and the occasional sheep.

At midnight it arrived at the Castle, where all was prepared.

During the month before the advent of the Big Freeze, the Castle dwellers stockpiled their food, ventured into the Forest and brought back as much wood as they could carry, and spent a fair amount of time knitting and weaving blankets. It was at this time of year that the Northern Traders would arrive, bringing their supplies of heavy wool cloth, thick arctic furs and salted fish, not forgetting the spicy foods that the Wendron Witches loved so much. The Northern Traders had an uncanny instinct for the timing of the Big Freeze, arriving about a month before it was due and leaving just before it set in. The five Traders who had sat in Sally Mullin's cafe on the night of the fire had been the last ones to leave, and so no one in the Castle was at all surprised by the arrival of the Big Freeze. In fact, the general opinion was that it was somewhat late, although the truth was that the last of the Northern Traders had left a little earlier than they had expected, due to unforeseen circumstances.

Silas, as ever, had forgotten that the Big Freeze was due and had found himself marooned in The Hole in the Wall Tavern after a huge snowdrift blocked the entrance. As he had nowhere else to go anyway, he settled down and decided to make the best of things while Alther and a few of the Ancients pursued their task of trying to find Simon.

The black rat in the Rat Office, who was awaiting Stanley's return, found himself marooned at the top of the iced-up East Gate Lookout Tower. The drainpipe had filled with water from a burst pipe and then promptly froze, blocking his way out. The rats in the Customer Office downstairs left him to it and went home.

The Supreme Custodian was also waiting for Stanley's return. Not only did he want information from the rat— where exactly Marcia Overstrand was—he was also anxiously awaiting the outcome of the message that the rat was to deliver. But nothing happened. From the day the rat was sent, a platoon of fully armed Custodian Guards was posted at the

Palace Gate, stamping their frozen feet and staring into the blizzard, waiting for the ExtraOrdinary Wizard to Appear. But Marcia did not return.

The Big Freeze set in. The Supreme Custodian, who had spent many hours boasting to DomDaniel about his brilliant idea of stripping the Message Rat of his Confidential status and sending a false message to Marcia, now did his best to avoid his Master. He spent as much time as he could in the Ladies' Washroom. The Supreme Custodian was not a superstitious man, but he was not a stupid man either, and it had not escaped his notice that any plans he had discussed while he was in the Ladies' Washroom had a habit of working out, though he had no idea why. He also enjoyed the comfort of the small stove, but most of all he relished the opportunity to *lurk*. The Supreme Custodian loved lurking. He had been one of those small boys who was always listening around a corner to other people's conversations, and consequently he was often able to have a hold over someone and was not afraid to use it to his advantage. It had served him well during his advancement up the ranks of the Custodian Guard and had played a large part in his appointment as Supreme Custodian.

And so, during the Big Freeze, the Supreme Custodian holed up in the washroom, lit the stove and lurked with glee, hiding behind the innocent-seeming door with the faded gold lettering and listening to conversations as people passed by. It was such a pleasure to see the blood drain from their faces as he jumped out and confronted them with whatever insulting comment they had just made about him. It was even more of a pleasure to call the Guard and have them marched straight off to the dungeons, especially if they went in for a bit of pleading. The Supreme Custodian liked a bit of pleading. So far he had had twenty-six people arrested and thrown into the dungeons for making rude comments about him, and it had never crossed his mind even once to wonder why he had yet to hear something nice being said.

But the most interesting project that occupied the Supreme Custodian was Simon Heap. Simon had been brought straight from the chapel to the Ladies' Washroom and chained to a pipe. As Jenna's adopted brother, the Supreme Custodian reckoned he would know where she had gone, and he was looking forward to persuading Simon Heap to tell him.

As the Big Freeze set in and neither the Message Rat nor Marcia returned to the Castle, Simon languished in the Ladies' Washroom, constantly questioned about Jenna's whereabouts. At first he was too terrified to talk, but the Supreme Custodian was a subtle man, and he set about gaining Simon's confidence. Whenever he had a spare moment, the unpleasant little man would prance into the washroom and prattle on to Simon about his tedious day, and Simon would listen politely, too scared to speak. After a while Simon dared to venture a few comments, and the Supreme Custodian seemed delighted to have a reaction from him, and began to bring him extra food and drink. And so Simon relaxed a little, and it was not long before he found himself confiding his desire to be the next ExtraOrdinary Wizard, and his disappointment with the way that Marcia had fled. It was not, he told the Supreme Custodian, the kind of thing that *he* would have done.

The Supreme Custodian listened approvingly. Here at last was a Heap who made some sense. And when he offered Simon the possibility of an Apprenticeship with the new Extra-Ordinary Wizard—"seeing as, and I know this will just remain between you and me, young Simon, the present boy is proving *most* unsatisfactory, despite our high hopes for him,"—Simon Heap began to see a new future for himself. A future where he might be respected and be able to use his Magykal talent, and not treated merely as "one of those wretched Heaps." So, late one evening, after the Supreme Custodian had sat down companionably beside him and offered him a hot drink, Simon Heap told him what he wanted to know—that Marcia and Jenna had gone to Aunt Zelda's cottage in the Marram Marshes.

"And where *exactly* would that be, lad?" asked the Supreme Custodian with a sharp smile on his face.

Simon had to confess he did not know *exactly*.

In a fit of temper the Supreme Custodian stormed out and went to see the Hunter, who listened in silence to the Supreme Custodian ranting on about the stupidity of all Heaps in general and of Simon Heap in particular.

"I mean, Gerald—" (For that was the Hunter's name. It was something he liked to keep quiet about, but to his irritation the Supreme Custodian used "Gerald" at every possible opportunity.) "—I mean," said the Supreme Custodian indignantly as he strode up and down the Hunter's sparsely furnished room in the barracks, waving his arms dramatically in the air, "how can anyone not know *exactly* where their aunt lives? How, Gerald, can he visit her if he doesn't know *exactly* where she lives?"

The Supreme Custodian was a dutiful visitor of his numerous aunts, most of whom wished that their nephew did not know *exactly* where they lived.

But Simon had provided enough information for the Hunter. As soon as the Supreme Custodian had gone, the Hunter set to work with his detailed maps and charts of the Marram Marshes and before long had pinpointed the likely whereabouts of Aunt Zelda's cottage. He was ready once again for the Chase.

And so, with some trepidation, the Hunter went to see DomDaniel.

DomDaniel was skulking at the top of the Wizard Tower, passing the Big Freeze by digging out the old Necromancy books that Alther had locked away in a cupboard and Summoning his library assistants, two short and extremely nasty Magogs. DomDaniel had found the Magogs after he had jumped from the Tower. Normally they lived far below the earth and consequently bore a close resemblance to huge blind worms with the addition of long, boneless arms. They had no legs but advanced over the ground on a trail of slime with a caterpillarlike movement, and were surprisingly fast when they wanted to be. The Magogs had no hair, were a yellowish-white color and appeared to have no eyes. They did in fact have one small eye that was also yellowish-white; it lay just above the only features in their face, which were two glistening round holes where a nose should be and a mouth slit. The slime they extruded was unpleasantly sticky and foul-smelling although DomDaniel himself found it quite agreeable.

Each Magog would probably have been about four feet tall if

you had stretched it out straight; although that was something no one had ever attempted. There were better ways to fill your days, like scratching your nails down a blackboard or eating a bucket of frog spawn. No one ever touched a Magog unless it was by mistake. Their slime had such a revolting quality to it that just remembering the smell of it was enough to make many people sick on the spot. Magogs hatched underground from larvae left in unsuspecting hibernating animals, such as hedge-hogs or dormice. They avoided tortoises as it was hard for the young Magogs to get out of the shells. Once the first rays of the spring sunshine had warmed the earth, the larvae would burst out, consume what was left of the animal and then burrow deeper into the ground until it reached a Magog chamber. DomDaniel had hundreds of Magog chambers around his hideout in the Badlands and always had a steady supply. They made superb Guards; they could deliver a bite that gave most people rapid blood poisoning and saw them off in a few hours, and a scratch from a Magog's claw would become so infected that it could never heal. But their greatest deterrent was how they looked: their bulbous yellowish-white head, apparently blind, and their constantly moving little jaw with its rows of spiked yellow teeth were gruesome and kept most people at bay.

The Magogs had arrived just before the Big Freeze. They

had terrified the Apprentice out of his wits, which had given DomDaniel some amusement and an excuse to leave the boy shivering out on the landing while he tried, yet again, to learn the Thirteen Times Tables.

The Magogs gave the Hunter a bit of a shock too. As he made it to the top of the spiral stairs and strode past the Apprentice on the landing, deliberately ignoring the boy, the Hunter slipped on the trail of Magog slime that led into DomDaniel's apartment. He just got his balance back in time, but not before he had heard a snigger coming from the Apprentice.

Before long the Apprentice had a little more to snigger about, for at last DomDaniel was shouting at someone other than him. He listened with delight to his Master's angry voice, which traveled extremely well through the heavy purple door.

"No, no, *No!*" DomDaniel was shouting. "You must think I am completely *mad* to let you go off again on a Hunt on your own. You are a bumbling *fool*, and if there was anyone else I could get to do the job, believe me, I *would*. You will wait until I *tell* you when to go. And then you will go under *my supervision*. Don't *interrupt!* No! I will *not* listen. Now *get out*—or would you like one of my Magogs to *assist* you?"

The Apprentice watched as the purple door was flung open and the Hunter made a quick exit, skidding over the slime and rattling down the stairs as fast as he could. After that the Apprentice almost managed to learn his Thirteen Times Tables. Well, he got up to thirteen times seven, which was his best yet.

Alther, who had been busy mixing up DomDaniel's pairs of socks, heard everything. He blew out the fire and followed the Hunter out of the Tower, where he Caused a huge snow-fall to drop from the Great Arch just as the Hunter walked under it. It was hours before anyone bothered to dig the Hunter out, but that was little consolation to Alther. Things were not looking good.

Deep in the frozen Forest, the Wendron Witches set out their traps in the hope of catching an unwary wolverine or two to tide them over the lean time ahead. Then they retired to the communal winter cave in the slate quarry, where they bur-rowed into their furs, told each other stories and kept a fire burning day and night.

The occupants of the tree house gathered around the wood-burning stove in the big hut and steadily ate their way through Galen's stores of nuts and berries. Sally Mullin hud-dled into a pile of wolverine furs and quietly mourned her cafe while comfort-eating her way through a huge pile of hazel-nuts. Sarah and Galen kept the stove going and talked about herbs and potions through the long cold days.

The four Heap boys made a snow camp down on the Forest floor some distance away from the tree house and took to living wild. They trapped and roasted squirrels and anything else they could find, much to Galen's disapproval, but she said nothing. It kept the boys occupied and out of the tree house, and it also conserved her winter food supplies, which were being rapidly nibbled through by Sally Mullin. Sarah visited the boys every day, and although at first she was worried about them being out on their own in the Forest, she was impressed by the network of igloos they built and noticed that some of the younger Wendron Witches had taken to dropping by with small offerings of food and drink. Soon it became rare for Sarah to find her boys without at least two or three young witches helping them cook a meal or just sitting around the campfire laughing and telling jokes. It surprised Sarah just how much fending for themselves had changed the boys—they all suddenly seemed so grown up, even the youngest, Jo-Jo, who was still only thirteen. After a while Sarah began to feel a bit of an interloper in their camp, but she persisted in visiting them every day, partly to keep an eye on them and partly because she had developed quite a taste for roast squirrel.

⊹⊱ 29 ⊰⊹
PYTHONS AND RATS

The morning after the arrival of the Big Freeze, Nicko opened the front door of the cottage to find a wall of snow before him. He set to work with Aunt Zelda's coal shovel and dug a tunnel about six feet long through the snow and into the bright winter sun. Jenna and Boy 412 came out through the tunnel, blinking in the sunlight.

"It's so bright," said Jenna. She shaded her eyes against the snow, which glinted almost painfully with a sparkling frost.

The Big Freeze had transformed the cottage into an enormous igloo. The marshland that surrounded them had become a wide arctic landscape, all the features changed by the windblown snowdrifts and the long shadows cast by the low winter sun. Maxie completed the picture by bounding out and rolling in the snow until he resembled an overexcited polar bear.

Jenna and Boy 412 helped Nicko dig a path down to the frozen Mott, then they raided Aunt Zelda's large stock of brooms and began the task of sweeping the snow off the ice so that they could skate all around the Mott. Jenna made a start while the two boys threw snowballs at each other. Boy 412 turned out to be a good shot and Nicko ended up looking rather like Maxie.

The ice was already about six inches thick and was as smooth and slippery as glass. A myriad of tiny bubbles was suspended in the frozen water, giving the ice a slightly cloudy appearance, but it was still clear enough to see the frozen strands of grass trapped within it and to see what lay beneath. And what lay beneath Jenna's feet as she swept away the first swathe of snow were the two unblinking yellow eyes of a giant snake, staring straight at her.

"Argh!" screamed Jenna.

"What's that, Jen?" asked Nicko.

"Eyes. *Snake eyes.* There's a massive snake underneath the ice."

Boy 412 and Nicko came over.

"Wow. It's *huge*," Nicko said.

Jenna knelt down and scraped away some more snow.

"Look," she said, "there's its tail. Right by its head. It must stretch all around the Mott."

"It can't," Nicko disagreed.

"It must."

"I suppose there might be more than one."

"Well, there's only one way to find out." Jenna picked up the broom and started sweeping. "Come on, get going," she told the boys. Nicko and Boy 412 reluctantly picked up their brooms and got going.

By the end of the afternoon they had discovered that there was indeed only one snake.

"It must be about a mile long," said Jenna as at last they got back to where they had started. The Marsh Python stared at them grumpily through the ice. It didn't like being looked at, particularly by *food*. Although the snake preferred goats and lynxes, it regarded anything on legs as food and had occasionally partaken of the odd traveler, if one had been so careless as to fall into a ditch and splash around too much. But generally it avoided the two-legged kind; it found their numerous wrappings indigestible, and it particularly disliked boots.

The Big Freeze set in. Aunt Zelda settled down to wait it out, just as she did every year, and informed the impatient Marcia that there was no chance whatsoever of Silas returning with her KeepSafe now. The Marram Marshes were completely cut off. Marcia would just have to wait for the Big Thaw like everyone else.

But the Big Thaw showed no sign of coming. Every night the north wind brought yet another howling blizzard to pile the drifts even deeper.

The temperatures plummeted and the Boggart was frozen out of his mud patch. He retreated to the hot spring bath hut, where he dozed contentedly in the steam.

The Marsh Python lay trapped in the Mott. It made do with eating whatever unwary fish and eels came its way and dreaming of the day it would be free to swallow as many goats as it could manage.

Nicko and Jenna went skating. At first they were happy to circle around the iced-up Mott and irritate the Marsh Python, but after a while they began to venture into the white landscape of the marsh. They would spend hours racing along the frozen ditches, listening to the crackle of the ice beneath them and sometimes to the mournful howl of the wind as it threatened to bring yet another fall of snow. Jenna noticed that all the sounds of the marsh creatures had disappeared. Gone were the busy rustlings of the marsh voles and the quiet splishings of the water snakes. The Quake Ooze Brownies were safely frozen far below the ground and made not a single shriek between them, while the Water Nixies were fast asleep, their suckers frozen to the underside of the ice, waiting for the thaw.

Long, quiet weeks passed at Keeper's Cottage and still the snow blew in from the north. While Jenna and Nicko spent hours outside skating and making ice slides around the Mott, Boy 412 stayed indoors. He still felt chilled if he stayed out for any length of time. It was as if some small part of him had not yet warmed through from the time he had been buried in the snow outside the Wizard Tower. Sometimes Jenna sat with him beside the fire. She liked Boy 412; although she didn't know why, seeing as he never spoke to her. She didn't take it personally, as Jenna knew he had not uttered a word to anyone since he had arrived at the cottage.

Jenna's main topic of conversation with him was Petroc Trelawney, who Boy 412 had taken a liking to.

Some afternoons Jenna would sit on the sofa beside Boy 412 while he watched her take the pet rock out of her pocket. Jenna would often sit by the fire with Petroc, as he reminded her of Silas. There was something about just holding the pebble that made her sure Silas would come back safely.

"Here, you hold Petroc," Jenna would say, putting the smooth gray pebble into Boy 412's grubby hand.

Petroc Trelawney liked Boy 412. He liked him because he was usually slightly sticky and smelled of food. Petroc Trelawney would stick out his four stumpy legs, open his eyes and lick Boy 412's hand. Mmm, he'd think, not bad. He could definitely taste eel, and was there a hint of cabbage lingering as a subtle aftertaste? Petroc Trelawney liked eel and would give Boy 412's palm another lick. His tongue was dry and slightly rasping, like a minute cat's tongue, and Boy 412 would laugh. It tickled.

"He likes you." Jenna would smile. "He's never licked *my* hand."

There were many days when Boy 412 just sat by the fire reading his way through Aunt Zelda's stock of books, immersing himself in a whole new world. Before he came to

Keeper's Cottage, Boy 412 had never read a book. He had
been taught to read in the Young Army but had only ever been
allowed to read long lists of Enemies, Orders of the Day and
Battle Plans. But now Aunt Zelda kept him supplied with a
happy mixture of adventure stories and Magyk books, which
Boy 412 soaked up like a sponge. It was on one of these days,
almost six weeks into the Big Freeze, when Jenna and Nicko
had decided to see whether they could skate all the way to the
Port, that Boy 412 noticed something.

He already knew that every morning, for some reason,
Aunt Zelda lit two lanterns and disappeared into the potion
cupboard under the stairs. At first Boy 412 had thought nothing of it. After all, it was dark in the potion cupboard and Aunt
Zelda had many potions to tend. He knew that the potions
that needed to be kept in darkness were the most unstable and
required constant attention; only the day before, Aunt Zelda
had spent hours filtering a muddied Amazonian Antidote that
had gone lumpy in the cold. But what Boy 412 noticed this
particular morning was how quiet it was in the potion cupboard, and he knew that Aunt Zelda was not generally a quiet
person. Whenever she walked past the Preserve Pots they rattled and jumped, and when she was in the kitchen the pots
and pans clanged and banged; so how, wondered Boy 412, did

she manage to be so quiet in the small confines of the potion cupboard? And why did she need *two* lanterns?

He put down his book and tiptoed over to the potion cupboard door. It was strangely silent considering it contained Aunt Zelda in close proximity to hundreds of little clinky bottles. Boy 412 knocked hesitantly on the door. There was no reply. He listened again. Silence. Boy 412 knew he should really just go back to his book but somehow *Thaumaturgy and Sortilage: Why Bother?* was not as interesting as what Aunt Zelda was up to. So Boy 412 pushed open the door and peered in.

The potion cupboard was empty.

For a moment, Boy 412 was half afraid that it was a joke and Aunt Zelda was going to jump out at him, but he soon realized that she was definitely not there. And then he saw why. The trapdoor was open, and the musty damp smell of the tunnel that Boy 412 remembered so well drifted up to him. Boy 412 hovered at the door, uncertain of what to do. It crossed his mind that Aunt Zelda might have fallen through the trapdoor by mistake and needed help, but he realized that if she *had* fallen, she would have got wedged halfway, as Aunt Zelda looked a good deal wider than the trapdoor did.

As he was wondering how Aunt Zelda had managed to squeeze herself through the trapdoor, Boy 412 saw the dim yellow glow of a lantern shining up through the open space in the floor. Soon he heard the heavy tread of Aunt Zelda's sensible boots on the sandy floor of the tunnel and her laborious breathing as she struggled up the steep incline toward the wooden ladder. As Aunt Zelda started to heave herself up the ladder, Boy 412 silently closed the cupboard door and scuttled back to his seat by the fire.

It was quite a few minutes later when an out-of-breath Aunt Zelda poked her head out of the potion cupboard a little suspiciously and saw Boy 412 reading *Thaumaturgy and Sortilage: Why Bother?* with avid interest.

Before Aunt Zelda had time to disappear back into the cupboard, the front door burst open. Nicko appeared with Jenna closely following. They threw down their skates and held up what looked like a dead rat.

"Look what we found," said Jenna.

Boy 412 pulled a face. He didn't like rats. He'd had to live with too many of them to enjoy their company.

"Leave it outside," said Aunt Zelda. "It's bad luck to bring a dead thing across the threshold unless you're going to eat it. And I don't fancy eating *that*."

"It's not dead, Aunt Zelda," said Jenna. "Look." She held out the brown streak of fur for Aunt Zelda to inspect. Aunt

Zelda poked at it warily.

"We found it outside that old shack," said Jenna. "You know the one, not far from the Port at the end of the marsh. There's a man there who lives with a donkey. And a lot of dead rats in cages. We looked through the window—it was horrible. And then he woke up and saw us, so me and Nicko went to run off and we saw this rat. I think he'd just escaped. So I picked him up and put him in my jacket and we ran for it. Well, skated for it. And the old man came out and yelled at us for taking his rat. But he couldn't catch us, could he, Nicko?"

"No," said Nicko, a man of few words.

"Anyway, I think it's the Message Rat with a message from Dad," said Jenna.

"*Never*," said Aunt Zelda. "That Message Rat was fat."

The rat in Jenna's hands let out a weak squeak of protest.

"And this one," said Aunt Zelda, poking the rat in the ribs, "is as thin as a rake. Well, I suppose you had better bring it in, whatever kind of rat it may be."

And that is how Stanley finally reached his destination, nearly six weeks after he had been sent out from the Rat Office. Like all good Message Rats he had lived up to the Rat Office slogan: *Nothing* stops a Message Rat.

But Stanley was not strong enough to deliver his message. He lay feebly on a cushion in front of the fire while Jenna fed him pureed eel. The rat had never been a great fan of eel, particularly the pureed variety, but after six weeks in a cage drinking only water and eating nothing at all, even pureed eel tasted wonderful. And lying on a cushion in front of a fire instead of shivering at the bottom of a filthy cage was even more wonderful. Even if Bert did sneak in the odd peck when no one was looking.

Marcia did the Speeke, Rattus Rattus command after Jenna insisted on it, but Stanley uttered not a word as he lay weakly on his cushion.

"I'm still not convinced it's the Message Rat," said Marcia a few days after Stanley had arrived and the rat had still not spoken. "That Message Rat did nothing *but* talk, if I remember rightly. And a load of drivel most of it was too."

Stanley gave Marcia his best frown, but it passed her by.

"It *is* him, Marcia," Jenna assured her. "I've kept loads of rats and I'm good at recognizing them. This one is definitely the Message Rat that we had before."

And so they all waited nervously for Stanley to recover enough to Speeke and deliver Silas's longed-for message. It was an anxious time. The rat developed a fever and became delirious, mumbling incoherently for hours on end and almost driving Marcia to distraction. Aunt Zelda made up copious amounts of willow bark infusions that Jenna patiently fed to the rat through a small dropper. After a long and fretful week, the rat's fever at last abated.

Late one afternoon, when Aunt Zelda was locked in the potion cupboard (she had taken to locking the door after the day Boy 412 had peeked inside) and Marcia was working out some mathematical spells at Aunt Zelda's desk, Stanley gave a cough and sat up. Maxie barked and Bert hissed with surprise, but the Message Rat ignored them.

He had a message to deliver.

⊹ 30 ⊹
MESSAGE FOR MARCIA

S*tanley soon had an expectant* audience gathered around him. He hobbled stiffly off the cushion, stood up and took a deep breath. Then he said in a shaky voice, "First I must ask. Is there anyone here answering to the name of Marcia Overstrand?"

"You know there is," said Marcia impatiently.

"I still have to ask, Your Honor. Part of the procedure," said the Message Rat. He continued. "I am come here to deliver a message to Marcia Overstrand, ex–ExtraOrdinary Wizard—"

"*What?*" gasped Marcia. "*Ex?* What does that idiot rat

mean, ex–ExtraOrdinary Wizard?"

"Calm down, Marcia," said Aunt Zelda. "Wait and see what he has to say."

Stanley carried on, "The message is sent at seven o'clock in the morning . . ." The rat paused to work out just how many days ago it had been sent. As a true professional, Stanley had kept a record of his time imprisoned in the cage by scratching a line for each day on one of the bars. He knew he had done thirty-nine days with Mad Jack, but he had no idea how many days he had spent delirious in front of the fire in Keeper's Cottage, " . . . er . . . a long time ago, by proxy, from one Silas Heap residing in the Castle—"

"What's proxy mean?" asked Nicko.

Stanley tapped his foot impatiently. He didn't like interruptions, especially when the message was so old that he was afraid he may not remember it. He coughed impatiently.

"Message begins:

> Dear Marcia,
>   I hope you are keeping well. I am well and am at the Castle. I would be grateful if you would meet me outside the Palace as soon as possible. There has been a development. I will be at the Palace Gate at

midnight, every night, until your arrival.
   Looking forward to seeing you,
   With best wishes,
   Silas Heap

"Message ends."

Stanley sat back down on his cushion and breathed a sigh of relief. Job done. He may have taken the longest time a Message Rat had ever taken to deliver a message, but he'd done it. He allowed himself a small smile even though he was still on duty.

There was silence for a moment, and then Marcia exploded. "Typical, just *typical!* He doesn't even make an effort to get back before the Big Freeze, then, when he finally does get around to sending a message, he doesn't bother to even *mention* my KeepSafe. I give up. I should have gone myself."

"But what about Simon?" asked Jenna anxiously. "And why hasn't Dad sent a message to *us* too?"

"Doesn't sound much like Dad anyway," grunted Nicko.

"No," agreed Marcia. "It was far too polite."

"Well, I suppose it *was* by proxy," said Aunt Zelda uncertainly.

"What does proxy mean?" Nicko asked again.

"It means a stand-in. Someone else gave the message to the Rat Office. Silas must have been unable to get there. Which is to be expected, I suppose. I wonder who the proxy was?"

Stanley said nothing, even though he knew perfectly well that the proxy was the Supreme Custodian. Although no longer a Confidential Rat, he was still bound by the Rat Office code. And that meant all conversations within the Rat Office were Highly Confidential. But the Message Rat felt awkward. These Wizard people had rescued him, looked after him and probably saved his life. Stanley shifted about and looked at the floor. Something was going on, he thought, and he didn't want to be part of it. This whole message had been a complete nightmare from start to finish.

Marcia walked over to the desk and slammed her book shut with a bang.

"How dare Silas ignore something as important as my KeepSafe?" she said angrily. "Does he not know that the whole point of an Ordinary Wizard is to serve the ExtraOrdinary Wizard? I will not put up with his insubordinate attitude *any* longer. I intend to find him and give him a piece of my mind."

"Marcia, is that wise?" asked Aunt Zelda quietly.

"I am still the ExtraOrdinary Wizard and I will *not* be kept away," Marcia declared.

"Well, I suggest you sleep on it," said Aunt Zelda sensibly. "Things always look better in the morning."

Later that night, Boy 412 lay in the flickering light of the fire, listening to Nicko's snuffles and Jenna's regular breathing. He had been woken up by Maxie's loud snores, which resonated through the ceiling. Maxie was meant to sleep downstairs but he still sneaked up to lie on Silas's bed if he thought he could get away with it. In fact, when Maxie started snoring downstairs, Boy 412 often gave the wolfhound a shove and helped him on his way. But that night Boy 412 realized that he was listening to something else apart from the snores of a wolfhound with sinus trouble.

Creaking floorboards above his head . . . stealthy footsteps on the stairs . . . the squeak of the second-to-last creaky step . . . Who was that? *What* was that? All the ghost stories that he had ever been told came back to Boy 412 as he heard the quiet swish of a cloak along the stone floor and knew that whoever, or *whatever*, it was had entered the same room.

Boy 412 sat up very slowly, his heart beating fast, and stared into the gloom. A dark figure was moving stealthily toward the book that Marcia had left on the desk. The figure picked up the book and tucked it into its cloak, then she saw the whites of Boy 412's eyes staring at her out of the darkness.

"It's me," whispered Marcia. She beckoned Boy 412 over to her. He slipped silently out of his quilt and padded across the stone floor to see what she wanted.

"How anyone is expected to sleep in the same room as that animal I do *not* understand," Marcia whispered crossly. Boy 412 smiled sheepishly. He didn't say that it was he who had pushed Maxie up the stairs in the first place.

"I'm Returning tonight," said Marcia. "I'm going to use the Midnight Minutes, just to make sure of things. You should remember that, the minutes on either side of midnight are the best time to Travel safely. Especially if there are those abroad who may wish you harm. Which I suspect there are. I shall make for the Palace Gate and sort that Silas Heap out. Now, what's the time?"

Marcia pulled out her timepiece.

"Two minutes to midnight. I will be back soon. Perhaps you could tell Zelda." Marcia looked at Boy 412 and remembered that he hadn't uttered a word since he had told them his rank and number in the Wizard Tower. "Oh, well, it doesn't matter if you don't. She'll guess where I've gone."

Boy 412 suddenly thought of something important. He fumbled in the pocket of his sweater and drew out the Charm that Marcia had given him when she had asked him to be her Apprentice. He held the tiny pair of silver wings in his palm and looked at them a little regretfully. They glinted silver and gold in the Magykal glow that was beginning to surround Marcia. Boy 412 offered the Charm back to Marcia—he thought he should no longer have it, since there was no way he was ever going to be her Apprentice—but Marcia shook her head and knelt down beside him.

"No," she whispered. "I still hope you will change your mind and decide to be my Apprentice. Think about it while I'm away. Now, it's one minute to midnight. Stand back."

The air around Marcia grew cold, and a shiver of strong Magyk swept around her and filled the air with an electric charge. Boy 412 retreated to the fireside, a little scared but fascinated too. Marcia closed her eyes and started to mutter something long and complicated in a language he had never heard before, and as he watched, Boy 412 saw the same Magykal haze appear that he had first seen when he was sitting in *Muriel* in the Deppen Ditch. Suddenly Marcia threw her cloak over herself so that she was covered from head to toe, and as she did so, the purple of the Magyk haze and the purple of the cloak mixed together. There was a loud hiss, like water dropping onto hot metal, and Marcia disappeared, leaving only a faint shadow that lingered for a few moments.

✳ ✳ ✳

At the Palace Gate, at twenty minutes past midnight, a platoon of Guards was on duty, just as it had been every night for the past fifty bitterly cold nights. The Guards were frozen and were expecting yet another long boring night doing nothing but stamping their feet and humoring the Supreme Custodian, who had some strange idea that the ex–ExtraOrdinary Wizard was going to turn up right there. Just like that. Of course she never had, and they didn't expect her to either. But still, every night he sent them out to wait and get their toes frozen into blocks of ice.

So when a faint purple shadow began to emerge in their midst, none of the Guards really believed what was happening.

"It's *her*," one of them whispered, half afraid of the Magyk that suddenly swirled in the air and sent uncomfortable charges of electricity through their black metal helmets. The Guards unsheathed their swords and watched as the hazy shadow composed itself into a tall figure wrapped in the purple cloak of an ExtraOrdinary Wizard.

Marcia Overstrand had Appeared right in the middle of the Supreme Custodian's trap. She was taken by surprise, and without her KeepSafe and the protection of the Midnight Minutes—for Marcia was twenty minutes late—she was not able to stop the Captain of the Guard from ripping the

Akhu Amulet from her neck.

Ten minutes later Marcia was lying at the bottom of Dungeon Number One, which was a deep, dark chimney buried in the foundations of the Castle. Marcia lay stunned, trapped in the middle of a Vortex of Shadows and Shades that DomDaniel had, with great pleasure, set up especially for her. That night was the worst night of Marcia's life. She lay helpless in a pool of foul water, resting on a pile of bones of the dungeon's previous occupants, tormented by the moaning and the screaming of the Shadows and Shades that whirled around her and drained her Magykal powers. It was not until the next morning—when, luckily, an Ancient ghost got lost and happened to pass through the wall of Dungeon Number One— that anyone apart from DomDaniel and the Supreme Custodian knew where she was.

The Ancient brought Alther to her, but there was nothing he could do except sit by her and encourage her to stay alive. Alther needed all his powers of persuasion, for Marcia was in despair. In a fit of temper with Silas she knew she had lost everything that Alther had fought for when he deposed DomDaniel. For once again DomDaniel had the Akhu Amulet tied around his fat neck, and it was he, not Marcia Overstrand, who truly was now the ExtraOrdinary Wizard.

THE RAT'S RETURN

A unt Zelda did not possess a timepiece or a clock. Timepieces never worked properly at Keeper's Cottage; there was too much Disturbance under the ground. Unfortunately, this was something that Aunt Zelda had never bothered to mention to Marcia as she herself was not too concerned with the exact time of day. If Aunt Zelda wanted to know the time, she would content herself with looking at the sundial and hoping that the sun was out, but she was much more concerned with the passing of the phases of the moon.

The day the Message Rat was rescued, Aunt Zelda had

taken Jenna for a walk around the island after it got dark. The snow was as deep as ever and had such a crisp covering of frost that Jenna was able to run lightly across the top, although Aunt Zelda in her big boots sank right down. They had walked along to the end of the island, away from the lights of the cottage, and Aunt Zelda had pointed up at the dark night sky, which was brushed with hundreds of thousands of brilliant stars, more than Jenna had ever seen before.

"Tonight," Aunt Zelda had said, "is the Dark of the Moon."

Jenna shivered. Not from the cold but from a strange feeling she got, standing out on the island in the middle of such an expanse of stars and darkness.

"Tonight, however hard you look, you will not see the moon," said Aunt Zelda. "No one on earth will see the moon tonight. It is not a night to venture out alone on the marsh, and if all the marsh creatures and spirits weren't safely frozen below the ground, we would be CharmLocked into the cottage by now. But I thought you would like to see the stars without the light of the moon. Your mother always liked looking at the stars."

Jenna gulped. "My *mother*? You mean, my mother when I was *born*?"

"Yes," said Aunt Zelda. "I mean the Queen. She loved the stars. I thought you might too."

"I do," breathed Jenna. "I always used to count them from my window at home if I couldn't get to sleep. But—how did you know my mother?"

"I used to see her every year," said Aunt Zelda. "Until she . . . well, until things changed. And her mother, your lovely grandmother, I saw her every year too."

Mother, grandmother . . . Jenna began to realize she had a whole family that she knew nothing about. But somehow Aunt Zelda did.

"Aunt Zelda," said Jenna slowly, daring at last to ask a question that had been bothering her ever since she had learned who she really was.

"Hmm?" Aunt Zelda was gazing out across the marsh.

"What about my father?"

"Your father? Ah, he was from the Far Countries. He left before you were born."

"He left?"

"He had a boat. He went off to get something or other," said Aunt Zelda vaguely. "He arrived back at the Port just after you were born with a ship full of treasures for you and your mother, so I heard. But when he was told the terrible news, he sailed away on the next tide."

"What—what was his name?" asked Jenna.

"No idea," said Aunt Zelda who, along with most people, had paid little attention to the identity of the Queen's consort. The Succession was passed from mother to daughter, leaving the men in the family to live their lives as they pleased.

Something in Aunt Zelda's voice caught Jenna's attention, and she turned away from the stars to look at her. Jenna caught her breath. She had never really noticed Aunt Zelda's eyes before, but now the bright piercing blue of the White Witch's eyes was cutting through the night, shining through the darkness and staring intently out at the marsh.

"Right," said Aunt Zelda suddenly, "time to go inside."

"But—"

"I'll tell you more in the summer. That's when they used to come, MidSummer Day. I'll take you there too."

"Where?" asked Jenna. "Take me where?"

"Come on," said Aunt Zelda. "I don't like the look of that shadow over there . . . "

Aunt Zelda grabbed Jenna's hand and ran back with her across the snow. Out on the marsh a ravenous Marsh Lynx stopped stalking and turned away. It was too weak now to give chase; had it been a few days earlier, it could have eaten well and seen the winter through. But now the Lynx slunk back to its snow hole and weakly chewed at its last frozen mouse.

After the Dark of the Moon, the first thin sliver of the new moon appeared in the sky. Each night it grew a little bigger. The skies were clear now that the snow had stopped falling, and every night Jenna watched the moon from the window, while the Shield Bugs moved dreamily in the Preserve Pots, waiting for their moment of freedom.

"Keep watching," Aunt Zelda told her. "As the moon grows it draws up the things from the ground. And the cottage draws in the people that wish to come here. The pull is strongest at the full moon, which is when you came."

But when the moon was a quarter full, Marcia had left.

"How come Marcia's *gone*?" Jenna asked Aunt Zelda the morning they discovered her departure. "I thought things came back when the moon was growing, not went away."

Aunt Zelda looked somewhat grumpy at Jenna's question. She was annoyed with Marcia for going so suddenly, and she didn't like anyone messing up her moon theories either.

"Sometimes," Aunt Zelda said mysteriously, "things must leave in order to return." She stomped off into her potion cupboard and firmly locked the door behind her.

Nicko made a sympathetic face at Jenna and waved her pair of skates at her.

"Race you to Big Bog." He grinned.

"Last one there's a dead rat." Jenna laughed.

Stanley woke up with a start at the words "dead rat" and opened his eyes just in time to see Nicko and Jenna grab their skates and disappear for the day.

By the time the full moon arrived and Marcia had still not returned, everyone was very worried.

"I told Marcia to sleep on it," said Aunt Zelda, "but oh, no, *she* gets herself all worked up over Silas and just ups and goes in the middle of the night. Not a word since. It really is too bad. I can understand Silas not getting back, what with the Big Freeze, but not Marcia."

"She might come back tonight," ventured Jenna, "seeing as it's the full moon."

"She might," said Aunt Zelda, "or she might not."

Marcia, of course, did not return that night. She spent it as she had spent the last ten nights, in the middle of the Vortex of Shadows and Shades, lying weakly in the pool of filthy water at the bottom of Dungeon Number One. Sitting next to her was Alther Mella, using all the ghostly Magyk he could to help keep Marcia alive. People rarely survived the actual fall into Dungeon Number One, and if they did, they did not last long, but soon sank below the foul water to join the bones that lay just beneath the surface. Without Alther, there is no doubt that the same fate would have befallen Marcia eventually.

That night, the night of the full moon, as the sun set and the moon rose in the sky, Jenna and Aunt Zelda wrapped themselves up in some quilts and kept watch at the window for Marcia. Jenna soon fell asleep, but Aunt Zelda kept watch all night until the rising of the sun and the setting of the full moon put an end to any faint hopes she may have had of Marcia returning.

The next day, the Message Rat decided he was strong enough to leave. There was a limit to how much pureed eel even a rat could stomach, and Stanley thought he had well and truly reached that limit.

However, before Stanley could leave, he either had to be commanded with another message or released with no message. So that morning he coughed a polite cough and said, "Excuse me, all." Everyone looked at the rat. He had been very quiet while he was recovering, and they were unused to hearing him speak.

"It is time I returned to the Rat Office. I am already some-what overdue. But I must ask, Do you require me to take a message?"

"Dad!" said Jenna. "Take one to Dad!"

"Who might Dad be?" asked the rat. "And where is he to be found?"

"We don't know," said Aunt Zelda snappily. "There is no message, thank you, Message Rat. You are released."

Stanley bowed, very much relieved.

"Thank you, Madam," he said. "And, ahem, thank you for your kindness. All of you. I am very grateful."

They all watched the rat run off over the snow, leaving small footprints and tailprints behind him.

"I wish we had sent a message," said Jenna wistfully.

"Best not," Aunt Zelda said. "There's something not quite right about that rat. Something different from last time."

"Well, he was a lot thinner," Nicko pointed out.

"Hmm," murmured Aunt Zelda. "Something's up. I can feel it."

Stanley had a good trip back to the Castle. It wasn't until he reached the Rat Office that things started to go wrong. He scampered up the recently defrosted drainpipe and knocked on the Rat Office door.

"Come in!" barked the black rat, only just back on duty after a belated rescue from the frozen Rat Office.

Stanley sidled in, well aware that he was going to have some explaining to do.

"*You!*" thundered the black rat. "At last. How dare you make a fool of me. Are you aware how *long* you have been away?"

"Er . . . two months," muttered Stanley. He was only too well aware how long he had been away and was beginning to wonder what Dawnie would have to say about it.

"*Er . . . two months, sir!*" yelled the black rat, thumping his tail on the desk in anger. "Are you aware just how *stupid* you have made me look?"

Stanley said nothing, thinking that at least some good had come out of his ghastly trip.

"You will pay for this," bellowed the black rat. "I will personally see that you never get another job as long as I am in charge here."

"But—"

"But, *sir!*" the black rat screamed. "What did I tell you? Call me *sir!*"

Stanley was silent. There were many things he could think

of calling the black rat, but "sir" was not one of them. Suddenly Stanley was aware of something behind him. He wheeled around to find himself staring at the largest pair of muscle-bound rats he had ever seen. They stood threateningly in the Rat Office doorway, cutting out the light and also any chance that Stanley might have had of making a run for it, which he suddenly felt an overpowering urge to do.

The black rat, however, looked pleased to see them.

"Ah, good. The boys have arrived. Take him away, boys."

"Where?" squeaked Stanley. "Where are you taking me?"

"Where . . . are . . . you . . . taking . . . me . . . *sir*," said the black rat through gritted teeth. "To the proxy who sent this message in the first place. He wishes to know where *exactly* you found the recipient. And as you are no longer a Confidential, you will of course have to tell him.

"Take him to the Supreme Custodian."

✢ 32 ✢
THE BIG THAW

The day after the Message Rat left, the Big Thaw set in. It happened first in the Marram Marshes, which were always a little warmer than anywhere else, and then it spread up the river, through the Forest and into the Castle. It was a great relief to everyone in the Castle, as they had been running out of food supplies due to the Custodian Army having looted many of the winter storerooms to provide DomDaniel with the ingredients for his frequent banquets.

The Big Thaw also came as a relief to a certain Message Rat

who was shivering glumly in a rat trap underneath the floor of the Ladies' Washroom. Stanley had been left there on account of his refusal to divulge the whereabouts of Aunt Zelda's cottage. He was not to know that the Hunter had already successfully worked it out from what Simon Heap had told the Supreme Custodian, neither was he to know that no one had any intention of setting him free, although Stanley had been around long enough to guess as much. The Message Rat kept himself going as best he could: he ate what he could catch, mainly spiders and cockroaches; he licked the drips from the thawing drain; and he found himself thinking almost fondly about Mad Jack. Dawnie, meanwhile, had given up on him and gone to live with her sister.

The Marram Marshes were now awash with water from the rapidly thawing snow. Soon the green of the grass began to show through, and the ground became heavy and wet. The ice in the Mott and the ditches was the last to thaw, but as the Marsh Python began to feel the temperature rise, he started to move about, flicking his tail impatiently and flexing his hundreds of stiffened ribs. Everyone at the cottage was waiting with bated breath for the giant snake to break free. They were not sure how hungry he might be, or how cross. To make sure that Maxie stayed inside, Nicko had tied the wolfhound to the table leg with a thick piece of rope. He was pretty sure that fresh wolfhound would be top of the menu for the Marsh Python once he was released from his icy prison.

It happened the third afternoon of the Big Thaw. Suddenly there was a loud *crack!* and the ice above the Marsh Python's powerful head shattered and sprayed up into the air. The snake reared up, and Jenna, who was the only one around, took refuge behind the chicken boat. The Marsh Python cast a glance in her direction but did not fancy chewing its way through her heavy boots, so it set off rather painfully and slowly around the Mott until it found the way out. It was then that it ran into a spot of bother: the giant snake had seized up. It was stuck in a circle. When it tried to bend in the other direction nothing seemed to work. All it could do was swim around and around the Mott. Every time it tried to turn off into the ditch that would lead it out into the marsh, its muscles refused to work.

For days the snake was forced to lie in the Mott, snapping at fish and glaring angrily at anyone who came near. Which no one did after it had flicked its long forked tongue out at Boy 412 and sent him flying. At last, one morning the early spring sun came out and warmed the snake up just enough for its stiffened muscles to relax. Creaking like a rusty gate, it swam off painfully in search of a few goats, and slowly over the next few days it *almost* straightened out. But not completely. To the end of its days, the Marsh Python had a tendency to swim to the right.

When the Big Thaw reached the Castle, DomDaniel took his two Magogs upriver to Bleak Creek where, in the dead of night, the three beings crossed a narrow mildewed gangplank and boarded his Darke ship, *The Vengeance*. There they waited some days until the high spring tide that DomDaniel needed to get his ship out of the creek floated them free.

The morning of the Big Thaw, the Supreme Custodian called a meeting of the Council of the Custodians, unaware that the day before he had forgotten to lock the door to the Ladies' Washroom. Simon was no longer chained to a pipe, for the Supreme Custodian had begun to see him more as a companion than a hostage, and Simon sat and waited patiently for his usual midmorning visit from him. Simon liked hearing the gossip about DomDaniel's unreasonable demands and temper tantrums and felt disappointed when the Supreme Custodian did not return at the normal time. He was not to know that the Supreme Custodian, who recently had become somewhat bored with Simon Heap's company, was at that moment gleefully plotting what DomDaniel called "Operation Compost Heap," which included the disposal of not only Jenna but the entire Heap family, including Simon.

After a while, more out of boredom than a desire to escape, Simon tried the door. To his amazement it opened, and he found himself staring into an empty corridor. Simon leaped back inside the washroom and slammed the door shut in a panic. What should he do? Should he escape? Did he *want* to escape?

He leaned against the door and thought things over. The only reason for staying was the Supreme Custodian's vague offer of becoming DomDaniel's Apprentice. But it had not been repeated. And Simon Heap had learned a lot from the Supreme Custodian in those six weeks he had spent in the Ladies' Washroom. At the top of the list was not to trust anything the Supreme Custodian said. Next on the list was to look after Number One. And, from now on, Number One in Simon Heap's life was definitely Simon Heap.

Simon opened the door again. The corridor was still deserted. He made his decision and strode out of the washroom.

Silas was wandering mournfully along Wizard Way, gazing up into the grubby windows above the shops and offices that

lined the Way, wondering if Simon might be held prisoner
somewhere in the dark recesses behind them. A platoon of
Guards marched briskly past, and Silas shrank back into a
doorway, clutching Marcia's KeepSafe, hoping it still worked.

"Psst," hissed Alther.

"What?" Silas jumped in surprise. He hadn't seen much of
Alther recently, as the ghost was spending most of his time
with Marcia in Dungeon Number One.

"How's Marcia today?" Silas whispered.

"She's been better," said Alther grimly.

"I really think we should let Zelda know," said Silas.

"Take my advice, Silas, and don't go *near* that Rat Office.
It's been taken over by DomDaniel's rats from the Badlands.
Vicious bunch of thugs. Don't worry now, I'll think of some-
thing," said Alther. "There must be a way to get her out."

Silas looked dejected. He missed Marcia more than he liked
to admit.

"Cheer up, Silas," said Alther. "I've got someone waiting
for you in the tavern. Found him wandering around the
Courthouse on my way back from Marcia. Smuggled him out
through the tunnel. Better hurry up before he changes his
mind and goes off again. He's a tricky one, your Simon."

"*Simon!*" Silas broke into a broad smile. "Alther, why didn't you say? Is he all right?"

"*Looks* all right," said Alther tersely.

Simon had spent nearly two weeks back with his family when, on the day before the full moon, Aunt Zelda stood on the cottage doorstep Listening to something far away.

"Boys, boys, not now," she said to Nicko and Boy 412, who were having a duel with some spare broom handles. "I need to concentrate."

Nicko and Boy 412 suspended their fight while Aunt Zelda became very still and her eyes took on a faraway look.

"Someone's coming," she said after a while. "I'm sending Boggart out."

"At last!" said Jenna. "I wonder if it's Dad or Marcia. Maybe Simon's with them? Or Mum? Maybe it's *everyone!*"

Maxie jumped up and bounded over to Jenna, his tail wagging madly. Sometimes Maxie seemed to understand exactly what Jenna was saying. Except when it was something like "Bath time, Maxie!" or "No more biscuits, Maxie!"

"Calm down, Maxie," said Aunt Zelda, rubbing the wolfhound's silky ears. "The trouble is it doesn't feel like anyone I know."

"Oh," said Jenna, "but who else knows we're here?"

"I don't know," replied Aunt Zelda. "But whoever it is, they're in the marshes now. Just arrived. I can feel it. Go and *lie down*, Maxie. Good boy. Now, where's that Boggart?"

Aunt Zelda gave a piercing whistle. The squat brown fig-ure climbed out of the Mott and waddled up the path to the cottage.

"Not so loud," he complained, rubbing his small round ears. "Goes right through me that does." He nodded to Jenna. "Evenin', miss."

"Hello, Boggart." Jenna smiled. The Boggart always made her smile.

"Boggart," said Aunt Zelda, "there's someone coming through the marshes. More than one perhaps. I'm not sure. Can you just nip off and find out who it is?"

"No trouble. Could do with a swim. Won't be long," said the Boggart. Jenna watched him waddle off down to the Mott and disappear into the water with a quiet splash.

"While we're waiting for Boggart we should get the Preserve Pots ready," said Aunt Zelda. "Just in case."

"But Dad said you made the cottage Enchanted after the Brownie raid," said Jenna. "Doesn't that mean we're safe?"

"Only against Brownies," said Aunt Zelda, "and even that's wearing off by now. Anyway, whoever is coming across the marsh feels a lot bigger than a Brownie to me."

Aunt Zelda went to find the *Shield Bug Preserves* spell book.

Jenna looked at the Preserve Pots, which were still lined up on the windowsills. Inside the thick green gloop the Shield Bugs were waiting. Most were sleeping, but some were slowly moving about as if they knew they might be needed. For who? wondered Jenna. Or *what*?

"Here we are," said Aunt Zelda as she appeared with the spell book and thumped it down on the table. She opened it at the first page and took out a small silver hammer, which she handed to Jenna.

"Right, here's the Activate," she said to her. "If you could just go round and tap each Pot with this, then they'll be Ready."

Jenna took the silver hammer and walked along the lines of Pots, tapping on every lid. As she did so, each Pot's inhabitant woke up and snapped to attention. Before long there was an army of fifty-six Shield Bugs waiting to be released. Jenna reached the last Pot, which contained the ex-millipede. She tapped the lid with the silver hammer. To her surprise, the lid flew off, and the Shield Bug shot out in a shower of green goo. It landed on Jenna's arm.

Jenna screamed.

The released Shield Bug crouched, sword at the ready, on Jenna's forearm. She stood frozen to the spot, waiting for the bug to turn and attack her, forgetting that the bug's only mission was to defend its Releaser from her enemies. Which it was busy looking for.

The Shield's green armored scales moved fluidly as it shifted about, sizing up the room. Its thick right arm held a razor-sharp sword that glinted in the candlelight and its short powerful legs moved restlessly as the bug shifted its weight from one large foot to the other while it sized up the potential enemies.

But the potential enemies were a disappointing lot.

There was a large patchwork tent with bright blue eyes staring at it.

"Just put your hand over the bug," the tent whispered to the Releaser. "It will curl up into a ball. Then we'll try and get it back into the Pot."

The Releaser looked at the sharp little sword the bug was waving around, and she hesitated.

"I'll do it if you like," said the tent and moved toward the bug. The bug swung around menacingly, and the tent stopped in her tracks, wondering what was wrong. They had Imprinted all the bugs, hadn't they? It should realize that none of them was the enemy. But this bug realized no such thing. It crouched on Jenna's arm, continuing its search.

Now it saw what it was looking for. Two young warriors carrying pikestaffs, poised to attack. And one of them was wearing a *red hat*. From a dim and distant previous life the Shield Bug remembered that red hat. It had done him wrong. The bug didn't know exactly what the wrong was, but that made no difference.

It had sighted the enemy.

With a fearsome screech, the bug leaped off Jenna's arm, flapping its heavy wings, and set off through the air with a metallic clattering noise. The bug was heading straight for Boy 412 like a tiny guided missile, its sword held high above its head. It was squealing loudly, its wide-open mouth showing rows of little pointed green teeth.

"Hit it!" yelled Aunt Zelda. "Quick, bop it on the head!"

Boy 412 gave a wild swipe with his broom handle at the advancing bug but missed. Nicko aimed a blow, but the bug swerved at the last moment, shrieking and waving its sword at Boy 412. Boy 412 stared in disbelief at the bug, terribly aware of the bug's pointy sword.

"Keep still!" said Aunt Zelda in a hoarse whisper. "Whatever you do, don't move."

Boy 412 watched, horrified, as the bug landed on his shoulder and advanced purposefully toward his neck, raising its sword like a dagger.

Jenna sprang forward.

"No!" she yelled. The bug turned toward its Releaser. It didn't understand what Jenna said, but as she clamped her hand over it, the bug sheathed its sword and curled itself obediently into a ball. Boy 412 sat down on the floor with a bump.

Aunt Zelda was ready with the empty Pot, and Jenna tried to stuff the curled-up Shield Bug into it. It wouldn't go in. First one arm stayed out, then another. Jenna folded both arms in, only to find that a big green foot had kicked its way out of the jar. Jenna pushed and squeezed, but the Shield Bug struggled and fought against going back into the Pot with all its might.

Jenna was afraid it might suddenly turn nasty and use its sword, but desperate as the bug was to stay out of the Pot, it never unsheathed its sword. The safety of its Releaser was its prime concern. And how could the Releaser be safe if its protector was back in its Pot?

"You'll have to let it stay out," sighed Aunt Zelda. "I've never known anyone able to put one back. I sometimes think they are more trouble than they're worth. Still, Marcia was very insistent. As always."

"But what about Boy 412?" asked Jenna. "If it stays out, won't it just keep attacking him?"

"Not now that you've taken it off him. It should be all right."

Boy 412 looked unimpressed. "Should" was not quite what he wanted to hear. "Definitely" was more what he had in mind.

The Shield Bug settled down on Jenna's shoulder. For a few minutes it eyed everyone suspiciously, but every time it made a move, Jenna put her hand over it, and soon the bug quieted down.

Until *something* scratched at the door.

Everyone froze.

Outside on the door *something* was scratching its claws down the door.

Scritch . . . scratch . . . scritch.

Maxie whined.

The Shield Bug stood up and unsheathed its sword. This time Jenna did not stop it. The bug hovered on her shoulder, poised to jump.

"Go see if it's a friend, Bert," said Aunt Zelda calmly. The duck waddled over to the door, cocked its head to one side and listened, then gave one short meow.

"It's a friend," said Aunt Zelda. "Must be the Boggart. Don't know why he's scratching like that though."

Aunt Zelda opened the door and screamed, "Boggart! Oh, Boggart!"

The Boggart lay bleeding on the doorstep.

Aunt Zelda knelt down by the Boggart, and everyone crowded around. "Boggart, Boggart, dear. What has happened?"

The Boggart said nothing. His eyes were closed, his fur dull and matted with blood. He slumped down onto the ground, having used his last ounce of strength to reach the cottage.

"Oh, Boggart . . . open your eyes, Boggart . . . " cried Aunt Zelda. There was no response. "Help me lift him, someone. Quick."

Nicko jumped forward and helped Aunt Zelda sit the Boggart up, but he was a slippery, heavy creature, and everyone's help was needed to get him inside. They carried the Boggart into the kitchen, trying not to notice the trail of blood that dripped onto the floor as they went, and they laid him on the kitchen table.

Aunt Zelda placed her hand on the Boggart's chest.

"He's still breathing," she said, "but only just. And his heart is fluttering like a bird. It's very weak." She stifled a sob, then shook herself and snapped into action.

"Jenna, talk to him while I get the Physik chest. Keep talking to him and let him know we're here. Don't let him slip away. Nicko, get some hot water from the pot."

Boy 412 went to help Aunt Zelda with the Physik chest, while Jenna held the Boggart's damp and muddy paws and talked to him in a low voice, hoping that she sounded calmer than she felt.

"Boggart, it's all right, Boggart. You'll be better soon. You will. Can you hear me, Boggart? Boggart? Squeeze my hand if you can hear me."

A very faint movement of the Boggart's webbed fingers brushed against Jenna's hand.

"That's it, Boggart. We're still here. You'll be all right. You will . . ."

Aunt Zelda and Boy 412 came back with a large wooden chest, which they set down on the floor. Nicko put a bowl of hot water on the table.

"Right," said Aunt Zelda. "Thank you, everyone. Now I'd like you to leave me and Boggart to get on with this. Go and keep Bert and Maxie company."

But they were unwilling to leave the Boggart.

"Go *on*," Aunt Zelda insisted.

Jenna reluctantly let go of the Boggart's floppy paw, then she followed Nicko and Boy 412 out of the kitchen. The door was closed firmly behind them.

Jenna, Nicko and Boy 412 sat glumly on the floor by the fire. Nicko cuddled up to Maxie. Jenna and Boy 412 just stared at the fire, deep in their own thoughts.

Boy 412 was thinking about his Magyk ring. If he gave the ring to Aunt Zelda, he thought, maybe it would cure the Boggart. But if he did give her the ring, she would want to know where he had found it. And something told Boy 412 that if she knew where he had found it, she would be mad. Really mad. And maybe send him away. Anyway, it was stealing, wasn't it? He had stolen the ring. It wasn't his. But it might save the Boggart . . .

The more Boy 412 thought about it, the more he knew what he had to do. He had to let Aunt Zelda have the dragon ring.

"Aunt Zelda said to leave her alone," said Jenna as Boy 412 got up and walked toward the closed kitchen door.

Boy 412 took no notice.

"*Don't*," snapped Jenna. She jumped up to stop him, but at that moment the kitchen door opened.

Aunt Zelda came out. Her face was white and drawn, and she had blood all over her apron.

"Boggart's been shot," she said.

✠ 33 ✠
WATCH AND WAIT

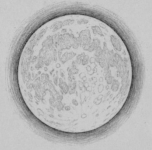

The bullet *was lying on* the kitchen table. A small lead ball with a tuft of Boggart fur still stuck to it, it sat menacingly in the middle of Aunt Zelda's newly scrubbed table.

The Boggart lay quietly in a tin bath on the floor, but he looked too small, thin and unnaturally clean to be the Boggart they all knew and loved. A broad bandage made of a torn sheet was wrapped around his middle, but already a red stain was spreading across the whiteness of the cloth.

His eyes fluttered slightly as Jenna, Nicko and Boy 412 crept into the kitchen.

"He's to be sponged down with warm water as often as we

can," said Aunt Zelda. "We mustn't let him dry out. But do not get the bullet wound wet. And he needs to be kept clean. No mud for at least three days. I've put some yarrow leaves under his bandage, and I'm just boiling him up some willow bark tea. It will take the pain away."

"But will he be all right?" asked Jenna.

"Yes, he'll be fine." Aunt Zelda allowed herself a small, strained smile as she stirred the willow bark around a large copper pan.

"But the bullet. I mean who would do this?" Jenna found her eyes drawn to the ball of black lead, an unwelcome and threatening intruder that posed too many nasty questions.

"I don't know," said Aunt Zelda in a low voice. "I've asked Boggart, but he's in no state to speak. I think we should keep watch tonight."

So, while Aunt Zelda tended the Boggart, Jenna, Nicko and Boy 412 took themselves and the Preserve Pots outside.

Once they were in the chill night air, Boy 412's Young Army training took over. He scouted around for somewhere that would give a good view of all the approaches to the island but at the same time give them somewhere to hide. He soon found what he was looking for. The chicken boat.

It was a good choice. At night the chickens were safely shut away in the hold of the boat, leaving the deck free. Boy 412 clambered up and crouched down behind the dilapidated wheelhouse, then he beckoned Jenna and Nicko to join him. They climbed into the chicken run and passed the Preserve Pots up to Boy 412. Then they joined him in the wheelhouse.

It was a cloudy night, and the moon was mostly hidden, but every now and then it appeared and shone a clear white light over the marshes, giving a good view for miles around. Boy 412 cast an expert eye over the landscape, checking for movement and telltale signs of disturbance just as he had been taught to by the ghastly Deputy Hunter, Catchpole. Boy 412 still remembered Catchpole with a shudder. He was an extremely tall man, which was one of the reasons he had never made it to be Hunter—he was just too visible. There were also many other reasons, such as his unpredictable temper; his habit of clicking his fingers when he got tense, which often gave him away just as he had reached his prey; and his dislike of too many baths, which had also saved those he hunted who had a keen sense of smell—provided the wind was blowing in the right direction. But the main reason Catchpole had never made it to Hunter was due to the simple fact that no one liked him.

Boy 412 didn't like him either, but he had learned a lot from him, once he had got used to the temper tantrums, the smell and the clicking. And one of the things that Boy 412 remembered was *watch and wait*. That's what Catchpole used to say over and over again, until it stuck in Boy 412's head like an irritating tune. Watch and wait, watch and wait, *watch and wait, boy.*

The theory was that if the watcher *waited* long enough, the prey would surely reveal itself. It may be only the slight movement of a small branch, the momentary rustling of leaves underfoot or the sudden disturbance of a small animal or bird, but the sign would surely come. All the watcher had to do was *wait* for it. And then, of course, recognize it when it came. That was the hardest part, and the bit that Boy 412 was not always very good at. But this time, he thought, this time without the pungent breath of the revolting Catchpole breathing down his neck, he could do it. He was sure he could.

It was cold up in the wheelhouse, but there was a pile of old sacks stacked up there, so they wrapped themselves in them and settled down to wait. And watch. And *wait*.

Although the marshes were still and calm, the clouds in the sky were racing past the moon, one moment obscuring it and plunging the landscape into gloom, the next rolling away and allowing the moonlight to flood over the marshland. It was in one of these moments, when the moonlight suddenly lit up the crisscross network of drainage ditches that covered the Marram Marshes, that Boy 412 saw something. Or he thought he did. Excited, he grabbed hold of Nicko and pointed in the direction where he thought he had seen something, but just at that moment the clouds covered the moon again. So, crouched in the wheelhouse, they waited. And watched and waited some more.

It seemed to take forever for the long, thin cloud to wander across the moon, and as they waited, Jenna knew that the last thing she wanted to see was someone, or something, making its way through the marsh. She wished that whoever it was who had shot the Boggart had suddenly remembered that they had left the kettle boiling on the fire and had decided to go home and take it off before their house burned down. But she knew they hadn't because suddenly the moon had come out from behind the cloud, and Boy 412 was pointing at something again.

At first Jenna couldn't see anything at all. The flat marshland stretched below her as she peered through the old wheelhouse like a fisherman searching the sea for the sign of a shoal of fish. And then she saw it. Slowly and steadily, a long black shape was making its way along one of the distant drainage ditches.

"It's a canoe . . ." whispered Nicko.

Jenna's spirits rose. "Is it Dad?"

"No," whispered Nicko, "there're *two* people. Maybe three. I can't be sure."

"I'll go and tell Aunt Zelda," said Jenna. She got up to go, but Boy 412 put his hand on her arm to stop her.

"What?" whispered Jenna.

Boy 412 shook his head and put his finger to his lips.

"I think he thinks you might make a noise and give us away," whispered Nicko. "Sound travels a long way over the marsh at night."

"Well, I wish he'd *say* so," said Jenna edgily.

So Jenna stayed in the wheelhouse and watched the canoe make steady progress, unerringly picking its way through the maze of ditches, passing by all the other islands and heading straight for theirs. As it came closer Jenna noticed that something about the figures looked horribly familiar. The larger figure in the front of the canoe had the concentrated look of a tiger stalking its prey. For a moment Jenna felt sorry for the prey until, with a jolt, she realized who that was.

It was *her*.

It was the Hunter, and he had come for *her*.

✠ 3 4 ✠
AMBUSH

As the canoe drew closer the watchers in the chicken boat could see the Hunter and his companions clearly. The Hunter sat in the front of the canoe paddling at a brisk pace and behind him was the Apprentice. And behind the Apprentice was a . . . Thing. The Thing squatted on the top of the canoe, casting its eye around the marsh and occasionally making a grab for a passing insect or bat. The Apprentice cowered in front of the Thing, but the Hunter appeared to take no notice. He had more important things to think about.

Jenna shuddered when she saw the Thing. It scared her almost more than the Hunter did. At least the Hunter was a human, albeit a deadly one. But what exactly was the creature squatting on the back of the canoe? To calm herself she lifted the Shield Bug off her shoulder, where it had been sitting quietly, and holding it carefully in the palm of her hand, she pointed out the approaching canoe and its grim trio.

"Enemies," she whispered. The Shield Bug understood. It followed Jenna's slightly trembling finger and locked its sharp green eyes, which had perfect night vision, on to the figures in the canoe.

The Shield Bug was happy.

It had an enemy.

It had a sword.

Soon the sword would meet the enemy.

Life was simple when you were a Shield Bug.

The boys let out the rest of the Shield Bugs. One by one, they undid each Preserve Pot lid. As they took each lid off, a Shield Bug leaped out in a shower of green gloop, sword at the ready. With each bug Nicko or Boy 412 pointed out the rapidly approaching canoe. Soon fifty-six Shield Bugs were lined up, crouching like coiled springs on the gunnels of the chicken boat. The fifty-seventh stayed on Jenna's shoulder, fiercely loyal to its Releaser.

And now all those on the chicken boat had to do was wait. And watch. And that is what, hearts thumping in their ears, they did. They watched the Hunter and the Apprentice change from shadowy shapes into the dreaded figures they had seen months earlier at the mouth of the Deppen Ditch, and they looked just as nasty and dangerous as they had then.

But the Thing remained a shadowy shape.

The canoe had reached a narrow ditch that would take it past the turning into the Mott. All three watchers held their breath as they waited for it to reach the turning. Maybe, thought Jenna, clutching at straws, maybe the Enchantment is working better than Aunt Zelda thinks and the Hunter can't see the cottage.

The canoe turned into the Mott. The Hunter could see the cottage only too well.

In his mind the Hunter rehearsed the three steps of the Plan:

STEP ONE: Secure the Queenling. Take prisoner and install in canoe under guard of accompanying Magog. Shoot only if necessary. Otherwise

return to DomDaniel, who wished to "do the job
himself" this time.
STEP TWO: *Shoot vermin, i.e., the witch woman*
and the Wizard boy. And the dog.
STEP THREE: *A little bit of private enterprise.*
Take the Young Army deserter prisoner.
Return to Young Army. Collect bounty.

Satisfied with his plan, the Hunter paddled noiselessly
along the Mott, heading for the landing stage.

Boy 412 saw him drawing near and motioned Jenna and
Nicko to stay still. He knew any movement would give them
away. In Boy 412's mind they had now progressed from
Watch and Wait to *Ambush*. And in *Ambush*, Boy 412 remem-
bered Catchpole telling him as he breathed down his neck,
Stillness Is All.

Until the *Instant of Action.*

The fifty-six Shield Bugs, lined up along the gunnels,
understood exactly what Boy 412 was doing. A large part of
the Charm with which they had been created had actually
been taken from the Young Army training manual. Boy 412
and the Shield Bugs were acting as one.

The Hunter, Apprentice and the Magog had no idea that

very soon they would be part of an *Instant of Action*. The Hunter had tied up at the landing stage and was busy trying to get the Apprentice out of the canoe without making any noise and without the boy falling into the water. Normally the Hunter would not have cared in the slightest if the Apprentice had fallen in. In fact, he might have given him a sly push if it hadn't been for the fact that the Apprentice would have made a loud splash and no doubt done a lot of squawking in the bargain. So, promising himself that he'd push the irritating little so-and-so into the next available cold water when he got the chance, the Hunter had silently eased himself out of the canoe and then pulled the Apprentice up onto the landing stage.

The Magog slunk down into the canoe, pulled its black hood over its blind-worm eye, which was troubled by the bright moonlight, and stayed put. What happened on the island was none of its business. It was there to take custody of the Princess and to act as a guard against the marsh creatures during the long journey. It had done its job remarkably well, apart from one irritating incident that had been as much the fault of the Apprentice as anything. But no Marsh Wraith or Brownie had dared approach the canoe with the Magog perched on it, and the slime the Magog extruded had covered the hull of the canoe and caused all the Water Nixies' suckers to slip off, burning them unpleasantly in the process.

The Hunter was pleased with the Hunt so far. He smiled his usual smile, which never reached his eyes. At last they were here at the White Witch's hideaway, after a grueling paddle across the marsh and that wasteful encounter with some stupid marsh animal who kept getting in the way. The Hunter's smile faded at the memory of their meeting with the Boggart. He did not approve of wasting bullets. You never knew when you might need the extra one. He cradled his pistol in his hand and very slowly and deliberately loaded a silver bullet.

Jenna saw the silver pistol glint in the moonlight. She saw the fifty-six Shield Bugs lined up ready for action and decided to keep her own bug beside her. Just in case. So she put her hand over the bug to quiet it. The bug obediently sheathed its sword and rolled into a ball. Jenna slipped the bug into her pocket. If the Hunter carried a pistol, then she would carry a bug.

With the Apprentice following in the Hunter's footsteps as he'd been instructed, the pair crept silently up the little path that led from the landing stage to the cottage, passing the chicken boat on its way. As they reached the chicken boat the Hunter stopped. He had heard something. Human heartbeats. Three sets of very fast human heartbeats. He raised his pistol . . .

Aaaeeeiiiigh!!

The scream of fifty-six Shield Bugs is a terrible scream. It dislocates the three tiny bones inside the ear and creates an incredible feeling of panic. Those who know about Shield Bugs will do the only thing they can: stuff their fingers in their ears and hope to control the panic. This is what the Hunter did; he stood completely still, put his fingers deep into his ears, and if he felt a flicker of panic, it did not trouble him for more than a moment.

The Apprentice of course knew nothing about Shield Bugs. So he did what anyone would do when confronted with a swarm of small green things flying toward you, waving scalpel-sharp swords and screeching so high that your ears felt like they would burst. He ran. Faster than he had ever run before, the Apprentice hurtled down to the Mott, hoping to get into the canoe and paddle to safety.

The Hunter knew that, given a choice, a Shield Bug will always chase a moving enemy and ignore a still one, which is exactly what happened. To the Hunter's great satisfaction, all fifty-six Shield Bugs decided that the enemy was the Apprentice and pursued him shrilly down to the Mott, where the terrified boy hurled himself into the freezing water to escape the clattering green swarm.

The intrepid Shield Bugs hurled themselves into the Mott after the Apprentice, doing what they had to do, following the enemy to the end, but unfortunately for them, the end they met was their own. As each bug hit the water it sank like a stone, its heavy green armor dragging it down to the sticky mud at the bottom of the Mott. The Apprentice, shocked and gasping with the cold, hauled himself out onto the bank and lay shivering under a bush, too afraid to move.

The Magog watched the scene with no apparent interest at all. Then, when all the fuss had died down, he started to trawl the depths of the mud with his long arms and pick out the drowned bugs one by one. He sat contentedly on the canoe, sucking the bugs dry and crunching them into a smooth green paste with his sharp yellow fangs—armor, swords and all—before he slowly sucked them down into his stomach.

The Hunter smiled and looked up at the wheelhouse of the chicken boat. He hadn't expected it to be this easy. All three of them waiting for him like sitting ducks.

"Are you going to come down, or am I going to come up and get you?" he asked coldly.

"Run," hissed Nicko to Jenna.

"What about *you*?"

"I'll be okay. It's you he's after. Just go. *Now*."

Nicko raised his voice and spoke to the Hunter. "Please don't shoot. I'll come down."

"Not just you, sonny. You're *all* coming down. The girl first."

Nicko pushed Jenna away. "*Go!*" he hissed.

Jenna seemed unable to move, unwilling to leave what felt like the safety of the chicken boat. Boy 412 recognized the terror on her face. He had felt like that so many times before in the Young Army, and he knew that unless he grabbed her, just as Boy 409 had once done for him to save him from a Forest wolverine, Jenna would be unable to move. And if he didn't grab her, the Hunter would. Quickly, Boy 412 propelled Jenna out of the wheelhouse, clasped her hand tightly and jumped with her off the far side of the chicken boat, away from the Hunter. As they landed on a pile of chicken dung mixed with straw, they heard the Hunter swear.

"Run!" hissed Nicko, looking down from the deck.

Boy 412 pulled Jenna to her feet, but she was still unwilling to go.

"We can't leave Nicko," she gasped.

"I'll be all right, Jen. Just go!" yelled Nicko, oblivious to the Hunter and his pistol.

The Hunter was tempted to shoot the Wizard boy there and then, but his priority was the Queenling, not Wizard scum. So, as Jenna and Boy 412 picked themselves up off the dung heap, clambered over the chicken wire and ran for their lives, the Hunter leaped after them as if his own life too depended on it.

Boy 412 kept hold of Jenna as he headed away from the Hunter, around the back of the cottage and into Aunt Zelda's fruit bushes. He had the advantage over the Hunter in that he knew the island, but that did not bother the Hunter. He was doing what he did best, tracking a prey and a young and terrified one at that. Easy. After all, where could they run to? It was only a matter of time before he got them.

Boy 412 and Jenna ducked and weaved through the bushes, leaving the Hunter struggling to find his way through the prickly plants, but all too soon Jenna and Boy 412 reached the end of the fruit bushes and reluctantly emerged into the exposed grassy space that led down to the duck pond. At that moment the moon came out from behind the clouds, and the Hunter saw his prey outlined against the backdrop of the marshes.

Boy 412 ran, pulling Jenna along with him, but the Hunter was slowly gaining on them and did not seem to tire, unlike Jenna, who felt she could not run another step. They skirted the duck pond and raced up to the grassy knoll at the end of the island. Horribly close behind them they could hear the footsteps of the Hunter, echoing as he too reached the knoll and sprinted over the hollow ground.

Boy 412 dodged this way and that between the small bush-es scattered about, dragging Jenna behind him, aware that the Hunter was almost near enough to reach out and grab her.

And then suddenly the Hunter *was* near enough. He lunged forward and dived at Jenna's feet.

"Jenna!" yelled Boy 412, pulling her out of the Hunter's grasp and jumping with her into a bush.

Jenna crashed into the bush after Boy 412, only to find that suddenly the bush wasn't there anymore, and she was tum-bling headlong into a dark, cold, endless space.

She landed with a jolt on a sandy floor. A moment later there was a thud, and Boy 412 lay sprawled in the darkness beside her.

Jenna sat up, dazed and aching, and rubbed the back of her head where she had hit the ground. Something very strange had happened. She tried to remember what it was. Not their escape from the Hunter, not the fall through the ground, but something even stranger. She shook her head to try to clear the fuzziness in her brain. That was it. She remembered.

Boy 412 had *spoken*.

☩ 35 ☩
GONE TO GROUND

Y ou can talk," *said Jenna*, rubbing the bump on her head.
"Of *course* I can talk," said Boy 412.

"But why haven't you, then? You haven't ever said *anything*.
Except for your name. I mean, number."

"That's all we were meant to say if we were captured. Rank
and number. Nothing else. So that's what I did."

"You weren't captured. You were *saved*," Jenna pointed out.

"I know," said Boy 412. "Well, I know that *now*. I didn't
then."

Jenna found it very strange to be actually having a conversation with Boy 412 after all this time. And even stranger to
be having it at the bottom of a pit in complete darkness.

"I wish we had a light," said Jenna. "I keep thinking the Hunter's going to creep up on us." She shivered.

Boy 412 reached up inside his hat, drew out his ring and slipped it onto his right index finger. It fitted perfectly. He cupped his other hand around the dragon ring, warming it and willing it to give out its golden glow. The ring responded, and a soft glow spread out from Boy 412's hands until he could clearly see Jenna looking at him through the darkness. Boy 412 felt very happy. The ring was brighter than ever, and soon it cast a warm circle of light around them as they sat on the sandy floor of the tunnel.

"That's amazing," said Jenna. "Where did you find it?"

"Down here," said Boy 412.

"What, you just found it? Just now?"

"No. I found it before."

"Before what?"

"Before—remember when we got lost in the haar?"

Jenna nodded.

"Well, I fell down here then. And I thought I was going to be stuck here forever. Until I found the ring. It's Magyk. It lit up and showed me the way out."

So that was what happened, thought Jenna. It made sense now. Boy 412 sitting smugly waiting for them when she and

Nicko finally found their way back, frozen and soaked after hours of wandering around looking for him. She had just *known* he had some kind of secret. And then all that time he had been walking around with the ring and never showing anyone. There was more to Boy 412 than met the eye.

"It's a beautiful ring," she said, gazing at the gold dragon curled around Boy 412's finger. "Can I hold it?"

A little reluctantly, Boy 412 took off the ring and gave it to Jenna. She cradled it carefully in her hands, but the light began to fade and the darkness drew in around them. Soon the light from the ring had completely died.

"Have you dropped it?" Boy 412 asked accusingly.

"No," said Jenna, "it's still here in my hand. But it doesn't work for me."

"Of course it works. It's a Magyk ring," said Boy 412. "Here, give it back. I'll show you." He took the ring and immediately the tunnel was filled with light. "See, it's easy."

"Easy for you," said Jenna, "but not for me."

"I don't see why," said Boy 412, puzzled.

But Jenna had seen why. She had seen it over and over again, growing up in a household of Wizards. And although Jenna knew only too well that she was not Magykal, she could tell who was.

"It's not the ring that's Magyk. It's *you*," she told Boy 412.

"I'm not Magyk," said Boy 412. He sounded so definite that Jenna didn't argue.

"Well, whatever you are, you'd better keep hold of the ring," she said. "So how do we get out?"

Boy 412 put the dragon ring on and set off along the tunnel, leading Jenna confidently through the twists and turns that had so confused him before, until at last they arrived at the top of the steps.

"Careful," he said. "I fell down these last time and nearly lost the ring."

At the bottom of the steps Jenna stopped. Something had made the hair on the back of her neck stand up.

"I've been here before," she whispered.

"When?" asked Boy 412, a bit put out. It was *his* place.

"In my dreams," muttered Jenna. "I know this place. I used to dream about it in the summer when I was at home. But it was bigger than this . . ."

"Come on," said Boy 412 briskly.

"I wonder if it *is* bigger, if there's an echo." Jenna raised her voice as she spoke.

there's an echo there's an echo there's an echo there's an echo there's an echo there's an echo . . . sounded all around them.

"Shhh," whispered Boy 412. "He might hear us. Through the ground. They train them to hear like dogs."

"Who?"

"*Hunters.*"

Jenna fell silent. She had forgotten about the Hunter, and now she didn't want to be reminded.

"There're pictures all over the walls," Jenna whispered to Boy 412, "and I know I've dreamed about *them*. They look really old. It's like they're telling a story."

Boy 412 hadn't taken much notice of the pictures before, but now he held his ring up to the smooth marble walls that formed this part of the tunnel. He could see simple, almost primitive shapes in deep blues, reds and yellows showing what seemed to be dragons, a boat being built, then a lighthouse and a shipwreck.

Jenna pointed to more shapes farther along the wall. "And these look like plans for a tower or something."

"It's the Wizard Tower," said Boy 412. "Look at the Pyramid on the top."

"I didn't know the Wizard Tower was so old," said Jenna, running her finger over the paint and thinking that maybe she was the first person to see the pictures for thousands of years.

"The Wizard Tower is very old," said Boy 412. "No one knows when it was built."

"How do *you* know?" asked Jenna, surprised that Boy 412 was so definite.

Boy 412 took a deep breath and said in a singsong voice, *"The Wizard Tower is an Ancient Monument. Precious resources are squandered by the ExtraOrdinary Wizard to keep the Tower in its garish state of opulence, resources that could be used for healing the sick or making the Castle a more secure place for all to live.* See, I can still remember it. We used to have to recite stuff like that every week in our Know Your Enemy lesson."

"Yuck," sympathized Jenna. "Hey, I bet Aunt Zelda would be interested in all this down here," she whispered as she followed Boy 412 along the tunnel.

"She knows all about it already," said Boy 412, remembering Aunt Zelda's disappearance from the potion cupboard. "And I think she knows that I know."

"Why? Did she say?" asked Jenna, wondering how she had missed all this.

"No," said Boy 412. "But she gave me a funny look."

"She gives everyone funny looks," Jenna pointed out. "It doesn't mean she thinks they've been down some secret tunnel."

They walked on a little farther. The line of pictures had just ended and they had reached some steep steps leading upward. Jenna's attention was caught by a small rock nestled beside the bottom step. She picked it up and showed it to Boy 412.

"Hey, look at this. Isn't it lovely?"

Jenna was holding a large egg-shaped green stone. It was slippery-smooth as though someone had just polished it, and it shone with a dull sheen in the light of the ring. The green had an iridescent quality to it, like a dragonfly's wing, and it lay heavily but perfectly balanced in her two cupped hands.

"It's so smooth," said Boy 412, stroking it gently.

"Here, you have it," said Jenna impulsively. "It can be your own pet rock. Like Petroc Trelawney, only bigger. We could ask Dad to get a spell for it when we go back to the Castle."

Boy 412 took the green rock. He wasn't sure what to say. No one had ever given him a present before. He put the rock into his secret pocket on the inside of his sheepskin jacket. Then he remembered what Aunt Zelda had said to him when he had brought her some herbs from the garden.

"Thank you," he said.

Something in the way he spoke reminded Jenna of Nicko. *Nicko.*

Nicko and the *Hunter*.

"We've got to get back," said Jenna anxiously.

Boy 412 nodded. He knew they had to go and face whatever may be waiting for them outside. He had just been enjoying feeling safe for a while.

But he knew it couldn't last.

✠ 36 ✠
FROZEN

T he trapdoor slowly rose a few inches, and Boy 412 peered out. A chill ran though him. The door to the potion cupboard had been thrown wide open, and he was looking straight at the heels of the Hunter's muddy brown boots.

Standing with his back to the potion cupboard, only a few feet away, was the figure of the Hunter, his green cloak thrown over his shoulder and his silver pistol held at the ready. He was facing the kitchen door, poised as if about to rush forward.

Boy 412 waited to see what the Hunter was about to do, but the man did nothing at all. He was, thought Boy 412, *waiting*. Probably for Aunt Zelda to walk out of the kitchen.

Willing Aunt Zelda to stay away, Boy 412 reached down and held his hand out for Jenna's Shield Bug.

Jenna stood anxiously on the ladder below him. She could tell that all was not well from how tense and still Boy 412 had become. When his hand reached down she took the rolled-up Shield Bug from her pocket and passed it up to Boy 412, as they had planned, sending it a silent good luck wish as she did so. Jenna had begun to like the bug and was sorry to see it go.

Carefully, Boy 412 took the bug and slowly pushed it through the open trapdoor. He set the tiny armored green ball down on the floor, making sure he kept hold of it, and pointed it in the right direction.

Straight at the Hunter.

Then he let go. At once the bug uncurled itself, locked its piercing green eyes on to the Hunter and unsheathed its sword with a small swishing noise. Boy 412 held his breath at the noise and hoped the Hunter had not heard, but the stocky man in green made no move. Boy 412 slowly breathed out and, with a flick of his finger, he sent the bug into the air, toward its target, with a shrill shriek.

The Hunter did nothing.

He didn't turn or even flinch as the bug landed on his shoulder and raised its sword to strike. Boy 412 was impressed. He knew the Hunter was tough, but surely this was taking things too far.

And then Aunt Zelda appeared.

"Look out!" yelled Boy 412. "The Hunter!"

Aunt Zelda jumped. Not because of the Hunter but because she had never heard Boy 412 speak before and so she had no idea who had spoken. Or where the unknown voice was coming from.

Then, to Boy 412's amazement, Aunt Zelda snatched the Shield Bug off the Hunter and tapped it to make it roll back into a ball.

And *still* the Hunter did nothing.

Briskly, Aunt Zelda put the bug into one of her many patchwork pockets and looked around her, wondering where the unfamiliar voice had come from. And then she caught sight of Boy 412 peering out from the slightly raised trapdoor.

"Is that *you*?" she gasped. "Thank goodness you're all right. Where's Jenna?"

"Here," said Boy 412, half afraid to speak in case the Hunter heard. But the Hunter gave no sign of having heard anything at all, and Aunt Zelda treated him as nothing more than an awkward piece of furniture as she walked around his immobile figure, lifted up the trapdoor and helped Boy 412 and Jenna out.

"What a wonderful sight, *both* of you safe," she said happily. "I was so worried."

"But—what about *him*." Boy 412 pointed to the Hunter.

"Frozen," said Aunt Zelda with an air of satisfaction. "Frozen solid and staying that way. Until I decide what to do with him."

"Where's Nicko? Is he all right?" asked Jenna as she clambered out.

"He's fine. He's gone after the Apprentice," said Aunt Zelda.

As Aunt Zelda finished speaking, the front door crashed open and the dripping-wet Apprentice was propelled inside, followed by an equally dripping-wet Nicko.

"Pig," spat Nicko, slamming the door. He let go of the boy and went over to the blazing fire to get dry.

The Apprentice dripped unhappily on the floor and looked over to the Hunter for help. He dripped even more unhappily when he saw what had happened. The Hunter stood Frozen in mid-lunge with his pistol, staring into space with empty eyes. The Apprentice gulped—a big woman in a patchwork tent was advancing purposefully toward him, and he knew only too well who it was from the Illustrated Enemy Cards he had had to study before he came on the Hunt.

It was the Mad White Witch, Zelda Zanuba Heap.

Not to mention the Wizard boy, Nickolas Benjamin Heap, and 412, the lowlife runaway deserter. They were all here, just as he had been told they would be. But where was the one they had really come for? Where was the *Queenling*?

The Apprentice looked around and caught sight of Jenna in the shadows behind Boy 412. He took in Jenna's gold circlet shining against her long dark hair and her violet eyes, just like the picture on the Enemy Card (drawn very skillfully by Linda Lane, the spy). The Queenling was a little taller than he had expected, but it was definitely her.

A sly smile played on the Apprentice's lips as he wondered if he could grab Jenna all by himself. How pleased his Master would be with him. Surely then his Master would forget all his past failures and would stop threatening to send him into the Young Army as an Expendable. Especially if he had succeeded where even the Hunter had failed.

He was going to do it.

Taking everyone by surprise, the Apprentice, although hampered by his sodden robes, flung himself forward and seized hold of Jenna. He was unexpectedly strong for his size, and he wrapped a wiry arm around her throat, almost choking her. Then he started to drag her toward the door.

Aunt Zelda made a move toward the Apprentice, and he flicked open his pocketknife, pressing it hard against Jenna's throat.

"Anyone tries to stop me, and she gets it," he snarled, propelling Jenna out the open door and down the path to the canoe and the waiting Magog. The Magog paid the scene no attention at all. It was immersed in liquifying its fifteenth drowned Shield Bug, and its duties did not commence until the prisoner was in the canoe.

She nearly was.

But Nicko was not going to let his sister go without a fight. He hurtled after the Apprentice and threw himself onto him. The Apprentice landed on top of Jenna, and there was a scream. A trickle of blood ran from underneath her.

Nicko yanked the Apprentice out of the way.

"Jen, Jen!" he gasped. "Are you hurt?"

Jenna had jumped up and was staring at the blood on the path.

"I—I don't think so," she stammered. "I think it's *him*. I think *he's* hurt."

"Serve him right," said Nicko, kicking the knife out of the Apprentice's reach.

Nicko and Jenna hauled the Apprentice to his feet. He had a small cut on his arm but apart from that seemed unharmed. But he was deathly white. The Apprentice was frightened by the sight of blood, particularly his own, but he was even more frightened at the thought of what the Wizards might do to him. As they dragged him back into the cottage the Apprentice made one last attempt to escape. He twisted out of Jenna's grasp and aimed a hefty kick at Nicko's shins.

A fight broke out. The Apprentice landed a nasty punch to Nicko's stomach and was just about to kick him again when Nicko twisted his arm painfully behind his back.

"Get out of that one," Nicko told him. "Don't think you can try and kidnap my sister and get away with it. *Pig.*"

"He'd never have got away with it," mocked Jenna. "He's too stupid."

The Apprentice hated being called stupid. That was all his Master ever called him. Stupid boy. Stupid birdbrain. Stupid beetlehead. He *hated* it.

"I'm not stupid." He gasped as Nicko tightened his grip on his arm. "I can do anything I want to. I could have shot her if

I'd wanted to. I already *have* shot something tonight. So there."

As soon as he said it, the Apprentice wished he hadn't. Four pairs of accusing eyes stared at him.

"What exactly do you mean?" Aunt Zelda asked him quietly. "You shot *something*?"

The Apprentice decided to brazen it out.

"None of your business. I can shoot what I like. And if I want to shoot some fat ball of fur that gets in my way when I am on official business, then I will."

There was a shocked silence. Nicko broke it.

"Boggart. He shot the Boggart. *Pig.*"

"*Ouch!*" yelled the Apprentice.

"No violence, please, Nicko," said Aunt Zelda. "Whatever he's done, he's just a boy."

"I'm not *just* a boy," said the Apprentice haughtily. "I am Apprentice to DomDaniel, the Supreme Wizard and Necromancer. I am the seventh son of a seventh son."

"What?" asked Aunt Zelda. "*What* did you say?"

"I am Apprentice to DomDaniel, the Supreme—"

"Not that. We know *that*. I can see the black stars on your belt only too well, thank you."

"I said," the Apprentice spoke proudly, pleased that at

last someone was taking him seriously, "that I am the seventh son of a seventh son. I am Magykal." Even though,
thought the Apprentice, it hasn't quite shown itself yet. But
it will.

"I don't believe you," Aunt Zelda said flatly. "I've never
seen anyone less like a seventh son of a seventh son in my
life."

"Well, I am," the Apprentice insisted sulkily. "I am
Septimus Heap."

⊹→ 37 ←⊹
SCRYING

He's lying," *Nicko said angrily*, pacing up and down while the Apprentice dripped dry slowly by the fire.

The Apprentice's green woolen robes gave off an unpleasant musty odor, which Aunt Zelda recognized as being the smell of failed spells and stale Darke Magyk. She opened a few jars of Stink Screen, and soon the air smelled pleasantly of lemon meringue pie.

"He's just saying it to upset us," said Nicko indignantly.

"That little pig's name is *not* Septimus Heap."

Jenna put her arm around Nicko. Boy 412 wished he understood what was happening.

"Who is *Septimus Heap?*" he asked.

"Our brother," said Nicko.

Boy 412 looked even more confused.

"He died when he was a baby," said Jenna. "If he had lived, he would have had amazing Magykal powers. Our dad was a seventh son, you see," Jenna told him, "but that doesn't always make you any more Magykal."

"It certainly didn't with Silas," muttered Aunt Zelda.

"When Dad married Mum they had six sons. They had Simon, Sam, Edd and Erik, Jo-Jo and Nicko. And then they had Septimus. So he was the seventh son of a seventh son. But he died. Just after he was born," said Jenna. She was remembering what Sarah had told her one summer night when she was tucked in her box bed. "I always thought he was my twin brother. But it turns out he wasn't . . ."

"Oh," said Boy 412, thinking how complicated it seemed to be to have a family.

"So he's definitely not our brother," Nicko was saying. "And even if he *was*, I wouldn't want him. He's no brother of mine."

"Well," said Aunt Zelda, "there's only one way to sort this out. We can see if he's telling the truth, which I very much doubt. Although I did always wonder about Septimus . . . It never seemed quite right somehow." She opened the door and checked the moon.

"A gibbous moon," she said. "Nearly full. Not a bad time to scry."

"What?" asked Jenna, Nicko and Boy 412 in unison.

"I'll show you," she said. "Come with me."

The duck pond was the last place they all expected to end up, but there they were, looking at the reflection of the moon in the still, black water, just as Aunt Zelda had told them to.

The Apprentice was wedged firmly between Nicko and Boy 412, in case he should try to make a run for it. Boy 412 was pleased that Nicko trusted him at last. Not so long ago, it was Nicko who was trying to stop *him* from making a run for it. And now here he was, watching exactly the kind of Magyk he had been warned about in the Young Army: a full moon and a White Witch, her piercing blue eyes blazing in the moonlight, waving her arms in the air and talking about dead babies. What Boy 412 found difficult to believe was not that this was happening, but the fact that to him it now seemed quite normal. Not only that, but he realized that the people he was standing around the duck pond with—Jenna, Nicko and Aunt Zelda—meant more to him than anyone ever had in his whole life. Apart from Boy 409, of course.

Except, thought Boy 412, he could do without the Apprentice. The Apprentice reminded him of most of the people who had tormented him in his previous life. *His previous life.* That, decided Boy 412, was how it was going to be. Whatever happened, he was never going back to the Young Army. *Never.*

Aunt Zelda spoke in a low voice. "Now I am going to ask the moon to show us Septimus Heap."

Boy 412 shivered and stared at the still, dark water of the pond. In the middle lay a perfect reflection of the moon, so detailed that the seas and mountains of the moon were clearer than he had ever seen before.

Aunt Zelda looked up at the moon and said, "Sister Moon, Sister Moon, show us, if you will, the seventh son of Silas and Sarah. Show us where he is now. Show us Septimus Heap."

Everyone held their breath and looked expectantly at the the surface of the pond. Jenna felt apprehensive. Septimus was *dead*. What would they see? A small bundle of bones? A tiny grave?

A silence fell. The reflection of the moon began to grow bigger until a huge white, almost perfect circle filled the duck pond. At first, vague shadows began to appear in the circle. Slowly they became more defined until they saw . . . their own reflections.

"See," said the Apprentice. "You asked to see me, and there I am. I *told* you."

"That doesn't mean anything," said Nicko indignantly. "It's just our reflections."

"Maybe. Maybe not," said Aunt Zelda thoughtfully.

"Can we see what happened to Septimus when he was born?" asked Jenna. "Then we'd know if he was still alive, wouldn't we?"

"Yes, we would. I'll ask. But it's much more difficult to see things from the past." Aunt Zelda took a deep breath and said, "Sister Moon, Sister Moon, show us, if you will, the first day of the life of Septimus Heap."

The Apprentice snuffled and coughed.

"Quiet, please," said Aunt Zelda.

Slowly their reflections disappeared from the surface of the water and were replaced by an exquisitely detailed scene, sharp and brilliant against the midnight darkness.

The scene was somewhere that Jenna and Nicko knew

well: their home back in the Castle. Like a tableau laid before them, the figures in the room were immobile, frozen in time. Sarah lay in a makeshift bed, holding a newborn baby, with Silas beside her. Jenna caught her breath. She had not realized how much she missed home until now. She glanced at Nicko, who had a look of concentration on his face that Jenna recognized as Nicko *not* looking upset.

Suddenly everyone gasped. The figures had begun to move. Silently and smoothly, like a moving photograph, they began to play out a scene before the entranced audience—entranced, except for one.

"My Master's Camera Obscura is a hundred times better than this old duck pond," the Apprentice said contemptuously.

"Shut *up*," hissed Nicko angrily.

The Apprentice sighed loudly and fidgeted about. It was all a load of rubbish, he thought. It's nothing to do with *me*.

The Apprentice was wrong. The events he was watching had changed his life.

The scene unfolded before them:

The Heaps' room looks subtly different. Everything is newer and cleaner. Sarah Heap is much younger too; her face is fuller and there is no sadness lingering in her eyes. In fact, she looks completely happy, holding her newborn baby, Septimus. Silas is also younger;

his hair is less straggly and his face less etched with worry. There are six little boys playing together quietly.

Jenna smiled wistfully, realizing that the smallest one with the mop of unruly hair must be Nicko. He looks so cute, she thought, jumping up and down, excited and wanting to see the baby.

Silas picks Nicko up and holds him up to see his new brother. Nicko reaches out a small, pudgy hand and gently strokes the baby's cheek. Silas says something to him and then puts him down to tod-dle off and play with his older brothers.

Now Silas is kissing Sarah and the baby good-bye. He stops and says something to Simon, the eldest, and then he is gone.

The picture fades away, the hours are passing.

Now the Heaps' room is lit by candlelight. Sarah is nursing the baby, and Simon is quietly reading a story to his younger brothers. A large figure in dark blue robes, the Matron Midwife, bustles into view. She takes the baby from Sarah and lays him in the wooden box that serves as his cot. With her back to Sarah she slips a small vial of black liquid from her pocket and dips her fin-ger into it. Then, glancing around her guiltily, the Midwife wipes her blackened finger along the baby's lips. At once, Septimus goes limp.

The Matron Midwife turns to Sarah, holding out the floppy baby to her. Sarah is distraught. She puts her mouth over her baby's to try to breathe life into him, but Septimus stays as limp as a rag. Soon Sarah too feels the effects of the drug. In a daze she collapses back against her pillows.

Watched by six horrified little boys, the Matron Midwife takes a huge roll of bandages out of her pocket and begins to wrap Septimus, starting with his feet and expertly working upward, until she reaches his head, where she stops for a moment and checks the baby's breathing. Satisfied, she continues with the bandaging, leaving his nose peeking out, until he looks like a tiny Egyptian mummy.

Suddenly the Matron Midwife makes for the door, taking Septimus with her. Sarah wills herself to wake from her drugged sleep just in time to see the Midwife throw open the door and bump into a shocked Silas, who has his cloak tightly wrapped around him. The Midwife pushes him aside and runs off down the corridor.

The corridors of The Ramblings are lit with brightly burning torches, which cast flickering shadows across the dark figure of the Matron Midwife as she runs, holding Septimus close. After a while she emerges into the snowy night and slows her pace, looking about anxiously. Hunched over the baby, she hurries along the deserted narrow streets until she reaches a wide-open space.

Boy 412 gasped. It was the dreaded Young Army Parade Ground.

The large dark figure moves over the snowy expanse of the parade ground, scuttling like a black beetle across a tablecloth. The guard at the barracks door salutes the Midwife and lets her in.

Inside the dismal barracks the Matron Midwife slows her pace. She walks carefully down a steep flight of narrow steps, which lead to a dank basement room full of empty cots lined up in ranks. It is what will soon become the Young Army nursery where all the orphaned and unwanted boy children from the Castle will be raised. (The girls will go to the Domestic Service Training Hall.) Already there are four unfortunate occupants. Three are triplet sons of a Guard who dared to make a joke about the Supreme Custodian's beard. The fourth is the Matron Midwife's own baby boy, six months old and being babysat in the nursery while she is at work. The babysitter, an old woman with a persistent cough, is slumped in her chair, dozing fitfully between coughing bouts. The Matron Midwife quickly places Septimus in an empty cot and unwinds his bandages. Septimus yawns and unclenches his tiny fists.

He is alive.

Jenna, Nicko, Boy 412 and Aunt Zelda stared at the scene before them in the pond, realizing that what the Apprentice had said now seemed to be all too true. Boy 412 had a nasty feeling in the pit of his stomach. He hated seeing the Young Army barracks again.

In the semidarkness of the Young Army nursery the Matron Midwife sits down wearily. She keeps glancing anxiously at the door as if waiting for someone to come in. No one appears.

A minute or two later she heaves herself up from her chair and goes over to the cot where her own baby is crying and picks the child up. At that moment the door is flung open, and the Matron Midwife wheels around, white-faced, frightened.

A tall woman in black stands in the doorway. Over her black, well-pressed robes she wears the starched white apron of a nurse, but around her waist is a blood-red belt showing the three black stars of DomDaniel.

She has come for Septimus Heap.

The Apprentice didn't like what he saw at all. He didn't want to see the lowlife family he was rescued from—they meant nothing to him. He didn't want to see what had happened to him as a baby either. What did that matter to him now? And he was sick of standing out in the cold with the enemy.

Angrily, the Apprentice kicked a duck sitting beside his feet, and booted the bird straight into the water. Bert landed with a splash in the middle of the pond, and the picture shattered into a thousand dancing fragments of light.

The spell was broken.

The Apprentice ran for it. Down to the Mott, along the path, racing as fast as he could, heading for the thin black canoe. He didn't get far. Bert, who had not taken kindly to being kicked into the pond, was after him. The Apprentice heard the flapping of the duck's powerful wings only a moment before he felt the peck of her beak on the back of his neck and the tug of his robes almost choking him. The duck took hold of his hood and pulled him toward Nicko.

"Oh, dear," said Aunt Zelda, sounding worried.

"I wouldn't bother about him," said Nicko angrily as he caught up with the Apprentice and got hold of him.

"I wasn't worried about *him*," said Aunt Zelda. "I was just hoping that Bert didn't strain her beak."

The Apprentice sat huddled in the corner by the fire, with Bert still hanging on to one of his dangling damp sleeves. Jenna had locked all the doors and Nicko had locked the windows, leaving Boy 412 to keep watch over the Apprentice while they went to see how the Boggart was.

The Boggart lay at the bottom of the tin bath, a small mound of damp brown fur against the white of the sheet that Aunt Zelda had laid underneath him. He half opened his eyes and regarded his visitors with a bleary, unfocused gaze.

"Hello, Boggart. Are you feeling better?" asked Jenna.

The Boggart did not respond. Aunt Zelda dipped a sponge

into a bucket of warm water and gently bathed him.

"Just keeping Boggart damp," she said. "A dry Boggart is not a happy Boggart."

"He's not looking good, is he?" Jenna whispered to Nicko as they tiptoed quietly out of the kitchen with Aunt Zelda.

The Hunter, still poised outside the kitchen door, regarded Jenna with a baleful stare as she appeared. His piercing pale blue eyes locked on to her and followed her across the room. But the rest of him was as immobile as ever.

Jenna felt the stare and glanced up. A cold shiver shot through her. "He's *looking* at me," she said. "His eyes are *following* me."

"Bother," tutted Aunt Zelda. "He's beginning to DeFrost. I'd better take this before it causes any more trouble."

Aunt Zelda pulled the silver pistol out of the Hunter's Frozen hand. His eyes flashed angrily as she expertly broke open the gun and removed a small silver ball from its chamber.

"Here you are," Aunt Zelda said, handing the silver bullet to Jenna. "It has been looking for you for ten years, and now its search is over. You are safe now."

Jenna smiled uncertainly and rolled the solid silver sphere around her palm with a sense of revulsion; although, she could not help but admire how perfect it was. Almost perfect. She lifted it up and squinted at a tiny nick in the ball. To her surprise there were two letters carved into the silver: I.P.

"What's I.P. mean?" Jenna asked Aunt Zelda. "Look, it's here on the bullet."

Aunt Zelda did not reply for a moment. She knew what the letters meant, but she was unsure about telling Jenna.

"I.P.," murmured Jenna, thinking it over. "I.P. . . ."

"Infant Princess," said Aunt Zelda. "A named bullet. A named bullet will always find its target. It doesn't matter how or when, but find you it will. As yours has done. But not in the way they intended."

"Oh," said Jenna quietly. "So the other one, the one for my mother, did it have . . . "

"Yes, it did. It had Q on it."

"Ah. Can I keep the pistol too?" asked Jenna.

Aunt Zelda looked surprised. "Well, I suppose so," she said. "If you really want to."

Jenna took the gun and held it as she had seen both the Hunter and the Assassin do, feeling its heavy weight in her hand and the strange sense of power holding it gave her.

"Thank you," she said to Aunt Zelda, handing the pistol

back to her. "Can you keep it safe for me. For now?"

The Hunter's eyes followed Aunt Zelda as she marched the pistol off to her Unstable Potions and Partikular Poisons cupboard and locked it away. They followed her back again as she walked up to him and felt his ears. The Hunter looked furious. His eyebrows twitched, and his eyes flashed angrily, but nothing else moved.

"Good," said Aunt Zelda, "his ears are still Frozen. He can't hear what we say yet. We've got to decide what we'll do with him before he DeFrosts."

"Can't you just ReFreeze him?" asked Jenna.

Aunt Zelda shook her head. "No," she replied regretfully. "You shouldn't ReFreeze someone once they start to DeFrost. It's not safe for them. They can get Freezer Burn. Or else go horribly soggy. Not a nice sight. But still, the Hunter's a dangerous man and he won't give up the Hunt. Ever. And somehow we have to stop him hunting us."

Jenna was thinking.

"We need," she said, "to make him forget everything. Even who he is." She chuckled. "We could make him think he's a lion tamer or something."

"And then he'd join a circus and find out that he wasn't, just after he'd put his head into a lion's mouth," Nicko finished.

"We must not use Magyk to endanger life," Aunt Zelda reminded them.

"He could be a clown, then," said Jenna. "He's scary enough."

"Well, I have heard there's a circus due in the Port any day now. I'm sure he'd find work." Aunt Zelda smiled. "They take all sorts, I'm told."

Aunt Zelda fetched an old, tattered book called Magyk Memories.

"You're good at this," she said, handing the book to Boy 412. "Can you find the right Charm for me? I think it's called Rogue Recollections."

Boy 412 leafed though the musty old book. It was one of those where most of the Charms had been lost, but toward the end of the book he found what he was looking for: a small, knotted handkerchief with some smudgy black writing along the hem.

"Good," said Aunt Zelda. "Perhaps you could do the spell for us, please?"

"Me?" asked Boy 412, surprised.

"If you wouldn't mind," replied Aunt Zelda. "My eyesight isn't up to it in this light." She reached up and checked the Hunter's ears. They were warm. The Hunter glared at her and narrowed his eyes in that familiar cold stare. No one took any notice.

"He can hear now," she said. "Best get this done before he can speak too."

Boy 412 carefully read the spell's instructions. Then he held the knotted handkerchief and said,

> Whatever your Historie may be
> 'tis lost to You when you see Me.

Boy 412 waved the handkerchief in front of the Hunter's angry eyes; then he undid the knot. With that, the Hunter's eyes went blank. His gaze was no longer threatening, but bewildered and maybe a little frightened.

"Good," said Aunt Zelda. "That seems to have worked well. Can you do the next bit now, please?"

Boy 412 said quietly,

> So listen to your new-sprung Ways,
> Remember Now your diff'rent Days.

Aunt Zelda planted herself in front of the Hunter and addressed him firmly. "This," she told him, "is the story of your life. You were born in a hovel down in the Port."

"You were a horrible child," Jenna told him. "And you had
pimples."

"No one liked you," added Nicko.

The Hunter began to look very unhappy.

"Except your dog," said Jenna, who was beginning to feel
just a bit sorry for him.

"Your dog died," said Nicko.

The Hunter looked devastated.

"*Nicko*," remonstrated Jenna. "Don't be mean."

"*Me?* What about *him?*"

And so the Hunter's horribly tragic life unfolded before
him. It was riddled with unfortunate coincidences, stupid mistakes and highly embarrassing moments that made his newly
DeFrosted ears go red at their sudden recollection. At last the
sad tale was finished off with his unhappy Apprenticeship to
an irascible clown known to all who worked for him as Dog
Breath.

The Apprentice watched with a mixture of glee and horror.
The Hunter had tormented him for so long, and the Apprentice
was glad to see someone was at last getting the better of him.
But he could not help but wonder what they were planning to
do to *him*.

As the sorry tale of the Hunter's past ended, Boy 412 reknotted the handkerchief and said,

What was your Life has gone away,
Another Past does now hold sway.

With some effort, they carried the Hunter outside like a large, unwieldy plank and set him up beside the Mott, so that he could finish DeFrosting out of the way. The Magog paid him no attention whatsoever, having just scooped its thirty-eighth Shield Bug out of the mud and being preoccupied with whether to take the wings off this one before it liquified it or not.

"Give me a nice garden gnome any day," said Aunt Zelda, regarding her new and, she hoped, temporary garden ornament with distaste. "But that's a job well done. Now all we've got to sort out is the Apprentice."

"Septimus . . ." mused Jenna. "I can't believe it. What will Mum and Dad say? He's so *horrible*."

"Well, I suppose growing up with DomDaniel hasn't done him any good," said Aunt Zelda.

"Boy 412 grew up in the Young Army, but he's okay," Jenna pointed out. "He would never have shot the Boggart."

"I know," agreed Aunt Zelda. "But maybe the Apprentice, er, Septimus will improve with time."

"Maybe," said Jenna doubtfully.

Sometime later, in the early hours of the morning, when Boy 412 had carefully tucked the green rock that Jenna gave him under his quilt to keep it warm and close to him—and just as they were at last settling down to sleep—there was a hesitant knock on the door.

Jenna sat up, scared. Who *was* it? She nudged Nicko and Boy 412 awake. Then she crept over to the window and silently drew back one of the shutters.

Nicko and Boy 412 stood by the door, armed with a broom and a heavy lamp.

The Apprentice sat up in his dark corner by the fire and smiled a smug smile. DomDaniel had sent a rescue party for him.

It was no rescue party, but Jenna went pale when she saw who it was.

"It's the *Hunter*," she whispered.

"He's not coming in," said Nicko. "No way."

But the Hunter knocked again, louder.

"Go away!" Jenna yelled at him.

Aunt Zelda came out from tending the Boggart.

"See what he wants," she said, "and we can send him on his way."

So, against all her instincts, Jenna opened the door to the Hunter.

She hardly recognized him. Although he still wore the uniform of a Hunter, he no longer looked like one. He had gathered his thick green cloak around him like a beggar with a blanket, and he stood in the doorway apologetically and slightly stooped.

"I am sorry to trouble you gentle folk at this late hour," he murmured. "But I fear I have lost my way. I wonder if you could direct me to the Port?"

"That way," said Jenna curtly, pointing out over the marshes.

The Hunter looked confused. "I am not very good at finding my way, miss. Where exactly would that be?"

"Follow the moon," Aunt Zelda told him. "She will guide you."

The Hunter bowed humbly.

"Thank you kindly, Madam. I wonder if I could trouble you by asking if there might be a circus due in town? I have hopes of obtaining a position there as a buffoon."

Jenna smothered a giggle.

"Yes, there is, as it happens," Aunt Zelda told him. "Er, would you wait a minute?" She disappeared into the kitchen and came back with a small bag containing some bread and cheese.

"Take this," she said, "and good luck with your new life."

The Hunter bowed again.

"Why, thank you kindly, Madam," he said and walked down to the Mott, passing the sleeping Magog and his thin black canoe without a flicker of recognition, and out over the bridge.

Four silent figures stood at the doorway and watched the solitary figure of the Hunter pick his way uncertainly across the Marram Marshes toward his new life in

FISHHEAD AND DURDLE'S
TRAVELING CIRCUS
AND MENAGERIE

until a cloud covered the moon and the marshes were once again plunged into darkness.

✢ 39 ✢
THE APPOINTMENT

L ater *that night the* Apprentice escaped through the cat
tunnel.

Bert, who still had all the instincts of a cat, liked to go wandering at night, and Aunt Zelda would leave the door on a
one-way CharmLock. This allowed Bert to go out, but nothing to come in. Not even Bert. Aunt Zelda was very careful
about stray Brownies and Marsh Wraiths.

So, when everyone except for the Apprentice had fallen
asleep and Bert had decided to go out for the night, the
Apprentice thought that he would follow her. It was a tight

squeeze, but the Apprentice, who was as thin as a snake and twice as wriggly, wormed his way through the narrow space. As he did so, the Darke Magyk which clung to his robes DisEnchanted the cat tunnel. Soon his flustered face emerged from the tunnel into the chill night air.

Bert met him with a sharp peck on the nose, but the Apprentice was not deterred. He was much more scared of getting stuck in the cat tunnel, with his feet still inside the house and his head on the outside, than he was of Bert. He had a feeling that no one would be in much of a hurry to pull him out if he did get stuck. So he ignored the angry duck and, with a huge effort, wriggled free.

The Apprentice made straight for the landing stage, closely pursued by Bert, who tried to grab his collar again, but this time the Apprentice was ready for her. Angrily, he swatted her away, sending her crashing to the ground and badly bruising a wing.

The Magog was lying full length in the canoe, sleeping while it digested all fifty-six Shield Bugs. The Apprentice warily stepped over it. To his relief the creature did not stir— digestion was something a Magog took very seriously. The smell of Magog slime caught in the back of the Apprentice's throat, but he picked up the slime-covered paddle and was soon away down the Mott, heading out toward the maze of winding channels that crisscrossed the Marram Marshes and would take him to the Deppen Ditch.

As he left the cottage behind and traveled into the wide moonlit expanse of the marshes, the Apprentice began to feel a little uneasy. With the Magog sleeping, the Apprentice felt horribly unprotected and he remembered all the terrifying stories he had heard about the marshes at night. He paddled the canoe as quietly as he was able to, afraid of disturbing something that may not want to be disturbed. Or, even worse, something that might be *waiting* to be disturbed. All around him he could hear the nighttime noises of the marsh. He heard the muffled underground shrieking of a pack of Brownies as they pulled an unsuspecting Marsh Cat down into the Quake Ooze. And then there was a nasty scrabbling and squelching noise as two large Water Nixies tried to clamp their sucker pads onto the bottom of the canoe and chew their way into it, but they slipped off soon enough thanks to the remnants of the Magog's slime.

Sometime after the Water Nixies had dropped off, a Marsh Moaner appeared. Although it was only a small wisp of white mist, it gave off a dank smell that reminded the Apprentice of the burrow in DomDaniel's hideout. The Marsh Moaner sat itself down behind the Apprentice and started tunelessly singing the most mournful and irritating song the Apprentice had ever heard. The tune whirled around and around inside his head—*"Weerrghh-derr-waaaah-dooooooooo . . . Weerrghh-derr-waaaah-dooooooooo . . . Weerrghh-derr-waaaah-dooooooooo . . ."*—until the Apprentice felt he might go mad.

He tried to bat the Moaner away with his paddle, but it went straight through the wailing scrap of mist, unbalanced the canoe and nearly sent the Apprentice tumbling out into the dark water. And still the awful tune went on, a little mockingly now that the Moaner knew it had the Apprentice's attention: *"Weerrghh-derr-waaaah-dooooooooo . . . Weerrghh-derr-waaaah-dooooooooo . . . ooooooooooooooooooooooooooooo . . ."*

"Stop it!" yelled the Apprentice, unable to stand the noise a moment longer. He stuffed his fingers into his ears and started singing in a voice loud enough to shut out the ghastly tune.

"I'm not listening, I'm not listening, I'm not listening," the Apprentice chanted at the top of his lungs while the triumphant Moaner swirled around the canoe, pleased with its night's work. It usually took the Marsh Moaner much longer to reduce a Young One to a gibbering wreck, but tonight it had struck lucky. Mission completed, the Marsh Moaner flattened

out into a thin sheet of mist and wafted off to spend the rest of the night contentedly hanging above its favorite bog.

The Apprentice paddled doggedly on, no longer caring about the succession of Marsh Wraiths, Bogle Bugs and a very tempting array of Marshfire that danced about his canoe for hours. By then the Apprentice did not mind what anything did, as long as it didn't *sing*.

As the sun rose over the far reaches of the Marram Marshes, the Apprentice realized he had become hopelessly lost. He was in the middle of a featureless expanse of marshland that all looked the same to him. He paddled wearily onward, not knowing what else to do, and it was midday before he reached a wide, straight stretch of water that looked as though it actually went somewhere, rather than petering out into yet another soggy morass. Exhausted, the Apprentice turned into what was the upper reaches of the Deppen Ditch and slowly headed toward the river. His discovery of the giant Marsh Python, lurking at the bottom of the Ditch and trying to straighten itself out, hardly even bothered the Apprentice. He was far too tired to care. He was also very determined. He had an appointment with DomDaniel, and *this* time he wasn't going to mess things up. Very soon the Queenling would be sorry. They would *all* be sorry. Particularly the duck.

＊ ＊ ＊

That morning, back at the cottage, no one could believe that the Apprentice had managed to squeeze out through the cat tunnel.

"I'd have thought his head was too big to fit through it," Jenna said scornfully.

Nicko went out to search the island, but he was soon back again. "The Hunter's canoe is gone," he said, "and that was a *fast* boat. He'll be far away by now."

"We've got to stop him," said Boy 412, who knew only too well just how dangerous a boy like the Apprentice could be, "before he tells anyone where we are, which he will do as soon as he can."

And so Jenna, Nicko and Boy 412 took *Muriel Two* and set off in pursuit of the Apprentice. As the pale spring sun rose over the Marram Marshes, sending long glancing shadows across the mires and bogs, the ungainly *Muriel Two* took them through the maze of cuts and ditches. She traveled slow and steady, far too slow for Nicko, who knew how quickly the Hunter's canoe must have covered the same distance. Nicko kept a watchful eye out for any sign of the sleek black canoe, half expecting to see it upturned in a Brownie Quake Ooze or drifting empty along a ditch, but to his disappointment he saw nothing apart from a long black log that only momentarily raised his hopes.

They stopped for a while to eat some goat cheese and sardine sandwiches beside the Marsh Moaners' bog. But they were left in peace as the Moaners were long gone, evaporated in the warmth of the rising sun.

It was early afternoon and a gray drizzle had set in when, at last, they paddled into the Deppen Ditch. The Marsh Python lay dozing in the mud, half covered with the sluggish water of the recently turned incoming tide. It ignored *Muriel Two*, much to the occupants' relief, and lay waiting for the fresh influx of fish that the rising tide would bring. The tide was very low, and the canoe sat well below the steep banks that rose up on either side of them, so it was not until they rounded the very last bend of the Deppen Ditch that Jenna, Nicko and Boy 412 saw what was waiting for them.

The *Vengeance*.

⊹ 40 ⊹
The Meeting

A shocked silence fell in the *Muriel Two* canoe.

Just a short paddle away, the *Vengeance* lay quietly at anchor in the early afternoon drizzle, still and steady in the middle of the river's deepwater channel. The massive black ship was a striking sight: its bow rose up like the steep side of a cliff, and with its tattered black sails furled, its two tall masts stood out like black bones against the overcast sky. An oppressive silence surrounded the ship in the gray light. No seagulls dared wheel around hoping for scraps. Small boats using the river saw the ship and hurried quietly along

the shallow waters by the riverbank, more willing to risk running aground than to go near the notorious *Vengeance*. A
heavy black cloud had formed above the masts, casting a dark
shadow over the entire ship, and from the stern a blood-red
flag with a line of three black stars fluttered ominously.

Nicko did not need the flag to tell him whose ship it was.
No other ship had ever been painted with the strong black
tar that DomDaniel used, and no other ship could have been
surrounded by such a malevolent atmosphere. He gestured
frantically to Jenna and Boy 412 to paddle backward, and a
moment later *Muriel Two* was safely hidden behind the last
bend of Deppen Ditch.

"What is it?" whispered Jenna.

"It's the *Vengeance*," whispered Nicko. "DomDaniel's ship.
I reckon it's waiting for the Apprentice. I bet that's where the
little toad has gone. Pass me the eyeglass, Jen."

Nicko put the telescope to his eye and saw exactly what
he had feared. There in the deep shadows cast by the steep
black sides of the hull was the Hunter's canoe. It lay bobbing in the water, empty and dwarfed by the bulk of the
Vengeance, tied to the foot of a long rope ladder that led up
to the ship's deck.

The Apprentice had kept his appointment.

"It's too late," said Nicko. "He's there. Oh, yuck, what's that? Oh, *disgusting*. That Thing's just slipped out from inside the canoe. It's so *slimy*. But it can certainly get up a rope ladder. It's like some gruesome monkey." Nicko shuddered.

"Can you see the Apprentice?" whispered Jenna.

Nicko swept the eyeglass up the rope ladder. He nodded. Sure enough, the Apprentice had almost reached the top, but he had stopped and was staring down in horror at the rapidly climbing Thing. In a matter of moments the Magog had reached the Apprentice and scuttled over him, leaving a trail of vivid yellow slime across the back of his robes. The Apprentice seemed to falter for a moment and almost loosen his grip on the ladder, but he struggled up the last few rungs and collapsed on the deck, where he lay unnoticed for some time.

Serves him right, thought Nicko.

They decided to take a closer look at the *Vengeance* on foot. They tied *Muriel Two* to a rock and walked along to the beach where they had had the midnight picnic the night of their escape from the Castle. As they rounded the bend Jenna got a shock. Someone was already there. She stopped dead and ducked back behind an old tree trunk. Boy 412 and Nicko bumped into her.

"What is it?" whispered Nicko.

"There's someone on the beach," whispered Jenna. "Maybe it's someone from the ship. Keeping guard."

Nicko peered around the tree trunk.

"It's not someone from the ship." He smiled.

"How do you know?" asked Jenna. "It could be."

"Because it's Alther."

Alther Mella was sitting on the beach, staring mournfully out into the drizzle. He had been there for days, hoping that someone from Keeper's Cottage would turn up. He needed to talk to them urgently.

"Alther?" whispered Jenna.

"Princess!" Alther's careworn face lit up. He wafted over to Jenna and enfolded her in a warm hug. "Well, I do believe you've grown since I last saw you."

Jenna put her fingers to her lips. "Shhh, they might hear us, Alther," she said.

Alther looked surprised. He wasn't used to Jenna telling him what to do.

"They can't hear me." He chuckled. "Not unless I want them to. And they can't hear you either—I've put up a Scream Screen. They won't hear a thing."

"Oh, Alther," said Jenna. "It is so lovely to see you. Isn't it, Nicko?"

Nicko had a big grin on his face. "It's great," he said.

Alther gave Boy 412 a quizzical look. "Here's someone else who's grown too." He smiled. "Those Young Army lads are always so painfully thin. It's nice to see you've filled out a bit. "

Boy 412 blushed.

"He's nice now too, Uncle Alther," Jenna told the ghost.

"I expect he was always nice, Princess," said Alther. "But you're not allowed to be nice in the Young Army. It's forbidden."

He smiled at Boy 412.

Boy 412 smiled shyly back.

They sat on the drizzly beach, just out of sight of the *Vengeance*.

"How's Mum and Dad?" asked Nicko.

"And Simon?" asked Jenna. "What about Simon?"

"Ah, Simon," said Alther. "Simon had deliberately slipped away from Sarah in the Forest. Seems he and Lucy Gringe had planned to secretly get married."

"What?" said Nicko. "Simon got *married*?"

"No. Gringe found out and shopped him to the Custodian Guards."

"Oh, no!" gasped Jenna and Nicko.

"Oh, don't worry yourselves about Simon," said Alther, strangely unsympathetic. "How he managed to spend all that time in the custody of the Supreme Custodian and come out looking like he'd had a holiday, I don't know. Although I have my suspicions."

"How do you mean, Uncle Alther?" asked Jenna.

"Oh, it's probably nothing, Princess." Alther seemed unwilling to say any more about Simon.

There was something Boy 412 wanted to ask but it felt odd talking to a ghost. But he had to ask, so he plucked up his courage and said, "Er, excuse me, but what's happened to Marcia? Is she all right?"

Alther sighed. "No," he said.

"No?" three voices asked at once.

"She was set up," Alther frowned. "Set up by the Supreme Custodian and the Rat Office. He's put his own rats in. Or rather DomDaniel's rats. And a vicious lot they are too. They used to run the spy network back at DomDaniel's place in the Badlands. They've got a very nasty reputation. Came in with the plague rats hundreds of years ago. Not nice."

"You mean our Message Rat was one of *them*?" asked Jenna, thinking of how she had rather liked him.

"No, no. He got marched off by the Rat Office heavies. He's disappeared. Poor rat. I wouldn't give much for his chances," said Alther.

"Oh. That's awful," said Jenna.

"And the message for Marcia wasn't from Silas either," said Alther.

"I didn't think it *was*," said Nicko.

"It was from the Supreme Custodian," Alther said. "So when Marcia turned up at the Palace Gate to meet Silas, the Custodian Guards were waiting for her. Of course that wouldn't have been a problem for Marcia if she had got her Midnight Minutes right, but her timepiece was twenty minutes slow. *And* she'd given away her KeepSafe. It's a bad business. DomDaniel has taken the Amulet, so I am afraid he's now . . . the ExtraOrdinary Wizard."

Jenna and Nicko were speechless. This was worse than anything they had feared.

"Excuse me," ventured Boy 412, who felt terrible. It was his fault. If he had been her Apprentice then he could have helped her. This never would have happened. "Marcia is still . . . alive, isn't she?"

Alther looked at Boy 412. His faded green eyes had a kindly expression as, using his unsettling habit of reading people's minds, he said, "You couldn't have done anything, lad. They would have got you too. She *was* in Dungeon Number One, but now—"

Boy 412 put his head in his hands in despair. He knew all about Dungeon Number One.

Alther put a ghostly arm around his shoulder. "Don't fret now," he told him. "I was with her for most of the time and she was doing all right. Kept going pretty well, I thought. All things considered. A few days ago I just popped out to check on various little . . . projects I have going on in DomDaniel's rooms at the Tower. When I got back to the dungeon she was gone. I've looked everywhere I can. I even have some of the Ancients looking. You know, the really old ghosts. But they're very faded and easily confused. Most of them don't know their way around the Castle very well anymore—they come up against a new wall or staircase and they're stuck. They can't work it out. I had to go and get one out of the kitchen midden yesterday. Apparently it used to be the Wizard's refectory. About five hundred years ago. Frankly the Ancients, sweet as they are, are more trouble than they are worth." Alther sighed. "Although I do wonder if . . ."

"If what?" asked Jenna.

"If she might be on the *Vengeance*. Unfortunately I can't get on the wretched ship to find out."

Alther was cross with himself. He would now advise any ExtraOrdinary Wizard to go to as many places as they could in their lifetime so that as a ghost they were not as thwarted as he had been. But it was too late for Alther to change what he had done while he was alive; he had to make the best of it now.

At least, when he was first appointed Apprentice, DomDaniel had insisted on taking Alther on a long and very unpleasant tour of the deepest dungeons. At the time Alther had never dreamed that one day he might come to be glad of it, but if only he had accepted an invitation to the launching party on the *Vengeance* . . . Alther remembered how, as one of some promising young potential Apprentices, he had been invited to a party on board DomDaniel's boat. Alther had turned down the invitation on account of the fact it was Alice Nettles's birthday. No women were allowed on the ship, and Alther was certainly not going to leave Alice alone on her birthday. At the party, the potential Apprentices had run riot and caused a great deal of damage to the ship, thus ensuring that they had no hope of being offered as much as a cleaning

job with the ExtraOrdinary Wizard. Not long afterward
Alther was offered the ExtraOrdinary Wizard Apprenticeship. Alther had never got the chance to visit the ship again.
After the disastrous party, DomDaniel took her up to Bleak
Creek for a refit. Bleak Creek was an eerie anchorage full of
abandoned and rotting ships. The Necromancer had liked it
so much that he left his ship there and visited every year for
his summer holiday.

The subdued group sat on the damp beach. They gloomily ate
the last of the damp goat cheese and sardine sandwiches and
drank the dregs from the flask of beetroot and carrot cordial.

"There are some times," said Alther reflectively, "when I
really miss not being able to eat anymore . . ."

"But this isn't one of them?" Jenna finished for him.

"Spot on, Princess."

Jenna fished Petroc Trelawney out of her pocket and offered
him a sticky mix of squashed sardine and goat cheese. Petroc
opened his eyes and looked at the offering. The pet rock was
surprised. This was the kind of food he usually got from Boy
412; Jenna always gave him biscuits. But he ate it anyway,
apart from a piece of goat cheese that stuck to his head and
then later to the inside of Jenna's pocket.

When they had finished chewing the last of the soggy sandwiches, Alther said seriously, "Now, down to business."

Three worried faces looked at the ghost.

"Listen to me, all of you. You must go *straight* back to Keeper's Cottage. I want you to tell Zelda to take you all to the Port first thing tomorrow morning. Alice—she is Chief Customs Officer down there now—is finding you a ship. You are to go to the Far Countries while I try and sort things out here."

"*But*—" gasped Jenna, Nicko and Boy 412.

Alther ignored their protest.

"I will meet you all at the Blue Anchor Tavern on the Harbor tomorrow morning. You *must* be there. Your mother and father are coming too, along with Simon. They are on their way down the river in my old boat, *Molly*. I am afraid that Sam, Erik and Edd and Jo-Jo have refused to leave the Forest—they have gone quite wild, but Morwenna will keep an eye on them."

There was an unhappy silence. No one liked what Alther had said.

"That's running away," Jenna said quietly. "We want to stay. And fight."

"I knew you'd say that," sighed Alther. "It is just what your mother would have said. But you *must* go now."

Nicko stood up.

"All right," he said reluctantly. "We'll see you tomorrow at the Port."

"Good," said Alther. "Now, be careful and I'll see you all tomorrow." He floated up and watched the three of them trail disconsolately back to the *Muriel Two*. Alther stayed watching until he was satisfied that they were making good progress along the Deppen Ditch and then he sped off along the river, flying low and fast, off to join *Molly*. Soon he was just a small speck in the distance.

Which was when the *Muriel Two* turned around and headed straight back toward the *Vengeance*.

✛ 4 1 ✛
THE VENGEANCE

There was much discussion in the *Muriel Two*.

"I really don't know about this. Marcia might not even be on the *Vengeance*."

"I bet she is, though."

"We've got to find her. I'm sure I could rescue her."

"Look, just because you've been in the Army doesn't mean you can go storming ships and rescuing people."

"It means you can *try*."

"He's right, Nicko."

"We'd never make it. They'll see us coming. Every ship always has a watch on board."

"But we could do that spell, you know the one . . . what was it?"

"Cause Yourself to be Unseen. Easy. Then we could paddle out to the ship and I'll climb up the rope ladder, and then—"

"Whoa, stop there. That's *dangerous*."

"Marcia rescued *me* when *I* was in danger."

"And *me*."

"All right. You win."

As the *Muriel Two* rounded the last bend of the Deppen Ditch, Boy 412 reached up into the pocket inside his red beanie hat and drew out the dragon ring.

"What's that ring?" asked Nicko.

"Um, it's Magyk. I found it. Under the ground."

"It looks a bit like the dragon on the Amulet," said Nicko.

"Yes," said Boy 412, "I thought that too." He slipped it on his finger and felt the ring grow warm. "Shall I do the spell, then?" he asked.

Jenna and Nicko nodded and Boy 412 began to chant:

Let me Fade into the Aire
Let all against me know not Where
Let them that Seeke me pass me by
Let Harme not reach me from their Eye.

Boy 412 slowly faded into the drizzle, leaving a canoe paddle hanging eerily in midair. Jenna took a deep breath and tried the spell for herself.

"You're still there, Jen," said Nicko. "Try again."

The third time was a charm. Jenna's canoe paddle now hovered in the air next to Boy 412's.

"Your turn, Nicko," said Jenna's voice.

"Hang on a minute," said Nicko. "I never did this one."

"Well, do your own, then," said Jenna. "It doesn't matter as long as it works."

"Well, er, I don't know if it *does* work. And it doesn't do the 'Harme not reach me' thing at all."

"*Nicko!*" protested Jenna.

"All right, all right. I'll try it."

"Not seen, Not heard . . . um . . . I can't remember the rest."

"Try 'Not seen, not heard, not a whisper, not a word,'" suggested Boy 412 from out of nowhere.

"Oh, yes. That's it. Thanks."

The spell worked. Nicko faded slowly away.

"You all right, Nicko?" asked Jenna. "I can't see you."

There was no reply.

"Nicko?"

Nicko's paddle waggled frantically up and down.

"We can't see him and he can't see us because his Unseen is different from ours," said Boy 412 slightly disapprovingly, "and we won't be able to hear him either, because it's mainly a silent spell. And it doesn't protect him."

"Not a lot of good, then," said Jenna.

"No," said Boy 412. "But I've got an idea. This should do it:

> Between the spells within our power,
> Give us one Harmonious Hour.

"There he is!" said Jenna, as the shadowy form of Nicko **Appeared**. "Nicko, can you see *us*?" she asked.

Nicko grinned and made a thumbs-up sign.

"Wow, you're *good*," Jenna told Boy 412.

It was becoming misty as Nicko, using the silent part of his spell, paddled them out from the Deppen Ditch into the open waters of the river. The water was calm and heavy, spotted with a fine drizzle. Nicko was careful to create as little disturbance as possible, just in case a pair of keen eyes from the crow's nest might be drawn to the strange swirls on the surface of the water, steadily making their way toward the ship.

Nicko made good progress, and soon the steep black sides

of the *Vengeance* reared up before them through the misty drizzle, and the Unseen *Muriel Two* reached the bottom of the rope ladder. They decided that Nicko would stay with the canoe while Jenna and Boy 412 tried to find out if Marcia was being held on the ship and, if possible, set her free. If they needed any help, Nicko would be ready. Jenna hoped they wouldn't. She knew that Nicko's spell would not protect him if he got into any trouble. Nicko held the canoe steady while first Jenna and then Boy 412 climbed uncertainly onto the ladder and started the long precarious climb to the *Vengeance*.

Nicko watched them with an uneasy feeling. He knew that Unseens can leave shadows and strange disturbances in the air, and a Necromancer like DomDaniel would have no trouble spotting them. But all Nicko could do was silently wish them luck. He had decided that if they did not come back by the time the tide had risen halfway up the Deppen Ditch, he would go in search of them, whether his spell protected him or not.

To pass the time, Nicko climbed into the Hunter's canoe. He may as well make the most of his wait, he thought, and sit in a decent boat. Even if it was a bit slimy. And *smelly*. But he'd smelled worse in some of the fishing boats he used to help out on.

✳   ✳   ✳

It was a long climb up the rope ladder and not an easy one. The ladder kept bumping against the ship's sticky black sides and Jenna was afraid that someone on board might hear them, but all was quiet above. So quiet that she began to wonder if it was some kind of ghost ship.

As they reached the top, Boy 412 made the mistake of looking down. He felt sick. His head swam with the giddy sensation of height, and he very nearly lost his grip on the rope ladder as his hands became suddenly clammy. The water was dizzyingly far away. The Hunter's canoe looked tiny, and for a moment he thought he saw someone sitting in it. Boy 412 shook his head. Don't look down, he told himself sternly. *Don't look down.*

Jenna had no fear of heights. She easily clambered up onto the *Vengeance* and hauled Boy 412 over the gap between ladder and deck. Boy 412 kept his eyes firmly fixed on Jenna's boots as he wriggled onto the deck and shakily stood up.

Jenna and Boy 412 looked around them.

The *Vengeance* was an eerie place. The heavy cloud hanging overhead cast a deep shadow over the entire ship, and the only sound they could hear was the quiet rhythmic creaking of the

ship itself as it rocked gently on the incoming tide. Jenna and
Boy 412 padded quietly along the deck, past neatly coiled
ropes, orderly lines of tarred barrels and the occasional can-
non pointing out menacingly over the Marram Marshes.
Apart from the oppressive blackness and a few traces of yellow
slime on the deck, the ship bore no clues as to who it belonged
to. However, when they reached the prow, a strong Darke
presence almost knocked Boy 412 off his feet. Jenna carried
on, unaware of anything, and Boy 412 followed her, not wanting to leave her alone.

The Darkenesse came from an imposing throne, set up
by the foremast, looking out to sea. It was a massive piece
of furniture, strangely out of place on the deck of a ship. It
was ornately carved from ebony and embellished with a
deep red gold leaf—and it contained DomDaniel, the
Necromancer, himself. Sitting bolt upright, his eyes closed,
his mouth slightly open and a low, wet gurgle emanating
from the back of his throat as he breathed in the drizzle,
DomDaniel was taking his afternoon nap. Underneath the
throne, like a faithful dog, lay a sleeping Thing in a pool of
yellow slime.

Suddenly Boy 412 clutched Jenna's arm so hard that she
nearly cried out. He pointed to DomDaniel's waist. Jenna

glanced down and then looked at Boy 412 in despair. So it was true. She had hardly been able to believe what Alther had told them but here, in front of her eyes, was the truth. Around DomDaniel's waist, almost hidden in his dark robes, was the ExtraOrdinary Wizard's belt. *Marcia's* ExtraOrdinary Wizard belt.

Jenna and Boy 412 stared at DomDaniel with a mixture of disgust and fascination. The Necromancer's fingers gripped the ebony arms of the throne; his thick yellow fingernails curved around the ends and clipped on to the wood like a set of claws. His face still had the telltale gray pallor it had acquired during his years spent Underground, before he had moved out into his lair in the Badlands. It was an unremarkable face in many ways—maybe the eyes were a little too deep set, and the mouth a little too cruel for it to be wholly pleasant—but it was the Darke that lay beneath that made Jenna and Boy 412 shudder as they gazed at it.

On his head DomDaniel wore a cylindrical black hat shaped like a short stovepipe, which, for some reason he did not understand, was always a little too big for him, regardless of how often he had a new one made to fit. This bothered DomDaniel more than he liked to admit, and he had become convinced that since his return to the Wizard Tower his head had started to shrink. While the Necromancer slept, the hat had slipped down and was now resting on the top of his whitish ears. The black hat was an old-fashioned Wizard hat, which no Wizard had worn, or had wanted to wear, since it had been associated with the great Wizard Inquisition many hundreds of years ago.

Above the throne a dark red silk canopy, emblazoned with a trio of black stars, hung heavily in the drizzle, dripping every now and then onto the hat and filling up the indentation in the top with a pool of water.

Boy 412 took hold of Jenna's hand. He remembered a small, moth-eaten pamphlet of Marcia's he had read one snowy afternoon called The Hypnotik Effect of the Darke, and he could feel Jenna being drawn in. He pulled her away from the sleeping figure toward an open hatch.

"Marcia's *here*," he whispered to Jenna. "I can feel her Presence."

As they reached the hatch there was a sound of footsteps running along the deck below and then rapidly climbing the ladder. Jenna and Boy 412 jumped back and a sailor holding a long, unlit torch ran up onto the deck. The sailor was a small, wiry man dressed in the usual Custodian black; unlike the Custodian Guards he was not shaven-headed but had long hair carefully tied back in a thin dark plait that straggled halfway down his back. He had baggy trousers that reached to just below his knee and a top with broad black and white stripes running across it. The sailor took out a tinder box, struck a spark and lit his torch. The torch flared to life, and a brilliant orange flame lit up the gray drizzly afternoon, casting dancing shadows across the deck. The sailor walked forward with the blazing torch and placed it in a holder on the prow of the ship. DomDaniel opened his eyes. His nap was over.

The sailor hovered nervously beside the throne, awaiting his instructions from the Necromancer.

"Are they returned?" came a low, hollow voice that made the hair on the back of Boy 412's neck stand up.

The sailor bowed, avoiding the Necromancer's gaze.

"The boy is returned, my lord. And your servant."

"Is that *all*?"

"Yes, my lord. But . . ."

"But *what*?"

"The boy says that he captured the Princess, sire."

"The *Queenling*. Well, well. *Wonders* will never *cease*. Bring them to me. *Now!*"

"Yes, my lord." The sailor bowed low.

"And—bring up the *prisoner*. She will be *interested* to see her erstwhile charge."

"Her what, sire?"

"The *Queenling*, wretch. Get them *all* up here. *Now!*"

The sailor disappeared through the hatchway, and soon Jenna and Boy 412 could feel movement below their feet. Deep in the hold of the ship, things were stirring. Sailors were tumbling from their hammocks, putting down their carvings, knottings or unfinished ships in bottles and turning out onto the lower deck to do DomDaniel's bidding.

DomDaniel eased off his throne, a little stiff from his doze in the chill drizzle, and blinked as a runnel of water from the top of his hat landed in his eye. Irritated, he kicked the sleeping Magog awake. The Thing oozed itself out from under the throne and followed DomDaniel along the deck, where the Necromancer stood, arms folded, a look of anticipation upon his face, waiting for those he had summoned.

Soon a heavy footfall could be heard below, and a few moments later half a dozen deckhands appeared and took up their positions as guard around DomDaniel. They were followed by the hesitant figure of the Apprentice. The boy looked white, and Jenna could see that his hands were trembling.

DomDaniel barely gave him a glance. His eyes were still fixed on the open hatch, waiting for his prize, the Princess, to appear.

But no one came.

Time seemed to slow down. The deckhands shifted about, unsure of what they were actually waiting for, and the Apprentice's nervous tic below his left eye started up. Every now and then he glanced up at his Master and quickly away again as if afraid DomDaniel may catch his eye. After what seemed an age DomDaniel demanded, "Well, where *is* she, boy?"

"Wh-who, sir?" stammered the Apprentice, although he knew perfectly well who the Necromancer meant.

"The *Queenling*, you beetlebrain. Who do you think I meant? Your idiot mother?"

"N-no, sir."

More footsteps were heard below.

"Ah," muttered DomDaniel. "At *last*."

But it was Marcia who was pushed out through the hatch by an accompanying Magog, who held her arm tightly in its long yellow claw. Marcia tried to shake it off, but the Thing was stuck to her like glue and had covered her with streaks of yellow slime. Marcia looked down at it in disgust, and she kept exactly the same expression on her face as she turned to meet DomDaniel's triumphant gaze. Even after a month locked away in the dark and with her Magykal powers drained from her, Marcia cut an impressive figure. Her dark hair, wild and unkempt, had an angry look to it; her salt-stained robes had a simple dignity and her purple python shoes were, as ever, spotless. Jenna could tell that she had unsettled DomDaniel.

"Ah, Miss Overstrand. So kind of you to drop by," he murmured.

Marcia did not reply.

"Well, Miss Overstrand, this is the reason I have been keeping you. I wanted you to see this little . . . *finale*. We have an interesting little bit of news for you, do we not, Septimus?" The Apprentice nodded uncertainly.

"My trusted Apprentice has been visiting some *friends* of yours, Miss Overstrand. In a *sweet* little cottage over there-abouts." DomDaniel waved his ring-encrusted hand toward the Marram Marshes.

Something in Marcia's expression changed.

"Ah, I see you know who I mean, Miss Overstrand. I rather *thought* you might. Now, my Apprentice here has reported a *successful* mission."

The Apprentice tried to say something but was waved quiet by his Master.

"Even *I* have not heard the full details. I am sure *you* would want to be the *first* to hear the good news. So now Septimus is going to tell us *all*. Aren't you, boy?"

The Apprentice stood up reluctantly. He looked very nervous. In a reedy voice, he started to speak hesitantly, "I . . . um . . ."

"Speak up, boy. No good if we can't hear a *word* you're saying, now *is* it?" DomDaniel told him.

"I . . . er, I have found the Princess. The Queenling."

There was an air of restlessness among the audience. Jenna got the impression that this news was not entirely welcome to the assembled deckhands, and she remembered Aunt Zelda telling her that DomDaniel would never win over the seafaring people.

"Go on, boy," prompted DomDaniel impatiently.

"I—the Hunter and me, we captured the cottage and, um, also the White Witch, Zelda Zanuba Heap, and the Wizard boy, Nickolas Benjamin Heap, *and* the Young Army deserter, Expendable Boy 412. And I *did* capture the Princess—the Queenling."

The Apprentice paused. A look of panic had appeared in

his eyes. What was he going to say? How was he going to explain away the lack of the Princess and the disappearance of the Hunter?

"You *did* capture the Queenling?" asked DomDaniel suspiciously.

"Yes, sir. I *did*. But . . ."

"But *what*?"

"But. Well, sir, after the Hunter was overpowered by the White Witch and left to become a buffoon—"

"A *buffoon*? Are you trying to be *funny* with me, *boy*? If you are, I would *not* advise it."

"No, sir. I am not trying to be funny at all, sir." The Apprentice had never felt less like being funny in his entire life. "After the Hunter left, sir, I managed to capture the Queenling single-handed, and I nearly got away but—"

"Nearly? You *nearly* got away?"

"Yes, sir. It was very close. I was attacked with a knife by the mad Wizard boy Nickolas Heap. He is very dangerous, sir. And the Queenling escaped."

"*Escaped?!*" roared DomDaniel, towering over the trembling Apprentice. "You come back and you call your mission a success? Some *success*. First you tell me that the wretched Hunter has become a *buffoon*, then you tell me that you were thwarted by a pathetic White Witch and some pesky runaway kids. And *now* you tell me that the Queenling has *escaped*. The whole point of the mission, *the whole point*, was to capture the upstart Queenling. So what part of it *exactly* do you call a *success*?"

"Well, we know where she is now," the Apprentice mumbled.

"We knew where she was *before*, boy. That was why you *went* there in the *first* place."

DomDaniel raised his eyes to heaven. What was wrong with his cabbagehead Apprentice? Surely the seventh son of a seventh son should have *some* Magyk about him by now? *Surely* he should have been strong enough to triumph over a ragtag group of hopeless Wizards holed up in the middle of nowhere? A feeling of rage bubbled up through DomDaniel.

"*Why?*" he screamed. "Why am I surrounded by fools?" Spitting with anger now, DomDaniel caught sight of Marcia's expression of contempt mixed with relief at the news she had just heard.

"Take the prisoner away!" he yelled. "Lock her up and throw away the key. She's *finished*."

"Not yet," Marcia replied quietly, deliberately turning her back on DomDaniel.

Suddenly, to Jenna's horror, Boy 412 stepped out from the shelter of the barrel and moved silently toward Marcia. Carefully, he slipped between the Thing and the deckhands who were pushing Marcia roughly back toward the hatch. The contemptuous expression in Marcia's eyes changed to astonishment, then rapidly to a studied blankness, and Boy 412 knew that she had seen him. Quickly, he took his dragon ring from his finger and pressed it into Marcia's hand. Marcia's green eyes met his as, unseen by the guards, she slipped the ring into her tunic pocket. Boy 412 did not linger. He turned away, and in his haste to get back to Jenna, he brushed against a deckhand.

"Halt!" shouted the man. "Who goes there?"

Everyone on the deck froze. Except for Boy 412, who darted away and grabbed hold of Jenna. It was time to go.

"Interlopers!" screamed DomDaniel. "I can see *shadows! Get them!!*"

In a panic the crew of the *Vengeance* looked around. They could see nothing. Had their Master finally gone mad? They had been expecting it long enough.

In the confusion, Jenna and Boy 412 made it back to the rope ladder and down to the canoes faster than they would have thought possible. Nicko had seen them coming. They were just in time—the Unseen was wearing off.

Above them the commotion on the ship raged as torches were lit and all possible hiding places were searched. Someone cut the rope ladder and, as the *Muriel Two* and the Hunter's canoe paddled away into the mist, it fell with a splash and sank into the dark waters of the rising tide.

✢ 42 ✢
THE STORM

*G*et them! I want them caught!"
DomDaniel's bellows of rage
echoed through the mist.

Jenna and Boy 412 paddled *Muriel
Two* as hard as they could toward the
Deppen Ditch, and Nicko, who would
not be parted from the Hunter's
canoe, followed them.

Another yell from DomDaniel
caught their attention: "Send the swimmers out. *Now!*"

There was a lull in the sounds emanating from the
Vengeance while the only two sailors on board who could
swim were pursued around the deck and caught. Two loud

splashes followed as they were thrown overboard to give chase.

The occupants of the canoes ignored the gasps coming from the water and pressed on toward the safety of the Marram Marshes. Far behind them the two swimmers, who had been knocked half unconscious by the huge drop, swam around in circles in a state of shock, realizing that what the old seafarers had told them was true: it was indeed unlucky for a sailor to know how to swim.

On the deck of the *Vengeance*, DomDaniel retreated to his throne. The deckhands had shrunk away after being made to throw two of their shipmates overboard, and DomDaniel had the deck to himself. A deep chill surrounded him as he sat on his throne and immersed himself in his Darke Magyk, chanting and wailing his way through a long and complicated Reverse Incantation.

DomDaniel was Summoning up the tides.

The incoming tide obeyed him. It gathered itself up from the sea and poured in, tumbling and churning past the Port, funneling itself up into the river, dragging with it dolphins and jellyfish, turtles and seals as they were all swept along with the irresistible current. The water rose. Higher and higher it climbed while the canoes struggled slowly across the surging river. As the canoes reached the mouth of the Deppen Ditch, it became even more difficult to control them in the tide race that was quickly filling up the Ditch.

"It's too rough," yelled Jenna over the rush of the water, fighting with her paddle against yet another eddy as *Muriel Two* pitched from side to side in the swirling waters. The flood tide carried the canoes along with it, taking them into the Ditch at breakneck speed, twisting and turning helplessly in the wild surge. As they were thrown along like so much flotsam and jetsam, Nicko could see that already the water was brimming to the top of the Ditch. He had never known anything like it before.

"Something's wrong," he yelled back at Jenna. "It shouldn't be like this!"

"It's him!" shouted Boy 412, waving his paddle in the direction of DomDaniel and immediately wishing he hadn't as *Muriel Two* lurched sickeningly to one side. "Listen!"

As the *Vengeance* had begun to rise high in the water and tug on her anchor chain, DomDaniel had changed his Commands and was shouting above the roar of the tide. "Blow! Blow! Blow!" he screamed. "Blow! Blow! Blow!"

The wind gathered and did what it was Commanded to do. It came in fast with a wild howl, throwing the surface of the water into waves and pitching the canoes violently from side to side. It blew away the mist and, perched high up in the water at the top of Deppen Ditch, Jenna, Nicko and Boy 412 could now see the *Vengeance* clearly.

The *Vengeance* could also see them.

On the prow of the ship DomDaniel took out his eyeglass and searched until he saw what he was looking for.

Canoes.

And as he studied the occupants his worst fears were realized. There was no mistaking the long dark hair and the golden circlet of the girl in the front of the strange green canoe. It was the *Queenling*. The Queenling had been on board his ship. She had been running around, under his very nose, and he had let her escape.

DomDaniel became strangely quiet as he gathered his energies and Summoned the most powerful Storm he could muster.

The Darke Magyk turned the howl of the wind into an ear-splitting shriek. Black storm clouds came sweeping in and piled high over the bleak expanse of the Marram Marshes. The late afternoon light grew dim, and dark cold waves began to break over the canoes.

"The water's coming in. I'm soaked," yelled Jenna as she

fought to keep control of *Muriel Two* while Boy 412 frantically bailed out the water. Nicko was having trouble in the
Hunter's canoe—a wave had just crashed over him and the
canoe was now awash. Another wave like that, thought
Nicko, and he'd be at the bottom of the Deppen Ditch.

And then suddenly there *was* no Deppen Ditch.

With a roar the banks of Deppen Ditch gave way. A massive wave surged through the breach and roared out across the
Marram Marshes, taking all with it: dolphins, turtles, jellyfish,
seals, swimmers . . . and two canoes.

The speed at which Nicko was traveling was faster than he
had ever dreamed possible. It was both terrifying and exciting
at once. But the Hunter's canoe rode the crest of the wave
lightly and easily, as though this was the moment it had been
waiting for.

Jenna and Boy 412 were not quite as thrilled as Nicko at
the turn of events. *Muriel Two* was a contrary old canoe, and
she did not take to this new way of traveling at all. They had
to fight hard to stop her from being rolled over by the massive
wave that was thundering across the marsh.

As the water spread across the marsh, the wave began to
lose some of its power, and Jenna and Boy 412 were able to
steer *Muriel Two* more easily. Nicko maneuvered the Hunter's

canoe along the wave toward them, deftly twisting and turning it as he went.

"That is the best thing ever!" he shouted above the rush of the water.

"You're crazy!" yelled Jenna, still struggling with her paddle to stop *Muriel Two* from tipping over.

The wave was fading fast now, slowing its pace and losing most of its power as the water that drove it sank into the wide expanse of the marshes, filling the ditches, the bogs, the slimes and the Ooze with clear, cold salt water and leaving an open sea behind it. Soon the wave was gone, and Jenna, Nicko and Boy 412 were adrift on an open sea that stretched into the distance as far as they could see, dotted with little islands here and there.

As they paddled the canoes in what they hoped was the right direction, a threatening darkness began to fall as the storm clouds gathered high above them. The temperature dropped sharply, and the air became charged with electricity. Soon a warning roll of thunder rumbled across the sky and large spots of heavy rain began to fall. Jenna looked out over the cold gray mass of water before them and wondered how they were going to find their way home.

In the distance on one of the farthest islands, Boy 412 saw

a flickering light. Aunt Zelda was lighting her storm candles and placing them in the windows.

The canoes picked up speed and headed home as the thunder rolled and sheets of silent lightning began to light up the sky.

Aunt Zelda's door was open. She was expecting them.

They tied the canoes to the boot scraper by the front door and walked into the strangely silent cottage. Aunt Zelda was in the kitchen with the Boggart.

"We're back!" yelled Jenna. Aunt Zelda came out of the kitchen, quietly closing the door behind her.

"Did you find him?" she asked.

"Find who?" said Jenna.

"The Apprentice boy. Septimus."

"Oh, *him*." So much had happened since they had set off that morning that Jenna had forgotten why they went in the first place.

"My goodness, you got back just in time. It's dark already," said Aunt Zelda, bustling over to close the door.

"Yes, it's—"

"Aargh!" screamed Aunt Zelda as she reached the door and saw the water lapping at the doorstep, not to mention two canoes bobbing up and down outside.

"We're flooded. The animals! They'll drown."

"They're all right," Jenna reassured her. "The chickens are all there on top of the chicken boat—we counted them. And the goat has climbed up onto the roof."

"The *roof?*"

"Yes, she was eating the thatch when we saw her."

"Oh. Oh, well."

"The ducks are fine and the rabbits . . . well, I think I saw them just kind of floating around."

"Floating around?" cried Aunt Zelda. "Rabbits don't float."

"*These* rabbits were. I passed quite a few, just lying on their backs. Like they were sunbathing."

"Sunbathing?" squeaked Aunt Zelda. "At night?"

"Aunt Zelda," said Jenna sternly, "forget the rabbits. There's a storm coming."

Aunt Zelda stopped fussing and surveyed the three damp figures in front of her.

"I'm sorry," she said. "What was I thinking about? Go and get dry by the fire."

While Jenna, Nicko and Boy 412 stood steaming by the fire, Aunt Zelda peered out into the night again. Then she quietly closed the cottage door.

"There's a Darkenesse out there," she whispered. "I should have noticed, but Boggart's been bad, very bad . . . and to think you've been out in it . . . on your own." Aunt Zelda shivered.

Jenna started to explain, "It's DomDaniel," she said. "He's—"

"He's what?"

"Horrible," Jenna said. "We saw him. On his ship."

"You *what?*" said Aunt Zelda, openmouthed, not daring to believe what she was hearing. "You saw *DomDaniel?* On the *Vengeance?* Where?"

"Near the Deppen Ditch. We just climbed up and—"

"Climbed up what?"

"The ladder. We got on the ship—"

"You—you've been on the *Vengeance?*" Aunt Zelda could hardly understand what she was hearing. Jenna noticed that her aunt had suddenly gone very pale, and her hands were trembling slightly.

"It's a bad ship," said Nicko. "Smells bad. Feels bad."

"*You* were on there too?"

"No," said Nicko, wishing now that he had been. "I would have gone, but my Unseen wasn't good enough, so I stayed behind. With the canoes."

It took Aunt Zelda a few seconds to take this all in. She looked at Boy 412.

"So you and Jenna have been on that Darke ship . . . on your own . . . in the middle of all that Darke Magyk. *Why?*"

"Oh, well, we met Alther—" Jenna tried to explain.

"*Alther?*"

"And he told us that Marcia—"

"*Marcia? What's Marcia* got to do with it?"

"She's been captured by DomDaniel," said Boy 412. "Alther said he thought she might be on the ship. And she was. We saw her."

"Oh, my. This just gets worse." Aunt Zelda collapsed into her chair by the fire. "That interfering old ghost should know better," snapped Aunt Zelda. "Sending three youngsters off to a Darke ship. What *was* he thinking of?"

"He didn't send us, really he didn't," said Boy 412. "He told us not to, but we had to *try* to rescue Marcia. But we couldn't though . . ."

"Marcia's captured," whispered Aunt Zelda. "This is bad." She stabbed at the fire with a poker, and a few flames shot into the air.

A long, loud rumble of thunder rolled across the sky right above the cottage, shaking it to its foundations. A wild gust of wind found its way through the windows, blowing out the storm candles and leaving only the flickering fire to light the room. A moment later a sudden downpour of hail clattered against the windows and fell down the chimney, putting out the fire with an angry hiss.

The cottage was plunged into darkness.

"The lanterns!" said Aunt Zelda, getting up and finding her way through the dark to the lantern cupboard.

Maxie whined and Bert hid her head under her one good wing.

"Bother, now where's the key?" muttered Aunt Zelda, scrabbling around in her pockets and finding nothing. "Bother, bother, bother."

Crack!

A bolt of lightning shot past the windows, illuminating the scene outside, and struck the water very close to the cottage.

"Missed," said Aunt Zelda grimly, "just."

Maxie yelped and burrowed under the rug.

Nicko was staring out the window. In the brief glare of the lightning he had seen something he had not wanted to see again.

"He's coming," he said quietly. "I saw the ship. In the

distance. Sailing over the marshes. He's coming *here*."

Everyone scrambled to the window. At first all they could see was the darkness of the approaching storm, but as they watched, staring into the night, a flicker of sheet lightning played across the clouds and showed them the sight that Nicko had glimpsed before.

Silhouetted against the lightning, still far away but with its sails flying in the howling wind, the huge Darke ship was cutting through the waves and heading toward the cottage.

The *Vengeance* was coming.

⊹ 43 ⊹
THE DRAGON BOAT

A unt Zelda was panicking.

"Where is the key? I can't find the *key*! Oh, here it is."
With shaking hands she drew the key out of one of her
patchwork pockets and opened the door to the lantern cupboard. She took out a lantern and gave it to Boy 412.

"You know where to go, don't you?" asked Aunt Zelda.
"The trapdoor in the potion cupboard?"

Boy 412 nodded.

"Go down into the tunnel. You'll be safe there. No one will find you. I'll make the trapdoor Disappear."

"But aren't *you* coming?" Jenna asked Aunt Zelda.

"No," she said quietly. "Boggart's very sick. I'm afraid he may not last if I move him. Don't worry about me. It's not *me* they want. Oh, look, take this, Jenna. You may as well have him with you." Aunt Zelda fished Jenna's Shield Bug out of yet another pocket and gave the rolled-up bug to her. Jenna tucked the bug into her jacket pocket.

"Now, go!"

Boy 412 hesitated, and another crack of lightning split the air.

"Go!" squeaked Aunt Zelda, waving her arms about like a demented windmill. "*Go!*"

Boy 412 opened the trapdoor in the potion cupboard and held the lantern high, his hand trembling a little, while Jenna scrambled down the ladder. Nicko hung back, wondering where Maxie had got to. He knew how much the wolfhound hated thunderstorms, and he wanted to take him with him.

"Maxie," he called out. "Maxie boy!" From underneath the rug a faint wolfhound whine came in reply.

Boy 412 was already halfway down the ladder.

"Come *on*," he told Nicko. Nicko was busy wrestling with

the recalcitrant wolfhound who refused to come out from what he considered to be the safest place in the world. Under the hearth rug.

"Hurry *up*," said Boy 412 impatiently, his head sticking back up through the trapdoor. What Nicko saw in that heap of smelly fur Boy 412 had no idea.

Nicko had grabbed hold of the spotted scarf that Maxie wore around his neck. He heaved the terrified dog out from under the rug and was dragging him across the floor. Maxie's claws made a hideous scraping noise on the stone flags and as Nicko shoved him into the dark potion cupboard he whined piteously. Maxie knew he must have been *very* bad to deserve this. He wondered what it was he had done. And why he hadn't enjoyed it more at the time.

In a flurry of fur and dribble, Maxie fell through the trapdoor and landed on Boy 412, knocking the lantern from his hand, putting it out and sending it rolling away down the steep incline.

"*Now* look what you've done," Boy 412 told the dog crossly as Nicko joined him at the bottom of the wooden ladder.

"What?" asked Nicko. "*What* have I done?"

"Not you. *Him*. Lost the lantern."

"Oh, we'll find it. Stop worrying. We're safe now." Nicko

hauled Maxie to his feet, and the wolfhound skittered down the sandy slope, his claws scrabbling on the rock underneath, dragging Nicko with him. They both slipped and slid down the steep slope, coming to rest in an unruly heap at the bottom of some steps.

"Ow!" said Nicko. "I think I've found the lantern."

"Good," said Boy 412 grumpily. He picked up the lantern, which sprang to life again and lit up the smooth marble walls of the tunnel.

"There're those pictures again," said Jenna. "Aren't they amazing?"

"How come everyone's been down here except for me?" complained Nicko. "No one asked if *I* might have liked to look at the pictures. Hey, there's a boat in this one, look."

"We know," said Boy 412 shortly. He put down the lantern and sat on the ground. He felt tired and wished Nicko would be quiet. But Nicko was excited by the tunnel.

"It's amazing down here," he said, staring at the hieroglyphs that ran along the wall as far as they could see in the flickering light of the lantern.

"I know," said Jenna. "Look, I really like this one. This circle thing with a dragon in it." She ran her hand over the small blue and gold image inscribed on the marble wall. Suddenly she felt the ground begin to shake. Boy 412 jumped to his feet.

"What's that?" he gulped.

A long, low rumble sent tremors up through their feet and reverberated through the air.

"It's moving!" gasped Jenna. "The tunnel wall is *moving*."

One side of the tunnel wall was parting, ponderously rolling back, leaving a wide-open space in front of them. Boy 412 held up the lantern. It flared into a brilliant white light and showed, to their astonishment, a vast subterranean Roman temple laid out before them. Beneath their feet was an intricate mosaic floor, and rising into the darkness were huge round marble columns. But that was not all.

"Oh."

"Wow."

"Phew." Nicko whistled. Maxie sat down and breathed respectful clouds of dog breath into the chill air.

In the middle of the temple, resting on the mosaic floor, lay the most beautiful boat anyone had ever seen.

The golden Dragon Boat of Hotep-Ra.

The huge green and gold head of the dragon reared up from the prow, its neck arched gracefully like a giant swan's. The body of the dragon was a broad open boat with a smooth hull of golden wood. Folded neatly back along the outside of the hull were the dragon's wings; great iridescent green folds shimmered as the multitude of green scales caught the light of the lantern. And at the stern of the Dragon Boat the green tail arched far up into the darkness of the temple, its golden barbed end almost hidden in the gloom.

"How did *that* get here?" breathed Nicko.

"Shipwrecked," said Boy 412.

Jenna and Nicko looked at Boy 412 in surprise. "How do *you* know?" they both asked.

"I read about it in *A Hundred Strange and Curious Tales for Bored Boys*. Aunt Zelda lent it to me. But I thought it was a legend. I never thought the Dragon Boat was *real*. Or that it was *here*."

"So what is it?" asked Jenna, entranced by the boat and getting the strangest feeling she had seen it somewhere before.

"It's the Dragon Boat of Hotep-Ra. Legend has it he was the Wizard who built Wizard Tower."

"He *did*," said Jenna. "Marcia told me."

"Oh. Well, there you are, then. The story said Hotep-Ra was a powerful Wizard in a Far Country and he had a dragon. But something happened and he had to leave quickly. So the dragon offered to become his boat, and she carried him safely to a new land."

"So that boat is—or was—a real dragon?" whispered Jenna, in case the boat could hear her.

"I suppose so," said Boy 412.

"Half boat, half dragon," muttered Nicko. "Weird. But why is she *here*?"

"She was wrecked off some rocks by the Port lighthouse," said Boy 412. "Hotep-Ra towed her into the marshes and had her pulled out of the water into a Roman temple that he found on a sacred island. He started rebuilding her, but he couldn't find any skilled craftsmen at the Port. It was a really rough place in those days."

"Still is," grunted Nicko, "and they're still no good at building boats either. If you want a proper boatbuilder you come upriver to the Castle. Everyone knows that."

"Well, that was what they told Hotep-Ra too," said Boy 412. "But when this oddly dressed man turned up at the Castle claiming to be a Wizard, they all laughed at him and refused to believe his stories about his amazing Dragon Boat. Until one day the Queen's daughter fell ill, and he saved her life. The Queen was so grateful that she helped him build the Wizard Tower. One summer he took her and her daughter out to the Marram Marshes to see the Dragon Boat. And they fell in love with it. After that Hotep-Ra had as many boatbuilders working on it as he wanted, and because the Queen loved the boat, and she liked Hotep-Ra too, she used to bring her daughter out every summer just to see how they were getting on. The story says the Queen still does that. Oh, er . . . well, not any more, of course."

There was a silence.

"Sorry. I didn't think," muttered Boy 412.

"Doesn't matter," said Jenna a little too brightly.

Nicko went over to the boat and expertly ran his hand over the gleaming golden wood of the hull.

"Nice repair," he said. "Someone knew what they were doing. Shame no one has sailed her since though. She's so beautiful."

He began to climb an old wooden ladder that was propped up against the hull.

"Well, don't just stand there, you two. Come and have a look!"

The inside of the boat was like no other boat anyone had ever seen. It was painted a deep lapis lazuli blue with hundreds of hieroglyphs running along the deck inscribed in gold.

"That old chest in Marcia's room at the Tower," said Boy 412 as he wandered along the deck, trailing his fingers along the polished wood, "it had the same kind of writing on it."

"Did it?" said Jenna doubtfully. As far as she remembered, Boy 412 had his eyes closed most of the time he was in the Wizard Tower.

"I saw it when the Assassin came in. I can still see it now in my head," said Boy 412, who was often troubled with a photographic memory of the most unfortunate of times.

They wandered along the deck of the Dragon Boat, past coiled green ropes, golden cleats and shackles, silver blocks and halyards and endless hieroglyphs. They passed by a small cabin with its deep blue doors firmly closed and carrying the same dragon symbol enclosed in a flattened oval shape that they had seen on the door in the tunnel, but none of them felt quite brave enough to open the doors and see what was below. They tiptoed past and, at last, reached the stern of the boat.

The tail of the dragon.

The massive tail arched high above them, disappearing into the gloom and making them all feel very small and a little vulnerable. All the Dragon Boat had to do was swish its tail down at them, and that, thought Boy 412 with a shiver, would be that.

Maxie had become very subdued and was walking obediently behind Nicko, his tail between his legs. He still had the feeling he had done something very wrong, and being on the Dragon Boat had not made him feel any better.

Nicko was at the stern of the boat, casting an expert eye over the tiller. It met with his approval. It was an elegant, smoothly curved piece of mahogany, carved so expertly that it fit into the hand as if it had known you forever.

Nicko decided to show Boy 412 how to steer.

"Look, you hold it like this," he said, taking hold of the tiller, "and then you push it to the right if you want the boat to go left, and you pull it to the left if you want the boat to go right. Easy."

"Doesn't sound very easy," said Boy 412 doubtfully. "Sounds back to front to me."

"See, like this." Nicko pushed the tiller to the right. It moved smoothly, turning the huge rudder at the stern in the opposite direction.

Boy 412 looked over the side of the boat.

"Oh, *that's* what it does," he said. "I see now."

"You try," said Nicko. "It makes more sense when you're holding it yourself." Boy 412 took the tiller in his right hand and stood beside it as Nicko had shown him.

The dragon's tail twitched.

Boy 412 jumped. "*What was that?*"

"Nothing," said Nicko. "Look, just push it away from you, like this . . ."

While Nicko was doing what he liked to do best, telling someone about how boats worked, Jenna had wandered up to the prow to look at the handsome golden dragon head. She gazed at it and found herself wondering why its eyes were closed. If she had a wonderful boat like this, thought Jenna, she would give the dragon two huge emeralds for eyes. It was no more than the dragon deserved. And then, on impulse, she wrapped her arms around the dragon's smooth green neck and laid her head against it. The neck felt smooth and surprisingly warm.

A shiver of recognition ran through the dragon at Jenna's touch. Distant memories came flooding back to the Dragon Boat . . .

Long days of convalescence after her terrible accident. Hotep-Ra bringing the beautiful young Queen from the Castle to visit her on MidSummer Day. Days turning into months dragging into years as the Dragon Boat lies on the floor of the temple and is slowly, so slowly, put back together by Hotep-Ra's boatbuilders. And each MidSummer Day the Queen, now accompanied by her baby daughter, visited the Dragon Boat. The years wearing on and still the boatbuilders have not finished. Endless lonely months when the builders disappear and leave her alone. And then Hotep-Ra becoming older and more frail, and when at last she is restored to her former glory, Hotep-Ra is too ill to see her. He orders the temple to be covered over with a huge mound of earth to protect her until the day she will again be needed, and she is plunged into darkness.

But the Queen does not forget what Hotep-Ra has told her—that she must visit the Dragon Boat each MidSummer Day. Every summer she comes to the island. She orders a simple cottage to be built for her ladies and herself to stay in, and every MidSummer Day she lights a lantern, takes it down into the temple and visits the boat she has come to love. As the years go by, each successive Queen pays a midsummer visit to the Dragon Boat, no longer knowing why, but doing it because her own mother did so before her, and because each new Queen grows to love the dragon too. The dragon loves each Queen in return, and although each one is different in her own way, they all possess the same distinctive, gentle touch, as does this one.

And so the centuries pass. The Queen's midsummer visit becomes a secret tradition, watched over by a succession of White Witches who live in the cottage, keeping the secret of the Dragon Boat and lighting the lanterns to help the dragon through her days. The dragon dozes the centuries away, buried under the island, hoping one day to be released and waiting for each magical MidSummer Day *when the Queen herself brings a lantern and pays her respects.*

Until one MidSummer Day ten years ago when the Queen did not come. The dragon was tormented with worry, but there was nothing to be done. Aunt Zelda kept the cottage ready for the advent of the Queen, should she ever arrive, and the dragon had waited, her spirits kept up by Aunt Zelda's daily visit with yet another freshly lit lantern. But what the dragon was really waiting for was the moment when the Queen would again throw her arms around her neck.

As she had just done.

The dragon opened her eyes in surprise. Jenna gasped. She must be dreaming, she thought. The dragon's eyes were indeed green, just as she had imagined, but they were not emeralds. They were living, seeing dragon eyes. Jenna let go of the dragon's neck and stepped back, and the dragon eyes followed her movement, taking a long look at the new Queen. It is a young one, thought the dragon, but none the worse for that. She bowed her head respectfully.

From the stern of the boat, Boy 412 saw the dragon bow her head, and he *knew* he was not imagining things. Neither was he imagining something else. The sound of running water.

"Look!" yelled Nicko.

A narrow dark gap had appeared in the wall between the two marble pillars holding up the roof. A small trickle of water had begun to pour ominously through the opening as if a sluice gate had been nudged open. As they watched, the trickle soon became a stream, with the gap opening wider and wider. Soon the mosaic floor of the temple was awash with water, and the stream pouring in had become a torrent.

With a thunderous roar, the earth bank outside gave way, and the wall between the two pillars collapsed. A river of mud and water swept into the cavern, churning around the Dragon Boat, lifting and rocking her from side to side, until suddenly she was floating free.

"She's afloat!" yelled Nicko excitedly.

Jenna stared down from the prow at the muddy water swirling below them and watched as the small wooden ladder was caught up in the flood and swept away. Far above her, Jenna became aware of some movement: slowly and painfully, with a neck stiff from all the years of waiting, the dragon was turning her head to see who, at last, was at the helm. She rested her deep-green eyes on her new Master, a surprisingly small figure in a red hat. He did not look anything like her last Master, Hotep-Ra, a tall dark man whose gold and platinum belt would flash in the sunlight glancing off the waves and whose purple cloak would fly wildly in the wind as they sped together over the ocean. But the dragon recognized the most important thing of all: the hand that once again held the tiller was Magykal.

It was time to go to sea once more.

The dragon reared her head, and the two massive leathery wings, which had been folded along the sides of the boat, began to loosen. Before her, for the first time in many hundreds of years, she could see open water.

Maxie growled, the hair on his neck standing up on end.

The boat began to move.

"What are you *doing*?" Jenna yelled at Boy 412.

Boy 412 shook his head. *He* wasn't doing anything. It was the *boat*.

"Let go!" Jenna yelled at him above the noise of the storm outside. "Let go of the tiller. It's *you* making this happen. *Let go!*"

But Boy 412 would not let go. Something kept his hand firmly on the tiller, guiding the Dragon Boat as she began to move between the two marble pillars, taking with her her new crew: Jenna, Nicko, Boy 412 and Maxie.

As the dragon's barbed tail cleared the confines of the temple, a loud creaking began on either side of the boat. The dragon was lifting her wings, unfurling and spreading each one like an enormous webbed hand stretching its long bony fingers, cracking and groaning as the leathery skin was pulled taut. The crew of the Dragon Boat stared into the night sky, amazed at the sight of the huge wings towering above the boat like two giant green sails.

The dragon's head reared up into the night, and her nostrils flared, breathing in the smell she had dreamed of all those years. The smell of the sea.

At last the dragon was free.

⊹⊦ 44 ⊦⊹
TO SEA

S teer *her into the waves!"* yelled Nicko as a wave caught the
side of the boat and crashed over them, soaking them
with freezing-cold water. But Boy 412 was struggling hard to
shift the tiller against the wind and the force of the water. The
gale screaming in his ears and the driving rain in his face did
not help either. Nicko threw himself at the tiller, and together
they put all their weight against it, pushing the tiller away from
them. The dragon set her wings to catch the wind, and the
boat slowly came around to face the oncoming waves.

Up at the prow, Jenna, soaked with the rain, was clinging to
the dragon's neck. The boat pitched up and down as it rode

through the waves, flinging her helplessly from side to side.

The dragon reared her head, breathing in the storm and lov-ing every minute of it. It was the start of a voyage, and a storm at the beginning of a voyage was always a good omen. But where did her new Master wish her to take him? The dragon turned her long green neck and looked back at this new Master at the helm, struggling with his shipmate, red hat sodden with the rain, rivulets of water teeming down his face.

Where do you wish me to go? asked the dragon's green eyes.

Boy 412 understood the look.

"Marcia?" he yelled at the top of his voice to Jenna and Nicko.

They nodded. *This* time they were going to do it.

"Marcia!" Boy 412 shouted at the dragon.

The dragon blinked uncomprehendingly. Where was Marcia? She had not heard of that country. Was it far away? The Queen would know.

Suddenly the dragon dipped her head and scooped Jenna up in the playful way she had done with so many Princesses over the centuries. But in the howling wind the effect was more ter-rifying than playful. Jenna found herself flying through the air above the surging waves, and a moment later, soaked by the sea spray, she was perched on top of the dragon's golden head, sitting just behind her ears and hanging on to them as though her life depended on it.

Where is Marcia, my lady? Is it a long voyage? Jenna heard the dragon ask hopefully, already looking forward to many happy months sailing the oceans with her new crew in search of the land of Marcia.

Jenna risked letting go of a surprisingly soft golden ear and pointed to the *Vengeance* which was coming up fast.

"Marcia's there. She's our ExtraOrdinary Wizard. And she's a prisoner on that ship. We want her back."

The dragon's voice came to her again, a little disappointed not to be traveling any farther. *Whatever you wish, my lady, it shall be done.*

Deep in the hold of the *Vengeance*, Marcia Overstrand sat listening to the Storm raging above her. On the little finger of her right hand, which was the only one on which it would fit, she wore the ring Boy 412 had given her. Marcia sat in the dark hold, turning over in her mind all the possible ways Boy 412 could have found the long-lost Dragon Ring of Hotep-Ra. None of them made much sense to her. However he had found it, the ring had done for Marcia the wonderful thing it used to do for Hotep-Ra. It had taken away her seasickness. It was also, Marcia knew, slowly restoring her Magykal strength. Little by little she could feel the Magyk returning, and as it did so, the Shadows that had haunted her and followed her from Dungeon Number One began to slink away. The effect of DomDaniel's terrible Vortex was disappearing. Marcia risked a small smile. It was the first time she had smiled for four long weeks.

Beside Marcia, her three seasick guards lay slumped in pathetically groaning heaps, wishing that they too had learned to swim. At least they would have been thrown overboard by now.

Far above Marcia, in the full force of the Storm he had created, DomDaniel was sitting bolt upright on his ebony throne, while his miserable Apprentice shivered beside him. The boy was meant to be helping his Master to prepare his final lightning Strike, but he was so seasick that all he could do was stare glassily ahead and give the occasional moan.

"Quiet, boy!" snapped DomDaniel, trying to concentrate on gathering the electrical forces together for the most powerful Strike he had ever done. Soon, thought DomDaniel triumphantly, not only would that interfering witch's nasty little cottage be gone but the whole island too, evaporated in a blinding flash. DomDaniel fingered the ExtraOrdinary Wizard Amulet, which was now back in its rightful place. It was back around *his* neck, not the scrawny neck of some half-baked stick insect woman Wizard.

DomDaniel laughed. It was all so *easy*.

"Ship ahoy, sire," a faint voice called down from the crow's nest. "Ship ahoy!"

DomDaniel cursed.

"*Don't interrupt!*" he shrieked above the howl of the wind and Caused the sailor to fall with a scream into the seething waters below.

But DomDaniel's concentration had been broken. And, as he tried to regain control of the elements for the final Strike, something caught his eye.

A small golden glow was coming out of the dark toward his ship. DomDaniel fumbled for his eyeglass and, raising it to his eye, could hardly believe what he saw.

It was impossible, he told himself, absolutely impossible. The Dragon Boat of Hotep-Ra did not exist. It was nothing more than a legend. DomDaniel blinked the rain out of his eyes and looked again. The wretched boat was heading straight for him. The green glint of the dragon's eyes shot through the dark and met his one-eyed gaze through the eyeglass. A cold shiver ran through the Necromancer. This, he decided, was the doing of Marcia Overstrand. A Projection of her fevered brain as she schemed against him, deep within his own ship. Had she learned *nothing*?

DomDaniel turned to his Magogs.

"Dispatch the prisoner," he snapped. "Now!"

The Magogs flicked their dirty yellow claws open and closed, and a thin sheen of slime appeared over their blind-worm heads, as it always did in moments of excitement. They hissed a question to their Master.

"Anyway you like," he replied. "I don't care. Do whatever you want, but just *do it. Fast!*"

The ghastly pair slithered off, dripping slime as they went, and disappeared belowdecks. They were pleased to get out of the storm, excited by the fun they had in store.

DomDaniel put away his eyeglass. He no longer needed it, for the Dragon Boat was quite near enough for him to easily see. He tapped his foot impatiently, waiting for what he took to be Marcia's Projection to disappear. However, to DomDaniel's dismay, it did not disappear. The Dragon Boat drew ever closer and appeared to be fixing him with a particularly nasty stare.

Edgily, the Necromancer started pacing the deck, oblivious to the squall of rain that suddenly poured down on him, and deaf to the noisy flapping of the last few remaining shreds of the sails. There was only one sound that DomDaniel wanted to hear, and that was the sound of Marcia Overstrand's last scream far below in the hold.

He listened intently. If there was one thing DomDaniel enjoyed, it was hearing the last scream of a human being. Any human being was good, but the last scream of the ex–ExtraOrdinary Wizard was particularly good. He rubbed his hands together, closed his eyes and waited.

Down in the depths of the *Vengeance* the Dragon Ring of Hotep-Ra was glowing brightly on Marcia's little finger, and her Magyk had returned enough for her to slip out of her chains. She had stolen away from her comatose guards and was climbing up the ladder out of the hold. As she stepped from the ladder and was about to make her way to the next one, she almost slipped on some yellow slime. Out of the gloom came the Magogs, straight for her, hissing with delight. They edged her into a corner, all the while clattering their excited pointy rows of yellow teeth at her. With a loud snap, they unsheathed their claws and advanced upon Marcia with glee, their little snake's tongues flicking in and out of their mouths.

Now, thought Marcia, was the time to discover if her Magyk really was returning.

"Congeal and Dry. Solidify!" Marcia muttered, pointing the finger bearing the Dragon Ring at the Magogs.

Like two slugs covered with salt, the Magogs suddenly

collapsed and shrank with a hiss. A very nasty crackling sound followed as their slime solidified and dried to a thick yellow crust. In a few moments all that was left of the Things were two withered black and yellow lumps lying at Marcia's feet, stuck fast to the deck. She stepped over them disdainfully, careful of her shoes, and continued her journey up to the top deck.

Marcia wanted her Amulet back, and she was going to get it.

Up on deck DomDaniel had lost patience with his Magogs. He cursed himself for thinking they would get rid of Marcia quickly. He should have realized. Magogs liked to take their time with their victims, and time was something DomDaniel did not have. He had Marcia's wretched Projection of the Dragon Boat looming toward him, and it was affecting his Magyk.

And so, as Marcia was about to climb the ladder that led up onto the deck, she heard a loud bellow from above, "A hundred crowns!" bawled DomDaniel. "No, a *thousand* crowns. A thousand crowns to the man who rids me of Marcia Overstrand! *Now!*"

Above her Marcia heard the sudden stampede of bare feet as all the sailors on deck made for the hatchway and ladder on which she was standing. Marcia leaped off and hid as best she could in the shadows, as the entire ship's crew pushed and fought their way down in an effort to be the first to reach the prisoner and claim the prize. From the shadows she watched them go, kicking, fighting and shoving one another out of the way. Then, as the melee disappeared down to the lower decks, she gathered her damp robes around her and climbed the ladder onto the open deck.

The cold wind took her breath away, but after the foul mugginess of the ship's hold, the fresh stormy air smelled wonderful. Quickly, Marcia hid behind a barrel and waited, considering her next move.

Marcia watched DomDaniel closely. He looked, she was pleased to see, sick. His normally gray features now had a bright green tinge to them, and his bulgy black eyes were staring up at something behind her. Marcia swung around to see what could possibly be turning DomDaniel so green.

It was the Dragon Boat of Hotep-Ra.

High above the *Vengeance*, with her green eyes flashing and lighting up DomDaniel's pallid face, the Dragon Boat was flying through the howling wind and the pouring rain. Her huge wings beat slowly and powerfully against the storm, lifting the golden boat and her three petrified crew into the night air, flying them toward Marcia Overstrand, who could not believe what she was seeing.

No one on the Dragon Boat could believe it either. When the Dragon had started to beat her wings against the wind and slowly lift herself out of the water, Nicko had been horrified; if there was one thing Nicko was sure about, it was that boats did not fly. Ever.

"Stoppit!" Nicko yelled in Boy 412's ear above the creaking of the huge wings, which swept slowly past them, sending leathery gusts of air into their faces. But Boy 412 was excited. He hung on tightly to the tiller, trusting the Dragon Boat to do what she did best.

"Stop what?" Boy 412 yelled back, gazing up at the wings, his eyes glowing and a broad grin on his face.

"It's you!" yelled Nicko. "I know it is. *You're* making her fly. *Stop*. Stop it now! She's out of control!"

Boy 412 shook his head. It was nothing to do with *him*. It was the Dragon Boat. *She* had decided to fly.

Jenna was holding on to the dragon's ears with a grip so tight her fingers were white. Far below she could see the waves crashing against the *Vengeance*, and as the Dragon Boat dipped toward the deck of the Darke ship, Jenna could also see the ghastly green face of DomDaniel staring up at her. Jenna quickly looked away from the Necromancer—his malevolent gaze made her feel chilled to the core and gave her a horrible feeling of despair. She shook her head to get rid of the Darke feeling, but a doubt stayed in her mind. How *were* they going to find Marcia? She glanced back at Boy 412. He had let go of the tiller and was looking over the side of the Dragon Boat, down toward the *Vengeance*. Then, as the Dragon Boat dipped and her shadow fell across the Necromancer below, Jenna suddenly knew what Boy 412 was doing. He was getting ready to jump ship. Boy 412 was steeling himself to go aboard the *Vengeance* and get Marcia.

"Don't!" Jenna yelled. "Don't jump! I can see Marcia!"

Marcia had stood up. She was still staring at the Dragon Boat in disbelief. Surely it was just a legend? But, as the dragon swooped down toward Marcia, her dragon eyes flashing a brilliant green and her nostrils sending out great jets of orange fire, Marcia could feel the heat of the flames and she knew that this was real.

The flames licked around DomDaniel's sodden robes and sent a pungent smell of burned wool into the air. Singed by the fire, DomDaniel fell back, and for a brief moment a faint ray of hope crossed the Necromancer's mind—maybe this was all a terrible nightmare. Because on the top of the dragon's head he could see something that was surely impossible: sitting there was the *Queenling*.

Jenna dared to let go of one of the dragon's ears and slipped her hand into her jacket pocket. DomDaniel was still staring at her, and she wanted him to stop—in fact, she was going to *make* him stop. Jenna's hand was shaking as she drew the Shield Bug out of her pocket and raised it up in the air. Suddenly, out of her hand flew what DomDaniel took to be a large green wasp. DomDaniel hated wasps. He staggered back as the insect flew toward him with a high-pitched shriek and landed on his shoulder, where it stung him on the neck. Hard.

DomDaniel screamed, and the Shield Bug stabbed at him again. He clapped his hand over the bug and, confused, it curled itself up into a ball and bounced down onto the deck, rolling off into a dark corner. DomDaniel collapsed onto the deck.

Marcia saw her chance and took it. In the light of the fire coming out of the dragon's flared nostrils, Marcia steeled herself to touch the prostrate Necromancer. With trembling fingers she searched through the folds of his sluglike neck and found what she was looking for. Alther's shoelace. Feeling extremely sick but even more determined, Marcia pulled at an end of the shoelace, hoping the knot would untie. It didn't. DomDaniel made a choking sound, and his hands flew up to his neck.

"You're strangling me," he gasped, and he too grabbed hold of the shoelace.

Alther's shoelace had done good service over the years, but it was not up to the task of resisting two powerful Wizards fighting over it. So it did what shoelaces often do. It broke.

The Amulet dropped to the deck, and Marcia swept it up in her grasp. DomDaniel lunged desperately after it, but Marcia was already retying the shoelace around her neck. As the knot was tied, the ExtraOrdinary Wizard belt Appeared around her waist, her robes glistened in the rain with Magyk, and Marcia stood up straight. She surveyed the scene with a triumphant smile—she had reclaimed her rightful place in the world. She was, once again, the ExtraOrdinary Wizard.

Enraged, DomDaniel staggered to his feet, screaming, "Guards, guards!" There was no response. The entire crew was deep in the bowels of the ship on a wild goose chase.

As Marcia prepared a Thunderflash to hurl at the increasingly hysterical DomDaniel, a familiar voice above her said, "Come on, Marcia. Hurry up. Get on here with me."

The dragon dipped her head down onto the deck, and, for once, Marcia did as she was told.

✢ 45 ✢
EBB TIDE

The *Dragon Boat flew slowly* over the flooded marshes, leaving the powerless *Vengeance* behind. As the storm died away the dragon dipped her wings and, a little out of practice, landed back on the water with a bump and a massive splash.

Jenna and Marcia, who were clinging tightly to the dragon's neck, were soaked.

Boy 412 and Nicko were knocked off their feet by the landing and sent sprawling across the deck, where they ended up in a tangled heap. They picked themselves up and Maxie shook himself dry. Nicko breathed a sigh of relief. There was no doubt in his mind—boats were not meant to fly.

Soon the clouds drifted away out to sea, and the moon appeared to light their way back home. The Dragon Boat glimmered green and gold in the moonlight, her wings held up to catch the wind as she sailed them home. From a small lighted window far across the water Aunt Zelda watched the scene, a little disheveled from dancing triumphantly around the kitchen and colliding with a pile of saucepans.

The Dragon Boat was reluctant to return to the temple. After her taste of freedom she dreaded the thought of being shut away underground again. She longed to turn around and head out to sea while she still could and sail away across the world with the young Queen, her new Master and the ExtraOrdinary Wizard. But her new Master had other ideas. He was taking her back again, back to her dry, dark prison. The dragon sighed and hung her head. Jenna and Marcia nearly fell off.

"What's going on up there?" asked Boy 412.

"She's sad," said Jenna.

"But you're free now, Marcia," said Boy 412.

"Not *Marcia*. The dragon," Jenna told him.

"How do you know?" asked Boy 412.

"Because I do. She talks to me. In my head."

"Oh, yes?" Nicko laughed.

"'Oh, yes' to you too. She's sad because she wants to go to sea. She doesn't want to go back into the temple. Back to prison, she calls it."

Marcia knew how the dragon felt.

"Tell her, Jenna," said Marcia, "that she will go to sea again. But not tonight. Tonight we'd all like to go home."

The Dragon Boat raised her head high, and this time Marcia *did* fall off. She slipped down the dragon's neck and landed with a bump on the deck. But Marcia didn't care; she didn't even complain. She just sat gazing up at the stars while the Dragon Boat sailed serenely across the Marram Marshes.

Nicko, who was keeping a lookout, was surprised to see a small and oddly familiar fishing boat in the distance. It was the chicken boat, floating out with the tide. He pointed it out to Boy 412. "Look, I've seen that boat before. Must be someone from the Castle fishing down here."

Boy 412 grinned. "They chose the wrong night to come out, didn't they?"

By the time they reached the island, the tide was rapidly ebbing and the water covering the marsh was becoming shallow.

Nicko took the tiller and guided the Dragon Boat into the course of the submerged Mott, passing the Roman temple as he did so. It was a striking sight. The marble of the temple glowed a luminous white as the moon shone upon it for the first time since Hotep-Ra had buried the Dragon Boat inside. All the earth banks and the wooden roof that he had built had been washed away, leaving the tall pillars standing clear in the brilliant moonlight.

Marcia was astounded.

"I had *no* idea this was here," she said. "No idea at *all*. You'd have thought *one* of the books in the Pyramid Library might have mentioned it. And as for the Dragon Boat . . . well, I always thought that was just a legend."

"Aunt Zelda knew," said Jenna.

"*Aunt Zelda?*" asked Marcia. "Why didn't she say so?"

"It's her job *not* to say. She's the Keeper of the island. The Queens, um, my mother, and my grandmother and great-grandmother and all the ones before them, they had to visit the dragon."

"*Did* they?" asked Marcia, amazed, "Why?"

"I don't know," said Jenna.

"Well, they never told *me*, or Alther come to that."

"Or DomDaniel," Jenna pointed out.

"No," said Marcia thoughtfully. "Maybe there are some things it is better for a Wizard not to know."

They tied the Dragon Boat up to the landing stage, and she settled down into the Mott like a giant swan easing herself onto her nest, slowly lowering her huge wings and folding them neatly along the side of her hull. She dipped her head to allow Jenna to slip down onto the deck, then the dragon gazed around her. It may not be the ocean, she thought, but the wide expanse of the Marram Marshes with its long, low horizon stretching as far as the eye could see was the next best thing. The dragon closed her eyes. The Queen had returned, and she could smell the sea. She was content.

Jenna sat and dangled her legs over the edge of the sleeping Dragon Boat, surveying the scene before her. The cottage looked as peaceful as ever, although maybe it was not quite as neat as when they had left it, due to the fact that the goat had munched its way through much of the roof and was still going strong. Most of the island was now out of the water, although it was covered with a mixture of mud and seaweed. Aunt Zelda, thought Jenna, would not be happy about the state of her garden.

When the water had ebbed from the landing stage, Marcia and the crew climbed out of the Dragon Boat and made their way up to the cottage, which was suspiciously quiet and the front door was slightly open. With a sense of foreboding, they peered inside.

Brownies.

Everywhere. The door to the Disenchanted cat tunnel was open and the place was crawling with Brownies. Up the walls, over the floor, stuck on the ceiling, packed tight into the potion cupboard, munching, chewing, tearing, pooing as they went through the cottage like a storm of locusts. At the sight of the humans, ten thousand Brownies started up their high-pitched squeals.

Aunt Zelda was out of the kitchen in a flash.

"*What?*" she gasped, trying to take it all in but seeing only an unusually disheveled Marcia standing in the middle of a heaving sea of Brownies. Why, thought Aunt Zelda, does Marcia always have to make things so *difficult?* Why on *earth* had she brought a load of Brownies back with her?

"Blasted Brownies!" bellowed Aunt Zelda, waving her arms about in an ineffectual way. "Out, out, *get out!*"

"Allow me, Zelda," Marcia shouted. "I'll do a quick Remove for you."

"*No!*" yelled Aunt Zelda. "I must do this myself, otherwise they will lose respect for me."

"Well, I wouldn't exactly call this respect," muttered Marcia, lifting her ruined shoes out of the sticky slime and inspecting the soles. She definitely had a hole in them somewhere. She could feel the slime seeping in between her toes.

Suddenly the shrieking stopped, and thousands of little red eyes all stared in terror at the thing a Brownie feared the most. A Boggart.

The Boggart.

With his fur clean and brushed, looking thin and small with the white sash of his bandage still tied around his middle, there was not quite as much Boggart as there had been. But he still had Boggart Breath. And, breathing Boggart Breath as he went, he waded through the Brownies, feeling his strength returning.

The Brownies saw him coming, and desperate to escape, they stupidly piled themselves up in the farthest corner away from the Boggart, higher and higher until every Quake Ooze Brownie but one, a young one out for the first time, was on the teetering pile in the far corner by the desk. Suddenly the young Brownie shot out from underneath the hearth rug. Its anxious red eyes shone from its pointy face and its bony fingers and toes clattered on the stone floor as, watched by everyone, it scuttled down the length of the room to join the pile.

It threw itself onto the slimy heap and joined the throng of little red eyes staring at the Boggart.

"Dunno why they don't just *leave*. Blasted Brownies," said the Boggart. "Still, there's bin a terrible storm. Don't suppose they wanter go out of a nice warm cottage. You seen that big ship out there stuck on the marshes sinkin' down into the mud? They're lucky all them Brownies is in 'ere an' not out there, busy draggin' 'em down inter the Ooze."

Everyone exchanged glances.

"Yes, aren't they just?" said Aunt Zelda who knew exactly which ship the Boggart was talking about, having been too engrossed watching everything from the kitchen window with the Boggart to have noticed the invasion of the Brownies.

"Yeah. Well, I'll be off now," said the Boggart. "Can't stand bein' so clean anymore. Just want ter find a nice bit a mud."

"Well, there's no shortage of that outside, Boggart," said Aunt Zelda.

"Yeah," said the Boggart. "Er, just wanter say thank you, Zelda, fer . . . well, fer lookin' after me, like. Ta. Them Brownies'll leave when I've gone. If you get any more trouble, just yell."

The Boggart waddled out of the door to spend a few happy

hours choosing a patch of mud to spend the rest of the night in. He was spoiled for choice.

As soon as he left, the Brownies became restless, their little red eyes exchanging glances and looking at the open door. When they were quite sure that the Boggart was really gone, a cacophony of excited shrieks started up and the pile suddenly collapsed in a spray of brown goo. Free of Boggart Breath at last, the Brownie pack headed for the door. It rushed down the island, streamed over the Mott bridge and headed out across the Marram Marshes. Straight for the stranded *Vengeance*.

"You know," said Aunt Zelda as she watched the Brownies disappear into the shadows of the marsh, "I almost feel sorry for them."

"What, the Brownies or the *Vengeance?*" asked Jenna.

"Both," said Aunt Zelda.

"Well, I don't," said Nicko. "They deserve each other."

Even so, no one wanted to watch what happened to the *Vengeance* that night. And no one wanted to talk about it either.

Later, after they had cleared as much brown goo out of the cottage as they could, Aunt Zelda surveyed the damage, determined to look on the bright side.

"It's really not so bad," she said. "The books are fine—well, at least they will be when they've all dried out and I can redo the potions. Most of them were coming up to their drink-by date anyway. And the really important ones are in the Safe. The Brownies didn't eat *all* the chairs like last time, and they didn't even poo on the table. So, all in all, it could have been worse. Much worse."

Marcia sat down and took off her wrecked purple python shoes. She put them by the fire to dry while she considered whether to do a Shoe Renew or not. Strictly speaking, Marcia knew she shouldn't. Magyk was not meant to be used for her own comfort. It was one thing to sort out her cloak, which was part of the tools of her trade, but she could hardly pretend that the pointy pythons were necessary for the performance of Magyk. So they sat steaming by the fire, giving off a faint but disagreeable smell of moldy snake.

"You can have my spare pair of galoshes," Aunt Zelda offered. "Much more practical for around here."

"Thank you, Zelda," said Marcia dismally. She hated galoshes.

"Oh, cheer up, Marcia," said Aunt Zelda irritatingly. "Worse things happen at sea."

⊹⊹ 46 ⊹⊹
A VISITOR

The next morning all that Jenna could see of the *Vengeance* was the top of the tallest mast sticking out of the marsh like a lone flagpole, from which fluttered the remnants of the tops'l. The remains of the *Vengeance* was not something Jenna wanted to look at, but like everyone in the cottage who woke up after her, she had to see with her own eyes what had happened to the Darke ship. Jenna closed the shutter and turned away. There was another boat that she would much rather see.

The Dragon Boat.

Jenna stepped out of the cottage into the early morning

spring sunshine. The Dragon Boat lay majestically in the Mott, floating high in the water, her neck stretched out and her golden head held aloft to catch the warmth of the first sunlight to fall upon her for hundreds of years. The shimmer of the green scales on the dragon's neck and tail and the glint of the gold on her hull made Jenna screw her eyes up against the glare. The dragon had her eyes half closed too. At first Jenna thought the dragon was still asleep, but then she realized that she was also shielding her eyes against the brightness of the light. Ever since Hotep-Ra had left her entombed under the earth, the only light the Dragon Boat had seen had been a dull glow from a lantern.

Jenna walked down the slope to the landing stage. The boat was big, much bigger than she remembered from the night before, and was wedged tightly into the Mott now that the floodwater had left the marshes. Jenna hoped the dragon did not feel trapped. She reached up on tiptoes to put her hand on the dragon's neck.

Good morning, my lady, the dragon's voice came to her.

"Good morning, Dragon," Jenna whispered. "I hope you're comfortable in the Mott."

There is water beneath me, and the air smells of salt and sunshine. What more could I wish for? asked the dragon.

"Nothing. Nothing at all," agreed Jenna. She sat down on the landing stage and watched the curls of the early morning mist disappear in the warmth of the sun. Then she leaned back contentedly against the Dragon Boat and listened to the dabblings and splashings of the various creatures in the Mott. Jenna had become used to all the underwater inhabitants by now. She no longer shuddered at the eels who made their way out along the Mott on their long journey to the Sargasso Sea. She didn't mind the Water Nixies too much, although she no longer paddled with bare feet in the mud, after one had stuck itself onto her big toe and Aunt Zelda had had to threaten it with the toasting fork to get it to drop off. Jenna even quite liked the Marsh Python, but that was probably because it had not returned since the Big Thaw. She knew the noises and splashes that each creature made, but as she sat in the sun, dreamily listening to the splish of a water rat and the gloop of a mudfish, she heard something she did not recognize.

The creature, whatever it was, moaned and groaned pathetically. Then it puffed, splashed and groaned some more. Jenna had never heard anything like it before. It also sounded rather large. Taking care to keep out of sight, Jenna crept behind the thick green tail of the Dragon Boat, which was curled up and resting on the landing stage; then she peered over to see what creature could possibly be making so much fuss.

It was the Apprentice.

He lay facedown on a tarry plank of wood that looked as though it had come from the *Vengeance* and was paddling it along the Mott using just his hands. He looked exhausted. His grubby green robes clung to him and steamed in the early morning warmth, and his lanky dark hair was straggling over his eyes. He seemed hardly to have the energy to raise his head and look where he was going.

"Oi!" yelled Jenna. "Go away." She picked up a rock to throw at him.

"No. Please don't," pleaded the boy.

Nicko appeared.

"What's up, Jen?" He followed Jenna's gaze. "Hey, *shove off*, you!" he yelled.

The Apprentice took no notice. He paddled his plank up to the landing stage and then just lay there, exhausted.

"What do you want?" asked Jenna.

"I . . . the ship . . . it's gone down. I escaped."

"Scum always floats to the surface," Nicko observed.

"We were covered in creatures. Brown, slimy . . . *things*." The boy shivered. "They pulled us down into the marsh. I couldn't breathe. Everyone's gone. Please help me."

Jenna stared at him, wavering. She had woken up early because she had been having nightmares full of screaming Brownies pulling her down into the marsh. Jenna shuddered. She didn't want to think about it. If she couldn't bear to even *think* about it, how much worse must it be for a boy who had actually been there?

The Apprentice could see that Jenna was hesitating. He tried again.

"I—I'm sorry for what I did to that animal of yours."

"The Boggart is not an *animal*," said Jenna indignantly. "And he is not *ours*. He is a creature of the marsh. He belongs to no one."

"Oh." The Apprentice could see he had made a mistake. He changed back to what had worked before.

"I'm sorry. I—I just . . . feel so scared."

Jenna relented.

"We can't just leave him lying on a plank," she said to Nicko.

"I don't see why not," said Nicko, "except I suppose he's polluting the Mott."

"We'd better take him inside," said Jenna. "Come on, give us a hand."

They helped the Apprentice off his plank and half carried, half led him up the path and into the cottage.

"Well, look what the cat dragged in" was Aunt Zelda's comment as Nicko and Jenna dumped the boy down in front of the fire, waking up a bleary-eyed Boy 412.

Boy 412 got up and moved away. He had seen a flicker of Darke Magyk as the Apprentice came in.

The Apprentice sat pale and shivering beside the fire. He looked ill.

"Don't let him out of your sight, Nicko," said Aunt Zelda. "I'll go and get him a hot drink."

Aunt Zelda came back with a mug of chamomile and cabbage tea. The Apprentice pulled a face but drank it down. At least it was hot.

When he had finished, Aunt Zelda said to him, "I think you had better tell us why you have come here. Or rather, you had better tell Madam Marcia. Marcia, we have a visitor."

Marcia was at the door, having just got back from an early morning walk around the island, partly to see what had happened to the *Vengeance* but mostly just to taste the sweet spring air and the even sweeter taste of freedom. Although Marcia was thin after almost five weeks' imprisonment and there were still dark shadows under her eyes, she looked much better than she had the night before. Her purple silk robes and tunic were fresh and clean, thanks to a complete Five-Minute DeepClean Spell, which she hoped had got rid of any traces of Darke Magyk. Darke Magyk was sticky stuff and Marcia had had to be particularly thorough. Her belt shone bright after its Pristine Polish and around her neck hung the Akhu Amulet. Marcia felt good. She had her Magyk back, once again she was ExtraOrdinary Wizard, and all was right with the world.

Apart from the galoshes.

Marcia kicked the offending articles of footwear off at the door and peered into the cottage, which seemed gloomy after the bright spring sunshine. There was a particular darkness by the fire, and it took a moment for Marcia to register who exactly was sitting there. When she realized who it was, her expression clouded.

"Ah, the rat from the sinking ship," she snapped.

The Apprentice said nothing. He looked shiftily at Marcia, his pitch-black eyes coming to rest on the Amulet.

"Don't touch him, anyone," warned Marcia.

Jenna was surprised at Marcia's tone, but she moved away from the Apprentice as did Nicko. Boy 412 went over to Marcia.

The Apprentice was left alone by the fire. He turned to face the disapproving circle that surrounded him. It was not meant to go like this. They were meant to feel sorry for him. The Queenling did. He had already won her over. And the mad

White Witch. It was just his luck that the interfering ex–ExtraOrdinary Wizard had turned up at the wrong moment. He scowled in frustration.

Jenna looked at the Apprentice. He looked different somehow, but she could not work out what it was. She put it down to his terrible night on a ship. Being dragged into the Quake Ooze by hundreds of screaming Brownies would be enough to give anyone the dark, haunted look in the boy's eyes.

But Marcia knew why the boy looked different. On her morning walk around the island she had seen the reason why, and it was a sight that had quite put her off her breakfast; although, admittedly, it did not take much to put Marcia off Aunt Zelda's breakfasts.

So when the Apprentice suddenly leaped to his feet and ran toward Marcia with his hands outstretched, poised to grab at her throat, Marcia was ready for him. She ripped the clutching fingers from the Amulet and hurled the Apprentice out the door with a resounding *crack* of a Thunderflash.

The boy lay sprawled, unconscious, on the path.

Everyone crowded around.

Aunt Zelda was shocked. "Marcia," she muttered, "I think you might have overdone it. He may be the most unpleasant boy I have ever had the misfortune to come across, but he's still only a boy."

"Not necessarily" was Marcia's grim reply. "And I haven't finished yet. Stand back, please, everyone."

"But," whispered Jenna, "he's our brother."

"I think not," said Marcia crisply.

Aunt Zelda put her hand on Marcia's arm. "Marcia. I know you're angry. You have every right to be after your time as a prisoner, but you mustn't take it out on a child."

"I'm not taking it out on a child, Zelda. You should know me better than that. This is no child. This is *DomDaniel*."

"*What?*"

"Anyway, Zelda, I am no Necromancer," Marcia told her. "I will never take a life. All I can do is to return him to where he was when he did this dreadful thing—to make sure that he does not profit from what he has done."

"No!" yelled the Apprentice-shaped DomDaniel.

He cursed the thin, reedy voice in which he was forced to speak. It had annoyed him enough to hear it when it had belonged to the wretched boy, but now that it belonged to him it was unbearable.

DomDaniel struggled to his feet. He could not believe the failure of his plan to retrieve the Amulet. He had had them all fooled. They had taken him in out of their misguided pity, and they would have looked after him too, until he found the right time to take back the Amulet. And then—ah, how different things would have been then. Desperately he gave it one last try. He threw himself to his knees.

"Please," he begged. "You've got it wrong. It's only me. I'm not—"

"Begone!" Marcia commanded him.

"*No!*" he screamed.

But Marcia continued:

Begone.
Back to where you were,
When you were
What you were!

And he was gone, back to the *Vengeance*, buried deep in the dark recesses of the mud and the Ooze.

Aunt Zelda looked upset. She still could not believe that the Apprentice really was DomDaniel. "That's a terrible thing to do, Marcia," she said. "Poor boy."

"Poor boy, my foot," snapped Marcia. "There's something you should see."

⊹ 47 ⊹
THE APPRENTICE

They set off at a brisk pace, Marcia striding ahead of them as best she could in her galoshes. Aunt Zelda had to break into a trot to keep up. She wore a look of dismay as she took in the destruction wrought by the floodwaters. There was mud, seaweed and slime everywhere. It hadn't looked so bad in the moonlight the previous night, and besides, she had been so relieved to see everyone actually *alive* that a bit of mud and mess hardly seemed to matter. But in the revealing light of the morning it looked miserable. Suddenly she gave a cry of dismay.

"The chicken boat has gone! My chickens, my poor little chickens!"

"There are more important things in life than chickens," Marcia declared, moving purposefully ahead.

"The rabbits!" wailed Aunt Zelda, suddenly realizing that the burrows must have all been swept away. "My poor bunnies, all gone."

"Oh, do be quiet, Zelda!" Marcia snapped irritably.

Not for the first time, Aunt Zelda thought that Marcia's return to the Wizard Tower could not come soon enough for her. Marcia led the way like a purple pied piper in full flight, marching across the mud, leading Jenna, Nicko, Boy 412 and a flustered Aunt Zelda to a spot beside the Mott just below the duck house.

As they neared their destination, Marcia stopped, wheeled around and said, "Now, I just want to tell you, this is not a pretty sight. In fact, maybe only Zelda should see this. I don't want to go giving you all nightmares."

"We've been having those already," declared Jenna. "I don't see what could be worse than *my* nightmares last night."

Boy 412 and Nicko nodded in agreement. They had both slept very badly the previous night.

"Very well, then," said Marcia. She stepped carefully across the mud behind the duck house and stopped by the Mott. "*This* is what I found this morning."

"Eurgh!" Jenna hid her face in her hands.

"Oh, oh, oh," gasped Aunt Zelda.

Boy 412 and Nicko were silent. They felt sick. Suddenly Nicko disappeared down to the Mott and *was* sick.

Lying on the muddy grass beside the Mott was what at first glance looked like an empty green sack. On second glance it looked like some strange unstuffed scarecrow. But on third glance, which Jenna only managed through her fingers covering her eyes, it was only too apparent what lay before them.

The empty body of the Apprentice.

Like a deflated balloon, the Apprentice lay, drained of all life and substance. His empty skin, still clad in its wet, salt-stained robes, lay strewn across the mud, discarded like an old banana skin.

"This," said Marcia, "is the *real* Apprentice. I found him this morning on my walk. Which is why I knew for sure that the 'Apprentice' you had sitting by the fire was an impostor."

"What happened to him?" Jenna whispered.

"He has been Consumed. It's an old and particularly nasty trick. One from the Cryptic archives," said Marcia gravely. "The ancient Necromancers used to do it all the time."

"Is there nothing we can do for the boy?" asked Aunt Zelda.

"It's too late, I'm afraid," replied Marcia. "He is nothing

more than a shadow now. By midday, he will be gone."

Aunt Zelda sniffed. "He had a tough life, poor little mite. Snatched from his family and Apprenticed to that awful man. I don't know what Sarah and Silas are going to say when they hear about this. It's a terrible thing. Poor Septimus."

"I know," agreed Marcia. "But there's nothing we can do for him now."

"Well, I shall sit with him—what's left of him—until he disappears," murmured Aunt Zelda.

A subdued party minus Aunt Zelda made their way back to the cottage, each occupied with his or her own thoughts. Aunt Zelda came back briefly and disappeared into the Unstable Potions and Partikular Poisons cupboard before returning to the duck house, but everyone else spent the rest of the morning quietly cleaning up the mud and setting the cottage to rights. Boy 412 was relieved to see that the green rock Jenna had given him had not been touched by the Brownies. It was still where he had put it, folded carefully into his quilt, in a warm corner beside the fireplace.

In the afternoon, after they had coaxed the goat down from the roof—or what was left of it—they decided to take Maxie for a walk on the marsh. As they were leaving, Marcia called out to Boy 412, "Can you help me with something, please?"

Boy 412 was only too happy to stay behind. Although he was used to Maxie by now, he still was not entirely happy in his company. He never could understand why Maxie would suddenly take it into his head to jump up and lick his face, and the sight of Maxie's glistening black nose and slobbery mouth always sent an unpleasant shiver through him. Try as he might, he just did not get the *point* of dogs. So Boy 412 happily waved Jenna and Nicko off to the marsh and went inside to see Marcia.

Marcia was sitting at Aunt Zelda's small desk. Having won the battle of the desk before she went away, Marcia was determined to regain control now that she was back again. Boy 412 noticed that all of Aunt Zelda's pens and notebooks had been dumped on the floor, apart from a few Marcia was busy Transforming into much smarter ones for her own use. She was doing this with a clear conscience as they had a definite Magykal purpose—at least Marcia hoped they were going to have—if all went as she planned.

"Ah, there you are," Marcia said in that businesslike way that always made Boy 412 feel as though he had done something wrong. She dumped a scruffy old book on the desk in front of her.

"What's your favorite color?" demanded Marcia. "Blue? Or red? I thought it might be red, seeing as you haven't taken that awful red hat off since you got here."

Boy 412 was taken aback. No one had ever bothered to ask him what his favorite color was. And, anyway, he wasn't even sure if he knew. Then he remembered the beautiful blue inside the Dragon Boat.

"Um, blue. Sort of deep blue."

"Ah, yes. I like that too. With some gold stars, don't you think?"

"Yes. Um, that's nice."

Marcia waved her hands over the book in front of her and muttered something. There was a loud rustling of paper as all the pages sorted themselves out. They got rid of Aunt Zelda's jottings and doodlings, and also her favorite recipe for cabbage stew, and they turned themselves into a brand-new, smooth, cream-colored paper, perfect for writing on. Then they bound themselves in lapis lazuli–colored leather complete with real gold stars and a purple spine that showed the diary belonged to the Apprentice of the ExtraOrdinary Wizard. As a final touch Marcia added a clasp of pure gold and a small silver key.

She opened the book to check that the spell had worked. Marcia was pleased to see that the first and last pages of the book were bright red, exactly the same color as Boy 412's hat. Written on the first page were the words: APPRENTICE DIARY.

"There," said Marcia, closing the book with a satisfying thump and turning the silver key in the lock. "It looks good, doesn't it?"

"Yes," said Boy 412, bemused. Why was she asking *him*?

Marcia looked Boy 412 in the eye.

"Now," she said, "I have something to return to you—your ring. Thank you. I will always remember what you did for me."

Marcia took the ring from a pocket in her belt and placed it carefully on the desk. Just seeing the gold dragon ring curled on the desk with its tail clasped in its mouth and its emerald eyes shining at him made Boy 412 feel very happy. But for some reason he hesitated to pick it up. He could tell there was something else that Marcia was about to say. And there was.

"Where did you get the ring?"

Immediately Boy 412 felt guilty. So he *had* done something wrong. That's what it was all about.

"I—I found it."

"Where?"

"I fell down into the tunnel. You know, the one that went to the Dragon Boat. Only I didn't know that then. It was dark. I couldn't see. And then I found the ring."

"Did you put the ring on?"

"Well, yes."

"And then what happened?"

"It—it lit up. So I could see where I was."

"And did it fit you?"

"No. Well, not at first. And then it did. It got smaller."

"Ah. I don't suppose it sang you a song, did it?"

Boy 412 had been staring intently at his feet up until then. But he glanced up at Marcia and caught a smile in her eyes. Was she making fun of him?

"Yes. As it happens, it did."

Marcia was thinking. She said nothing for so long that Boy 412 felt he had to speak.

"Are you cross with me?"

"Why should I be cross with you?" she replied.

"Because I took the ring. It belongs to the dragon, doesn't it?"

"No, it belongs to the Dragon Master." Marcia smiled.

Boy 412 was worried now. Who was the Dragon Master? Would he be angry? Was he very *big*? What would he do to him when he found out he had his ring?

"Could you . . ." he asked hesitantly, "could you give it back to the Dragon Master? And tell him I'm sorry I took it?" He pushed the ring back across the desk toward Marcia.

"Very well," she said solemnly, picking the ring up. "I'll give it back to the Dragon Master."

Boy 412 sighed. He had loved the ring, and just being close to it had made him feel happy, but he wasn't surprised to hear that it belonged to someone else. It was too beautiful for him.

Marcia looked at the Dragon Ring for a few moments. Then she held it out to Boy 412.

"Here"—she smiled—"is your ring."

Boy 412 stared at her, uncomprehending.

"*You* are the Dragon Master," said Marcia. "It is your ring. Oh, yes, and the person who took it says to tell you he's sorry."

Boy 412 was speechless. He stared at the ring lying in his hand. It was *his*.

"*You* are the Dragon Master," repeated Marcia, "because the ring chose you. It doesn't sing for just anyone, you know. And it was *your* finger it chose to fit, not mine."

"Why?" breathed Boy 412. "Why me?"

"You have astonishing Magykal power. I told you before. Maybe now you'll believe me." She smiled.

"I—I thought the power came from the ring."

"No. It comes from you. Don't forget, the Dragon Boat recognized you even without the ring. She *knew*. Remember, it was last worn by Hotep-Ra, the first ExtraOrdinary Wizard. It's been waiting a long time to find someone like him."

"But that's because it's been stuck in a secret tunnel for hundreds of years."

"Not necessarily," said Marcia mysteriously. "Things have a habit of working out, you know. Eventually."

Boy 412 was beginning to think that Marcia was right.

"So is the answer still no?"

"No?" asked Boy 412.

"To being my Apprentice. Has what I've told you changed your mind? Will you be my Apprentice? Please?"

Boy 412 fumbled in his sweater pocket and pulled out the Charm that Marcia had given him when she had first asked him to be her Apprentice. He looked at the tiny silver wings. They shone as brightly as ever and the words on them still said, FLY FREE WITH ME.

Boy 412 smiled.

"Yes," he said. "I would like to be your Apprentice. Very much."

✦ 48 ✦
THE APPRENTICE SUPPER

I t *had not been easy* to bring the Apprentice back. But Aunt Zelda had done it. Her own Drastic Drops and Urgent Ungent had had some effect, but not for long; soon the Apprentice had begun to slip away again. It was then that she had decided there was only one thing for it: Vigor Volts.

The Vigor Volts were a bit of a gamble, as Aunt Zelda had modified the potion from a Darke recipe she had found in the attic when she had moved in. She had no idea how the Darke part of it would work, but something told her that maybe this was what was needed. A touch of Darkenesse. With some trepidation, Aunt Zelda had unscrewed the lid. A brilliant blue-white light shot out from the tiny brown glass bottle and almost blinded her. Aunt Zelda waited until the spots had disappeared from her eyes, then carefully dropped a tiny amount of the electric blue gel onto the Apprentice's tongue. She crossed her fingers, something a White Witch does not do lightly, and held her breath. For a minute. Suddenly the Apprentice had sat up, looked at her with eyes open so wide that she could see almost nothing but white, taken a huge, sighing intake of breath and then lain down in the straw, curled up and gone to sleep.

The Vigor Volts had worked, but Aunt Zelda knew there was something she had to do before he could fully recover. She had to Release him from the clutches of his Master. And so she had sat by the duck pond and, as the sun set and the deep orange full moon rose low on the broad horizon of the Marram Marshes, Aunt Zelda did her own bit of scrying. There were one or two things she wanted to know.

Night had fallen and the moon was high in the sky. Aunt Zelda walked home slowly, leaving the Apprentice in a deep sleep. She knew he would need to sleep for many days before he could be moved from the duckhouse. Aunt Zelda also knew he would be with her for a while longer. It was time that she had another stray to look after, now that Boy 412 had recovered so well.

Her blue eyes glittering in the dark, Aunt Zelda picked her way along the Mott path, engrossed by the images she had seen in the duck pond, trying to understand their meaning. So preoccupied was she that she did not look up until she had almost reached the landing stage in front of the cottage. She was not pleased by the sight that met her.

The Mott, thought Aunt Zelda irritably, was a mess. There were just too many boats cluttering up the place. As if the Hunter's rancid canoe and the tatty old *Muriel Two* weren't bad enough, there was now, parked on the other side of the bridge, a decrepit old fishing boat that contained an equally decrepit old ghost.

Aunt Zelda marched over to the ghost and spoke to him very loudly and very slowly, in the voice she always used when addressing ghosts. Particularly old ones. The old ghost was remarkably polite to Aunt Zelda, considering she had just woken him up with a very rude question.

"No, Madam," he said graciously. "I'm sorry to disappoint you. I'm not one of those awful old sailors off that evil ship. I am, or I suppose I should, strictly speaking, say that I was,

Alther Mella, ExtraOrdinary Wizard. At your service, Madam."

"Really?" said Aunt Zelda. "You don't look a bit like I expected."

"I'll take that as a compliment," said Alther graciously. "Excuse my rudeness in not alighting from my boat to greet you, but I have to stay in my dear old boat *Molly*, otherwise I will be Returned. But it is a pleasure to meet you, Madam. I take it you are Zelda Heap."

"Zelda!" Silas called out from the cottage.

Aunt Zelda looked up at the cottage, puzzled. All the lanterns and candles were blazing, and it seemed to be full of people.

"Silas?" she yelled. "What are *you* doing here?"

"Stay there," he shouted. "Don't come in. We'll be out in a minute!" He disappeared into the cottage, and Aunt Zelda heard him say, "No, Marcia, I've told her to stay outside. Anyway, I'm sure Zelda wouldn't *dream* of interfering. No, I *don't* know if there are any more cabbages. Why do you want *ten* cabbages anyway?"

Aunt Zelda turned to Alther, who was lounging comfortably in the prow of the fishing boat. "*Why* can't I go in?" she demanded. "What's going on? How did Silas get here?"

"It's a long story, Zelda," said the ghost.

"You may as well tell me," said Aunt Zelda, "as I don't suppose anyone else will bother to. They seem too busy raiding my entire stock of cabbages."

"Well," said Alther, "I was in DomDaniel's rooms one day attending to some, er, business, when the Hunter came and told him he had found out where you all were. I knew you were safe while the Big Freeze lasted, but when the Big Thaw arrived I thought you would be in trouble. I was right. As soon as the thaw came, DomDaniel shot off to Bleak Creek and picked up that ghastly ship of his, ready to bring the Hunter down here. I arranged for my dear friend Alice at the Port to have a ship ready and waiting to take you all somewhere safe. Silas insisted that *all* the Heaps had to go, so I offered him *Molly* to travel in down to the Port. Jannit Maarten had her laid up at the boatyard, but Silas got her in the water. Jannit wasn't very happy about the state *Molly* was in, but we couldn't wait around for any repairs. We stopped off at the Forest and picked up Sarah; she was very upset because none of the boys would come. We set off without them, and we were making good time until we had a small technical problem—a large technical problem, actually. Silas put his foot through the bottom of the boat. While we were repairing it we got overtaken by the *Vengeance*. Lucky not to be spotted, really. Sarah was in a terrible state about that—she thought all was lost. And then, to crown it all, we got caught up in the Storm and swept onto the marshes. Not one of my most enjoyable trips in *Molly*. But here we are, and while we were just messing about in a boat, you seem to have dealt with everything most satisfactorily yourselves."

"Apart from the mud," muttered Aunt Zelda.

"Indeed," agreed Alther. "But in my experience Darke Magyk always leaves some kind of dirt behind. It could be worse."

Aunt Zelda did not reply. She was somewhat distracted by the din coming from the cottage. Suddenly there was a loud crash followed by raised voices.

"Alther, what *is* going on in there?" demanded Aunt Zelda. "I'm only gone for a few hours, then I come back to find some kind of party going on and I'm not even allowed back into my own home. Marcia has gone too far this time if you ask me."

"It's an Apprentice Supper," said Alther. "For the Young Army lad. He's just become Marcia's Apprentice."

"Really? That's *wonderful* news," said Aunt Zelda, brightening. "Perfect news in fact. But you know, I always hoped he would."

"Did you?" said Alther, beginning to warm to Aunt Zelda. "I always did too."

"Still," sighed Aunt Zelda, "I could have done without this supper lark. I had a nice quiet bean and eel stew planned for tonight."

"Got to have the Apprentice Supper tonight, Zelda," Alther said. "It must be held on the day the Apprentice accepts a Wizard's offer. Otherwise the contract between the Wizard and the Apprentice is void. And you can't make the contract again—you only get one chance. No supper, no contract, no Apprentice."

"Oh, I know," said Aunt Zelda airily.

"When Marcia was Apprenticed to me," said Alther nostalgically, "I remember we had quite a night. We had all the Wizards there, and there were a lot more in those days too. That supper was something we talked about for years afterward. We had it in the Hall of the Wizard Tower—you ever been there, Zelda?"

Aunt Zelda shook her head. The Wizard Tower was somewhere she would have liked to have visited, but when Silas was briefly Alther's Apprentice she had been too busy taking over as Keeper of the Dragon Boat from the previous White Witch, Betty Crackle, who had let things go somewhat.

"Ah, well, let's hope you get to see it one day. It is a wonderful place," he said, remembering the luxury and Magyk that had surrounded them all then. A little different, thought Alther, from a makeshift party beside a fishing boat.

"Well, I have every hope that Marcia will be going back very soon," said Aunt Zelda. "Now that we seem to have got rid of that awful DomDaniel man."

"I was Apprenticed to that awful DomDaniel man, you know," Alther continued, "and all I got for my Apprentice Supper was a cheese sandwich. I can tell you, Zelda, I regretted eating that cheese sandwich more than anything else I had ever done in my life. It bound me to that man for years and years."

"Until you pushed him off the Wizard Tower." Aunt Zelda chuckled.

"I didn't push him. He *jumped*," protested Alther. Yet *again*. And not, he suspected, for the last time.

"Well, good for you, whatever happened," said Aunt Zelda, distracted by the babble of excited voices coming from the open doors and windows of the cottage. Above the hubbub came Marcia's unmistakable bossy tones:

"No, let *Sarah* take that one, Silas. You'll only drop it."

"Well, put it down, then, if it's *that* hot."

"Mind my shoes, will you? And get that dog off for good-ness' sake."

"Wretched duck. Always under my feet. Eurgh, is that duck poo I've just trodden on?"

And finally: "And now I'd like my Apprentice to lead the way, please."

Boy 412 came out the door, holding a lantern. He was fol-lowed by Silas and Simon, who were carrying the table and chairs, then Sarah and Jenna with an assortment of plates, glasses, bottles, and Nicko who had a basket piled high with ten cabbages. He had no idea why he had a basket of cabbages, and he was not going to ask either. He had already trodden on Marcia's brand-new purple python shoes (there was no way she would be wearing *galoshes* to her Apprentice's Supper), and was keeping out of her way.

Marcia followed, carefully stepping over the mud, carry-ing the blue leather Apprentice Diary she had Made for Boy 412.

As the party emerged from the cottage, the last of the clouds cleared away and the moon rode high in the sky, cast-ing a silver light over the procession as it made its way to the landing stage. Silas and Simon set the table down next to Alther's boat, *Molly*, and put a large white cloth over it, then

Marcia directed how everything should be set out. Nicko had to put the basket of cabbages in the middle of the table just where Marcia told him to.

Marcia clapped her hands for silence.

"This is," she said, "an important evening for all of us, and I would like to welcome my Apprentice."

Everyone clapped politely.

"I'm not one for long speeches," Marcia continued.

"That's not how I remember it," Alther whispered to Aunt Zelda, who was sitting next to him in the boat so that he did not feel left out of the party. She nudged him companionably, forgetting for a moment that he was a ghost, and her arm went right through him and her elbow hit *Molly*'s mast.

"Ouch!" Aunt Zelda yelped. "Oh, sorry, Marcia. Do go on."

"Thank you, Zelda, I will. I just want to say that I have spent ten years looking for an Apprentice, and although I have met many Hopefuls, I have never found what I was looking for, until now."

Marcia turned to Boy 412 and smiled. "So, thank you for agreeing to be my Apprentice for the next seven years and a day. Thank you very much. It's going to be a wonderful time for us both."

Boy 412, who was sitting next to Marcia, blushed bright

red as Marcia handed him his Apprentice Diary. He held the diary tightly with his clammy hands, leaving two slightly grubby handprints on the porous blue leather, which would never come off and would always remind him of the evening that changed his life forever.

"Nicko," said Marcia, "hand the cabbages out, will you?"

Nicko looked at Marcia with the same expression he used for Maxie when he had done something particularly silly. But he said nothing. He picked up the basket of cabbages and walked around the table and started handing them out.

"Er, thank you, Nicko," said Silas as he took the proffered cabbage and held it awkwardly in his hands, wondering quite what to do with it.

"No!" snapped Marcia. "Don't *give* it to them. Put the cabbages on the *plates.*"

Nicko gave Marcia another Maxie look (this time it was the I-wish-you-hadn't-pooed-*there* look), then quickly dumped a cabbage on each plate.

When everyone, including Maxie, had a cabbage, Marcia raised her hands for silence.

"This is a suit-yourself supper. Each cabbage is Primed to willingly Transform itself into whatever you would most like

to eat. Just place your hand on the cabbage and decide what
you would like."

There was an excited buzz as everyone decided what they
were going to have and Transformed their cabbages.

"It's a criminal waste of good cabbages," Aunt Zelda whispered to Alther. "I shall just have cabbage casserole."

"Now that you have all decided," said Marcia loudly over
the hubbub, "there is one last thing to be said."

"Get a move on, Marcia!" Silas called out. "My fish pie's
getting cold."

Marcia gave Silas a withering look.

"It is traditional," she continued, "that in return for the
seven years and a day of his life that the Apprentice offers the
Wizard, the Wizard offers something to the Apprentice."
Marcia turned to Boy 412, who was sitting almost hidden
behind a huge plate of eel stew and dumplings just like Aunt
Zelda always made.

"What would you like from me?" Marcia asked him. "Ask
me anything you like. I will do my best to give it to you."

Boy 412 gazed at his plate. Then he looked at all the people gathered around him and thought how different his life
had become since he had met them. He felt so happy that
there was really nothing else he wanted. Except for one thing.

One big, impossible thing that he was almost too scared to think about.

"Anything you like," Marcia said softly. "Anything you want at all."

Boy 412 gulped.

"I want," he said quietly, "to know who I am."

✣ 49 ✣
SEPTIMUS HEAP

U*nnoticed on the chimney pot* of Keeper's Cottage, a storm petrel perched. He had been blown in the night before and had been watching the Apprentice Supper with great interest. And now, he noted with a feeling of fondness, Aunt Zelda was about to do what the petrel had always considered she had a particular gift for.

"It's the perfect night for it," Aunt Zelda was saying as she stood on the bridge over the Mott. "There's a beautiful full moon, and I've never known the Mott to be so still. Can everyone fit on the bridge? Shuffle up a bit, Marcia, and make room for Simon."

Simon didn't look as if he wanted to be made room for.

"Oh, don't bother about me," he mumbled. "Why break the habit of a lifetime?"

"*What* did you say, Simon?" asked Silas.

"Nothing."

"Let him be, Silas," said Sarah. "He's had a tough time recently."

"We've all had a tough time recently, Sarah. But *we* don't go around moaning about it."

Aunt Zelda tapped the handrail of the bridge irritably.

"*If* everybody has quite finished bickering, I would like to remind you that we are about to try to answer an important question. All right, everybody?"

Silence descended on the group. Along with Aunt Zelda, Boy 412, Sarah, Silas, Marcia, Jenna, Nicko and Simon were all squashed onto the small bridge that went over the Mott. Behind them was the Dragon Boat, her head raised high and arched over them, her deep green eyes staring intently at the reflection of the moon swimming in the still waters of the Mott.

In front of them, pushed back a little to allow the reflection of the moon to be seen, was *Molly* with Alther sitting in the prow, observing the scene with interest.

Simon hung back on the edge of the bridge. He didn't see what the fuss was about. Who cared where some Young Army brat came from? Especially a Young Army brat who had stolen his lifelong dream from him. Boy 412's parentage was the last thing Simon cared about, or was ever likely to as far as he could imagine. So, as Aunt Zelda started to call upon the moon, Simon deliberately turned his back.

"Sister Moon, Sister Moon," said Aunt Zelda softly, "Show us, if you will, the family of Boy 412 of the Young Army."

Exactly as before in the duck pond, the reflection of the moon began to grow bigger until a huge round white circle filled the Mott. At first, vague shadows began to appear in the circle; slowly they became more defined until everyone watching saw . . . their own reflections.

There was a murmur of disappointment from everyone except Marcia, who had noticed something no one else had, and from Boy 412, whose voice seemed to have stopped working. His heart was pounding somewhere high in his throat, and his legs felt as though they might turn into parsnip puree at any moment. He wished he had never asked to see who he was. He didn't think he really wanted to know. Suppose his family was horrible? Suppose they *were* the Young Army, like he had been told? Suppose it was DomDaniel himself? Just as he was about to tell Aunt Zelda that he had changed his mind, that he didn't care who he was anymore, thank you, Aunt Zelda spoke.

"Things," Aunt Zelda reminded everyone on the bridge, "are not always as they seem. Remember, the moon always shows us the truth. How we see the truth is up to us, not the moon."

She turned to Boy 412, who stood beside her. "Tell me," she asked him, "what would you *really* like to see?"

The answer Boy 412 gave was not the one he had expected to give.

"I want to see my mother," he whispered.

"Sister Moon, Sister Moon," said Aunt Zelda softly, "show us, if you will, the mother of Boy 412 of the Young Army."

The white disk of the moon filled the Mott. Once more, vague shadows began to appear until they saw . . . their own reflections, *again*. There was a collective moan of protest, but it was quickly cut short. Something different was happening. One by one, people were disappearing from the reflection.

First Boy 412 himself disappeared. Then Simon, Jenna, Nicko and Silas went. Then Marcia's reflection faded, followed by Aunt Zelda's.

Suddenly Sarah Heap found herself looking at her own

reflection in the moon, waiting for it to fade like all the others had done. But it did not fade. It grew stronger and more defined, until Sarah Heap was standing alone in the middle of the white disk of the moon. Everyone could see that it was no longer just a reflection. It was the answer.

Boy 412 gazed at the picture of Sarah, transfixed. How could Sarah Heap be his mother? *How?*

Sarah raised her eyes from the Mott and looked at Boy 412.

"Septimus?" she half whispered.

There was something Aunt Zelda wanted to show Sarah.

"Sister Moon, Sister Moon," said Aunt Zelda, "show us, if you will, the seventh son of Sarah and Silas Heap. Show us *Septimus Heap.*"

Slowly the image of Sarah Heap faded away and was replaced by—

Boy 412.

There was a gasp, even from Marcia, who had guessed who Boy 412 was a few minutes earlier. Only she had noticed that her image had disappeared from the reflection of Boy 412's family.

"Septimus?" Sarah knelt down beside Boy 412 and looked at him searchingly. Boy 412's eyes stared into hers, and Sarah said, "You know, I do believe your eyes are beginning to turn green, just like your father's. And mine. And your brothers'."

"Are they?" asked Boy 412. "Really?"

Sarah reached out and placed her hand on Septimus's red hat. "Would you mind if I took this off?" she asked.

Boy 412 shook his head. That's what mothers were for. To fiddle about with your hat.

Gently, Sarah lifted off Boy 412's hat for the first time since Marcia had crammed it onto his head at Sally Mullin's bunkhouse. Straw-colored tufts of curly hair sprang up as Septimus shook his head like a dog shaking off water and a boy shaking off his old life, his old fears and his old name.

He was becoming who he really was.

Septimus Heap.

What Aunt Zelda
Saw in
the Duck Pond

We are back in the Young Army nursery.

In the semidarkness of the nursery the Matron Midwife puts the baby Septimus in a cot and sits down wearily. She keeps glancing anxiously at the door as if waiting for someone to come in. No one appears.

A minute or two later she heaves herself up from her chair and goes over to the cot where her own baby is crying and picks the child up. At that moment the door is flung open, and the Matron Midwife wheels around, white-faced, frightened.

A tall woman in black stands in the doorway. Over her black, well-pressed robes she wears the starched white apron of a nurse, but around her waist is a blood-red belt showing the three black stars of DomDaniel.

She has come for Septimus Heap.

The Nurse is late. She got lost on her way to the nursery, and now she is flustered and afraid. DomDaniel does not tolerate lateness. She sees the Matron Midwife with a baby, just as she has been told she would. She does not know that the Matron Midwife is holding her own child in her arms and that Septimus Heap is asleep in a cot in the dim shadows of the nursery. The Nurse runs over to the Midwife and seizes the baby from her. The Midwife protests. She tries to wrest her baby back from the Nurse, but her desperation is more than matched by the Nurse's determination to make it back to the boat in time for the tide.

The taller, younger Nurse wins. She bundles up the baby in a long red cloth emblazoned with three black stars and runs out, pursued by the screaming Midwife who now knows exactly how Sarah Heap felt only a few hours ago. The Midwife is forced to give up her chase at the barracks door where the Nurse, flaunting her three black stars, has the Matron Midwife arrested by the guard, and disappears into the night, triumphantly carrying off the Midwife's own child to DomDaniel.

Back in the nursery the old woman who is meant to be babysitting wakes up. Coughing and wheezing, she gets up and makes up four nighttime bottles for her charges. One each for the triplets—Boys 409, 410 and 411—and one for the newest recruit to the

Young Army, twelve-hours-old Septimus Heap, destined to be known for the next ten years as Boy 412.

Aunt Zelda sighed. This was as she had expected. Next she asked the moon to follow the Midwife's child. There was something else she needed to know.

The Nurse just makes it back to the boat in time. A Thing stands at the stern of the boat and sculls her across the river using the old fishermen's way with just one oar. On the other side she is met by a Darke horseman, riding a huge black horse. He pulls the Nurse and the child up behind him and canters off into the night. They have a long and uncomfortable ride ahead of them.

By the time they reach DomDaniel's lair high up in the old slate quarries of the Badlands, the Midwife's baby is screaming and the Nurse has a terrible headache. DomDaniel is waiting to see his prize, which he takes to be Septimus Heap, the seventh son of a seventh son. The Apprentice that every Wizard and every Necromancer dreams of. The Apprentice who will give him the power to return him to the Castle and take back what is rightfully his.

He looks at the screaming baby with distaste. The screams make his head ache and his ears ring. It is a big baby for a newborn, thinks DomDaniel, and an ugly one too. He doesn't like it very much. The Necromancer has an air of disappointment about him as he tells the Nurse to take the baby away.

The Nurse puts the baby in the waiting cot and goes to bed. She feels too ill to get up the next day, and no one bothers to feed the Midwife's son until well into the next night. There is no Apprentice Supper for this Apprentice.

Aunt Zelda sat by the duck pond and smiled. The Apprentice is free of his Darke Master. Septimus Heap is alive, and has found his family. The Princess is safe. She remembered something Marcia often said: things *do* have a habit of working out. Eventually.

AFTER . . .

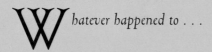

GRINGE, THE GATEKEEPER

Gringe remained the North Gate Gatekeeper throughout all the upheavals at the Castle. Although he would rather have jumped into a vat of boiling oil than admit it, Gringe loved his job, and it gave his family a secure home in the gatehouse after many years of living rough under the Castle walls. The day that Marcia had given him a half crown turned out to be an important day for Gringe. That day, for the first and only time ever, Gringe kept some of the bridge money—Marcia's half crown, to be exact. There was something about the thick, solid silver disk lying warm and heavy in the palm of his hand that made Gringe reluctant to put it into the toll box. So he slipped it into his pocket, telling himself he would add it to the day's takings that night. But Gringe could not bring himself to part with the half crown. And so the half crown sat in his pocket for many months until Gringe began to consider it his own.

And there the half crown would have stayed had it not been for a notice Gringe found nailed up on the North Gate one cold morning almost a year later:

Young Army Conscription Edict
All boys aged eleven to sixteen
years who are not apprenticed to
a recognized trade are to report
to the Young Army Barracks
at 0600 hours tomorrow

Gringe felt sick. His son, Rupert, had celebrated his eleventh birthday the previous day. Mrs. Gringe was hysterical when she saw the notice. Gringe felt hysterical too, but when he saw Rupert, white-faced, reading the notice, he decided he had to stay calm. He shoved his hands in his pockets and thought. And when, out of habit, his hand closed around

Marcia's half crown, Gringe knew he had the answer.

As soon as the boatyard was open that morning, they had a new apprentice: Rupert Gringe, whose father had just secured a seven-year apprenticeship with Jannit Maarten, a herring-boat builder, for the substantial down payment of a half crown.

THE MATRON MIDWIFE

After the Matron Midwife was arrested, she was taken to the Castle Asylum for Deluded and Distressed Persons due to her distraught state of mind and preoccupation with baby-snatching, which was not considered to be a healthy preoccupation for a Midwife to have. After spending a few years there she was allowed to leave because the Asylum was becoming overcrowded. There had been a huge increase in deluded and distressed people since the Supreme Custodian had taken over the Castle, and the Matron Midwife was now neither deluded nor distressed enough to merit a place. And so Agnes Meredith, former Matron Midwife, now unemployed bag lady, packed her many bags and set off to search for her lost son, Merrin.

THE NIGHT SERVANT

The Supreme Custodian's Night Servant was thrown into a dungeon after dropping the Crown and adding another dent to it. He was released a week later by mistake and went to work in the Palace kitchens as an undercook peeling potatoes, which he was good at, and soon progressed to be chief potato-peeler. He enjoyed his job. No one minded if he dropped a potato.

JUDGE ALICE NETTLES

Alice Nettles first met Alther Mella when she was a trainee advocate at the Castle Court. Alther had yet to become DomDaniel's Apprentice, but Alice could tell that Alther was special. Even after Alther became the ExtraOrdinary Wizard and was much talked about as "that awful Apprentice who pushed his Master from the Tower," Alice kept seeing him. She knew that Alther was incapable of killing anything, even an irritating ant. Shortly after Alther became ExtraOrdinary Wizard, Alice achieved her ambition of becoming a judge. Soon their separate careers began to keep Alther and Alice increasingly busy, and they never saw as much of each other as they would have liked to, something that Alice always regretted.

It was a terrible double blow to Alice when, in the space of a few days, the Custodians not only killed the dearest friend she had ever had but also took away her life's work when they banned women from the Courthouse. Alice left the Castle and went to stay with her brother in the Port. After some time she recovered enough from Alther's death to take a job as legal advisor to the Customs House.

It was after a long day dealing with a tricky problem involving a smuggled camel and a traveling circus that Alice repaired to the Blue Anchor Tavern before she returned to her brother's house. It was there, to her delight, that she finally met the ghost of Alther Mella.

THE ASSASSIN

The Assassin suffered complete memory loss after being hit by Marcia's Thunderflash. She was also quite badly burned. When the Hunter had collected the pistol from the Assassin, he had left her lying where he found her, unconscious on Marcia's carpet. DomDaniel had had her thrown out into the snow, but she was found by the night street sweepers and taken to the Nuns'

Hospice. She eventually recovered and stayed on at the Hospice, working as a helper. Luckily for her, her memory never returned.

LINDA LANE

Linda Lane was given a new identity and moved into some luxurious rooms overlooking the river to reward her for finding the Princess. However, some months later she was recognized by the family of one of her previous victims, and late one night as she sat on her balcony with a glass of her favorite wine supplied by the Supreme Custodian, Linda Lane was pushed off and fell into the fast-flowing river. She was never found.

THE YOUNGEST KITCHEN MAID

After the youngest Kitchen Maid started having nightmares about wolves, her sleep became so badly disturbed that she often fell asleep at work. One day she dozed off while she was meant to be turning the spit and a whole sheep went up in flames; it was only the prompt action of the chief potato-peeler that saved her from the same fate as the sheep. The youngest Kitchen Maid was demoted to assistant potato-peeler, but three weeks later she ran away with the chief potato-peeler to start a better life in the Port.

THE FIVE NORTHERN TRADERS

After their hurried exit from Sally Mullin's Tea and Ale House, the five Northern Traders spent the night on their ship, stowing away their wares and preparing to leave on the early morning high tide. They had been caught up in unpleasant changes of government before and had no wish to stay around and see what happened this time. In the Traders' experience it was always a nasty business. As they sailed past the smoldering remains of Sally Mullin's Tea and Ale House the next morning, they knew they were right. But they gave little thought to Sally as they set off down the river, planning their voyage south to escape the Big Freeze and looking forward to the warmer climes of the Far Countries. The Northern Traders had seen it all before, and did not doubt they would see it all again.

THE WASHING-UP BOY

The Washing-up Boy employed by Sally Mullin was convinced that it was his fault the Tea and Ale House burned down. He was sure he must have left the tea towels drying too close to the fire just as he had done before. But he was not one to let these things trouble him for long. The Washing-Up Boy believed that every setback was an opportunity in disguise. And so he built a small hut on wheels and every day he trundled it down to the Custodian Guard barracks and sold meat pies and sausages to the Guards. The contents of his pies and sausages varied and depended on what the Washing-up Boy could get hold of, but he worked hard, making the pies late into the night, and did a brisk trade all day. If people began to notice that their cats and dogs were disappearing at an alarming rate, no one thought to link it with the sudden appearance of the Washing-up Boy's meat pie hut. And, when the ranks of the Custodian Guards were devastated by food poisoning, it was the barracks' Canteen Cook who was blamed. The Washing-up Boy prospered and never, ever, ate one of his own meat pies or sausages.

Rupert Gringe

Rupert Gringe was the best apprentice Jannit Maarten had ever had. Jannit built shallow-draught herring boats, which could fish the waters near the shore and trap the shoals of herring by running them up against the sand banks just outside the Port. Any herring fisherman in possession of a Jannit Maarten boat was sure of a good living, and it soon became known that if Rupert Gringe had worked on the boat, you were lucky—the boat would sit well in the water and run fast with the wind. Jannit recognized talent when she saw it, and she soon trusted Rupert to work on his own. The first boat Rupert built entirely by himself was *Muriel*. He painted her a dark green like the depths of the river and gave her deep red sails like the late summer sunsets over the sea.

Lucy Gringe

Lucy Gringe had met Simon Heap at a dance class for young ladies and gentlemen when they were both fourteen. Mrs. Gringe had sent Lucy along to keep her out of trouble for the summer. (Simon had gone to the class by mistake. Silas, who had some trouble with reading and often got his letters mixed up, had thought it was a Trance class and had made the mistake of mentioning it to Sarah one evening. Simon overheard, and after much pestering, Silas had enrolled him in the class.)

Lucy loved the way Simon was determined to be the best dancer in the class, just as Simon was always determined to be the best at everything. And she liked his green Wizard eyes and his curly blond hair too. Simon had no idea why he liked a *girl* all of a sudden, but for some reason he found he could not stop thinking about Lucy. Lucy and Simon continued to see each other whenever they could, but kept their meetings secret. They knew neither of their families would approve.

The day Lucy ran away to get married to Simon Heap was the best and worst day of her life. It was the best day right up until the Guards burst into the Chapel and took him away. After that Lucy didn't care what happened to her. Gringe came and took her home. He locked her up at the top of the gatehouse tower to stop her running away and begged her to forget about Simon Heap. Lucy refused and would not speak to her father at all. Gringe was heartbroken. He had only done what he thought best for his daughter.

JENNA'S SHIELD BUG

When the ex-millipede fell off DomDaniel it bounced and ended up on top of a barrel. The barrel was washed overboard as the *Vengeance* was pulled down into the Quake Ooze. It floated off to the Port where it fetched up on the town beach. The Shield Bug dried out its wings and flew off to a nearby field where a traveling circus had just arrived. For some reason it took a particular dislike to an inoffensive buffoon, and it caused great amusement to the audience every night as the bug chased the buffoon around the ring.

THE SWIMMERS AND THE CHICKEN BOAT

The two swimmers who were thrown from the *Vengeance* were lucky to survive. Jake and Barry Parfitt, whose mother had insisted on teaching them to swim before they became seafarers, were not particularly strong swimmers, and it was all they could do to keep their heads above water as the storm raged around them. They were beginning to give up hope when Barry saw a fishing boat coming toward them. Although there appeared to be no one on board the fishing boat, there was an unusual gangplank hanging down from the deck. With their last ounce of strength Jake and Barry pulled themselves up onto the gangplank and collapsed onto the deck, where they found themselves surrounded by chickens. But they didn't care what they were surrounded by as long as it wasn't water.

When the waters eventually ebbed from the Marram Marshes, Jake, Barry and the chickens came to rest on one of the marsh islands. They decided to stay put, out of the way of DomDaniel, and soon there was a thriving chicken farm some miles away from Draggen Island.

THE MESSAGE RAT

Stanley was eventually rescued from his prison under the floorboards of the Ladies' Washroom by one of the old Rat Office rats who had heard what had happened to him. He spent some time recovering at the rat's nest at the top of the East Gate gatehouse tower, where Lucy Gringe took to feeding him biscuits and confiding her troubles to him. In Stanley's opinion, Lucy Gringe had had a lucky escape. If anyone had ever asked Stanley, he would have told them that Wizards in general, and Wizards called Heap in particular, were nothing but trouble. But no one ever did ask.